STORM

Nicholas Carter lives near Bristol and has been a journalist in the West Country for seventeen years. He is a member of The Sealed Knot. His first novel in this series, *Turncoat's Drum*, is also available from Pan Books. The third novel *And King's Men Crow* is published in hardback by Macmillan.

Also by Nicholas Carter

Turncoat's Drum
And King's Men Crow

NICHOLAS CARTER

STORMING PARTY

THE

SHADOW

ON THE

CROWN

Part Two

PAN BOOKS

First published 1996 by Macmillan

This edition published 1997 by Pan Books
an imprint of Macmillan Publishers Ltd
25 Eccleston Place London SW1W 9NF
and Basingstoke

Associated companies throughout the world

ISBN 0 330 33861 7

1 3 5 7 9 8 6 4 2

A CIP catalogue record for this book is available from the British Library.

Typeset by Parker Typesetting Service, Leicester
Printed by Mackays of Chatham plc, Chatham, Kent

DRAMATIS PERSONAE

MENTIONED IN HISTORY

King Charles I
Prince Rupert of the Rhine, his nephew
Prince Maurice, Rupert's younger brother
Sir Ralph Hopton, Royalist General in the West, former comrade of Sir William Waller
Sir William Waller, Parliamentary General in the West
Colonel Nathaniel Fiennes, Governor of Bristol for the Parliament
Colonel John Birch, Colonel Alexander Popham, West Country Parliamentarian soldiers

UNMENTIONED IN HISTORY

Parliamentarian

William Sparrow, Cornet, McNabb's troop of horse
Major Archibald McNabb, Scots officer of horse, serving with Waller
Major Tobias Fulke, a gallant but rather elderly gentleman
Sir Gilbert Morrison, MP, former colonel of militia, wool merchant and turncoat, Governor in waiting of the Royal Westward Society of Oceanic Venturers
Captain Jamie Morrison, his son, serving in militia
Bella Marguerite Morrison, his daughter
Mary Keziah Pitt, her maid and confidante
Master Algernon Starling, clerk to Sir Gilbert
Zachary, Eli, Mordecai and Jeremiah Pitt, serving in militia or the Morrison household

Colston Muffet, sergeant, Merrick's Regiment, serving with Waller
Hereward Gillingfeather, as above, an agitator, William Butcher, as above, sharpshooter
Captain Gallen Fey, master of Parliament's ship *Conqueror*
Lieutenants Richard Pine and Phileas Rhodes, seamen Jacob Late, 'Evergreen' Slater and David Swale, members of the crew

Royalist

Captain Hugo Telling, officer of horse, Prince Maurice's regiment
Jack Cady, Ned Jacobs, his troopers of horse
Colonel Scipio Porthcurn, officer of Cornish foot
Jethro Polruan, Denzil Petherton, Judd Downderry, Simon Shevick, Issac Thrush, Gideon Wooly, Cornish foot soldiers
Anthony St John Dyle, Lord Clavincale, Royalist entrepreneur and magnate
Colonel Nybb, his mercenary bodyguard
Captain Valentine Cruickshank, master of the *Messalina's Purse*, a privateer
Caleb, his half-witted son
Edward Callow, mate of the *Messalina's Purse*
Count Orlando de Meola, a Spanish gentleman adventurer
Emilio de Rodriguez, his companion in arms
Captain Martin Breech, Sergeant Joshua Lawton, turncoat dragoons
'Deaf' Jacob Kreutzfeld, German mercenary gunner serving wherever he may
Colonel Augustus Potts, Royalist artillery officer
Colonel Sparkes, sickly Royalist officer of foot
Elder Sergeant Cully Oates, one of his veteran troops
Ross 'Roy' Dunblane, Laird of Tullymallock, Scots Royalist Lord
Margaret, Lady Ramsay, widow of the Royalist squire
Sir Marmaduke Ramsay, and mother of Thomas Ramsay
Anneliese Ramsay, her remaining daughter
Findlay, their gamekeeper and sharpshooter
Matilda Dawkins, a Royalist camp follower
Ambrosio de Meola St Corelli, an Italian surgeon serving with Hopton, cousin to Count de Meola

'Twas a bewtyfull peece of danger, to see so many fires incessentlye in the darck'
Bernard de Gomme, Prince Rupert's fireworker, on the siege of Bristol

PART ONE

PRISONERS OF FORTUNE

BY

ROUNDWAY DOWN,

13 JULY 1643

Most of the surviving foot were too shocked to raise their swords. Baffled and bewildered by the irresistible enemy cavalry, the Roundheads left standing were being herded like cattle, gallows fodder penned on their narrow Golgotha. Their dwindling regiments pulsed and shrank with every successive volley, each savage, swirling charge.

The dazed survivors of Sir William Waller's infantry seemed unable to master their pikes, let alone prime and fire their brittle muskets. They had been overawed by these howling imps of Hell, demonic half-men and their bellowing familiars. Overborne by legions of screaming Cavaliers who had risen from the chalky escarpments like the children of the Hydra to scour their own russet-coated cavalry from the field, and chase them like so many stampeding sheep over Roundway's treacherous cliffs.

Their mortified commander, dumbfounded by the loss of his carefully collected army, had spurred off hard on the heels of his broken horse. Waller was an experienced general who knew well enough when a battle was lost, but that afternoon had been the most shattering experience of his hard career. He had witnessed nothing less than the total eclipse of his hopes and fortunes. The slow soldiers he left behind watched him go, his face whiter than his gaping shirt collar, a feeble flag of surrender.

The Parliamentarian regiments stared in drop-jawed disbelief as the colours they had followed all those long summer weeks were taken out to the rear, rolled and wrapped around their ash staffs. Crying cornets on fresh horses stowed the flags behind their knees and galloped off, running the gauntlet of the scattered Cavaliers who fired their pistols and screamed at them to surrender. The Royalist riders had spurred their tired mounts after them but soon gave up in disgust. There would be colours enough on the field, with five regiments of enemy foot standing forlorn on their hill, a green island in a sudden whirlpool of colour, completely surrounded by the resurgent King's men.

Against all expectation, Charles Stewart's Western army had refused to lie down and die on the broad downs above Devizes. Sir Ralph Hopton's hard-fighting Cornish Royalists had shut themselves up in the town while the cavalry galloped off for help. The crafty Royalist general had wasted time discussing terms he had no intention of keeping while he waited for the relief column. Prince Maurice's battered horse regiments had ridden through the night and the following day, returned precious hours later to surprise and spoil the Parliamentarians' premature victory celebrations.

An army Sir William Waller had imagined to be dead and buried, ready to collapse in shameful ruin, had risen from the green downs like a majestic phoenix and scattered his Godly forces like a flock of larks in a thunderstorm. Seeing the extent of the disaster about to engulf them, the rest of the officers had peeled away from their rooted regiments like flies from a dead donkey, and followed the colours off the field.

'Fight on, lads.' A wounded major yelled idiocies to his confused congregation, gaping in bewilderment at their catastrophic reversal of fortune. 'We'll be back with the Bristol garrison, and save you yet!'

'Save yourself, sir!' an elderly pikeman shouted in reply.

'I'll bring the Bristol boys back!' the officer yelled hysterically, tears running through his sooty moustaches.

'Bring 'em back?' a flaxen-headed Londoner sneered. 'Forty soddin' miles either way?'

His elder sergeant, a lean, weatherbeaten veteran called Colston Muffet, raised his chin a notch, nodded at the enemy cavalry hurrying to re-form over the northern edge of the down.

'That's what our friends have done, seemingly. All the way to Oxford and back. I wouldn't have believed it if I wasn't seein' it for myself.'

'God curse them all to the fiery pit,' another musketeer growled, wiping his red mouth on his dirty sleeve. 'They must have signed pacts with Satan himself, to get back here that quick!'

For once Muffet, the iron-haired veteran, found he had to agree with Gillingfeather, the principal regimental agitator and campfire preacher.

'It's us as is for the pit, my friend,' he said under his breath.

The isolated regiments stood like forgotten monuments on the windblown plateau, a shuffling Stonehenge of green and red coats. They watched in horror as the Cornish infantry they had bottled up in Devizes the previous week hurried up the hill from the south, eager to avenge themselves on their erstwhile masters. The Cornish sally trapped the forlorn Roundhead foot between the town and the rapidly re-forming Royalist cavalry brigades manoeuvring to the north. Some of the more enthusiastic Cornish had already seized a battery of Waller's guns and had turned the smoking culverins and sakers on their previous owners, sitting targets now along their bloody ridge. Here and there individuals and small groups tried to escape, dashing for the cover of some hidden gully or chalky cliff. They were pursued by Royalist dragoons on dusty nags, firing from the saddle like hunters after wounded game.

The dumbstruck soldiers bickered over what could have gone wrong. Most blamed the Earl of Essex for allowing the Royalists the time to organize the unexpected relief column. The lacklustre earl commanded the main Parliamentarian field army based on Reading. How had he come to allow three thousand enemy cavalry to ride away right under his nose? The cursing troops watched their mortified commanders spur away from the stricken field, taking what little was left of their honour and pride with them.

'Fuck only knows how they did it, but they're here all right,' was Long Col's phlegmy assessment of the situation. He spat into the trampled grass.

'I don't like the look of this now, Col,' the young musketeer muttered, watching the enemy forces pulsing out of the town and over the downs. 'I don't like the look of this one bit.'

No drum. No bugle. No bawled orders. The Parliamentarian infantry standing in forlorn clumps on the hill had been swallowed up in the throat-tightening silence, punctuated only by the eerie, agonized clatter of their abandoned weapons.

'Baa!' The shrill cry echoed over the nervous regiments, rattling the frightened mass of red-handed rebels. A lone officer tramped through their bewildered ranks, laughing at their chalky faces and pinched expressions.

'Baa!' he bawled, nodding hysterically. 'Baa baa!' The sullen soldiers stared at him or shoved him away with an oath, as if they were reluctant to be caught in the vicinity of such a careless madman. A heavyset cavalryman who had lost his horse barged through the muttering files, clamped a bloody hand over the witless captain's trembling shoulder.

'Jamie, for God's sake shut that racket. What's the matter with you?'

William Sparrow cuffed his comrade on the back of his new buff coat, smiled wearily at the demented youngster. He had known Jamie Morrison since boyhood, a sickly youth whom his merchant father had practically press-ganged into the militia, frogmarched up to Bristol from his home in the hills.

'Never mind all your books and bars now, boy,' Sir Gilbert had told the would-be lawyer, 'there's a war on and there's many a name to be made.' The sullen soldiers on the hill could have invented a few names for the poor lad now.

''E's lost his head, that's what,' the elderly pikeman commented, serenely puffing on his pipe as if he was on guard duty behind Bristol's walls and not standing in a field surrounded by six thousand of the King's best men. 'I've seen it 'afore.'

'Will he be all right?' William asked, blinking rapidly against the last rays of the sun.

'Who's to say?' the pikeman asked, shrugging his shoulder and making his well-worn weapon twitch like a skeleton's arm.

'Baa!' Jamie Morrison bawled. 'Baa baa baa!'

*

With the ragged Parliamentarians safely surrounded and almost certainly surrendered, the Cornish infantry who had been penned up in Devizes since the previous weekend swarmed out of the town, trampled their own barricades in their rush up the hill. The bawling troopers brought the more belligerent citizens out of their cellars, and they joined the excited mob hurrying up the steep slopes to complete the encirclement of their desperate enemy. The sweating banshees in their patched coats and worn boots looked for all the world like the boarding parties of a pirate fleet, a bandit army vomited from the wild country away to the west. They fell gleefully on the dead and wounded littering the lower slopes, tore boots from cold feet and emptied purses into their dirty paws. They ransacked the abandoned camp, tore great oak wains into splinters to get their hands on the food and finery within. The ringleaders shoved their way into the mute mass of men on the crest, cursing them stupid in their own hellish dialects, hoarsely ordering the bewildered Roundheads to drop their redundant weapons.

There were precious few Parliamentarian field officers left to hold the sorry mob together now. Far too few to give the inevitable surrender any veneer of ceremony or respectability.

The laws of war were peculiarly punctilious on the finer points of capitulation, the etiquette of the underdog – but the savagely triumphant Cornish swarming like sackclothed locusts over Runaway Hill had no time for bowing and scraping, for rolled colours and tucked drums.

'Get 'em down, yer beef-witted bastards! Drop yer ironmongery and take quarter!'

'Better do as 'e sez, lads. Easy now,' the elderly sergeant advised, opening his gnarled paw and letting his pike-prop drop to the grass.

One enormous musketeer in a faded red suit, attracted by the bizarre cry of the shell-shocked officer, barged his way through a flock of frightened rebels and hauled the daft youth up by his lapels.

'Stow that noise or I'll cut your throat and drink yer blood!' the Cornish giant bellowed, throwing the sheepish captain against his shocked troopers. His cronies hurrying behind him laughed.

'Get on now, Jethro, you know you never touches blood afore the sun goes down!'

'Ah, but it'll be down soon,' he leered, dropping his victim into the trampled grass.

Sparrow winced at his friend's treatment but took three steps back from the trouble, desperate to hide his cavalryman's garb amongst the tightly packed pikemen. He recognized the red-haired brute from Lansdown. He'd thought he'd killed him with that sword blow, left him for dead. Here he was returned to haunt him in his beastly bloody red suit.

'Baa!' Jamie said weakly, pawing at the tangle of broken boots and bare feet. The berserking warrior knocked their muskets and pikes aside, glared at the frightened Roundhead troops as they backed away from their abandoned weapons and crestfallen captain.

'Drop it, laddie,' he growled, 'and that sword. Empty your pockets, you miserable vermin!'

His cronies fell in behind him, relieved the foolish prisoners of coats and boots and breeches. They tore snapsacks open, ran their daggers up the hems of torn tunics to find hidden coins. A rangy Cornish fighter spied a fowling piece among the firewood heap of abandoned muskets, whistled to his mates.

'A long rifle, eh? Who's the sharpshooter?'

A bandaged pikeman hurried over, held the barrel to his broken nose.

'I took a graze, and my brother Michael worse,' he accused, eyeing the miserable captives. 'Who's the bugger who had such sport yesterday, eh?' He thumped a white-haired musketeer in the chest. 'What about you, Grand-pappy? See far enough to fire this, could you? What about you? Come on, don't be bashful!' He menaced the fearful crowd with the butt of his pike, his beady eyes rimmed red with exhaustion. His murderous enquiries were interrupted by the noisy arrival of their commander, a tall colonel in black breeches and doublet riding a horse to match.

'Polruan, Shevick! Damn your eyes, we're to round them up, not lay them out! Get out of there, you brutes,' he yelled, lashing about his spirited mount to clear a passage through the confused scrummage.

Colonel Scipio Porthcurn had been obliged to commandeer a runaway horse to keep up with his bloody bandits, the worst rascals in a battle-hardened army. They were hot enough now all right, after spending the past days bottled up in Devizes like wasps in a jam pot. Now they were out, stinging who they might. He'd be hoarse by nightfall, and be thankful he suffered no worse, given this set of stab-in-the-back scoundrels.

'They've surrendered, damn you!' Porthcurn yelled.

'They'm saucy bastards, and one of 'em had this!' Shevick shouted, brandishing Billy Butcher's fowling piece. The cockney dyer's apprentice had claimed six victims with it that week alone. He had followed Muffet's advice and made sure he was well away from the damned thing when they had eventually put up their hands.

'Leave these men be or I'll hang you up by your tongue, you filthy ape!'

Polruan snatched off his greasy red Montero cap, exhibited the caked wound where his ear had been. 'They shoots me bliddy ear off and you're tellin' me to forgive and forget?' he snorted.

'You lost your flap on Lansdown, you Hell-spawned beggar!' Porthcurn replied, refusing to give an inch before his renegade regiment's blustering champion. 'Now leave off that looting and fall in. These men are to be escorted back to the castle.' He slumped in the saddle, eyed the great press of prisoners.

'Sir Ralph Hopton has let it be known that any man who enlists in the King's army will be fully pardoned for any previous service.'

Many hundreds of them would have heard similar offers already, perhaps more than once. They had all heard the stories about the filthy conditions at the jails back in Oxford, the brutal governors who would sell a man into slavery for a few coppers in commission. Serve with the Cornish, though? The Papist heathens who had invaded their prosperous shires, cut a swath of destruction through Devon and Somerset?

Porthcurn sensed their hesitation, nodded sourly. 'You've got the night to think about it. I'll be around again in the morning,' he shouted, spurring off down the hill to find the rest of his men.

BY

DEVIZES CASTLE,

13 JULY 1643

The unexpectedly victorious Cornish regiments had disintegrated even more rapidly than their Parliamentarian counterparts up on the hill. Pikemen and musketeers, captains and corporals, gunners and tinkers had fallen out to plunder the richly provisioned enemy camp and despoil the poor unfortunates who could not hide themselves away. The furious townsfolk of Devizes had joined in the plundering, loudly proclaiming they were off to fetch back their own property – allegedly stolen by the arrogant, wicked and cowardly rebels.

'Where's your King Jesus now?' a fat innkeeper who had never even seen a Roundhead bawled at the prisoners as they shuffled through the streets. 'He's turned his back on you, not so cocky now, boys!' the fat man leered.

Hereward Gillingfeather barged his way through the shuffling ranks, jabbed his sooty finger into the innkeeper's barrel chest. 'They may have turned our guns on us but they'll never turn our God!' the agitator bawled.

The burgher quailed, looked over his shoulder for support and found none. The few Cornish soldiers who had been detailed to guard the prisoners seemed too concerned with looking over their own shoulders and casting covetous glances at the hill to offer any practical assistance with the saucy Roundheads.

Muffet stepped over, laid his heavily veined hand on his furious comrade's twitching shoulder. 'Leave it now, Gilly.'

Colonel Porthcurn, cursing his absent soldiers, spurred over to put a halt to the acrimonious exchange. Why was it he had been commissioned to keep this pack of dogs but was all too frequently obliged to bark himself?

'Get back in line there,' he cried, hoping his voice alone could control the increasingly surly prisoners. 'And you people get about your business, you poisonous scum!' The bitter crowd parted around the demon officer and his coal-black horse, went on up the hill while the prisoners were marched into the battered town, trampling the debris knocked loose by their own guns. Here and there a door opened to admit a scuttling relative, some foolhardy son or uncle who had taken his chances with Waller. Others slipped away unnoticed down rubble-strewn alleys, stripping off their soldiers' coats as they went. Muffet eyed the available exits, but the scowling colonel on the big stallion seemed to be keeping an especially sharp eye on his section, and before they could think twice they had marched beneath the moss-encrusted portcullis of Devizes Castle. Prisoners indeed.

'Officers fall out to the right, if there are any of you left,' a grinning dragoon called cheerily, as the shuffling files passed under the gatehouse and into the shadowed courtyard.

'Oy! Not you!' The dragoon laid his carbine across Sparrow's broad chest, shook his head.

'I'm an officer!' Sparrow insisted, tugging at his cavalry issue buff coat and knotted sash.

'And I'm the Queen Mother! Bugger off back in line before I lose my temper!'

'Baa!' Jamie said wearily, his wide eyes rolling alarmingly in their sooty sockets.

'Baa! to you too and all.'

'I'm cornet to Major McNabb,' William insisted, trying to sound as if he must therefore be third in line to the Earl of Essex himself.

'Cornet? Where's your bloddy flag, then? Drop it, did you?'

'I did not!' Sparrow cried. 'It was taken, same as everyone else's!'

'Baa!' Jamie added.

'Hah! That sounds true enough. Late to the battle and early to leave, eh?'

'I got knocked off, I took cover with the foot!' William told the disbelieving dragoon.

'Bad move, son. They weren't goin' nowhere once your pals had buggered off. Standing there solid like a bunch of bloody statues, what did they expect? Now fuck off with your mad mate before I lose my rag.'

William frowned, stamped off over the cobbled yard after his friends.

'OY!'

William wheeled round, relieved the idiot dragoon had changed his mind. He smiled broadly.

'You can git them bloody boots off and all. You look about my size!' the bow-legged dragoon called ironically.

William limped over the cobbles clutching the dragoon's broken-down ankle boots. Not much of an exchange even if they fitted, which William doubted. Colston Muffet grinned at him.

'I should hang onto 'em if I were you. They'll have us

marching to Oxford tomorrow, and you'll be thankful of 'em then!'

William slumped down against an empty barrel, examined his holed stockings. He sat back, blinking rapidly. 'God's wounds, I must have had 'em on too long,' he complained, wafting the foul stink from his face. Jamie had fallen asleep at his feet, curled up like a miller's dog in front of a fire. The rest regarded him sourly, glad of the momentary quiet.

'Oxford, you say,' Sparrow said flatly. 'That must be what, a hundred miles?'

'If you go the pretty way, aye. We'll be going straight down the London road, mark my words,' Muffet replied, making himself comfortable on a discarded saddle.

'I don't fancy that,' Billy Butcher observed.

'A nest of idolatrous heathens and fornicating whore's melts,' Gillingfeather added. 'The cradle of the Antichrist wherein the beasts do walk upon their hind legs and . . .'

'I think we get the general idea, Gilly,' Muffet agreed, watching the agitated agitator stamp up to the rugged wall as if he could think out the bricks. Gillingfeather was a lightly built but wiry Londoner, his arms and chest covered in a shockingly profuse mat of dark hair. The simian thatch seemed strangely out of place with his pious pronouncements, and Gillingfeather was in the habit of buttoning his shirt sleeves at all times to hide his hairy arms.

'What about it, you know, what he said?' Zachary Pitt, a swarthy farmer from the Mendip Hills, enquired, nodding at the more experienced men sitting about him.

'What who said? That Colonel?' Muffet snapped. 'It's up to you, lad, but I'd rather enlist for another twenty-years war over in Germany than sign on with that damned crew!'

There was a murmur of agreement from the prisoners

in the corner of the yard. Zachary wasn't convinced. He and his brothers had joined the Chipping Marleward trained band a few weeks before. They hadn't particularly enquired which side the militia would be fighting on. Didn't seem to make much difference, as long as you were winning.

'Oxford, though. Locked up God knows how long?' he fretted miserably. He had heartily despised his few days' training, locked up in Bristol's lousy stews. He was an unashamed countryman, used to windy hills and open downs. He couldn't be doing with narrow streets and squinting shutters, great flocks of pestilent people. He had been enjoying the army's sojourn on Roundway's breathtaking heights, up until that afternoon that was. Now he gazed miserably at the survivors of his west country regiment, wondered how bad service with the Cornish could be.

'But if he's won, like, the King I mean,' the farmer muttered unhappily, 'he'll hang us all as rebels and traitors!'

'You should have thought of that before you joined up, my lad!' Gillingfeather barked.

'Who says he's won, anyway?' Muffet asked more reasonably. 'He may have got the better of us this battle but he's a good way from winning the war.'

The Pitt brothers looked away gloomily, evidently unconvinced by the Londoner's argument.

'There's more than one army fighting for Parliament,' Muffet asserted.

'There's the Earl of Essex, for one,' Billy Butcher put in smugly. He and his colleagues had enlisted in one of the regiments raised for the Puritan nobleman at the very outbreak of the war. Ten months on they were among the only survivors of Merrick's foot, one of the dozens of forgotten formations whose taste of glory had turned out to be all too brief and all too bitter.

'Essex, you say? Hah! He's been sitting on his fat arse since Etch-Hill,' the elderly pikeman snorted.

Muffet ignored the all too familiar joke about the Earl's rumoured reluctance to come to grips with the King, and itemized the other Parliamentarian commanders whose fame had filtered through to the poor armies in the west.

'The Earl of Manchester's got another army up Lincoln way with that Cromwell feller.'

Several of the prisoners were vaguely familiar with the names although they hadn't the faintest idea where on God's green earth Lincoln might be.

'And then there's the Lord Fairfax and his son Sir Thomas. The last news sheet I saw said they'll be cocks of the north any day now.'

William glanced up at the ragged prisoners, nodded resignedly.

'You don't want to believe all you read in the news sheets, believe you me,' he said with feeling. His missing finger throbbed, a feeble echo of his old career. He watched the slow blood oozing into the dirty dressing he had clamped to his wound. His handwriting had been damn near unreadable before, God knows what his master Percival Greesham, Printer by the grace of God, would make of his three-fingered scrawl now. He stared miserably at his grumbling colleagues, watched Muffet stride between the crouching men trying to stir up some spirit.

'Stick together, that's the thing,' Long Col said authoritatively. 'Me and Gilly here, and young Billy besides, we've been at it since we joined Merrick's back last year. You go choppin' and changin', you'll see us again soon enough. And we're none of us fond of a turncoat.'

Zachary sighed heavily, glanced down at their captain, blissfully asleep at their feet. Baa to you too, he thought sourly.

Twelve miles from that miserable castle, his lordship Anthony St John Dyle endured his own tiresome imprisonment in a smelly, clattering coach drawn by four of the most broken-winded nags in the King's household. The impudent driver had steered the stuffy coach into every pothole he had seen and a few others besides. Their tortuous route had taken them down every back lane and over every hump-backed bridge on the west road, and he was still a good fifty miles from his destination. It was the height of summer for a start, and the poor rutted tracks were little more than dustbowls. Stiflingly hot, it was as much as the red-faced peasants could do to give you a good day as they passed the coach, heads cast down in their abject misery.

He wasn't even sure who he was supposed to be meeting. Some wily grocer with ideas above his station, the young lord imagined. What was his name, Masterson? Morrison. That was it. He had been sent on a secret mission, to rendezvous with the principal West Country magnates. The honest merchants and tireless tradesmen who were (God willing) going to breathe new life into the King's cause, and find new ways of raising coin for his impoverished armies. A new treaty with the West Country merchant adventurers, to set up a new trading empire based on the small ports the King's army had captured along the Bristol Channel. If only they had held on to

Bristol itself, they would have had a second city to rival the capital, compete with the wretched merchants in rebel-held London. Now that would be a treaty worth travelling for.

The corpulent nobleman had been bored to distraction during the tedious trip, made doubly trying by the fact he was obliged to put up with the boorish Captain Nybb for company. The giant rogue claimed to be a colonel, with years of experience with the Saxons on the Continent, but Clavincale had paid handsomely for his savage services, and so Nybb had been prepared to overlook his temporary demotion. Nybb was a handy enough swordsman in case of trouble but he was completely baffled by the intrigues of a jealous court, and seemed unconcerned with the importance of establishing the right connections to the King, or even more importantly, his Queen.

The heavily powdered gentleman waved his lavender-drenched handkerchief in front of his fleshy nose, peered out of the window at the dark countryside.

'Where in the name of all the hells are we?' he snorted. 'I would have thought we would have been there by now!'

'Ya, vir can'ter be'ridden anywhere you liken'oo, mineer,' Nybb growled in his pot-pourri camp dialect. A bizarre hotchpotch of German, Spanish, Swedish, French and Latin built around a questionable English framework. His lordship had to pick and pan his meanings from his bodyguard's pan-European drivel.

'See yer roader's klecked mitt soldiers!' Nybb made a brushing motion with his hairy paw. He elaborated with a series of guttural oaths and nodded familiarly at the young courtier. His lordship sighed, settled back in the over-stuffed seat. Nybb yawned. The hairy ape squatted like a vile toad, lifting his behind to honour every jangling pothole with a revolting fart. Like so many of the rogues who had learned their bandit trade on the continent, Nybb had little time for the niceties of polite society. He had served just about every nation including the damned Turks, fighting throughout Germany's ruinous wars. He had even brought back a huge set of Hussar wings from the King of Poland, sturdy parallel poles studded with eagles' feathers.

'I'ken ridden avaster mitt ze flugzeuge,' he had offered, whistling and blowing through his multi-coloured moustaches to demonstrate the noise the elaborate wings made when galloping down on a terrified foe.

'I don't think that will be necessary,' his lordship had simpered. 'Besides, they won't fit in the coach.'

When the King had raised his standard at Nottingham Nybb had taken the first ship he could get, returned to an England he barely recognized (and a language he hardly understood) to offer his sword to his sovereign. For a price. He had raised and lost a company of desperadoes, feckless ruffians more used to plundering than charging sober blocks of Roundhead horse. They had enjoyed shriekingly good sport on Edgehill, but had drifted away during the subsequent stalemate as the battered armies threaded their way down through the Midlands and came to rest around their winter bases, the rebel Earl of Essex on the outskirts of London and the King at Oxford. Nybb was not comfortable sitting out long sieges, and as the last of his men had ridden off a few nights before, aiming their nags for their homes away in the west, he had decided it was time for a change, and had taken service instead with the young nobleman. The King's most trusted and obedient servant, Anthony St John Dyle, eldest son of the Earl of Dartland, and third Baron Clavincale.

The coach clattered to a halt outside a brightly lit inn, and the weary gentleman perked up at once. Nybb clambered down to reconnoitre, thrust his massive head back through the window.

'Ya, all ist klah. Comme mitt Ich and ye will stretcher de leg bonnes, eh?'

Clavincale followed his barely comprehensible advice, stepped down into the bustling courtyard as the panting team tossed their heads and pawed the dry earth. The driver was clambering down from the running-board, the enormous bundle of greasy reins thrown over his shoulder. The leather reeked, the horses steamed and the inn breathed stale beer. Clavincale held his handkerchief to his offended nose, stepped over to a splattered ruffian in a buff coat, busy fastening the girths under his charger's muddy belly. The blond youth rapped his cane on the brute's shoulder, stepped back in alarm as the insolent dog leapt around with an oath.

'Your pardon, sir. I thought the stable boys were making sport,' he mumbled, not nearly apologetic enough for Clavincale's liking.

'The White Horse, eh?' he asked, noticing the creaking inn sign as he averted his nose from the rider's bated breath.

'Right enough, sir.'

'Die weise pferde,' Captain Nybb translated.

'Devizes is that way, sir.' The stranger pointed back down the road, misunderstanding the gruff captain. 'Can't miss it, with the battle and all.'

'Ah yes, the battle.' Clavincale sighed. General Hopton shut up in the town with the triumphant Roundheads about to force his ignominious surrender. The whole of the west lost at a stroke. He wondered if he would have any treaty left to sign, or any merchants daring enough to defy the all-conquering Parliament in these wilder parts of the King's troubled realm.

'I'm off with the news now, sir, if you'll allow me to get on.'

'Ah, he's surrendered, then. All his army?'

'All but the horse, sir. They got off to Bristol down Roughridge Cliff, so they say.'

The fool was mistaken. Why would the Royalist cavalry flee towards the west?

'Hopton surrendered?' he queried.

The cavalryman shook his head.

'Surrendered? He won, sir! Begging your pardon, like. It's Waller's lost, sir, not us.'

Clavincale couldn't believe his ears. 'All his foot?'

'And every gun besides.'

His lordship's small blue eyes glittered with mischief and delight.

'How many have we captured?' he enquired as the rider adjusted his stirrup straps and prepared to mount.

'At least two thousand, by my reckoning. Now if I may, sir?'

'Yes yes, on your way my good man. Here,' he fished a penny from his purse, handed it up to the cavalryman. 'Have that for your trouble.'

The rider weighed the coin in his fist, nodded wearily.

'Thanks very much, sir,' he muttered.

'Two thousand? Two thousand, you say?'

The scout picked up his reins and nudged the big horse out of the yard. Clavincale stood amongst its steaming droppings for a moment, lost in thought. He waved Nybb back aboard the coach, clapped his chubby hands.

'Driver! Never mind the horses now! On to Devizes, as quick as you like!'

BY

BITTERWELL HILL,

CHIPPING MARLEWARD, SOMERSET, 13 JULY 1643

The weary chestnut had cast his shoe at the bottom of the hill, and the bleary-eyed boy could do little except poke his dirty hoof in well-intentioned but helpless agitation.

'I'm sorry, miss, I ain't the tools out yere like,' he explained, running his crusty sleeve across his nose. They had barely rested the last two days, rushing about the county as if the little dog cart was carrying a load of gunpowder through a firework display. The youngster regarded his mistress warily. She was pining for her lost lover of a Royalist captain, and it was only a matter of time before she exploded into an all too familiar tantrum. He peeped over the splintered running-board at her, holding his breath in the still evening air as if the slightest gasp from her miserable servant could set her off.

Bella Marguerite Morrison tapped her slipper on the potholed road, frowned at the rickety contraption in which she seemed to have spent the last six months of her tiresome life. She scowled at her young escort, who was almost fainting with fatigue, hopping from one foot to the other as if he had an urgent appointment alongside the nearest tree.

'We've come fifty miles only to break down on our own doorstep,' she breathed.

'Ain't it a bugger, miss, beg pardon, miss.' Jeremiah Pitt shuddered, weary and resigned to his humble role.

It was a bugger all right, running around after this desperately determined damsel when he ought to be helping his sister Mary Keziah search for their absent father. Old Gregory had hobbled off to take extra clothes and provisions to his three elder boys serving in the village trained band. Somehow, he had got himself caught up in the scuffle at Claverton Ford and he hadn't been seen since. Mistress Bella had at first agreed to join their fruitless search, but had then decided to extend their horizons by taking a well-deserved holiday in Chippenham.

They had arrived in the town just after it had been liberated by Sir William Waller's Parliamentary army – the army about to take the field with singularly disastrous consequences on Roundway Down. Bella's captivating presence – with the added incentive of a share in her father's reputed fortune – had brought officers and gentlemen in from all around. Her temporary headquarters in the town had been packed with eager young men hungry to steal a peek (and a little more besides) at the glorious girl. But no sooner than she had settled in Bella had been off again – much to the bitter disappointment of several eligible bachelors. The moment she had heard the shocking news about the capture and imprisonment of her favourite Royalist captain on Lansdown's bloody ridge she had dropped everything to be by his side. She had hurried back to Bath, where she and Jeremiah had spent a hot and humid day touring the town in a fruitless attempt to track down her wandering sweetheart. Poor Hugo had been marched off with the rest of the prisoners, but despite Bella's frantic searching they had not managed to secure the joyous reunion she had set her heart on.

Bella had lied, bribed, pouted and cajoled her way in to the various military headquarters in the town, but the wretched staff seemed to be in an utter frenzy and none could spare the time to help the wailing beauty find her fancyman.

'You want the adjutant general,' a flustered staff officer had snapped. 'He has the full list of all the officers taken.'

'And where is he?'

'On Roundway with Waller.'

'But I've just come from there!'

'Then you'll have to go straight back again won't you, my little honey blob?' the surly oaf had snorted.

Bella had decided against returning to the army. Hugo was in the town somewhere, his poor heart in his mouth, and it was her duty to get him out. The thought of the wretched, sensitive youth locked in a horrid mossy cell quite unnerved her. Besides, Bath was only twelve miles from home, and if anyone knew what to do it would be her father. Sir Gilbert Morrison had an answer for everything, and a notorious soft spot for his haphazard daughter. If she could only drag him away from his wretched business worries for a moment, he might find a way to release her precious captain.

'I'll walk the rest of the way,' she snapped, snatching her bag from the buggy. Jeremiah Pitt dropped the tired chestnut's leg, straightened up with alarm. 'Walk, miss? You?'

'I've got legs, haven't I?' Bella snapped.

Jeremiah raised his eyebrows. Oh yes, she had legs all right. The best set of pins this side of the Mendips.

'I know this hill well enough. God knows I keep getting dragged back here!' she said to herself as Jeremiah nodded in distraction. 'I'll send somebody down for the cart.'

'Why don't I go and—'

'I've waited long enough,' she cried. 'Hugo's relying on me now.'

The youngster unhitched the horse, collected his meagre belongings from the cart and led the limping animal on up the slope. His mistress had hurried on, and was already wreathed in the darkness, a grey ghost in her well-worn riding cloak.

'Miss Bella, wait on, miss, please!'

'I can't wait around for you, Jeremiah. You bring the horse on, I'll go ahead to find Father.'

The boy frowned in tearful exasperation, not the first young male to be left in such a wretched state in Bella Morrison's wake.

'Miss Bella, wait for me!' he howled, tugging the lame horse on up the hill.

Jeremiah had been forced to let the animal rest at the silent summit, staring into the whispering woods as the night things croaked and scampered in the undergrowth. He had to lean against the poor beast's chest as it hopped and slid down the other side. Thirty minutes later the boy led the chestnut across the narrow bridge at the foot of the hill, the tired animal tossing its head as they reached the sleeping village. The boy came to an exhausted halt, listened to the night sounds. The subdued clack of a nightjar, wasn't it?

No.

He tilted his head and made out the faint clatter of hoofs. Somebody was riding down the hill behind him. Jeremiah turned, peered back the way he had come. The hoofs drummed on the parched road, and the boy edged the lame chestnut onto the verge out of their way. He held the snorting beast's wet nose as the riders coagulated out of the gloom, clustering together to cross the ancient bridge. Jeremiah could make out their dust-grey riding jackets, but had no idea whose side they were on.

'Whoa now, lads,' the leader called, reining his sweating nag to a halt and leering down at the nervous youth. 'Seems we've found the other half of that cart,' he called. Jeremiah smiled weakly at them. Five riders with pinched, sooty faces barely visible under broad felt hats. Jeremiah had been around the camps long enough to know dragoons when he saw them. Highly mobile infantry who rode around the battlefields on their lumpy but reliable ponies, leaping off to fire ragged volleys before leaping back on and spurring off out of trouble. They spurred alongside, hemming him in between the sweating chestnut and the hedge. Jeremiah noticed they had swaddled their cheap saddles in bolts of bright cloth. He realized with a start they were Miss Bella's dresses. Her best, left packed on the cart the other side of the hill. By God, she'd be furious with them!

'Cart took a bit of a tumble, seemingly,' the leader growled, bending over his saddle to squint at the boy. 'So you won't be needin' that beast now, will yer?'

'It's Mistress Bella's horse, and that's her best frock,' Jeremiah said shakily. He was a good twenty yards from the nearest house, squat and shuttered along the lane there.

'I'd like to see her in it,' the dragoon replied.

'Or out,' one of his cronies called with a cackle.

'Hand him over now, lad,' the leader said menacingly.

'You can see he's lame,' Jeremiah insisted.

'Not as lame as he's going to be.' The dragoon peeled his coat away from his slack right arm, revealed the carbine resting along his thigh. 'Now. Hand him over,' he suggested, the moonlight glinting on his off-white teeth.

Night had fallen slowly high on the hill above the village, pushing bands of deep blue out over the horizons. The old oaks and beeches of Kilmersden Wood threw jagged shadows over the road and seemed to crowd in after their black children like a many-trunked army. Owls glided between mossy boughs, eyed scurrying moles. Foxes and badgers skittered in the nettle- and bramble-choked hollows, paused every now and then to sniff the breeze and eye the big house over the wild lawns, safe behind its girdle of trees, its live log stockade.

Margaret, Lady Ramsay, stared out at the silently accusing woods, crowding in on her lonely home like a crown of thorns. She was a formidably built but handsome woman, her luxuriant ash-blonde hair caught up in a brisk bun, the sternly clipped roots veined with silver.

'Shall I turn the bugger out of doors, ma'am?'

Lady Ramsay turned slowly, smiled wearily at the gravely concerned gamekeeper. Findlay was her prop now, a fiery-eyed and intensely loyal retainer, the terror of those wild woods the Ramsays had called home. Home no longer. Not if that whining, insinuating rogue Morrison had his way.

Turned out of his own home by the fluctuating fortunes of war, Morrison had fetched up at Kilmersden Hall, greedy as a leech to feed on what little was left of the Ramsays' perilously extended estate. The merry oaf had stuffed his fat paws in his mealy mouth, offering shocked sympathy to the grieving widow. He had hinted and teased all evening, apparently as stricken with grief over her husband's death on Lansdown Ridge as she was herself.

Incredulous at the equally pitiful fate of her son, shot while riding into the Royalist camp the night before that bloody battle. By mistake. How could anybody shoot somebody down by mistake? What cruel fates had picked on the Ramsays? What great God above had set their family on such a bloody course?

The wily merchant had choked on his own indignation, questioned his own 'truly and deeply held beliefs'.

'Madam, it is as wicked and unjust a fate as I have ever heard,' he had said, crocodile tears springing into his mobile eyes. Unable to bear her grief and shame any longer, Lady Ramsay had begged to be excused, left him to his cold feast in the empty lounge.

The house echoed with its own emptiness, as if it had swallowed a bellyful of silence. Her daughter Anneliese, all she had left now, long since abed. All lights extinguished apart from the dim candles they held against the gathering darkness. A house without life, a mausoleum of lost hopes and desperate dreams. Old Ramsay had been a dreamer, a good man, but a dreamer none the less. Now he and his poor son had gone, this great pile was nothing but a gravestone around her neck, bound to drain away what little cash they had left.

Findlay tactfully turned away as the bitter tears stung her eyes. Lady Ramsay scowled herself still, willed her features to stone.

'It's too late for that,' she said huskily. Too late indeed. Their unbidden guest was waiting in the lounge, drinking her brandy and fortifying himself with a pullet. Waiting for her return, ready to fume and rage and lament her loss with the brutal sympathy of a slaughterman. What did the damned man have in mind? How had he put it? The King had owed her husband much, for such faultless service.

'Ah, owed, owed,' he had intoned. 'Would that he owed me more.'

The blustering bounder's stage whisper had clanged in her head like a culverin in a cathedral. Lady Ramsay had lost the merchant's meaning for a moment in the choppy sea of his barely controlled sentiments. She ran over their poisoned conversation once more, trying to imagine how Ramsay could ever have been taken in by such a blustering bounder.

'Owed? Owed whom?' she had asked, hideously bewildered.

'Why me, madam, for what little it's worth.'

She had blinked rapidly, confused by the unexpected pitfalls of their one-sided conversation.

'I mean, madam, if only I had lent your dear departed husband a little extra, maybe it would have helped the King's cause even more. Paid for the extra company of foot, the extra troop of horse that could have made all the difference.'

Lady Ramsay ignored his bluster. 'You lent my husband money?'

The merchant had waved his pudgy hands, pished and pshawed. 'A mere trifle.'

'How much?'

'A hundred pounds or so.'

'A hundred pounds,' she repeated stonily.

'Or so.'

Lady Ramsay listened in disbelief as he outlined the details of her late husband's debt. The Ramsays had held their house for the King despite the power of the local wool magnates, most of whom had sided with the rebel Parliament. The war had severely curtailed the Ramsays' slim business opportunities, and blocked their access to the

Bristol markets. Despite their failing incomes her husband had insisted on keeping the small but dedicated garrison paid. Most of the men had melted away by now or taken service with the Royalist army as it marched on the great crusade through the west, leaving the Ramsay household penniless and vulnerable. A draughty pile garrisoned by a middle-aged widow, her young daughter and a handful of decayed servants. And Findlay, of course. The sharpshooter was worth a dozen men alone with his six-foot fowling piece.

One hundred pounds? They had never been rich, despite the luxurious trappings they appeared to enjoy at Kilmersden Hall. How was she going to pay the grasping merchant?

'Honesty, madam. A virtue indeed, but misplaced in time of war. Your husband would have done better to keep the men in arrears, and ensured their continued loyalty,' Sir Gilbert had said silkily, biting his fat lip in mock concern.

' "Hang on to your money," I told him. "Let the rascals wait for their pay." But he wouldn't have it. "Gilbert," he said, "you must lend me another two hundred." '

'Two hundred? You said one hundred!'

'Or so, I said, madam. Two hundred in addition to the nine hundred and fifty already rendered.'

The richly furnished room had swung around like a lantern on the prow of a storm-tossed galleon.

'Nine hundred and fifty?'

'Call it a square twelve hundred and be done,' Sir Gilbert had offered generously. 'I'm not one to lose sleep over a few pennies.'

'My husband owes you twelve hundred pounds?' she had asked, light headed.

'I have his markers for a little over that sum, madam,' Sir Gilbert confirmed, gravely. 'I hesitate to burden you with the miserable details at a time like this.'

'But Sir Gilbert—' Her voice had broken, and she had wrestled with her suddenly dry throat. 'Sir Gilbert, you must know I have no opportunity at present for repaying such a sum.'

He had thrown up his hands in horror, shaken his fleshy head.

'There's no rush, no rush at all! Haven't you already done me a good turn, opening your house to a poor fugitive of this vile war? Why, this house, I already think of it as home. A home from home,' the merchant added hastily. Lady Ramsay shuddered at the prospect. He crossed the room, held her arm as if she was made of porcelain. 'There will be plenty of time to discuss . . . all that needs must be done,' he had concluded.

Needs must be done. The phrase echoed in her head like a broadside. Findlay coughed, reminded her of his beady-eyed presence.

'With your permission then, my lady, I'll take a turn around the grounds. There's odd folk abroad tonight, the road's busy,' he said quietly. 'Something's up away with the war and all.'

She nodded wretchedly. Odd folk on the roads? By God, she and Anneliese would be joining them, if the merchant proved true to his word. She watched the lean gamekeeper bow and take his leave. Overcome by his unflinching loyalty, Lady Ramsay burst into a squall of bitter tears.

Bella had reached the village some twenty minutes before her groom, and made her way along the narrow High

Street to her father's town house. A three-storeyed crate leaning drunkenly above the silent street, as lifeless as a gravestone. She had knocked and peered in at the grimed window, rattled the locked door. Her father was away again. Where? He wouldn't dare show his face in Bristol, not after his drastic about-face those weeks before. Sir Gilbert had been commissioned by the Parliament to raise a regiment of yeomen from the hills round about. As it turned out he had barely mustered a single company, but he had claimed pay and provision for the regiment anyway.

'We're bound to get a few more, by and by,' he had told his shocked daughter. 'Someone's bound to turn up sooner or later.' As the Royalist army had moved remorselessly closer, Sir Gilbert had decided it was time to rethink his responsibilities. 'Give the King another chance, God bless him. Monarchs don't grow on trees, you know,' he had explained airily. He was hardly likely to be greeted with open arms by Nathaniel Fiennes, the dour Roundhead colonel charged with holding the port of Bristol against the invading Royalists.

Bella had stood in the cold street, wondered at his whereabouts. She clicked her fingers. Kilmersden Hall, of course. Her father had already been forced to take refuge in the manor house once. A convenient if rather hostile bolt-hole, in case of trouble. It was another half an hour's walk, at least. Back over the bridge and right up the hill. Bella sighed, gathered up her skirts and marched on, indefatigably, into the night.

She heard the boy's feeble screams from the end of the lane, ducked into the shadows beneath the securely fastened shutters of the last cottage in the straggling village street. Bella had heard young Jeremiah whining often enough to know his small voice, almost lost amongst the guttural threats of men and the frightened whimperings of a horse. Bella peered around a mossy brick wall, squinted at the altercation along the lane. A group of riders seemed to be trying to force poor Jerry through a hedge. They were thrusting and kicking, pulling at the lame chestnut's bridle as the boy hung on grimly from the other side. Bella bristled, marched out from behind her rudimentary cover. The horse thieves saw her coming, hung back from their quarry in a loose, steaming scrummage. Jeremiah yanked the frightened chestnut's head around, forcing the beast to back into the dragoon nags. The bearded leader held up his carbine, snarled in frustration.

'You'll stay back, missy, if you know what's good for you,' he leered.

'They want the horse, Miss Bella!' Jeremiah yodelled. The dragoons urged their horses forward, blocking the narrow lane. Bella came to a nervous halt, tried to maintain her withering stare.

'Get out of my way, you louts, or I'll call the militia out!' she challenged them, blue eyes blazing in the darkness.

'That's a laugh!' One of the bedraggled riders hooted with laughter. 'We've just seen what's left of your precious militia rounded up on Runaway Hill!'

The leader spurred his pony ahead, peered at the girl's richly brocaded gown, peeping from beneath her travelling cloak.

'And who might you be, miss?'

Bella glanced from one rider to another, shook her head.

'I'm Mary Pitt,' the girl replied, naming her absent maid.

Bella had left the poor girl in Chippenham, mooning over that hulking oaf William Sparrow. What had the lout said, all the militia rounded up? William was with the militia on Roundway. He had asked Bella to marry him, but she could hardly marry poor William when she had so many gentlemen of quality paying her court. She had been quite relieved to discover her own maid had harboured a soft spot for the ambitious apprentice. They were far more suited. Mary would mend his bruised feelings quickly enough.

'Oh, but I do love him, miss,' she had cried on being told of Bella's imminent departure to Bath. 'Don't take me away from him, miss, not now I've got him!' Well, Mary was welcome to him.

She blinked rapidly, remembered where she was.

The dragoon smiled grimly. Several of his teeth were missing, the rest curled like a rabid dog's in his suggestively moving mouth.

'He said Bella. You're no Mary!' the rider retorted.

'Maybe that's her finery we found on the road there, Jack,' another rider called.

'Mislaid it, did you, miss? Your father knows you're abroad at this hour, does he?'

'Of course he does. He's just coming now with all the men,' Bella snapped.

The dragoon squatted in his cheap saddle, eyed the road behind her twitching head. 'I don't 'ear 'em,' he said casually. 'You 'ear 'em, Michael?'

'That I don't,' one of the riders replied in his rich Devon brogue.

'I think she's been tellin' tales,' the leader said. 'I think we ought to take this . . .'

The shot cracked around the village, bounded off into

the night like a snarling wolf. The startled dragoons hunched over their saddles, pulled pistols from their coats. The leader bowed lower and lower, his frightened pony hoofing the road. In the agonizing silence, they could hear the cold splash of his blood over his boots.

'Drop 'em, right now!' an enormous voice roared from the bushes. Devon Michael raised his pistol, fired blind. The leader's startled horse bolted, tipping the dead rider from his saddle. Bella leapt into the hedge. The four survivors tilted their heads, eyed the dripping willows lined along the stream. A thin plume of smoke rose like a whisper from the trees. Still no more shots. The battle-hardened dragoons slid out of their saddles, Devon Michael gathering the reins while the rest ducked down behind the verge. A one-man ambush, they'd run into many similar traps, ranging all over the country. Green troops would bolt, hang on to their hats and hide. These men were fighters. Renegades and cut-throats, but fighters all the same. The last of Captain Nybb's brave troop, on their way back home for a little well-earned rest. The only trouble was, they'd forgotten to ask their formidable captain's permission for their little excursion.

Jeremiah wriggled free from the deserter's vile grip and followed Bella through the hedge. He lay alongside the girl on the far side of the tangled vegetation, trembling with cold and fear.

'Who is it?' he whispered.

Bella shook her head, too terrified to speak. The shot was still vibrating through her skull. She peeped between the jagged brambles at the dead man hanging from his pony like a sack of turnips, the stubby carbine lying forgotten in the roadside mulch. She heard the surviving dragoons hissing instructions to each other.

'Bob, you get yerself back toward the bridge a way there,' Devon Michael ordered, peering over the ponies' quivering backs towards the trees. 'Joseph Hosay, you get along that away.' The dragoons ducked along the lane, flitting skilfully from one piece of cover to another. Devon Michael peered at the trees. No way the sniper could back off without revealing his position. Unless he'd already . . .

The second shot came from the bridge. A wiry dragoon in a worsted coat staggered back a few steps, clutching his throat. Devon Michael gripped the reins in his teeth, raised his carbine. Damn him, he was good, whoever he was. Two shots in under a minute. Unless there were more than one. Bob Finch lay twitching along the lane, his dirty fists opening and closing in a heap of cold horse dung. Devon Michael squinted into the gloom, watched for the movement from the bridge. Travis, the last dragoon, aimed his pistol and fired at the deserted structure. Devon Michael could hear shouts from the alerted village, saw squares of light fall into the street. No time. He cursed under his breath, swung himself into the saddle. The other dragoons doubled back to their ponies, grasped at the reins. They ducked down low over their saddles, rode back for the bridge. Travis drew his sword, held the dimly gleaming blade in front of him. Ten yards. Five. He saw the shadowy sniper leap up from the stiff bulrushes against the bridge and swing a heavy branch like a club. Devon Michael noticed he had laid his long gun on the bank, away from the water. Only a man who knew his business and loved what he knew would have discarded the fowling piece, trusted to a bit of wood to fight three mounted opponents.

He'd pay for that piece of insolence. Devon Michael reined in hard, damn near toppling his ragged pony. He watched as Travis took one swipe at the tall stranger as he cantered past toward the sanctuary of the far bank. The sniper swung the branch, cracked Travis' knee. The rider howled. Joseph Hosay spurred on, over the bridge and off into the night. Devon Michael cursed, scissored out of the saddle and aimed his carbine at the stranger as he stood poised by the cold parapet. Three yards off, a perfect target. Caught like a coney in a wire.

'I thought so. A gamekeep, a master's man,' he snarled.

The tall stranger straightened, caught his breath. Devon Michael took a wary step closer, the carbine's black eye aimed at the gamekeeper's chest.

'Who do you serve then, matey? Go shootin' my men down for sport?'

'Who do *you* serve?' the sniper asked coldly.

'I serve, sir, I serve,' the dragoon replied. 'Only now and again we don't serve nobody but ourselves.' He raised the carbine another notch, watched the gamekeeper's pale face tighten. A good man, but a dead man all the same.

Findlay flinched as the shot rang out, waited for the impact of the heavy bullet. No time to jump aside, not from this range. He opened his eyes as the heavily built dragoon leaned forward, his dirty face contorted in bewildered agony. The gamekeeper reacted at once. He darted forward, kicked the man's carbine to one side as the dirty desperado pulled the trigger. The stray ball tore through the bulrushes and splashed into the water. The dragoon cursed, sprawled face down in the mud. Findlay stared down at the twitching corpse, a heavy stain spreading slowly from the neat hole in his dusty coat. The gamekeeper looked up slowly, watched the shocked girl step closer cradling a smoking carbine in her arms. He could hear people running from the village to see what the disturbance was about, perhaps catch themselves a stray horse. He breathed a plume of vapour, nodded sourly as he recognized the girl. Morrison's daughter. The hated merchant's most valuable asset. Walk away from one Morrison slap bang into another. They were like weeds, this damn family.

Findlay had needed some space and some air all right. Stuck in the hollow house with his distraught mistress and that bastarding hound of a merchant, he would have ended up shooting the swine himself if he had been forced to listen to his humble blusterings much longer. He had been agitated by reports of an unusual number of strangers roaming over the road along the bottom of the hill, and had decided to cool his temper with a walk around the grounds. He had gone further than he intended, leaving the house alone on its lonely hill, and had just turned back when he had heard the commotion by the bridge. Deserters or some such scum. Looting some poor lad's horse, and then threatening his sparky mistress. He hadn't realized it was her. Findlay frowned, knew it wouldn't have made any difference if he had. He couldn't have stood by while a gang of looters plundered the poor girl. And now she had saved his life and put him in her debt. In her family's debt. The gamekeeper strode toward the crying girl, lifted the heavy carbine from her white hands.

'Another second he'd have plugged me for sure,' he said bluntly. 'I owe you, miss.'

Bella gaped at him as if he was babbling in tongues, deafened by the shots and her own fright. She had pulled the carbine from beneath the dead dragoon's body, pursued her craven enemy down the hill. The carbine had leapt so much when she pulled the trigger she had been terrified she had missed his broad bear's back. Bella had peered through the stinking smoke, watched the big dragoon fold up on himself like a slaughtered calf.

'We'd best get you up to your father,' Findlay growled, picking his trusty gun from the parapet. He led the stunned girl away, called the frightened boy from his cover behind the hedge.

'Pick up those pistols and get a hold of the ponies if you can,' Findlay ordered. 'They might come in handy.'

Jeremiah Pitt squeezed his way through the hedge, stared down at the sprawled bodies. He tottered for a moment, and fell back into the hedge in a dead faint. Findlay squeezed the dumb girl's arm, motioned her to wait while he walked over to the boy, bent down and lifted him on to his shoulder like a sack of rabbits. He snorted with the effort, shook his head. It took you funny sometimes, seeing your first body. If this war went on much longer, he'd be seeing more, sure as eggs was eggs.

BY

DEVIZES CASTLE,

14 JULY 1643

Scipio Porthcurn wiped the dregs of his all too short sleep from his eyes, blinked at the enormous musketeer framed by the dwarfed doorway. The brute's knock must have woken half the castle, but it was certainly an improvement on Jethro Polruan's usual bear-pit behaviour. The one-eared giant leered in greeting, touched his meaty paw to his ragged Montero cap in a fit of uncharacteristic courtesy.

'Gennlemuns to see you, sur,' he growled, nodding over his shoulder, as if the colonel could possibly see anything beyond his unwashed bulk.

'Tell the candle-wasting bastard to bother someone else. If he's an officer, I'm the queen of Sheba!' Porthcurn growled, dropping his exhausted head back on his crooked arm. He had been detailed to organize guards for the prisoners taken on Roundway, a thankless task seeing as how most of his men had made themselves scarce to join in the frenzied plundering on the ridge above the town. The prisoners had become surlier by the minute as well, loudly demanding their rights and a hot meal into the bargain. The mutinous screws. Polruan stepped into the room, making way for a blubbery blond youth in an immaculate grey suit liberally plastered in lawn and lace. His collars and cuffs could have kept a Flanders whore in underwear for a twelvemonth. The dandy had practically stuffed his handkerchief into his mouth against Polruan's raucous body odours, and was signalling the heavy musketeer away with expressive flicks of his narrow, womanly wrist. Colonel Porthcurn shoved himself to his tired feet, watched the young gentleman edge into the dank room followed by a heavily built bodyguard with more scars than a blind dog.

'Colonel Porthquorn? I'm delighted to make your acquaintance,' the dandy simpered. 'Can I be the first to congratulate you on this noble victory?' he enquired, taking a disdainful look about the barely furnished room. Porthcurn frowned as the corpulent newcomer picked at the frills hanging from his limp white wrist.

'We were in the town,' he said guardedly. 'It was my Lord Wilmot's cavalry as won the day for us, sir,' he added as an afterthought. Another young snotnose down from Oxford for a bit of glory? After a little nick, a small scar to wear on his powdered cheek to show off to the ladies in some perfumed cloister? Colonel Porthcurn, a plain farmer's son from north Cornwall, had little time for such posturing mannequins.

'All the same, sir. Your gallant men arrived to complete the rebels' discomfiture, is that not the case?' The gentleman waited while Polruan closed the door behind him, and beamed at the Cornish officer with brotherly familiarity.

'Please excuse my manners. I have been away from court too long. I am, sir, Anthony St John Dyle, Lord Clavincale, don't you know.'

Porthcurn didn't know. He grunted something noncommittal, tilted his black head to study the dandy's scowling bodyguard. Here was a man after his own kind. A bloody brawler if he wasn't much mistaken.

'Don't I know you, sir?' Porthcurn asked slyly.

'Mebbe, mineer. Cap'n Nybb's the name. Mucker a mine, then, ja?'

Porthcurn frowned, nodded. 'Wittstock, back in '36,' the colonel remembered. 'You were riding a big white horse with Polish feathers on your back!'

Nybb grinned broadly. 'Ja, hosen oder schleime! Wittstock!' He slapped his greasy breeches, recalled the battle. 'Mitt Generale Hatzfeld, auf dem laager top of that hill, ja, mineer!'

Porthcurn held his breath, smiled. 'I rode with General King that day. Up the hill.'

Nybb caught his meaning, shook his scarred head from side to side. 'Nicht mitt der Sachsens, eh, mineer? Ah, alle ist kla! Der Sachsens plenty kaput, eh?'

'I saw you ride through my troop. We lost a few good men that day.'

Nybb pursed his lips, ran his broad thumb along a puckered scar below his ear. 'Ja, mineer. C'est la guerre, mon ami!'

Clavincale gave a small cough, and smiled sweetly at his formidable bodyguard.

'Ah, it's always nice to meet one's former comrades,' he said shortly.

'We weren't comrades, sir. We were enemies. We fought up and down that hill, that day.'

Nybb nodded in agreement. 'And never a penny of money for it,' he sang quietly.

Porthcurn sighed.

'Well, now. And what can I do for you gentlemen? The staff officers are away across the courtyard.'

Clavincale eased his well-upholstered behind over the edge of Porthcurn's commandeered desk, selected a sheaf of creased papers bound with pink ribbon from his leather portfolio. He selected a sheet, passed it over to the swarthy Cornishman. Porthcurn eyed the small, carefully printed characters and studied the heavily embossed seal within a flaking crater of red wax. A Royal Commission, signed by King Charles himself. Porthcurn eyed the narrow script, reluctant to reveal his bewilderment. The damn paper said everything and nothing!

'My credentials, sir. A somewhat unusual array, as you have evidently noticed.'

Porthcurn nodded.

'In a nutshell, sir, I am an agent of the crown. I am to gather intelligence and use my family's considerable influence in any manner likely to be of assistance to our Sovereign.'

'A licence to do whatever need be done,' Porthcurn read aloud.

Clavincale raised an eyebrow, nodded. 'Whatever need be done indeed. My particular specialities are not on the field of battle, but are no less important for all of that,' he added rather waspishly.

The colonel scratched the heavy stubble on his jaw and shook his head.

'Well, as my particular specialities are very much confined to the field of battle, I can't see how I can be of any assistance to you, sir.'

Clavincale patted the tightly stretched thigh of his immaculate grey breeches, nodded briskly.

'Well, I'll come to the point, sir. You have been put in charge of these rogues, these Roundhead prisoners?' Porthcurn agreed he had. 'Well, therein lies the difficulty. I don't know whether you have heard of Major Scrope? Josiah Scrope? No matter, sir, he's no more than half man at best. A beast, sir. The Butcher of Buckingham, they call him at Oxford.' Porthcurn frowned, wondering what some boorish Roundhead major had to do with him.

'Unfortunately for our brave cause, Major Scrope has inveigled his way to the command of the prison there. He has friends within the Queen's circle of influence.' Clavincale lowered his voice as if the Catholic Spitfire Henrietta Maria herself was eavesdropping at the door.

'He's on our side?' Porthcurn asked.

Clavincale clicked his tongue.

'More's the pity. The fellow's a complete bounder, sir. No breeding at all. A common butcher, sir.'

'I don't see what it's got to—'

The blond youth raised his white hand daintily, gave the colonel a short smile. 'The King is in a quandary, sir. He has agreed to the man's appointment to please the Queen, God protect her from all harm,' he breathed. 'But his treatment of the prisoners is causing His Majesty dire distress, and losing him friends in both the Houses. We are handing the enemy gossip columnists a perfect opportunity to highlight what they see as the tyranny of Charles Stewart. In short, Colonel, the Roundheads fear our good Major Scrope so much they are actually fighting harder! They believe if they are to die under the lash in Oxford they might just as well take a few of our chaps with them!' Clavincale rolled his blue eyes for emphasis.

Porthcurn ran his broad thumb along his big nose, completely bewildered. 'You want the man shot, is that it?'

Clavincale gasped in horror. 'Shot? One of our own loyal officers? No, sir, not at all, sir. You mistake me, sir. It's just the King feels we should house our prisoners elsewhere, until we can find a more suitable assignment for the man.'

Porthcurn nodded. 'Where? Here? My regiment are fighters, sir, not gaolers. They'll not thank you for—'

'Again, sir, you mistake me,' Clavincale interrupted. 'I don't intend to turn this castle into a prison for the course of the war. I have foreseen an opportunity to ship them off, out of the way.'

'Out of the way?'

'Precisely.'

'Precisely where, out of the way?'

Clavincale shrugged his fashionably narrow shoulders. 'Oh, somewhere safe and sound. Where they can't escape to take up arms against the King. You don't want them taking up arms against the King again, do you, Porthquorn?'

'No, sir. But I can't imagine anywhere where they . . .' Oh yes he could. He could imagine only too well. 'Not the Indies?'

Clavincale frowned as if he had never heard of the place.

'No, no, no.' The nobleman clicked his tongue in annoyance. 'I have many friends amongst our trusted allies overseas, ambassadors and envoys and so on,' he said airily. 'They are always on the lookout for good men to serve abroad.'

Porthcurn scowled. Did this popinjay mean to sell the prisoners off as galley slaves?

Clavincale eyed him warily, smiled shortly.

'Their Imperial Majesties in Spain and Portugal would be more than willing to take the scum off our hands, Porthquorn,' he said sharply. 'We'll march them off down south to start with. They'll be safe enough there now your General Hopton has cleared the west, and there will be plenty of work to put them to.'

'Where?'

'Sherborne Castle, for a start. All enemy prisoners in these parts are being dispatched to a general rendezvous, and sent on from there.'

Porthcurn paused, took another look at the lord's unquestionable authorization. He'd not be party to sending men to the Indies, or condemn them to sweat out the rest of their lives in some Godforsaken Spanish garrison no matter what Clavincale's credentials said. They would be no better off than some indentured slave on some tobacco plantation, cutting sugar cane under a pitiless Caribbean sun. He'd heard stories about service on the Spanish main from some of the old mariners back home in Cornwall. A fit man would last six months, if he was lucky. A sick man wouldn't last hours under that ferocious heat.

'I shall have to discuss the matter with General Hopton,' he said briskly.

Clavincale closed his eyes as if he was in pain. 'I have already discussed the matter with General Hopton's staff. I see no reason for you to question my array. Kindly have the prisoners paraded for my inspection in one quarter of an hour.'

'But . . .'

'Colonel Porthquorn,' Clavincale snapped, 'must I take this matter higher? I have already explained the circumstances of the situation at Oxford. The bulk of these men must go elsewhere. I hear several hundred have already come to their senses and re-enlisted with the King?'

Porthcurn nodded. Several hundred scoundrels had changed sides for the moment, yes. They'd be off, though, the first chance they could get.

'Well, then. We must confine our attentions to the rest. Rebels and ringleaders, sir, I've no time for them. And I am rather surprised to find you so concerned for your enemy's welfare.'

The surly crew in the far corner of the courtyard climbed wearily to their feet as the dragoons elbowed their way through the packed ranks, knocked the prisoners aside with their halberds. The belligerent sergeant who had stolen William's boots returned their malicious stares with interest and kicked the reluctant wanderers awake.

'On your feet, you lot. And you, matey!'

'You've got my boots, you pigeon-toed dwarf!' William cursed. 'How can I stand up in these?' He held the dragoon's battered footwear up for inspection. They were clearly several sizes too small for the hulking cavalryman.

'Never mind that, you crop-headed bastard. Get up against the wall with the rest of 'em!'

'You said officers were to be quartered elsewhere!' William insisted, sticking to his guns as the rest of the prisoners shuffled into line for the inspection party, already picking their way across the crowded courtyard.

'Fuck off out of it before I clock you one,' the dragoon snarled.

'Sergeant Lawton!' The dragoon officer with the inspection party called the vindictive man away, hissed some instructions into his ear. William frowned, glanced at Long Col, who was keenly watching the Royalist officers as they pointed and prodded their way through the hungry mob.

'They've had all the recruits they're going to get,' he said under his breath. 'What's up now?'

Captain Breech, the dragoon officer in temporary charge of the prisoners, had already made his rounds, cursing and cajoling the exhausted scarecrows in the courtyard into taking the King's shilling.

'Free pardon for all and sixpence a man. A gallon of good ale and a hot meal into the bargain, what do you say, boys?'

'I'd rather serve in hell than with those bastard Cornish!' a wounded veteran had shouted from the back.

The dragoon officer had tactfully brought his own men with him rather than the despised invaders from the far west. He nodded his head conspiratorially.

'The general's already planning to raise more regiments round about. You won't have to serve with the Cornish,' he had reassured the waverers. 'We'll march everyone through the tower there. There'll be those of you who want to enlist but don't want to feel they're letting their mates down. If you're one of those, just stay in the tower while the rest march on through. Let the silly buggers go to Oxford if they want.'

'You'll get no recruits here, mate,' the elderly pikeman had predicted.

But when the shuffling crowd had completed the manoeuvre through the lower storey of the crumbling tower, it was clear to all Captain Breech's recruitment drive had been a worthwhile effort. Some two hundred and eighty prisoners had remained in the tower or filed out quietly into another part of the rambling castle. Amongst them were the Pitt brothers, terrified of being locked up in a narrow cell at Oxford. Bill Butcher the dyer's apprentice sneered and told-you-so'd, but William couldn't find it in his heart to blame his old friends.

'Will's right,' Long Col had agreed with a puff on his cold clay-pipe stem. 'They'd not stand it in Oxford.' William had frowned, wondered if he would be able to stand it in their place. He knew though, he knew without thinking, that there was no way on earth he would have stayed in the tower. He had made his choices months before. He'd not change his mind now, like his damned weathercock of a master had done. Sir Gilbert Morrison might be sitting pretty, counting his money with his new Royalist friends, but he'd never be able to hold his head up in Bristol, or Chipping Marleward come to that. William Sparrow might not become a knight or a great lord or leader, but he was no damned turncoat. He wasn't about to follow the merchant's cowardly example and change horses at the first fence.

Sparrow had gloomily resumed his seat on the old barrel, picked at the grubby bandage he had wrapped around his missing finger. A bloody memento from Roundway. He had barely felt the sword cut through his gauntlet, but now, hours later, the missing digit throbbed as if he had dipped it in the molten lead back at his master's workshop in Bristol. He wondered how old Percy Gresham was managing without him. No doubt the old crab had hired a new apprentice from the Bristol stews. He'd have no time for William were he ever to get himself home again. Sparrow rested his stubbled chin on his aching palm and sighed heavily. His rapidly diminishing employment prospects weren't his only concern. He had Mary Keziah to worry about now, as well as himself. He wondered how long his new sweetheart would manage without him. She was stuck back in Chippenham waiting for news. Hadn't he told her something about getting married that day? Running to find a preacher while the army took to its heels, hah! She'd wander on back after her mistress, find somebody else in the end.

William had been slumped in gloomy imaginings when

Captain Breech had returned with the inspection party. Peacock officers in all their finery, sorting through the remainder of the prisoners like shrewd farmers at market.

They didn't seem interested in the gangly youngsters, the coughing apprentices or the groaning wounded. The dandified gentlemen picked only the fit men.

'And fit men means we're to be worked,' Long Col predicted sourly. The lean veteran broke into a fit of dry coughing, bent over like an old crab as the Royalist gentlemen made their way into the corner of the courtyard. Butcher and Gillingfeather hung their heads on their chests, stared miserably at the cobbles. William twitched, watched their particular approach. The dragoon captain was escorting a young lord in a smart grey suit, and a scarred ruffian who looked as if he had been fighting from the age of five. Sparrow fidgeted under their hawk-eyed inspection.

'Here's a strapping lad,' Captain Breech observed. 'Fancies himself as an officer, so I'm told.' Sparrow kept quiet for once. The white-faced lord regarded him over the scented handkerchief he had pressed to his nose. He nodded once, and looked down at the helplessly disabled musketeers.

'Are these men sick, Captain?' the dandy enquired.

Captain Breech frowned. 'They weren't an hour ago. The hairy one's always on about something or other. A regular coxcomb, he is.'

Gillingfeather stopped coughing and looked up, his mad eyes rolling.

'The old one's no use. He sounds like a broken-winded nag. You, boy.' The lord aimed his slim shoe at Billy Butcher's behind. 'How old are you?'

The apprentice broke into a fit of coughing. The lord held the handkerchief higher.

'He's play acting, my lord,' Breech said. 'They're the worst scoundrels of the lot.'

'Take his name, Captain.'

Long Col looked up over the worn sleeve of his old coat. 'We stay together,' he said slowly. 'Take one you take us all.' The blond-haired youngster gave a short smile.

'I'm sure you'll be very happy,' he simpered, and continued his tour of their ragged ranks.

BY

KILMERSDEN HALL,

CHIPPING MARLEWARD, SOMERSET, 14 JULY 1643

Bella had arrived at Kilmersden Hall shivering in a horse blanket, exhausted and distraught after the horrifying ambush near the bridge. Findlay had helped her into the scullery with grumpy concern, fetched her a tot of brandy as the family stood staring in their nightclothes and shawls. The gamekeeper had explained what had happened, how he had come upon Miss Bella here being mauled by a gang of ruffians. Three of the said ruffians were now being loaded on to the Ramsays' cart in Chipping Marleward, two more had sloped off into the night. Findlay had caught two of their horses, and helped himself to their abandoned weapons. Bella's looted and somewhat bedraggled clothing had been tossed on a kitchen table, forgotten for now.

'I saved her, and she saved me,' he'd reported gruffly. 'If she hadn't plugged that big bugger, I'd be in me winding-sheet now, that's the truth of it.'

They had been mesmerized by her mad chase across the country, her narrow escape from the bandit horsemen. Sir Gilbert had been at once appalled and thrilled his wilful daughter had caused such a stir. She was no stay at home sewing woman. She was no cold-blooded fish content to hide away with an embroidery while the world whirled by. My, Sir Gilbert thought quickly, she would make a great catch for a stout-hearted man. Prince Rupert, or his younger brother Maurice, perhaps. If only he could invite them down to Chipping Marleward, they would be delighted with her. On the other hand though, she had been out on her own in the dead of night, off on some errand after her fancy captain. Sir Gilbert bristled. She could have been captured by bandits and held to ransom, sold off to the pirates to trade with the Turks! Damn the girl, was she quite unhinged? He had stood in the chill kitchen, torn between throwing his arms about her heaving shoulders and throttling her.

Having snatched a few hours' sleep Bella had risen early, apparently none the worse for her cross-country ordeal. She had spent most of her time since her eventful arrival urging her father to do something on wretched Hugo's behalf. He was the only man who could save the poor lamb. Sir Gilbert, angry and brooding at the untimely intrusion into his delicately poised affairs, had waved her away in distracted annoyance. Plotting rescue missions on behalf of some uppity officer hadn't figured high on his list of priorities. The wily merchant had flung his arms around her, of course, called her his chick, his own true heart. In front of Lady Ramsay, that was. In front of Findlay and Anneliese and the gawping servants, he had been a picture of fatherly concern.

But as soon as he had shut the door on them to comfort his obviously distressed daughter he had flung her on the divan in a fury, stamped around the room hissing horribly.

'Where in the name of all the hells have you been?' the merchant had demanded, red face pressed close to her tear-stained cheek. 'The last I heard you were taking the waters at Chippenham, holding court like Cleopatra! I tell you this, my girl, that's the last time you go anywhere without my say so!'

'I was perfectly safe in Chippenham,' Bella had sniffed defiantly.

'And then you decide to chase off across the country after some whippersnapper of a captain?'

'He needs me, Father. Nobody else is interested in getting him out. You haven't seen the conditions in which they keep the prisoners – the damp, the rats . . .'

'And what am I supposed to do, go to Waller and ask for him back? Use your sense, girl,' he had snapped. 'I've adjusted my allegiance, remembered my duty at last. They'd shoot me on sight!'

Bella had eyed her father balefully.

'Well, I'll go, then. You give me a letter offering to pay for his release!'

'*Pay?* What with? All I have is what I stand up in!' Sir Gilbert lied. In actual fact, his worldly fortune, satisfyingly enriched by the tidy profit he had made from his last wool delivery to Bristol, was currently residing in a grubby chest beneath his bed in Lady Ramsay's guest room. You needed ready cash at a time like this. Everything in a flux and dirty soldiers taking whatever they wanted. He had abandoned his house back in the village, taken shelter at the hall with his principal asset: three thousand pounds in coin. His second asset, his remarkable and fetchingly annoyed daughter Bella, tapped her slipper on the floorboards in a furious tattoo.

'We can't just leave him there, it must be hell for him. Tied up, horrid food . . .'

She had been plaguing her father about poor Hugo's plight when the messenger had arrived post-haste from Devizes. His cataclysmic dispatch confirmed the dead dragoon's sly assertion about the fate of the local militias: Waller had been utterly defeated by a sudden rush of Royalist cavalry from Oxford, his carefully nurtured army scattered. General Hopton's victorious Royalist army was the only remaining power in the west, and he was poised to strike at will.

Sir Gilbert Morrison stood proud, thumbs braced under his best coat as the mud-splattered messenger stuttered through his dispatch. The merchant had set himself up like a galleon under full sail, his generously upholstered body straining every seam as he digested the villain's news. Although he had respectfully placed himself behind Lady Ramsay's chair in the sumptuously appointed lounge, the bewildered messenger seemed drawn to his gloating presence, and addressed most of his remarks to the jolly gentleman rather than the scowling matron.

'Waller defeated at last. Praise the Lord for an unlooked-for mercy,' the lady of the house said, clamping her mouth against a sudden upsurge of misery. Not even news of the total and utter overthrow of all the King's enemies could compensate her grievous loss. The trivial, accidental deaths of her dithering but doting husband and desperately despondent son. Gone now, gone for ever. They hadn't died in the hour of a great victory, or perished at bay, holding out in some vitally important fortress. The King wouldn't have known who they were or what they had done, he could not have guessed how much the family had suffered and sacrificed for the sake of his. Two more unknown soldiers, blasted like crows on some forgotten hillside. Her slaughtered menfolk were the price of the King's triumph, Lady Ramsay thought bitterly. Charles

Stewart's victory had sounded the death knell of the Ramsays, and worse, much worse than that, had threatened to leave the poor survivors without a name, robbed of their men and of their honour. Packed up and picked over by this wine-guzzling merchant and his damned markers. What had Marmaduke been thinking of, borrowing money from their sworn snake of an enemy? Lady Ramsay closed her eyes against a pearled tear.

'Glory Hallelujah!' Sir Gilbert seconded, easing his way around the chair and pressing a sixpence on the bedraggled messenger. 'Here's something for your trouble, my lad.' The messenger took the coin, and backed out of the door which Findlay held open for him. He had a long ride ahead of him, taking the news of the fabulous victory on Roundway Down away into the far west. The gamekeeper glanced sourly at Sir Gilbert as he strode around the room, hands clasped behind his broad back. Lady Ramsay glanced up at her rosily complexioned guest, fought to control her spite.

'Did you not hear the messenger, Sir Gilbert?' she snapped. 'Your own son among those taken.' The formidable widow positively shook with indignation. The merchant sighed, rubbed his greasy chins distractedly.

'I heard aright, ma'am. And I hope it will teach him a lesson. I warned him not to go gallivanting off with those militia boys. No good will come of it, I told him.' He nodded at his daughter, sitting stiffly alongside her friend Anneliese Ramsay on the velvet-backed settle. Bella's hazel eyes were flickering with impatience, and the impudent girl looked ready to question his imaginative recollection of that particular conversation. Her shocking experience the previous evening had clearly affected her usually considerable powers of speech. The merchant held her eye for a moment, slapped the back of Lady Ramsay's chair.

'"Jamie," I said, "I haven't spent all that money on your ejication to have you up and join the army! You leave those meddling Roundheads be, and get yourself back to your books."'

Lady Ramsay sucked in her cheeks, white with anger as the merchant elaborated on his theme.

'I'll give him a piece of my mind, when I catch up with the rascal.'

'Thank the Lord you will enjoy that opportunity,' Lady Ramsay muttered.

The merchant frowned, then winked at his daughter. Bella was showing every sign of exploding into another of her strawberry tantrums. She eyed her effortlessly elastic father balefully. She of all people should have been used to his alarming about-faces by now. Sir Gilbert was so exasperatingly sincere to a cause, it quite baffled the uninitiated, persuaded the gullible to forget that today's avowed enemy had been yesterday's sworn ally.

Bella shook out the creases in her tired gown, raised her eyebrows at her grinning father. He had turned the tables again, transformed himself from a black rook to white bishop in one move, a single stately turn around the quiet room. Lady Ramsay watched her guest nod and chuckle to himself, glanced at his daughter sitting straight on the settle. The widow almost felt sorry for the girl; she couldn't help her father, after all.

'Forgive me, Sir Gilbert,' Lady Ramsay commented, meaning he should not be obliged to do any such thing, 'I can understand the difficulty in persuading a son to fall in line exactly with his parents' wishes, but I find it hard to imagine you could have condescended to your daughter's alarming anabasis around the countryside.'

Sir Gilbert sucked his generous lips for a moment, wondering what the old trout was getting at now. Bella held her breath as her father's doubtful grin was slowly replaced by a toothy smile.

'I think you'd better tell Lady Ramsay, don't you, my dear?'

Bella fidgeted, her smooth golden cheeks flushing in exasperated embarrassment.

'Why, your search for this young buck of yours!'

Bella closed her eyes for a moment, then turned and caught Lady Ramsay's miserable glance.

'The young gentleman who was here . . . you recall the wounded captain, madam,' she said falteringly. Lady Ramsay remembered the fellow. A glaring, insolent wretch who had been hurt in the cavalry fight at Chewton. The Ramsays had opened their house to the wounded of both sides after her late husband had agreed a truce with the local Parliamentary leader Sir Gilbert. The young captain had followed the girl about like a scolded dog until they had fallen out. He had left the hall in a vile temper, and taken most of the surviving wounded with him. The merchant, however, had stayed a little longer, and by the time he had eventually departed for his home down the hill, he had become as if by divine intervention a convinced and convincing Royalist. Lady Ramsay nodded sourly.

'Hugo . . . Captain Telling was captured on Lansdown Ridge. He was taken to Bath with the rest of the prisoners,' Bella explained.

'And my Bella's tried everything to get him out,' Sir Gilbert elaborated. 'They had developed a certain affection,' he added tenderly.

Lady Ramsay could well believe it.

'And your daughter assumed she could persuade Sir

William Waller to release the fellow in order that he might have another joust at him in a few weeks' time? I wonder why he would ever think of such a thing,' she asked airily.

'Why indeed,' Sir Gilbert agreed. 'Indeed, madam, I'll go further, I'll tell you why he might agree,' he went on grandly. 'If we were to write to the generals for an exchange, they might be interested. Our Jamie for young Hugo,' he said neatly.

'I cannot imagine either Sir William Waller or Sir Ralph Hopton would be particularly disposed to arranging exchanges to suit *you*, Sir Gilbert,' Lady Ramsay observed primly.

Her barb struck home. The merchant nodded soberly, concealing his irritation behind a vacuous smile. She would never let him forget he was a common tradesman, not even if he filled her house with trinkets and trifles and dressed up like one of those rosewater-scented gentlemen from Oxford. He swore under his breath, more determined than ever to impress on the old battleaxe he was as well connected and influential as her own dear departed husband. A broad hint he had friends in high places, that he wasn't just some bumbling huckster made good. By God, these Ramsays weren't the only blue-blooded brood in the West Country!

'Maybe not me, madam,' he allowed, 'but I am presently involved in negotiations with a gentleman from His Majesty's court at Oxford who possesses rather more clout, if you'll excuse the expression. He is on his way here even now. I am sure he would be only too pleased to offer his assistance in the matter.'

He'd let her get to him, told her more of his business than he had meant to. Clavincale's agent had sworn him to secrecy and all. Damn the old witch to hell!

Lady Ramsay sighed heavily, wondering which treacherous, insinuating toad the merchant was referring to. Sir Gilbert had already inveigled his way into her late husband's affairs, secured monies from the Parliament and managed to switch his wandering allegiance in the space of a few short weeks. She had no doubt he would manage to pull off a relatively straightforward exchange of prisoners. And then he would be free to turn his hateful attention back on her and poor distraught Anneliese. She shuddered at the thought.

While Bella Morrison fretted up at Kilmersden Hall, the object of her desperate quest lay on a padded couch with his head resting in a whore's lap. Hugo opened his eyes, beamed up at the girl, her pretty face framed by a wild mane of red hair. He let his eyes wander down her fine narrow neck, her smooth throat and fragrant, naked chest. He couldn't resist propping himself up to ease his lips around her alert nipples.

'I thought I was dreaming,' he said around the stiff pink thimble. 'I've dreamt about you so many times, stuck here.'

'I thought you needed your sleep,' Matilda Dawkins said huskily. 'How's the eye?'

The eye is fine, thank you very much, he thought, feasting on her apricot-down breasts.

Matilda smiled, relishing the warmth, the sticky fragrance of their abandoned lovemaking. He wasn't the best charger she'd had, but he certainly didn't refuse many fences. She hadn't seen the young captain since he was captured at the Battle of Lansdown, and it had been pure chance to find him under guard at the Happy Monk Inn off Cheap Street in Bath. One of half a dozen or so young bloods moping about under the dull eye of a listless musketeer. Matilda didn't know who had been more surprised, the despondent officer in his dirty brown coat or her, frolicking on the arm of Major Fulke from Strode's regiment. The gallant old gentleman's company had been detailed to guard the Royalist prisoners, scattered in the town houses and hostelries round about. How poor Hugo had stared! What a fuss the silly boy had made, jumping around the snug as if he owned her!

'What are you doing with the enemy?' he had snorted, his moustache twitching in the middle of his haggard face. He ignored Major Fulke's warning growl, prodded her bare arm. 'Where's my coat and where's my horse?'

'Let her be, sir, you won't raise your fist to a lady in my presence,' Major Fulke had snapped, his blood up despite his advancing years. Hugo had glared at the white-haired old gentleman, his weatherworn face proof of his long campaigns on the Continent. The youngster had rolled his sea-grey eyes, cocked his head in defiance.

'Lady? She's no lady but a common polecat! She took my coat and my—'

Fulke brought his greasy gauntlet across the youth's shouting mouth, knocking him back against a table where his comrades were playing cards. Hugo had steadied himself, wiped his bloody mouth.

'Have a care, sir, I'll not have ladies insulted,' Fulke insisted. A captain from the Earl of Caernarvon's horse laid his bandaged hand over Hugo's shoulder, held the furious youth back.

'A girl's got to make a livin', you know,' Matilda had told him, angry at being embarrassed in front of her new patron. Major Fulke was a kindly old gent really. Heart of gold and no wife. He paid her well and didn't keep her up all night snuffling and bumping into her bruised buttocks. Matilda had left her regular customers among the Royalist army back in Devizes. Caught up like moles in a trap, they had seemed to be on the very verge of surrender. None of them had seemed to possess the time, money or inclination to spend the last moments of their freedom lying with her, so she had gathered up her few belongings and walked out of the besieged town. Matilda hadn't liked the look of the great Roundhead camp on top of the hill. It was lousy with black-coated preachers and hard-faced cows waiting to cut her nose for her. Instead she had hitched a ride on a wagon to Chippenham, and then gone on to take the waters and meet a fine gentleman in Bath. She had met a gentleman all right. Major Fulke was a grand prize, and had already treated her to a new dress on the grounds her old one was becoming a little ragged around the hem. She had sewn a few shillings into the lining and all, in the last couple of days. The elderly Roundhead officer had ushered her through the snug, and taken her up to his room overlooking a clatty alley. He had spent an age clambering out of his armour, clanking about the narrow room resting his breastplate here, his cuirassier helmet there. Muttering on about the war, gossip and rumours from the battle. By the time he had come to bed she had been forced to pinch herself to stay awake.

'I'm sorry about that young upstart, my dear,' Fulke had said tenderly. 'Upsetting you like that.'

'Don't you worry about him, lover,' she had winked back. 'You cuddle down here and have a go on these.'

That had been three hours ago. He was up there snoring now, with a bit of luck. Matilda had slipped out of bed, thrown a shawl around her shoulders and hurried down the creaking stairs to the snug. A two-minute conversation and a sixpence had secured the guard's cooperation. He had unlocked the door, ducked inside the muggy room and returned a moment later with her drowsy lover, his lip all puffed and bruised. She had taken him into the landlord's best room, pushed a chair against the door, and fastened herself on the thin youth like a succubus. Drained his manly liquors like a vampire. Hugo had sweated and shivered, writhed like an eel under her energetic embrace. She had been forced to shush him several times, warning him he'd have the guards and officers down on them in a trice if he wasn't more careful. Matilda had left off at last, cradled his narrow head in her lap while he got his breath back. His slack mouth looked as if it had been on the receiving end of several more gauntlets, his poor lips chewed ragged by the voracious wanton.

Hugo prised himself up, rummaged under the couch for his breeches.

'Where are you goin'?' she asked drowsily. 'Come on back an' cuddle.'

Hugo tiptoed to the shuttered window, peered through the slats. He tugged his shirt over his painfully thin chest and buckled his belt.

'Hugo, come on back, my little house dove.'

The Royalist captain turned, held his finger to his lips. 'I think I can make it to the stable, cut a horse loose and be off before they know,' he hissed.

Matilda swung her long legs over the couch, crossed the room in an instant.

'Oh no. I didn't say anythin' about takin' off across the country,' she said, catching hold of his sleeve. 'The Major says there's been a battle. All sorts of folk loose on the road.'

Hugo glared at her. 'Are you mad? I've already been cooped up in here over a week!' The thin youth snorted. 'Of course there's been a battle. They're only waiting to round up Hopton's men and they'll march us all in chains to London!' Hugo exclaimed.

Matilda shook her tawny mane. 'I don't mind goin' behind his back, for old times' sake, but I'll not let you run off and make a fool of him!'

'He's a doddering old Roundhead who's too useless to do anything but beat up a few prisoners,' he argued. 'I'm surprised you can bring yourself to . . .'

Matilda flushed, her dark eyes flashing dangerously. Hugo twitched by the window, poised to run.

'He's clean and kind and he pays,' she breathed. 'Lucky yours was on the house, I don't see you carrying a purse around with you!'

'They stole it from me, the saucy knaves.'

'Well, you're not going anywhere and that's flat. I'll be here to keep an eye on you.' She winked, tugging her shawl around her neck. 'Touch that window and I'll scream the place down, so help me.'

Hugo frowned, shuffled out of the room after her. The sleepy musketeer collected another sixpence from the girl and saw her temporary charge back into his snug cell. The snores of his comrades rattled the pots on their shelves. The musketeer closed and locked the door, slipped the key back inside his loose coat. Matilda smiled at him.

'Give us that shillin' back and you can suck on these, my darlin',' she breathed seductively, opening the shawl with a wink.

'Yer on!' the musketeer replied with a lucky leer.

*

The mad crash of boots and the jangle of spurs brought Hugo around with a start. What a dream that had been! He could practically taste her lips! Rolling and wrestling on the couch with Matilda, the red-haired minx who had . . .

'ON YOUR FEET!' A bedraggled musketeer in a grey coat charged into the room, menaced the sleepy occupants with his gun. He'd lit his match, held it in his grubby fist for emphasis. Major Fulke strode into the room, his face red beneath its thatch of white hair. Hugo sat up, glared at him. He must have heard Matilda return to bed, beaten the truth of their passionate liaison out of her.

'You're to be moved, right now. Back to Bristol,' the major reported. 'Collect all your belongings and form up in the alley.'

'What's up now?' the captain from Caernarvon's horse called petulantly. 'I don't see why you get us up so early!'

'You're off to Bristol, gentlemen. Bath is being evacuated.'

'The plague, is it?'

'A plague, aye. Sir William's been beaten, up at Devizes. He's retreating on Bristol with all his horse and you're going with him.' The major's speech was drowned out by their huzzahs and cheers. The energetic captain jumped on a chair and danced a jig. Bottles smashed and loosened pots dropped from the leaning shelves like mortar rounds.

'Waller's lost! Huzzah for Hopton!' they chorused, dancing around the snug under the baleful glare of the old major.

Sir Gilbert strode over to the map board which had been tacked to the oak panels on the lounge walls. The Ramsays' draughty hall doubled as a formidable fortress as well as a home, and the lounge had been sandbagged as effectively as the rest of the house. The merchant took a quick look at the map, ran his pudgy index finger along the blue inked roads, east and west.

'Well, if that scoundrel's right Hopton will be free to march straight to Oxford, join up with the King for a descent on London,' he declared. 'The Earl of Essex is sitting on his arse at Reading, doing nothing. The war will be over in a few weeks.'

Findlay nodded dismally alongside.

'Or he could double back, look, trap Waller between him and Wales.'

Sir Gilbert poo-poohed the gamekeeper's suggestion.

'You might be a damn good shot, my friend, but when it comes to grand strategy, leave it to those who know. Hopton will make for London, mark my words!'

BY
LAWFORD'S GATE,

BRISTOL, 15 JULY 1643

The dusty cavalry looked as if they had charged through a windmill, hacked sacks of flour up on Roundway Hill rather than living, breathing Royalists. The riders were slumped in their saddles, their tired horses kicking up spiteful storms of grit as troop after troop passed under the historic gatehouse, to be swallowed up by a force-fed town. There had been precious few to cheer Parliament's hopeful forces out of Bristol all those weeks before, and so the exhausted cavalry were hardly surprised to see the walls deserted for their ignominious return.

The divided populace had little enthusiasm for any cause but their own, and they closed their shutters and hurried indoors as the weary riders made their way along Old Market toward the monolithic grey castle. Sir William Waller hardly noticed the frightened faces, the hostile glances from the shadows. He stared straight ahead, pulled at his fleshy nose every once in a while as his staff officers muttered comments, pointed out the labourers busy about the defences. By God, they would need them now, the principal Parliamentarian army in the west shattered like a porcelain vase.

Algernon Starling was practically alone on the breezy battlements, keeping a careful mental note of Waller's forces and their condition. A pencil and paper would have suited the clerk better, but Starling had no intention of being caught and hanged as a spy. Bristol had more than enough spies already. The black-suited clerk gazed down at the shuffling columns, estimated their strengths by counting colours. As far as he could make out (and God knew he was no soldier) Waller had about fifteen to twenty troops of cavalry left, all of them very weak. He shielded his dark eyes and gazed out over the smoky suburbs toward the green hills on the horizon, but there was no sign of the foot regiments. All he could see were occasional knots of frightened soldiers, hurrying in without arms, or helping their disabled colleagues. Starling whistled. So the early reports of the battle had not been exaggerated. Roundway Down had seen the complete destruction of Waller's army.

He glanced unconcernedly along the long walls, spotted the occasional militiaman marking time along the battlements. The towers and forts bristled with cannon of all calibres, but there seemed few trained gunners who knew how to use them. The governor, Nathaniel Fiennes, had barely two thousand men to hold five miles of defences, and only a fool would have trusted the solid citizens of Bristol to exert themselves in their retention. Starling hurried down the steep stair into the quiet backstreets, made his way along the refuse-strewn alleys to the main street. The decrepit town houses looked like fat old men bending down, their creaking lower storeys bulging under the weight of beam and brick above. Tottering chimneys and leaded windows clustered like crab's eyes above sooty sills. Starling stood in the shadows, watched the sad procession of Roundhead cavalry clatter along the cobbled road. They'd be lame all the sooner, driven on like this. A good job his master Sir Gilbert had given him a hundred pounds in coin to buy remounts. They would fetch a handsome price now, with half the cavalry in desperate need of fresh horses. Starling was to have a sixpence in commission on each sale. A tidy sum, no denying. He rubbed his hands and looked up as a Scots officer cursed his lumbering piebald. The beast seemed to be knitting, tripping over its hairy hoofs. The officer tore off his lobster-pot helmet, jabbed his spurs into the piebald's flank.

'By your seat, sir, the horse is not yours,' Starling called conversationally.

The officer glared down at him, his bright red hair cropped closely on his hot head.

'You're right enough there,' the officer snarled, pulling at the reins.

'If I'm not mistaken, sir, the animal belonged to one Sparrow, an apprentice?'

The officer gave up the unequal struggle with the stubborn horse, slumped in his saddle. 'Aye. D'ken the man hisself?'

Starling nodded soberly. 'Am I to understand Master Sparrow has not returned from Roundway?'

The Scot rubbed his gauntlet over his nose. 'He has not, though we didn't mark his fall, mind you. I lent him my horse before the battle, which is why I'm riding this damned beastie!' The officer shrugged. 'Ah well, he saved me at least. If I'd been on my own horse I would have been first over yon cliff with the Lobsters there.' He nodded to the heavily armoured cuirassiers trotting past, boiled red inside their steel shells. The armoured regiment had stood one charge on Roundway, but had collapsed in the face of a renewed assault by the irresistible Royalist cavalry. They had been driven over one of Roundway's treacherous cliffs, more than eighty of them breaking their necks in the terrible fall.

'Well, sir, thank the Lord you've come to Bristol. I'm not sure the garrison could have stood without you!' Starling called craftily.

The Scots officer snorted. 'They'll have to, my friend,' he replied, 'we're not bloody stopping!'

The stocky governor paced his headquarters in Bristol Keep, his busy hands clasped behind his back as if he couldn't trust them to behave. Nathaniel Fiennes was a heavily built, raw-boned man, with quick brown eyes and a generous mouth. Today, though, he had compressed his lips into a thin red line, clamped his teeth shut against the stream of unmanly profanities which threatened to vomit from his belly. Sir William Waller, the senior Parliamentary commander in the west, was standing, half hunched over the map table, staring at the swirling colours and contours as if he was replaying the recent disaster all over again. He swept a quill this way and that over the pitiless map as he should have dusted the outnumbered and exhausted Royalists from the downs. The general shook his head, wiped his beard with a clammy palm.

'They must have grown wings, they must have flown back from Oxford,' he muttered. Sir Arthur Haselrig, the commander of the heavily armoured Lobsters regiment, nodded in agreement. He had been knocked out of his saddle by the furious enemy charge, and had been on the verge of surrendering his sword when he had by chance been rescued by a stray troop of his own men. He wondered how the old castle had managed to swallow up their shame and misery.

'All my foot, my guns, my powder, every wagon and cart besides,' Waller went on, shaking his head in disbelief.

'Well, gentlemen, you can well imagine what the House will make of it.'

Nathaniel Fiennes' busy eyes protruded from his rugged face. 'Did I not warn you, sir, did I not beseech you to have a care for the army?' he asked, his voice thick with emotion. 'You have taken hundreds of men from the walls and lost them on Roundway. Now you say you are for Gloucester. What am I to do?'

The assembled officers stared at the wretched governor, appalled at his outburst but unable to condemn his pessimism.

Waller hung his head. 'There will be survivors, sir, stragglers.'

'I would rather turn them away than let them amongst my men,' Fiennes snorted, growing increasingly bitter at his gloomy prospects. 'They would infect the rest, undermine their confidence with their tales from Roundway. Most of my men are new to the colours, how do you imagine they'll stand if they hear the details of your defeat?'

Waller bristled, stung beyond endurance by the governor's defeatist whining. 'Most of my men were new to the colours,' he snapped. 'They fought well enough while they were able!'

Fiennes snorted, turned away from the cluttered table to gaze out of the broad gallery which commanded a view of the sluggish Avon. One of the rivers which protected his city of sand.

'We will send reinforcements from the Earl of Essex,' Waller declared resolutely.

'The earl would rather see us all defeated than you triumphant,' Fiennes bit back stubbornly.

Waller had little heart left to challenge that ugly

rumour. The bitter feud between the principal Roundhead general and his insubordinate subordinate in the west had bubbled and fumed for months. Waller knew full well the earl would rather cut off his toes than send his rival a single company of men. The camp gossips had already tried and convicted the ponderous nobleman for failing to intercept the Royalist cavalry at Oxford, and for allowing them out of his own back door to fall on Waller's shocked army. There had been moves at Westminster to advance Sir William over the Puritan earl, award his dutiful service with the principal command of Parliament's armies.

Roundway had dashed any such schemes into the dust.

'Well, whatever the case, my lords, Hopton won't be ready to march for weeks, the knocks he's had,' Haselrig commented, trying to encourage the pale governor, who stood by, chewing the cuff of his worn buff coat in distraction.

Fiennes looked up sharply. 'Nobody expected the King's cavalry to fly back from Oxford but they flew all the same,' he responded sourly.

Waller frowned, stung by this unfamiliar criticism.

'And *Hopton* will be the least of our worries,' Fiennes continued, jabbing a chewed finger at the spreadeagled map. 'If Essex won't move, the King can disengage in the east and finish us off once and for all! What if *you know who* marches west?'

'You know who?' Waller grated, knowing full well whom the nervous governor was referring to.

'Rupert.' Fiennes whispered the prince's name as if it was a spell in itself, a talisman of the King's irresistible victory. Fiennes looked from one to the other, challenging the dusty officers to dispute his assessment. Waller ran his hand over his face and thumbed grit from his tired eyes.

'Rupert,' he said wearily. 'Rupert Rupert Rupert. He is but a man, sir. He is not a beast of air and darkness!' The wretched governor didn't look at all convinced. 'An impetuous youth who makes up now for his long imprisonment in an Imperial fortress. A cool head and calm courage, sir, will hold him in check.'

The fiery prince, son of the Elector Palatinate, had already taken a hand in the endless wars in Germany. He had led a pitifully small army against the mighty Austrian empire, and had lost it in a blink of an eye at Vlotho on the Weser. He had then endured three years of comfortable confinement listening to endless lectures from his exasperated captors, who had urged the dashing young prince to put aside his father's hopeless quarrel and see reason. Rupert, typically, had refused to be swayed from the family cause and he now appeared just as determined to serve his uncle, Charles Stewart, in his just war on his rebel subjects.

'Whatever the situation, gentlemen, it is imperative we hold Bristol,' Waller continued. 'It is still possible the enemy might tarry awhile before they march. The King might yet make a move on London, Essex would be bound to gainsay him.'

Fiennes raised his reddish eyebrows. Waller thrust his chin out defiantly, thumped the map table.

'You must take advantage of every moment, sir. Recruit your men, train them while you can. See to your walls. I will go north, and ensure Gloucester is put into an adequate state of defence.'

Fiennes nodded sourly. 'In case Bristol falls, eh?'

'Bristol will not fall,' Waller grated. 'It cannot fall.'

*

Nathaniel Fiennes was hardly alone in his superstitious dread of the awesome prince. Rupert had already proved the bane of Parliament's cause. He was gloomily reported as being a master of disguise, a witch's familiar able to converse with the beasts of the dark woods and the birds of the air. He was a crack shot, an expert swordsman and a superb horseman. Quick and inquisitive, he could speak five languages and curse like a trooper in a dozen more. He had fought his first battle when hardly more than a boy, commanded armies in his teens and knew all the intricate arts of siege craft, mining and artillery. Unfortunately for the handsome prince, however, he possessed all the tact and courtly accomplishments of a red-hot cannonball.

Lovely young noblewomen and comfortably married matrons made fools of themselves slipping him notes and letters of breathless affection while their husbands chewed their moustaches in barely restrained jealousy. The prince and his dour younger brother Maurice could have cut a swath through the beautiful women crowded into the King's court at Oxford, but they rarely slept in the same bed twice and could barely find time to snatch a hot meal let alone sample the scented cleavages hopefully paraded for their Teutonic attention. The brothers were soldiers first and foremost, and cared nothing for the gossip and scandal of a bored court. Rupert would shout down his elders, generals who remembered the boy back when he was little more than a fugitive toddler in Bohemia. He would yawn and splutter, shake his head as cautious counsels were urged on the doubting King. Thick skinned, unblinking and as immovable as a hundred thousand cast-iron horses, Rupert in truth had as many enemies at Oxford as he had in Westminster. As long as he continued winning the King's war for him, he was all-powerful, but woe betide the arrogant prince if he should lose his magical touch. Knives had been sharpened for Rupert's despised back ever since the heady days of the previous autumn, when the King had raised his standard at Nottingham. A hundred men prayed for the day they would use them to cut their despised champion down to size.

Midnight in Oxford, and the quads and cloisters were lit for dancing and drinking, ancient colleges and humble alehouses alike celebrating the King's remarkable victory at Roundway. Fountains gushed ruby wine, stone jars rolled beneath unsteady feet. Lords and ladies swayed down panelled passages, tipping their drinks over their fantastical outfits. Courtiers and ambassadors bowed and waved, their befuddled heads weighed down with ridiculous headdresses. Courtesans and colonels pirouetted in candlelit chambers, their eyes fluttering and wandering behind sly black masks. Below stairs drunken soldiers and whores caroused in every room, relieved themselves noisily down the cellar steps or over their snoring comrades. The few Puritan-minded folk round about shook their heads and stopped their ears against these horrors of Babylon, these horned imps of Satan whistling and wenching the witching hours away.

Rupert had no time for their flattery, fashion or fornication, but he had whooped with the rest of them at the marvellous news from Devizes. King Charles, almost tipsy with delight at this sudden improvement in his fortunes, had gloated over the unexpected dispatch, danced a little jig as he devoured the details.

'Sir Ar-Arthur Haselrig, re-re-rescued by his own me-me-me-men as he fumbled with his sword knot trying to su-su-su, to su-su-su—'

'Submit, sire?'

'Surrender!' the King cried, tears of delight springing into his eyes.

'So much for these crabs of his, this tinpot cavalry we have heard so much about!' Lord Digby sneered, gulping his wine from a jewelled goblet.

'Lobsters, Di-Di-Digby, not crabs! Armoured from head to toe, the most fantastical sight to see on a ba-ba-battlefield,' the King stammered happily. He wiped his forked beard, glanced at his worshipping councillors. 'Ah, brave Sir Arthur! Had he been victualled as well as f-f-fortified he could have withstood a siege of seven y-years!' The King's courtiers shrieked with laughter at His Majesty's rare jest. Digby had to be helped up from the floor where he had fallen in a fit of helpless mirth, spilling what was left of his wine over his white breeches.

Rupert scowled at the repulsive toadies, crossed the room to the enormous map table. England and Scotland, luridly green and dissected by roads and rivers. Ireland, across the water but never far from the King's Machiavellian scheming, a jagged head with a single blue eye. The war-torn isles of Britain, studded by towns and cities, fortresses and magazines. Bristling with tiny flags, infested with armies like crawling beetles on a well-scythed meadow.

The prince dragged his arm across the table, hurling a great sheaf of plans and orders and arrays to the floor in a flutter of creased paper. The startled courtiers gaped round at him as he jammed his dagger into the heart of the table.

'General Hopton must immediately move on Bristol!'

he declared, a harsh black-pated crow, demonically handsome in his fine suit of red velvet. White-haired earls and gouty generals muttered and blinked at the wilful prince, urged His Majesty to stabilize, consolidate, regroup. Rupert had closed his eyes, clicked his tongue or burst into peals of laughter at the thoroughly sensible schemes advanced by the senior officers.

'My lord Wilmot will screen Oxford with his cavalry while I march west with the pick of the army. I will rendezvous with Hopton and take Bristol by the end of the month,' he boasted in his barely accented English.

'You'd leave us open to attack from Essex! We daren't spare the men!' a florid old warrior snorted from the back.

'Essex is a snail, carrying this House of Commons around on his back,' Rupert snarled. 'He'll not move an inch!'

'You can't be certain of that, my lord.'

'I can!' And he could. They rolled their eyes and cursed him hollow, but none dared argue with him.

Having won his point he had collected his hat, bowed to his uncle and strode off down the oak-panelled hallway with spurs jingling and scabbard scraping the worn boards. King Charles soothed and comforted his remaining officers whose brittle feathers had once again been given a severe ruffling by the upstart German. Rupert wouldn't have given a bean for their outraged protests. He stalked down the corridor and took a flight of marble steps six at a time. Ladies in waiting swooned, guards came to ragged attention and presented their halberds as he stormed down the steps to the crowded courtyard. He snatched up the reins of his charger from a startled groom, leapt into the saddle and aimed the black stallion through the crowds singing and dancing about the courtyard.

'Out of my way, you dolts!' he yelled. 'Make way there!'

Prince Rupert was coming to Bristol, whether poor old Nathaniel Fiennes was ready or not.

BY

KILMERSDEN HALL,

CHIPPING MARLEWARD, SOMERSET, 16 JULY 1643

Anthony St John Dyle bent forward and lifted the leather curtain flap to peer out of the window. The coach as usual smelt like a marl pit, and seemed to have attracted every bluebottle, mosquito and midge from the Somerset wetlands he had spied from the top of the hill. Lord Clavincale had little idea of the geography of the Mendips, but he had become all too familiar with the ruts and bumps in the dreadfully unkempt road. He took a quick peek at the ranked willows and drooping undergrowth along the track, and dropped the curtain back with a shudder. What a hateful wilderness! He had half a mind to have the driver turn the coach around and find more sensible accommodation in Bath – newly liberated from the quaking rebels. Perhaps he could find time in his pressing schedule for a few days to take the waters, wash the grime of the road from his bruised body. Mind you, flies, dirt and dust were hardly surprising travelling companions, now that he had ventured this far off the beaten track. He had resumed his journey that morning, following hard on the heels of the Cornish army as they harried the last Parliamentarian stragglers west toward their base in Bristol. The noisy Cornish – as rough and ready a set of blood-thirsty barbarians as Lord Clavincale had ever set eyes on – kicked up a storm of sand and grit as they traipsed along after Prince Maurice's cavalry, hurrying to stay in contact with the insignificant Roundhead rearguards. The disorderly soldiers smelled like wet bears and drank, squabbled and fought long into the night. Captain Nybb had been in his element, taking the opportunity to look up some of his old cronies from the German wars. He had returned that dawn with a head like an anvil and breath that would have taken the veneer from the coachwork. He had staggered back just in time for their departure and not even the dire state of the well-trampled road had disturbed his repose. The unshaven wretch was squatting opposite, his great stubbled head knocking against the rear of the coach as he snored and snarled in his ale-addled sleep. They reached the great crossroads before Bath, and quickly became entangled in a hopeless traffic jam which had blocked the narrow lanes in three directions. It seemed as if the entire Royalist army was running around in circles trying to find the quickest route to the west. Clavincale doubted the enemy would ever again find the courage to challenge their savage enthusiasm.

'It's not for war they hurry, mineer,' Nybb had replied, opening one blazing red eye for a moment. 'Nor yea nor nay neither. They want der loots, boy!'

De loose boy? What was the great ape jabbering about now?

The King's army – delivered from oblivion on Roundway – seemed to sense victory in the air with every westward step. The surly, disobedient rogues were hurrying along to make sure they collected their share of the plunder they reckoned they deserved. The general advance had become a free for all, a mad stampede as each company raced its nearest rivals for the right of the first night in the wealthy spa. There wouldn't be much left for latecomers, once the officers had regained control of their desperate men, turned brigands back to soldiers once more. Bath itself had fallen without a shot along with half a dozen smaller garrisons as news of the Roundheads' disastrous defeat spread like wildfire around the western counties. Clavincale could see the evidence for himself, read the faces of these wild-eyed men. One quick thrust to the heart, and the tottering Roundhead rebellion would be finished for ever!

He fidgeted impatiently inside the broiling coach, fanned his face with his scented handkerchief as he fretted over the delay. Outside the coach, mounted officers cursed and bawled as they tried to extract their troops from the chaos. They rode to and fro, prodding and flogging the Cornish horde on over the crossroads. The tangled column seemed to shake itself out, rumble and pulse along the narrow lanes allowing the crazy convoy of carts and wagons to rumble forward once more. Clavincale's driver whipped his tired team through the cursing stragglers and took the left fork, turning the creaking, overheating coach away from the great packed mass of sweating men and animals. He made good time along the narrow track to the south and up into the hills.

Midday now, and hotter than hell in the rumbling grumbling coach. Clavincale rubbed his left buttock, sighed sourly as Nybb dribbled drunken camp German. Another half day's journey on rotten roads to keep his appointment with this merchant fellow, Morrison. He made himself comfortable, considered his mission. The rude fellow was reputed to be the craftiest huckster in the west, according to the reports he had studied during his long, hot ride from Oxford.

Clavincale frowned, imagined the fun they would be having back at the King's court now. Celebrating a victory like true Cavaliers. The meeting had better be worth his while, dragging him so far away from the riotous celebrations his cronies at Oxford would be enjoying. He couldn't imagine the locals found any reason to stay up much after dark around here. He had seen decrepit farms and overgrown orchards, the occasional straggling village, but nothing of any interest to offer a gentleman of refinement. This Morrison fellow was a damned braggart, a self-made man who had dragged himself up from the gutter. Clavincale dabbed his lips thoughtfully. A huckster perhaps, but a shrewd trader who had made a fortune from Bristol's wharfs and quays, from the silly sheep wandering the rolling hills round about. The man had already taken six hundred pounds in gold from Parliament to equip a regiment, and had apparently offered to do the same in the name of the King. A worthy partner then, but a man to watch. Clavincale closed his eyes, and tried not to think about the horrid journey.

Once he had completed his business with Morrison, he might be able to catch up with the convoy he had dispatched from Devizes. Several wagon-loads of assorted goods taken from the houses of a number of wealthy rebels thereabouts, as well as the pick of the items he had bought from the Cornish. The soldiers had been keen enough to loot the Roundhead camp, but they could hardly carry the enormous heap of trinkets around with them. They had been shrewd enough to organize a sale of their looted goods outside the town, offering bargains to travellers and townsfolk alike in return for more readily transported coin or provision. Or drink. Clavincale had distributed several barrels of brandy and dozens of stone jars of good sweet cider as he haggled the dirty soldiers down. By the end of the sale he had barely opened his purse, relying on brandy and barter to secure the best bargains. The canny nobleman, touring the impromptu and rather raucous market with Captain Nybb, had picked up clocks, plate, good linen, ornate armour and a selection of Italian crafted luggage. He had also purchased twenty good horses from a squad of loutish Cornish musketeers who had no idea of their real value, and had completed his purchases with a rather nice coach and four some dragoons had managed to hide away in a nearby barn. He had sent the valuable convoy back to Oxford with his own best regards for His Majesty. That little lot should fetch a pretty penny for the King's impecunious cause, less his own modest commission of course.

And then there were the prisoners. They would be marching by now, but not to Oxford. A hundred and more sound fellows picked from the shuffling mass of misguided rebels packed into Devizes Castle. Good sound-limbed fellows who seemed to have got it into their heads they were to be sold as slaves to the Americas. There was no question of that. As long as they didn't misbehave for their new masters, of course.

As well as his all-powerful commission from the King, Clavincale was also working for the Spanish and Portuguese ambassadors, constantly on the lookout for promising men to fill their hard-pressed *tercios* or crew their embattled galleons. His assignment from the *French* court was, as one would have expected, rather more subtle. He was to keep an eye out for any art treasures which might find their way on to the market during these gravely troubled times. He saw himself as a champion of the arts, his mission to save great paintings or embroideries from the hands of the wild English mobs, and ship them off to the Continent. The whole operation was delightfully neat and a marvellous source of income for his lordship. Neither he nor his family were in any particular need of the ready cash, but only a fool would allow such an excellent opportunity to make money and secure a few more titles to go to waste.

Clavincale's father – the notorious judge 'Black Bob' Dyle – owned huge tracts of land in Dorset and Devon, and so he had set up a cosy naval base in the heart of their territory, the tiny and remote fishing harbour of Penmethock. The villagers were diehard Royalists and sworn servants of the Dyle family, and he could call out the whole population if necessary to load his busy privateer, the *Messalina's Purse.* The sleek cutter didn't look much, but she packed ten guns and could out-run most of the interfering Parliamentary fleet which patrolled the English Channel. The shallow draught allowed the craft to be sailed right in with the breakers, very handy for depositing cargoes on windy beaches. The goods he dealt with tended to be smallish but rather valuable, so there was no need to hire a clumsy great merchantman. Once safely out to sea the *Messalina* could sail where she pleased, put in to any number of Continental ports. The treasures he had collected on behalf of His Majesty (not forgetting his modest commission) would be unloaded and replaced with indispensable war *matériel*: muskets, swords, powder, brandy and wine. It was like most grand designs, a remarkably simple scheme, and highly profitable both to His Majesty and to Lord Clavincale.

The portly nobleman grinned as he calculated his profit margin for the trip. A tidy sum so far, and a treaty with this Morrison fellow would be the icing on the cake. Winning over the merchant and his like-minded friends in the West Country, and setting them up as a counterweight to the commercial domination of London . . . ah, he might even be awarded an earldom by his grateful sovereign. The only fly in the ointment was the distance those damned prisoners would have to march. Why couldn't Roundway have been fought nearer a friendly port? It was at least seventy miles from Devizes to the lonely cove at Penmethock. They would be obliged to make good time and possibly march by night in order to avoid running into patrols from the few Parliamentary garrisons left in the western counties. That would mean easier opportunities for the rogues to run off into the woods, if they had a run left in them that is. The prisoners would be tired out by the time they reached the coast. No doubt some of the wretches would have developed blisters or turned their ankles or caught the plague, and would end up hobbling like scarecrows by the time they boarded. Clavincale was also concerned at exactly how many prisoners could be packed into the hold. Fifty? Sixty? Still, Captain Cruickshank, his chief of seaborne operations, would see to the tiresome details. All he had to do was get the wretched rebels down to the coast and agree a suitable price with the hawk-featured clerks from the Spanish embassy. Once the prisoners were aboard ship they would have little opportunity to protest at their destination. The Spanish High Command had little time for troublemakers and deserters, especially as they were up to their wildly unfashionable ruffed collars in a filthy war with France. He had heard the punishments they handed out to their troops could be spectacularly barbaric. Something to do with the Inquisition, Clavincale supposed.

*

The noisy appearance of the two young missies startled the elderly gardener, who was just then buried to his waist in a writhing forest of brambles. Bates did his best to keep the grounds in order, but you couldn't keep a lawn in good condition with troops and dirty great horses marching all over it. Now most of the garrison of Kilmersden Hall had taken to its heels, the new feller – merchant Morrison – had decided it was time they tackled the unkempt shrubberies and towering weeds. Bates had dropped his clippers at the sudden alarm, thinking for a moment the wretched soldiers had come back, shouting and bawling as they ransacked the mansion. He squinted toward the great house from which the young ladies had emerged, the young mistress dark and drawn, the other, that honey blob Miss Bella, as fresh and ripe as a good eating apple. The gardener ducked down into the untameable undergrowth, tilted his head to eavesdrop as the girls stalked past.

'I wouldn't marry your brother if he was the last man on earth!' Anneliese Ramsay trumpeted, sending a brace of tame peacocks cooing for cover under the overgrown shrubbery. Kilmersden Hall had been justly famed for its lawns and gardens, its flower beds and borders. Before the war that was. Now the ha-ha doubled as a moat, the ornamental pond had been diverted around a gun emplacement and a stand of fine timber had been chopped down to create a broader field of fire for the Elizabethan robinet which had been dug in at the rear of the rambling mansion. Anneliese had joined her friend Bella on an afternoon stroll around the abandoned works. The stifling heat and their dismal surroundings had set both girls on edge. The dark girl had taken hold of Bella's arm, turning her friend towards her with more determination than she had meant.

'Ouch, you're pinching!' Bella snapped, equally short tempered. She wrenched her arm away and glared at her old friend, who glared defiantly back at her.

'What on earth is the matter?' Bella snorted. 'All I said was I hope Jamie will be all right!'

Anneliese rearranged her sharp features, sighed miserably. Bella stood back, breathing deeply. Perhaps it was the weather. Pitiless sun and not even the merest shaving of a breeze. The girls had been stifled by the torpid heat of the old house, and had hoped to freshen themselves with a walk before dinner. Bella had obviously hit a nerve, chattering on about her poor brother.

'I'm sorry, Bella,' Anneliese sighed. 'It's just . . . your father goes on . . . Your father can be trying at times,' she said in a gentler tone.

Bella snorted. 'My father is the most trying man in England! He's more trying than all these squabbling MPs and lords and earls and generals put together!' she joked, smiled shortly. 'But you know that well enough already. What has he been saying?'

Anneliese shrugged, picked a drooping rose bloom from the nearest bed.

'Nothing. Nothing at all.'

'He's been saying something! He's spent the last three days locked in with your mother, talking business,' Bella added quickly. She hadn't meant to imply any impropriety. Surely her father hadn't set his cap at Lady Ramsay? With her husband and poor dumb son barely cold in their graves? Not even Sir Gilbert could be that crass. Could he? Bella walked on a few steps alone, bit her lip. He might not be interested in the widow, but he might still have set his sights on a marriage. Jamie and Anneliese. They had known each other since childhood, and they had always been friendly enough. Neither her absent brother nor her preoccupied friend could ever have been described as overly demonstrative. They might actually make a good match. Bella suppressed a giggle, turned to watch Anneliese gathering up her skirts to join her.

'Your father . . .' Anneliese hesitated, looked awkward.

'My father what?'

'He and my mother have been discussing the future . . . of the house and everything.'

Bella nodded.

'From what little Mother tells me . . . it appears my father owed your father some money.'

Bella shrugged, embarrassed.

'Half Somerset owes my father money. It can't be very much, Annie, your family has the house, remember. We're merely refugees,' she observed airily.

Anneliese shook her head, her narrow face quite set. She had lost a good deal of weight since the shocking death of her father and brother on Lansdown Hill, and her once attractive features had been cruelly undermined. Her usually lively eyes were bleary, the skin beneath shadowed and smudged. Her cheeks were pale and drawn tight about her barely visible mouth. She compressed her lips even more, shook her head resignedly.

'He owed him a great deal of money, Bella, more than we have,' she insisted.

Bella began to take her meaning. 'Then they are talking business, settling your late father's affairs.'

'How can Mother settle his affairs? The garrison is all gone apart from Findlay, we've barely a bean left to pay the servants, let alone your father.' Bitter tears ran down her hollow cheeks. 'We've been ruined,' she croaked.

Bella stepped over to her friend, slipped her arms

around the sobbing girl's shoulders. 'Annie, Annie, come along now. You have the house, all your fine furniture and . . .'

'We don't have it. Your father has it. He is merely awaiting an opportune moment to take up the deeds.'

Bella blinked in sympathy, felt the dark girl shudder against her.

'My father wouldn't . . . couldn't stand by and let you lose your home,' Bella insisted. 'After you have taken us in off the road twice already? I shan't allow it! He wouldn't dare contemplate it!'

Anneliese looked up slowly, nodded miserably. 'No. He wouldn't,' she agreed with a croak. 'He's got something else in mind.'

Marriage. Anneliese and Jamie. The enormity of her father's ambition staggered her. Surely he wouldn't force Jamie on the poor girl at a time like this? No, not even Sir Gilbert would dare behave with such a complete disregard for the stricken family.

'I hear Mother crying in her room, every night. She won't repeat the details.'

'Of course she's upset . . .'

'It's more than that! She looks at me as if— Oh, I don't know!'

Bella embraced her friend, held on to her as if she was in danger of shivering out of her pale skin. The full extent of her father's scheming was beginning to dawn on her. The more she thought about it, the more obvious it was. Jamie and Anneliese. The warring clans united by marriage. The Morrisons would get the name and prestige they craved, the Ramsays the cash to maintain their enormous draughty pile on the top of the hill. That's how Sir Gilbert would see it, at any rate. Bella swallowed hard, ashamed of her own dismal part in the whole abominable affair. She had pestered her father into writing to the local commanders, urging them to arrange an exchange of prisoners. Jamie for Hugo. Her own brave captain would be freed from his grievous imprisonment so he could spend time with her. Careless, carefree Bella. They would go for endless rides together, lie in the long grass like the peasants she had watched from the shelter of the hayricks down in the village, while their horses cropped the turf and flicked their tails. And Jamie would be returned to them so he could be dusted off and married off to the first desperate daughter their grasping father could corner. The selfish simplicity of the scheme both appalled and fascinated her. She looked over her friend's trembling shoulder, and gazed at the massive mansion framed majestically behind them. Rearing over the gardens, the hill, like a giant monument to money and riches. With a small thrill of excitement she pictured parties and balls, dinners and dances. Sumptuous feasts and merry-making with all the people round about eating their fill and drinking their health. They could all live here, all together! There were dozens of rooms. She and Anneliese could arrange the banquets and order the dancing, send for players from Bath and Bristol. They could all be happy, if the wretched war would leave them alone for a while. Anneliese blew her nose, snagged Bella's wandering attention.

'It'll be all right,' Bella promised.

'Will it?' Anneliese asked, faintly. They turned together, watched Anneliese's young maid hurrying down the path after them. They hadn't noticed the gardener as they passed, busy clipping the brambles from the overgrown flowerbeds. He must have heard it all.

'Miss Annie, miss! Your mother wants to see you, straight away if you will!' the maid shrieked. Anneliese sighed.

Bella squeezed her hand and watched her tread mournfully back along the overgrown path. The gardener tipped his cap as she swept by, turned to gaze at Bella.

'What d'you think you're staring at?' Bella snapped, following her friend into the house.

Anneliese Ramsay knocked softly, eased the study door open. It had been her late father's den, his sanctuary from a domineering wife and pressing business which he had never been able to settle satisfactorily. Sir Marmaduke had been a kindly, careworn man, concerned to do the best he could for his family and dependants. But he had been superseded by businessmen with more cunning and more money, persuaded to sign chits and markers he no longer had the resources to guarantee. If he had been alive now, he would have been Sir Gilbert's creature, Anneliese thought with a shudder. He had held the hall for almost a year against a hostile village, maintained the King's cause in the dark months at the beginning of the war – only to lose everything to a lardy-necked buffoon with a sly tongue and quicker wits.

Her somewhat more formidable mother Lady Ramsay had stood right behind her man throughout those long winter weeks, fortified poor Ramsay's resolve. And now he was dead. Blasted to atoms on Lansdown, and her poor brother Thomas shot down carrying messages into the King's camp.

Perhaps it was the memory of her mother's domination of the household which made Lady Ramsay's ill-concealed distress all the more shocking. Anneliese stared at her, sitting straight by the fire and avoiding her gaze. Sir Gilbert was standing behind her with his fat hands resting on the back of her chair as if he would turn her this way or that, tip her over into the grate if he cared to. The merchant beamed, waved her in to her dead father's room as if he already owned the place.

'Come in, child, come in. And close the door behind you,' Sir Gilbert ordered crisply.

PART TWO

NEEDS MUST WHEN THE DEVIL DRIVES

BY

BLACK HORSE FERRY,

BESIDE THE RIVER AVON NEAR BRISTOL, 16 JULY 1643

The guards from Strode's regiment looked ready to bolt. They would fall out and scamper up every slope and hillock to spy out the countryside, desperately afraid they would see dust clouds on the horizons, discover the King's wild horsemen charging after them. Rumour had doubled, trebled the size of the enemy army bearing down after them. A straggler from Nathaniel Fiennes' regiment swore he had seen ten thousand cavalry lined up on Roundway like the host of Hell itself. The frightened soldier was helping to drag a litter carrying his wounded mate, injured by a ball from one of their own cannon, fired indiscriminately into the terrified mob of Roundhead infantry. Splattered in blood and grovelling in the grass, the Royalist cavalry had swept by the pitiful fugitives after more deserving targets. The scattered survivors had run for their lives, scuttled away from the scene of the catastrophe while they still could. The soldiers' fearful reports had sapped what little confidence Strode's men had left. They shambled along beside the prisoners, jumping out of their coats every time a cock crowed or a rook called. Only the iron will of their white-haired old major stopped them from taking to their heels, hiding themselves away in the lush woods which lined the river valley.

The slow-moving column had left the road for fear of probing enemy patrols, and were making their way toward Bristol along the Avon, crossing one lush water-meadow after another. They rounded a majestic bend in the river, and saw a huddle of cottages around a riverside inn. The village had grown up beside a shallow stretch of the river where an aged ferryman poled a splintered barge between the willow-ranked banks. Major Fulke had ridden the length of the column, urging his men to hurry and cursing the prisoners to the very pits of Hell.

'We ought to drown 'em!' a frightened musketeer called. 'Slowin' us down, they are!'

'Well, march faster, damn you!' Fulke snarled back, peering over the trampled meadow seeking any signs of pursuit. The green woods seemed quiet enough, but they were perilously exposed on the endlessly winding bank.

The bulk of the regiment and a hundred or so stragglers had already slipped away, hurrying for shelter inside Bristol's walls. He had been detailed to guard the prisoners, and had only been given the message to evacuate Bath at the last minute. As it was he had barely got his command away from the city before the Royalist outriders had forced the east gate and ridden in triumph around the abbey, firing their pistols to wake the dead. Fulke frowned, pulled his horse alongside the overloaded wagon which carried what was left of their baggage. They had scrambled away with what little they could.

Matilda was sitting alongside the driver, her skirt pulled up to cool her bronzed legs. Fulke licked his lips as she waved cheerily to him. Did the girl think they were out for a picnic?

'Toby! There you are,' she called. 'Why don't you tie the horse up and sit along with me for a while, eh?' the tireless creature asked with a wink. Fulke felt his boiled body flush beneath his clanking armour. He shook his head.

'I'm a little busy now, my dear. Bristol's not far.'

Matilda sighed, patted her skirts. 'I've never seen Bristol. Do they have many markets and shops up there?'

'I wouldn't know, my dear,' Fulke muttered. He looked up sharply at the sudden commotion ahead. One of the prisoners shouting the odds at his bewildered guard. Fulke tipped his forehead to the adoring girl and spurred along the column. The upstart in the brown coat again, bawling at one of his musketeers. The rest of the prisoners had crowded in, spoiling for a fight and anxious to waste precious time.

'Sergeant Grantly! Get these men moving!'

The heavily burdened musketeer prodded the young prisoner back with his musket butt as the rest of the guards closed up behind him, itching for a chance to drop their wretched charges and hurry on back to Bristol.

'Sergeant Grantly!' Fulke called.

The musketeer tilted his head at his hot-headed opponent.

'One more word out of you, my son, and I'll knock yer pretty teeth down yer bloody gob!'

'Give me a sword and we'll see who loses his teeth,' Telling snarled back as his fellow prisoners jeered and shouted.

Major Fulke scowled at the ferocious youngster he had struck with his glove the day before.

'Making remarks, sir,' Grantly called without taking his eyes from the prisoner.

'Remarks?'

'About the young lady, sir.'

Fulke bristled. 'Is that right?'

Telling glared up at the old gentleman, chin jutting. 'He made the remarks,' Telling argued, 'not me.'

'I don't want to hear your nonsense! Get on walking before I flog the lot of you!' Fulke ordered, drawing his weapon from the leather holster along his armoured thigh.

'Seems this young whippersnapper's taken a leaning on your lady, sir,' Grantly added, anxious to stoke the trouble and be rid of the dratted prisoners once and for all.

Fulke's florid face paled visibly. 'Am I to understand you know the lady?' he asked coldly.

Telling shrugged. 'Better than you'd know,' he declared to a chorus of encouragement from other prisoners.

The wagon had caught up with the rest of the party by now, and Matilda peered over at the commotion, guessing the heated debate had something to do with her.

'Hands up who's had her, boys!' shouted one of the prisoners from the anonymity of the back. Telling turned angrily. Grantly guffawed, held his hand up still clutching his burning match. Fulke squinted at his robust sergeant. Both prisoners and guards were chuckling with delight at the officers' evident embarrassment. It seemed their sweetheart had wandered from the paths of true love.

'She shagged out your boys and now she's started on ours!' the straggler from Fiennes' regiment shouted. Fulke twisted in his saddle to catch the culprit.

'Toby . . . don't let them talk to me so,' Matilda called, standing up on the running-board to get a better look at her accusers.

'Get yer drawers off, darlin'.'

'Who said that?'

'You can shut your gob and all, Ebenezer Bell! It takes you half an hour to find yours, let alone do anything with it!' Matilda shrieked at the red-faced musketeer. His colleagues collapsed with laughter. Telling shoved past the chuckling sergeant, held up his hand toward the furious red-head. Fulke brought his gauntlet down on his outstretched arm and Telling yelled in pain.

'I've told you before, sir, you'll not touch her ever more!' Fulke snarled down at the youngster as he nursed his wrist.

Telling glared spitefully at the old man on the prancing horse. 'Get down from that flea-bitten pit-pony and I'll make you pay for that,' he snarled back.

'Toby!' Matilda called warningly, the prisoners taking up her cry like an insane chorus.

'Toooobbbbyyyyyy! Toooobbyyyyy!'

Fulke swore and swung himself from the horse.

'Hugo, don't you dare lay a finger on him!' Matilda shouted from her splintered balcony on the wagon. Fulke shoved his men aside and stood nose to nose with the young Cavalier.

'I might just do that!'

'Go on, sir, bang him one for us!'

'Give him a sword!' Fulke bawled.

'Toby . . . don't you dare fight him for me! He's only a lad . . . Hugo, please don't hurt him!' Matilda called hopelessly, torn between her affection for the kindly old gent and her somewhat more animal attraction to the handsome captain. Grantly drew his sword, a plain soldier's tuck, and thrust the simple iron hilt at Telling. Fulke stepped back as the prisoners and guards edged back to form a hollow ring. He drew his own Walloon sword, the basket hilt and steel crosspiece dented and scarred with long and vigorous use. Telling swung the heavy tuck this way and that, squinted at the blade. As he expected it was as blunt as a butter knife and badly notched where the lousy sergeant had cut down boughs for his breakfast fire. He looked up as the white-haired major strode forward and swung his three-foot blade at his head. Telling just had time to raise his awkward blade and deflect the blow.

Ah, it was like that, was it?

Fulke drew back and slashed at his shoulder, and Telling danced backwards as the crowd whooped and whistled. Matilda stood alone on the wagon, hands clamped over her mouth but peeping nervously over her fingers. Fulke caught his breath, dangled the razor blade before Telling's face.

'Life in the old dog yet, eh, boy?' Fulke wanted to know.

Telling sneered. 'You're welcome to your life, as long as you don't sniff around my bitch!' he called.

'Who are you calling a bitch? I'm not your bitch or anyone else's!' Matilda screeched from the wagon. Fulke lunged and clipped Telling's arm. The worn brown fustian of his borrowed coat parted, drawing after it a bright blob of blood. Telling stood back, eyes blazing.

'You old goat! You'll pay for that,' he snarled. He crouched down, lunged with his right but threw the heavy hilted tuck into his left. Fulke brought his blade slashing down to his left as Telling pirouetted neatly, ducked down and brought the borrowed sword around like a scythe. Fulke took the blow on his left leg. His rolled-top leather boot absorbed the worst of the blow, but not enough to stop him buckling up at the knees. Fulke parried, over-balanced and fell on his face. Telling stepped closer and brought the blade down against the flushed skin on the major's neck.

'HUGO!' Matilda screamed.

The captain paused, the blunt blade resting against the old man's throat. Fulke cursed and rolled aside, sat up and examined his boot. He looked up, furious, as the officer menaced him with the borrowed sword.

'That's enough, back in line,' the major growled. Grantly stepped forward and helped the old gentleman to his feet. Fulke hopped experimentally, glowered at his opponent. Telling returned his stare and held on to the sword. The sergeant held his hand out.

'Give it back, boyo, before we shoot you down like a dog.'

'Do it!' Fulke barked.

The crowd of sweaty, tired, frightened men broke up once more, the prisoners taking their places inside a cordon of jumpy guards. Matilda had slumped down on the wagon to take refuge in a flood of embarrassed tears. Hugo snorted something under his breath and handed the heavy sword back to the belligerent sergeant.

'Get back in line and get a move on,' Fulke hissed as Ebenezer Bell held on to his horse for him. He clenched his teeth and swung himself into the saddle. As he did so he saw a flash of metal from the woods across the meadow. He straightened himself on the nervous horse and squinted back the way his troubled company had marched. Two, three, four horsemen appeared from the dense foliage. They walked their horses, evidently as interested in his command as the colonel was in theirs.

'Cavalry!' he yelled. 'Have a care!'

The frightened guards milled like headless chickens as the excited prisoners stood on tiptoes, shielded their eyes to spot their saviours. Fulke took in the situation in an instant, the silly argument forgotten in the heat of the moment. They were on the southern bank of the Avon, the broad meadow sweeping away before them. The nearest cover was a stand of timber a good mile over the empty grassland and halfway up the gently sloping valley. They would never make it. He peered around over the broad and unconcerned river. Far too deep to wade. Fulke shielded his eyes and stared at the small knot of villagers who had gathered to watch the trouble from the safety of the opposite bank. He followed their gaze and spotted the ferryman and his barge. The old man was enjoying the fun, leaning on his pole two hundred yards downstream. On his side of the river!

'Run to the ferry! Everybody on the ferry!' the resourceful old veteran bellowed. 'Keep an eye on the prisoners, I'll shoot down the first dog that tries to run for it!'

The startled guards needed no further urging. They kicked and shoved and prodded their charges along the bank, sweating and shouting with their bandoliers clinking and swinging on their chests. The prisoners were packed together, half striding half running under their fearful and trigger-happy masters. Fulke urged his horse alongside the wagon, helped Matilda climb up behind his back. The driver had dropped his reins and was running across the meadow after the prisoners, holding on to his hat as his dirty smock billowed around his unwashed white legs. Matilda closed her arms about his armoured waist as the game old bird spurred his horse after his troops. He reached the barge first, just as the dozy old ferryman realized their intentions and tried to pole himself away from the bank. Fulke brandished his pistol at the frightened old man.

'Wait there, you mangy hound, you'll not run out on my men!' he shouted.

The ferryman cursed but held the barge steady. Across the river the interested spectators screamed and fled for their homes like a flock of startled chickens. Fulke looked up, watched his men hurry along the bank prodding the prisoners with them.

'Why don't we leave 'em, sir, it'll be quicker!' Grantly called, his face flushed the colour of his coat.

Fulke frowned. 'I'll not abandon my charges to the first flock of coxcombs that happen along,' he snarled. 'Get 'em on the boat!' he ordered.

Grantly shook his head, but lent a ready hand manhandling the prisoners aboard the bobbing barge. Fulke peered along the bank toward the woods. At least sixty riders had emerged from the foliage, and were evidently unsure about how to proceed. Even as he watched, however, the troop accelerated away after them. Fulke could see the sun glint on their swords and breastplates.

'Steady, boys,' he called. 'Watch the prisoners, not those buggers!' Fulke helped Matilda clamber to the ground and waved her on to the barge after the men.

'Don't do anything silly, Toby!' she called despairingly as she was hauled aboard by Ebenezer Bell. The pursuing Royalist cavalry whooped and whistled as they galloped over the meadow, following the broad river as it turned majestically toward the north. A hundred yards now, and the major could pick out the colours of their coats and scarves. The ferryman had poled the boat away from the bank. Fulke dismounted with difficulty, felt his knee grate in angry protest. He slapped the beast on the rump and it cantered away gratefully, kicking its back legs as it went. The old man scrambled down the crumbling bank and hauled himself over the gunwale, straightened up with difficulty beside a press of anxious musketeers.

'Ready, boys!' he called, knowing they were by the way

they nudged and shoved each other for the best vantage points, burning matches poised over their musket pans. The ferryman raised his wet pole again, shoved it deep into the quaking lilies. The horsemen closed in, trampled the abandoned bank, shouting in impotent fury.

'Fire!' Fulke roared. Seven muskets belched smoke. The retorts rebounded over the river and echoed around the deserted village on the far bank. One of the riders slumped in his seat while his comrades emptied their pistols at the loaded barge. One of the prisoners screamed and staggered but was held up by the press of men crowded onto the narrow deck. His comrades shouted in anger and fear, holding the man upright as he coughed and choked on his own blood. Fulke waved his fist at the furious Royalist cavalry milling on the opposite bank. The barge glided across the water, out of range of their pistols.

Telling swore under his breath. The captain from Caernarvon's horse stood in front of him gasping his last, opening and shutting his white mouth like a stranded fish. The prisoners held him up like a colour, watched grimly as their friends shouted and bawled from the far bank. Hugo ducked down to the dirty deck, lost in a forest of dirty boots and broken-down shoes. He crawled between the shouting men, weaved between thrusting knees and stamping feet, and shouldered his way to the wooden rail which ran the length of the flat-bottomed barge.

Most of the musketeers at the stern had fired, those toward the bow still menaced the prisoners. Telling saw his chance. While the chuckling guards were reloading their cumbersome muskets on the crowded stern he ducked under the rail and dived into the water. The guards shouted a warning. A shot rang out, clipped one of the prisoner's hands and thudded into the worn planking of the deck. There was an instant uproar as prisoners and guards jostled and struggled. More shots. A prisoner toppled overboard. A guard was pushed after him, windmilling his arms as he tried to regain his balance. Fulke turned away from the desperate pack of prisoners, watched the fugitive splash and dive beneath the massed lily pads. He aimed slowly. The barge tipped as the struggle continued. Guards who had fired their weapons were forced to lay about them with the butts to keep the prisoners from over-running them completely. Fulke closed one eye and squeezed the trigger, just as Matilda fell against him, tipping his arm and sending the pistol ball smacking into the water a foot from the barge. He glared round at the crying girl, ground his teeth together in contempt.

'You stupid slut, you spoiled my aim!' he snarled, turning away to watch the fugitive swim under the lily pads and drag himself out on the crumbling bank. Half a dozen of the cavalry had dismounted to help him out. The rest fired their pistols at the escaping barge.

'I tripped, my dear,' Matilda lied, steadying herself on the major's arm. He thrust her away, glared at the bedraggled youth who had pulled himself out on the far bank. The youth turned, waved cheekily at his erstwhile captors.

Hugo Telling was free.

BY
SHERBORNE CASTLE,
DORSET, 18 JULY 1643

William Sparrow had marched so far on his badly blistered feet he no longer felt any pain, merely a creeping numbness which had seeped up the marrow of his shins, drained his thighs and loosened his pelvis. He felt as if his bowels might drop out at any moment, his shredded muscles had so little hold. He had walked most of the way in bare feet, his stockings and hose long since worn to sticky rags. He imagined they had marched to the ends of the earth, that they were bound to reach the sea soon or drop over the rim of the world. The bewildered cornet looked about him, sought out the familiar faces in the shuffling column. Colston Muffet trudged on as if the endless miles were a happy diversion on a summer afternoon. His lean back was bent almost double and his breath came in harsh gasps but he kept up a lively pace for all that. Billy Butcher hobbled behind, his feet in as serious a state as Sparrow's, while Gillingfeather stalked the rutted tracks like an avenging angel, hissing pious incantations or humming psalms with an occasional vindictive glance at the Royalist dragoons who had been detailed to escort them. Three nights and three days they had been walking, and the prickly dragoon captain had warned them they were barely halfway to their destination. Captain Breech had gathered them all together the first night out and paraded his entire troop for the prisoners to see.

'There they are, boys. Your guides for the journey. Should you step out of the column without permission they will immediately shoot you in the back.' The dragoons had snickered and grinned, but their captain had turned his baleful young face on them. 'Should you gentlemen miss your mark and allow one of these scoundrels to get away,' he said conversationally, 'the entire troop will forfeit its arrears of pay.' The dragoons had gasped at the prospect. They hadn't received a shilling since Christmas. The captain had drawn himself up on his captured horse, stared at the sullen mob of dirty faces.

'One hundred and six of you left Devizes, one hundred and six will fall in at Penmethock.'

'Penmezick?' Butcher had repeated. 'Where in all bleedin' Hell's Penmezick?'

'I have been ordered to deliver one hundred and six of you, and that is what I shall do. Those unable to march will be carried by their neighbours. Do I make myself clear?' At least half of Breech's command had served Parliament as well as the King, and he was anxious the long march didn't turn into some good-natured ramble. He had been promised twenty pounds for his trouble, if he could deliver the men on time.

'It's all right for him, up on that horse,' Butcher moaned, limping alongside Sparrow and nodding his sunburnt head at the arrogant captain. 'Why don't he get off and have a go at it?' Muffet hobbled on in silence, saving his energy.

The ragged column had left Devizes before dawn on 15 July, and set off towards Warminster. They had followed lonely lanes and trudged across the wild hillsides that skirted Salisbury Plain. The next day they had passed through Boreham, attracting curious stares from the townsfolk, and followed the cart tracks on to Mere. The men had already been dropping with fatigue, but Breech had beaten them awake an hour before dawn and watched them wade across the merry little River Stour. The freezing water had brought Sparrow's feet to life in an instant, and he had chewed his lips raw that morning as they marched over the heaths and hills between Wincanton and Shaftesbury. They were still short of Sherborne as the sun went down, but Breech trotted up and down the lines urging them on to one final effort.

'There'll be hot food and a rest at the castle. Keep the rendezvous and we'll all be happy.' The exhausted column shuffled along the dusty verges of the main road and reached the town by nightfall. They were billeted in the courtyard of the castle, which had been a Royalist beacon in south Somerset since the previous September when a small garrison of seven hundred men had managed to beat off an amateur army of over seven thousand West Country Roundheads. The castle had been designated as a clearing house for hundreds of rebels captured during General Hopton's victorious advance from Cornwall, and also served as a training depot for new contingents being sent north as reinforcements. Breech was as good as his word, for shortly after they arrived the dazed Roundheads were each given a bowl of broth, a hunk of cheese and a loaf. Sparrow tore at his food, the first proper meal he had enjoyed since the night before Roundway.

'Steady on, lad. Take smaller bites or you'll puke it all back up again,' Muffet said through a mouthful of bread. Sparrow ignored his advice, gobbled his meal and puked it all back up again.

'There you are,' Muffet commented. 'Your stomach's shrunk, see?'

'Ah, he could do with losing some weight,' Billy Butcher joked, spooning the last of his broth into his mouth.

Sparrow tugged at the flimsy basket of rags he had tied around his feet, picked at the bloody strips of skin between his toes.

'Vinegar. That's what you want on those,' Gillingfeather advised.

'Vinegar? You want to see me hop all the way to the sea?' William cursed under his breath. He knew well enough not to use profane language in front of the Londoner. He wouldn't hear the end of it.

'It'll harden your feet up, laddie. Too long sitting behind your desk is your trouble.'

William wished he was behind his desk now. Writing his pamphlets, mixing the inks or sorting the slugs of type. Why on earth had he ever volunteered for this? He'd been carried about the countryside on a half-wild horse to be hacked and jabbed at by enemy soldiers who seemed much more at home with their swords and pistols than he was. He had lost a finger already, been ridden over twice and penned up like a belligerent bull. To add insult to injury he had been looted by that ape-armed bastard Sergeant Lawton and denied his rightful status as an officer. Now it appeared they were to be sold into slavery. He could hardly believe his ears.

'Cornwall, see, what's Cornwall got?' Muffet asked quietly, fixing his ever-present clay pipe in his mouth despite the fact the dragoons had stolen all his tobacco. 'I'll tell you,' he went on. 'Tin. That's what it's got. They're plannin' on sending us down the mines!'

'Mines? What, underground?' Billy Butcher snorted.

'That's where mines usually are,' Muffet agreed. 'They'll send us to do the miners' work while the buggers get sent up and join Hopton! Be a regular holiday for them, wouldn't it?'

'They wouldn't dare!' Sparrow protested. 'There's rules for looking after prisoners.'

'They're Royalists, not Romans!' Muffet scowled.

'It's all the same to them what happens to us. We're filthy rebels serving ungrateful traitors, remember?'

'Ah, you're not having second thoughts, Colston?' Gillingfeather asked. 'The Lord of Hosts is our strength, he'll not abandon us to the wolves of Babylon.'

'I'm not having second thoughts, I'm just saying,' Muffet said sternly, before his fanatical companion could elaborate on his theme. 'You could tell that Cornish colonel didn't like it, whatever they had in mind for us. The black-haired bugger on the big horse.'

'Arguing the toss they were,' Butcher agreed. 'Him and that fancy house-dove in all the finery.'

'I didn't like the look of him, picking us over as if we were so many colts.'

'The thing is, boys,' Muffet whispered, 'if we're going to do anything about it, we'd best do it sooner rather than later!'

'Make a run for it, you mean?' Butcher asked loudly.

'Shush, you damned plover! Why don't you go and ask if you can exercise the captain's horse, take us along for the ride?'

Butcher looked peeved. 'I was only askin',' he said sourly.

William leaned back against the cold castle wall, listened to the low hum of the conversation slide by. He didn't like the idea of trying to escape with the guards facing the prospect of losing their pay if they succeeded. They couldn't be that far from the sea, and you could bet they would be extra vigilant now they were only a day or so from their destination. William sighed, thought fleetingly of poor Mary, lost and lonely back in Chippenham. What was she doing now? Looking for him, he imagined. Some hope. She'd find somebody else quick enough, she'd been forward enough with him. He closed his eyes and tried to picture her face, and fell immediately into a deep, dreamless sleep.

They were up before dawn the next day, refreshed with a pail of water and the remains of the previous night's bread. Captain Breech trotted along the column threatening and cajoling the guards and men.

'You'll be bathing your feet in the sea tonight, boys. One more push and we're there!'

'I'll give him one more push, I'll push my bleedin' musket right up his arse,' Billy Butcher muttered from the ranks.

Muffet eyed the young captain, nodded sourly. 'Mark him well, mate. That's one damned Royalist who'd better not find himself opposite me again.'

The muttered threats and curses died away as the column got underway, shuffling out of the gate under the curious eyes of a company of Cornish recruits. They booed and whistled as the prisoners trudged by, bellowed jokes in their own wild dialect. William tried to ignore them, but their blustering scorn stung him worse than his blistered feet. He stared at the dusty road, followed the man in front. Another twenty miles.

BY

KILMERSDEN HALL,

CHIPPING MARLEWARD, SOMERSET, 18 JULY 1643

Sir Gilbert Morrison watched the coach negotiate the arched gate and crunch the gravel along the winding drive. He had ordered all the servants out to cut the grass and clear the overgrown flowerbeds, and tidy up some of the rubble around the unsightly gun emplacements that fool Ramsay had dug in his once fine lawn. He had been all over the hall, making a careful inventory of all the furniture, hangings, paintings and plate. He anticipated that Lady Ramsay would go along with his proposals rather than throw them all back in his face, but it wouldn't do any harm to have a figure to hand in case she changed her mind. There was always the possibility the headstrong widow would allow her heart to rule her head and insist on selling everything so that what was left of her family could hang on to the empty shell of the hall.

The merchant had completed his tour of the house and had then visited the outhouses and stables. Findlay's horse was worth a bob or two, but the poor coach horses Ramsay had left were long overdue at the knacker's yard. The Ramsays had let their grounds go to rack and ruin as well. Good grazing land spoilt by poor drainage, and stands of good timber which had been allowed to grow wild, too closely for effective management. By God the estate was crying out for a man with a head on his shoulders, not a gourd full of fancy schemes and impossible dreams. So many treasures, so many familiar riches, and yet the family had been unable to keep their heads above water. Ramsay had left his estates to go to pot, just as King Charles had lost control of his Parliament, and by definition, the country. No financial acumen, you see, that was the root of the problem. Good business brains didn't grow from seed, after all.

Sir Gilbert had decided to act before it was too late, before Lady Ramsay had agreed to any of his little life-saving schemes. He had rounded up all the servants and marched them out with hoes and rakes to tidy up some of the rubbish which had accumulated during the long state of siege the house had endured. One of the lazy faggots must have carried tales to the house, because Lady Ramsay had appeared shortly after breakfast loudly demanding to know what he thought he was doing ordering her staff around.

'Protecting your good name and reputation, madam,' he had replied, quick as a flash. 'You wouldn't want to give Lord Clavinçale the impression we have let everything slip just because there is a war on!' He took off his hat and admired the view. 'The house may have had a garrison, but it doesn't have to look like a barracks, you know!'

The austere widow had compressed her lips, watched the miserable servants sweating in the sun as they cleared brambles and clipped the hedges.

'I would consider it most courteous, sir, if you cared to consult me before you took it upon yourself to invite your guests to my house, and then presumed to instruct my staff in their duties,' she said woodenly.

Sir Gilbert frowned in mock concern.

'Of course, my dear lady! Please excuse me if I have caused the least offence to your good self. I did not want to burden you with tiresome details when you have so many more pressing matters to attend to,' he said pointedly. She had not yet given her decision on the delicate matter of how Sir Marmaduke's debt was to be settled. He was not unduly concerned, however. As far as he saw it the widow had two choices. She could decide to spite him, sell the house and all the contents and settle the debt in ready cash. She could then say goodbye and good riddance to Sir Gilbert, but she and her daughter would be forced to move elsewhere. Abandon the family home and throw themselves on the mercy of some relative or friend. Perhaps they could take in needlework to pay their way, he couldn't imagine any other ways they could make a living. Well, perhaps one other. He sniggered to himself, pulled at his nose to disguise his amusement.

He had of course come up with a far more suitable solution to Lady Ramsay's predicament. There was no need for the poor widow to be thrown out of her home! For her daughter to wander the roads like any waif or stray without any prospects whatsoever. They had the house and the prestige, he had the money. And money was what was needed, at times like these. These Royalists and nobles were all the same. They didn't understand, they couldn't control, they had no concept of the money supply. You would have imagined these in-bred buffoons would have realized by now, would have put aside their snobbery and conceit and got around the table with the men in the know, the men with the money. Money made the world go around. Money bought power and soldiers, powder and cannons. Money paid troops and equipped fleets. Money kept everybody going, from the humblest farmer on the wildest hill to the King himself, safe, snug and smug up at Oxford. Perhaps this Lord Clavincale, this emissary from

His Majesty Charles Stewart, would understand the importance of people like him.

The money men. The men of tomorrow.

Lord Clavincale waited for Captain Nybb to adjust the steps, and clambered out of the coach into the bright afternoon sunshine. He glanced up at the household gathered on the steps. Were those sandbags there beside the door? Dear Lord, where had he ventured? The nobleman found his feet on the freshly raked gravel, beamed at the family assembled for his welcome. A short, red-faced man with a lively mop of closely clipped grey curls stepped down to meet him, opening his arms in welcome.

'My lord Clavincale! I hope your journey was not too tiresome!' Sir Gilbert called cheerily.

'On the contrary, sir, it was a most welcome diversion from Oxford! Who would have imagined in the midst of these wild hills of yours one would find such splendour?'

Sir Gilbert beamed at the powdered gentleman, recognizing an accomplished liar when he saw one. The merchant bowed, presented the lady of the house, formidable as ever in her widow's weeds.

'May I present Lady Ramsay, widow of the late and lamented Cavalier and Knight Sir Marmaduke Ramsay.'

Clavincale caught the woman's eye for a moment, bowed deeply.

'Lady Ramsay has very kindly opened her door to me and my family during these times of strife and crisis. A true Samaritan, sir, to whom the whole of Somerset, in fact the whole of England, owe an enormous debt of gratitude.'

Clavincale smiled broadly. The merchant could talk the hind legs off a donkey!

'Madam. May I present my most sincere condolences on your tragic loss. His Majesty King Charles has bidden me to express his own sincere regret and deep appreciation of the sacrifice your family has made in his true cause.'

Lady Ramsay nodded, her stern face set.

'May I also present Miss Ramsay, and my own daughter Miss Morrison.'

Clavincale smiled at the washed-out rag of a girl in the black dress and turned to the merchant's daughter. He blinked quickly, struggled to control his smile of surprise and delight. The girl was an absolute picture! Light auburn hair with veins of honey blonde and rich seams of gold, cheeky hazel eyes and a rather sensuous mouth. Her skin was lightly tanned, and so completely out of kelter with the trendsetters at Oxford, but wonderfully fresh nevertheless. Her complexion was perfect, her pretty nose slightly turned up at the end. Lady Ramsay noticed his careful scrutiny of the girl, the momentary attention which he tried to disguise by exaggerating his subsequent admiring look around the house and grounds.

'What a truly wonderful prospect,' Clavincale said fruitily.

'The bravest house in the Mendips, sir. The King won't find a truer family to his noble cause,' Sir Gilbert elaborated, stepping aside to reveal the servants and gardeners lined up as if for inspection. Findlay stood at the end of the tired rank, his fowling piece in his brown fist.

'This is Findlay, Lady Ramsay's loyal gamekeeper.'

Clavincale studied the gamekeeper's grey eyes, focused somewhere in the middle distance. A surly devil, to be sure. He examined the gamekeeper's six-foot fowling piece, nodded approvingly.

'I imagine you must be a crack shot, with a musket like that,' he commented.

'Good enough, sir.'

'I am trying to persuade Lady Ramsay to spare him as my sergeant major of foot,' Sir Gilbert interjected.

Clavincale nodded. 'You have begun recruiting already, sir?'

'I never stopped, sir, I never stopped. Regiments don't grow from seed, as well you know.' Sir Gilbert braced his thumbs behind the buff coat he had chosen for the occasion, surveyed the empty grounds as if the trees concealed several companies of crack troops which he had merely to whistle to attention.

'I am delighted to hear it,' Clavincale replied, stealing another look at the gamekeeper. So this was the sniper who had killed a brace of Nybb's deserters? They had heard all about the ambush during their overnight stay down the hill in Chipping Marleward. The landlord of the Blue Boar had inflated his part in the affair and the number of renegades, but the captain had recognized Jack Knoll's bloodstained riding coat and drawn his own conclusions. Two men with as many shots. A soldier worth cultivating, Clavincale thought. No wonder this rogue Morrison had already tried to sign him up. And if this was the sniper then this *Bella* Bella was the girl who had shot down that rogue Michael! By God, the girl must have some spirit!

'May I apologize once again for not being at home when you called, my lord, but I am sure you understand I felt my duty lay elsewhere.'

Clavincale had stolen another glance at the merchant's captivating daughter, idly tugging a rose from the flowerbed, and missed what her father had said.

'I beg your pardon, sir?'

'I mean, sir, my duty to these ladies, deprived of their menfolk by cruel fate.'

'Your compassion does you credit, sir,' Clavincale agreed.

Sir Gilbert beamed. This was going to be easy, he thought.

'Shall we go on indoors? Lady Ramsay has had the cooks prepare some refreshments.' Another lie. The wretched hag the Ramsays saw fit to employ in that capacity could barely boil an egg. Instead he had ordered Bella and Anneliese down to the kitchen to see what they could come up with. He watched the two girls sweep into the hall followed by the formidable Lady Ramsay. Clavincale watched Bella bend down to retrieve the blossom she had inadvertently dropped on the marble floor.

'Allow me, my dear.' The nobleman slipped between the girls and picked the stem between his gloved fingers. He handed it back to Bella, who fluttered her eyelashes in appreciation.

Steady on, girl, Morrison thought. Don't overdo it!

It took Sir Gilbert about three minutes to work out he had been completely wrong about Clavincale. He had imagined he was some younger son of an impoverished earl, too stupid to have gotten himself into the King's inner council and too weak kneed to go out and fight for his honour. The expensive clothing, the cologne and the limp handkerchief would fool a few people, but it didn't deceive Sir Gilbert. This aristocrat was rich and clever and every bit as slippery as he was. The merchant had studied him carefully as he nibbled his meal and sipped his wine, exchanging stilted small-talk with Lady Ramsay. Every now and then he would look up and smile at Bella, sitting alongside Anneliese and making the poor girl look even more miserable in comparison. How dare Lady Ramsay prevaricate over the marriage! Jamie was good enough for her whey-faced daughter any day of the week! After dinner the ladies had excused themselves and left the men to get down to the business of the day. Sir Gilbert listened to the nobleman outline the gist of the King's proposal. The terms of the treaty which would inject some desperately needed cash into the King's fight to regain his crown. In short, that the merchant houses in the west should be aided and encouraged in any manner possible, to enable them to mount a challenge to the commercial domination of their revolted colleagues in London. Sir Gilbert pursed his generous lips and nodded.

'Quite right. A splendid scheme. Please pass on my admiration and congratulations to His Majesty for formulating such an excellent plan.'

Clavincale smiled. The plan had had nothing to do with His Majesty, as they both knew full well.

'The question is, how does the King propose to advance our fortune over our former colleagues in London?'

The young courtier paused for a moment. 'I don't suppose I am giving away too many state secrets when I tell you Bristol will shortly be besieged by all the forces the King can muster.'

Sir Gilbert nodded. 'My own intelligence from the city is that Waller has left for Evesham and Colonel Fiennes has but two thousand men to hold the walls,' he reported.

The young lord made a dismissive gesture with his rose-pink hand. 'I don't imagine Bristol will prove to be too tough a nut to crack, especially for a commander of Prince Rupert's stature.'

So it was true, Rupert was on his way west. If only he could get young Bella up to meet *him*. Sir Gilbert was sure the moody prince would find his daughter as irresistible as every other young buck round about. Now that would be a marriage worth putting himself out for. Allied to the exiled Royal House of Bohemia. They had all the names and titles one could wish, but they didn't have any money either. It was common gossip that Rupert's father Frederick, the so-called Winter King of Bohemia, hadn't even been able to pay his milk bills. His exiled family were the impoverished darlings of the Protestant cause, blessed with a whole tribe of handsome sons and beautiful daughters. Pity the father had been such a loser.

'If Bristol should fall, local merchants such as yourself will once again have the opportunity of operating through a major port.'

That was true enough. Lonely little harbours like Minehead or Watchet made excellent bases for the Somerset small fry, but the bigger merchant houses could not make a decent operating profit making do with their limited facilities. Besides, most of the principal traders had warehouses in Bristol. Bristol was the second port in the land after London, the nub of half a dozen vital trade routes. He who controlled the Bristol trade could sit back and rake in a fortune in taxes and revenues.

'The port will be a decided boost for business,' Sir Gilbert agreed, 'but I am still not clear exactly how King Charles means to encourage our commercial efforts.'

Clavincale smiled, drummed his fingers on Sir Marmaduke's fine inlaid table.

'His Majesty proposes to issue a Royal Charter for Bristol as the staple port of the great trade houses. The Levant company, the Eastland Company and so on. This will open up all sorts of trading possibilities for the King's loyal West Country merchants, would it not?'

Sir Gilbert bit at his thumbnail, nodded. It would open possibilities all right.

'Of course, His Majesty would need to rely on the goodwill and cooperation of such a body.'

And a good percentage of the profits as well, no doubt. Still, business was business, and Sir Gilbert had never expected to be given something for nothing.

'If such a body could be brought into existence, it would need a figurehead, a guiding light. A man with the gifts and experience to recognize and understand the needs of both parties. To be able to liaise between the two, and balance the interests of the kingdom with its merchant adventurers,' Clavincale explained smoothly.

Sir Gilbert's eyes flashed momentarily. A foot in both camps. Merchant of the high seas and trusted commander to the King.

'The governorship of Bristol?' the merchant wondered aloud.

Clavincale raised his eyebrows. This rogue had ambition! 'Perhaps governor, perhaps mayor, perhaps some other suitable title could be offered. For the right man.'

'Of course. This governor or mayor or lord lieutenant, he would be the senior partner within the consortium, and possibly be responsible for civil affairs in the county, collection of taxes, raising, clothing and equipping new forces for His Majesty?' Sir Gilbert enquired.

'The post would certainly be a demanding one,' Clavincale chuckled.

'Not a job for the faint hearted!'

'Assuredly not!'

'Or for a common Somerset trader.'

The nobleman paused, nodded seriously. 'A title would be the least His grateful Majesty could provide,' Clavincale said guardedly. He had to hand it to the merchant, Morrison knew what he wanted and he played to his strengths. He had understood the basic flaw with the King's situation: he didn't have the money or resources to wage the war as effectively as Parliament. In the long run, the King must raise more cash for more troops, or his cause would collapse. Neither Lord Clavincale nor this grubby huckster wanted that.

'Well, then,' Sir Gilbert said briskly. 'I think we have a reasonable basis for negotiation, don't you?'

The scoundrel drove a hard bargain, by God! Clavincale swilled the last of the late Sir Marmaduke's best brandy, and drank a toast to their treaty. In return for helping to set up and acting as President of the Royal Westward Oceanic Venturers Sir Gilbert was to become Baron Morrison of Marleward. Baron Morrison of Guttersnipe! Clavincale had tried to haggle him down but the merchant had realized the importance of his position and stubbornly stuck to his guns.

'I don't imagine you've come all the way down here to take the waters, my lord,' the merchant had observed shrewdly. 'The creation of a West Country trading cartel could put thousands of pounds into the King's purse. No doubt His Majesty will see fit to reward your own enterprise on his behalf.'

Clavincale had smiled faintly, rather alarmed at this boorish oaf's well of detailed information. Was it possible he had caught wind of Clavincale's promised dukedom? Did he have contacts at court as well as in Bristol's coffee houses? Lord Marleward it was.

Titles were becoming more meaningless by the day as King Charles showered awards on those he could trust – or thought he could trust. Knight, duke, marquess or earl. A man could create his own pedigree, as long as he had ready cash for the King's coffers or reinforcements for his armies. Morrison, with his inside knowledge of Bristol's commerce and a whole regiment of connections in the west, wouldn't be the only commoner to finish the war as a nobleman, lording it over another man's land into the bargain. Of course, the new lord would be expected to keep the crucial West Country merchants in line, and to provide the King with a rich source of revenues. In addition to his mercantile skill, Sir Gilbert would also accept a commission from the King to raise and equip a regiment of foot from the hills roundabout to be paid and equipped from the consortium profits. And that wasn't all.

His son was to be released from his imprisonment at Devizes and returned post-haste to Somerset, where he would be made a knight. With Sir Gilbert and his son raised to the peerage, Lady Ramsay could have no reservations about the marriage of young Sir James to her daughter Anneliese. Sir Gilbert had apparently discussed the match at some length with the austere widow. No wonder the old girl looked so glum! Opening her doors to the wretched bounder was one thing, welcoming him as a part of the family quite another. The happy couple would of course continue to live at Kilmersden Hall with the dowager Lady Ramsay occupying the vacant wing of the vast mansion. There was plenty of room after all. As a consequence of the marriage any debts owed by Sir Marmaduke's estate to the latter gentleman would be taken as settled in full. A dowry would not be required. Sir Gilbert gulped his brandy, his twinkling eyes burning with the powerful fumes. He felt like dancing a jig around the room, but he managed to show some decorum.

'Well then, here's to us. A clean slate, a fresh start.'

'To the early and complete victory of the King,' Clavincale cried.

'God bless him!'

Bella Morrison had hovered in the hall as long as she was able without drawing attention to herself. Lady Ramsay had long since stalked back to her room and Anneliese had run off crying again. It must be terrible to lose a father and a brother, but life must go on, after all. Bella scolded herself, tried to imagine what life would be like without Sir Gilbert's constant scheming and her tiresome brother's selfish whining. Absolute bliss, she imagined.

Anneliese had refused to discuss her two-hour ordeal with Sir Gilbert and Lady Ramsay, and had pointedly avoided Bella ever since. The merchant's daughter tapped her slipper in agitation, turned and paced back down the richly furnished hallway. It was no good Anneliese taking it out on her! If her stupid parent hadn't gone borrowing so much money from her father her family wouldn't owe them anything! Lady Ramsay could turn them out to wander back to the cold house down in the village! Bella hadn't been party to the plotting, hadn't helped make any plans for her former friend. And even if she had, it wasn't as if Jamie would be that bad a match when you came right down to it. In fact, Anneliese's objections to the marriage had begun to sound very much like out and out snobbery! By finding fault with Jamie's family background, she was by definition finding fault with hers! Hah! As if any man worth his salt would come after Anneliese Ramsay before they came after her! She had let herself go to pieces since her father's death, she looked little more than a hag with her eyes all red and ringed! How dare she suggest Bella wasn't good enough for a decent marriage? Did the wretched girl expect her to be satisfied with the milkman? With an inky-fingered idiot like William Sparrow? By God, they were all in it together, putting her down, looking down their noses at her! She'd show them!

The study door opened and Lord Clavincale stepped out into the gloomy hallway. It was getting late, and Bates was still making his rounds lighting the lamps around the silent house. Bella froze alongside an ornate and rather daring statue, and watched the nobleman close the door and lean against it, rolling his eyes with a sigh.

She knew how he felt. Two hours with Sir Gilbert was enough to test anybody. Bella coughed politely. Clavincale looked up sharply, squinted into the gloom, and picked her out in the shadows. He smiled broadly.

'Miss Bella, it's you. I thought at first I must be seeing things, Venus herself coming to life before my tired eyes.' He stepped along the hall, bowed slightly as Bella emerged from the shadows, blushing deeply. Clavincale allowed his eyes to roam around her slim waist, noting the rather creased blue dress was at least two years behind the current fashion in Oxford. He looked up and completed a slow reconnaissance of her cleavage, which seemed to have made some rather satisfying advances since dinner. Clavincale dragged his eyes away from her delightful chest and caught her eye. She was boldly returning his stare, so much more interesting than those lettuce-leaf lovers who averted their eyes and giggled the moment a man looked at them.

'An afternoon with Father can be rather an ordeal,' she said smoothly.

Clavincale raised his eyebrows. She wasn't joking. He frowned good naturedly.

'Not such an ordeal as to prevent me from inviting you to take a turn around the grounds, my dear lady.'

Bella liked the sound of a real-life lord calling her lady. She smiled and held out her arm. Clavincale noted her long fingers were bare save for one small gold band, and that the fingernails had been rather fetchingly chewed. She seemed almost elemental, so much more real than the painted harlots back at Court. Her arm was warm, he felt the skin beneath his richly embroidered coat prickle as he guided the girl down the hall and past Bates, nodding and muttering as he continued his rounds with a lighted taper. They walked down the steps and out along the path, admiring the sunset. The heather had turned from tawny gold to a deep mauve as the sun sank behind the hills, the shadowed trees hissing in the light summer breeze. Looking up at the black and blue sky, they saw the first stars twinkling like elven lanterns, guiding their way around the quiet grounds. This western excursion of his was turning out to be a delightful holiday!

'I don't suppose I dare ask what you two have been discussing for so long,' Bella said archly.

Clavincale grinned like a schoolboy, bewitched by her daring wit. This was no silly sister content to wander around like a ghost. Hardly seen and never heard. She had views and ideas of her own. What a stir she would create at Oxford, what a name he would make amongst all the boastful soldiers and captains, turning up with a vision like this on his arm! It would almost be worth having Sir Gilbert as a father-in-law. Well, perhaps not.

'Business, my dear, business.'

'Did he mention the exchange?' Bella asked innocently.

'Exchange? Oh yes, your brother. Captured at Roundway fighting for the Roundheads.'

'Father thought he could be exchanged for a Royalist captain of our acquaintance. Do you know Hugo Telling? He is in Prince Maurice's regiment of horse.'

Clavincale disliked the military, braggarts and bounders the lot of them. He particularly disliked the Teutonic Terrors, the Princes of the Palatinate, Rupert and Maurice. They were the darlings of the court at the moment, unbeatable, irresistible. They were seen as the King's great hope, his best generals and bravest commanders. The handsome princes with their scarves and flashing looks put hard-working courtiers like himself very much in the shade.

'Your father mentioned something about it,' he said stiffly.

Bella realized she had struck a nerve. 'It seems a pity for them to be wasting away, when they could so easily be exchanged,' she said casually. 'What difference could it possibly make to the outcome of the war? It's all so very tiresome.'

Clavincale frowned and said nothing. They had reached a small copse, broody and bristling in the half light. Two months before Bella and Hugo had walked the same path. He had taken liberties Bella was not prepared to allow, and she had been obliged to knee him in the groin and trample his hat for his insolence. Hugo had left the hall shortly afterwards, his wounds recovering well enough but his pride in tatters. Bella knew the path very well, even in the slivered silver light. She paused, breathed deeply.

'I will write to the commander in Devizes first thing in the morning.'

'What about Hugo? He was in Bath the last I heard,' Bella insisted knowingly.

Clavincale sighed. 'You and Hu . . . Captain Telling, have an understanding?'

'Oh no,' Bella said with a chuckle. 'He's just a friend.'

'I see.'

'It's just he had promised to take me to Oxford. I would so dearly love to see Oxford, but what with Father being so busy . . . '

Clavincale swallowed, admired her features bathed in the moonlight flickering through the trees.

'You want to go to Oxford?'

'It's so dull being stuck at home here. I have always wanted to travel, see something of the world. Father seems to be too . . . '

'But I am sure your father would agree to you travelling with me, with your maids and any chaperone he might wish to appoint, of course.'

Bella looked up eagerly at the besotted lord, his pale, powdered face glowing unhealthily. Maid? Chaperone?

'Do you think he would? I don't know what I would give to see Oxford!'

Clavincale felt his shirt tighten about his throat. He eased a finger beneath his fashionable collar and smiled awkwardly.

'I'll speak to him in the morning. It is imperative I return to Oxford to consult the King on . . . what your father and I have discussed.'

Bella stamped her foot with excitement, gazed at the young lord as he stood fidgeting alongside her. Clavincale twitched, his throat dry. He hadn't felt as ill at ease with a wench since he had lost his virginity in a London whore-house back in '35. Bella seemed to sense his indecision. She stood on tiptoe, kissed his cheek in so demure a manner the poor lord almost mistook himself. He swivelled around, tugged her forward once more, and kissed her clumsily over her mouth. Bella stood back from him, whispered.

'Softly, love. Kiss me softly.'

Clavincale's eyes watered and his legs went.

BY

CHIPPING MARLEWARD,

SOMERSET, 19 JULY 1643

Jeremiah Pitt gathered his mistress had recovered from her midnight ordeal at the hands of the deserter dragoons. She had dashed into their gloomy cottage in the High Street, swinging around the worn door like an Oriental acrobat. His mother had been gathering up an enormous bag of laundry, and could hardly see the girl over the fortifications of sheets and underclothing.

'Molly Pritchard, if I've told you once I've told you a thousand times! It's no good chasing round 'ere like a constipated 'en, God's only given me one pair of 'ands, you know!'

Jeremiah threw himself out of his absent father's chair and beamed at the visitor. 'It's not Molly, Ma, it's Miss Bella!' he sang.

Mistress Pitt threw a brawny red arm over the offending obstacle, compressing the bundle enough to recognize their guest for herself.

'Lawks! I'm sorry, Miss Bella, if I'd known it—'

'That's all right, Mrs Pitt,' Bella snapped, peering about the narrow unfurnished room as if she expected to find it jammed with Roundhead spies. 'Is Mary at home?'

Mrs and Master Pitt looked over their shoulders as the maid in question appeared on the staircase, peering beneath the beams at the unannounced intruder.

'Miss Bella,' Mary Keziah said rather stiffly, as her fly-by-night mistress regained her breath. 'I've been looking for you all over,' she lied quietly.

'Mary! Where on earth have you been?' Bella scolded gently, waving her missing maid down into the scullery. The girl closed her eyes for a moment, recoiled at her diabolically vivid impressions of Roundway Down. It was as if the raw memories of her ordeal had been tattooed on her eyelids for ever. A filthy landscape of broken men and horses she would never shake free. Where on earth had she been? As far as Mary Keziah was concerned, she had endured a guided tour of Hell itself.

Mary Keziah and her mistress had parted company in Chippenham, the day before the disastrous battle. Bella had left to find and free her Royalist fancyman while her maid had hung on for news of William. He had told her it would be over in a matter of days, that Waller would force the wild Cornish to surrender, and then be free to march east, trapping the King between his forces and the Earl of Essex's main force. Like so many of William's grand schemes, Waller's victory march had been strangled in its own garlands.

Mary had hurried downstairs to listen to the terrified stragglers describe the disaster inflicted on Sir William's forces, fists clenched in stunned disbelief as they gasped the hideous details. The Roundhead army in which her new beau served as a cavalry cornet had been completely and utterly routed. Terrified her sweetheart had been killed, Mary had cadged a lift to the fatal hillside with a family of what she had taken to be concerned relatives. In fact, the gap-toothed wolves had turned out to be looters, hurrying to the battlefield to pick the pockets of the dead and wounded. They had whipped their undernourished horses until they were blanketed in bloody foam, snorting painfully as they hauled the wagon up the slaughtered slopes. Mary Keziah had watched in horrified disgust as they leapt from the creaking cart and fell to hungrily, plundering the bodies which lay ransacked and rotting in the sun. Nauseated by the sights and sounds of the stricken field, Mary Keziah had staggered away from the stinking carnage, wandered blindly into an irate Cornishman whose regiment had been detailed to help bury the bodies. She had screamed in horror as his black horse had reared up over her, his dark hair and scowling features plastered in chalk dust.

'What's wrong with you, girl, aren't they stiff enough for you yet?' he had leered.

Mary Keziah, stung by his accusation, had found her voice at last, and choked out her story. Her sweetheart had ridden to the battle but hadn't been seen since. The truculent officer had moderated his tone and finally taken her under his wing, escorting her around the bloody downs between heaps of stripped bodies. Mary Keziah had barely been able to peek at the slashed and gouged corpses, the purulent yellow flesh reminding her of slaughtered poultry on a butcher's slab.

'The cavalry were over this side, not that they stood that long. Do you know which regiment he served in?' Mary Keziah hadn't known. The kindly colonel had walked her past groups of his grinning men and up the slope to the very edge of the downs. She had wondered what he meant to do, bringing her so far away from the bloated dead and the wrecked camp. Looking back the way they had come, Mary Keziah imagined she was staring at a green beach, disfigured by a stinking high-water mark of flotsam and jetsam vomited by a scouring tide of war. Mary had looked away quickly, gratefully swallowing the cleaner air blowing from the west. She had gazed at the superb view, the peaceful patchwork fields of Wiltshire laid out neatly between the shimmering horizons, calming her violated spirit.

Mary had squinted into the sun, sure she had spotted a sudden movement in the glimmering haze. And then her hands had flown to her mouth, her frail form shuddering with revulsion as she picked out the sooty smears disfiguring the heavens.

The glorious summer sky had been dotted and dashed by solitary crows, winging in one after the other to gorge on the slaughter. Flocks of noisy rooks had flapped and tumbled as they pursued the silent crows down to the corpse-heavy hill.

'Down there,' the swarthy colonel had snapped, irritated by her bewilderment. Mary Keziah had swallowed weakly, peeked over the edge of the cliff, and seen more looters and burial parties moving this way and that between heaps of broken-backed horses and discarded equipment. 'The Lobsters lost eighty or so down there. Was he in Haselrig's?'

'He was in McNabb's!' Mary Keziah moaned, clutching her mouth at the revolting shambles at the foot of the cliff. 'He had to carry the flag!'

'Cornet to McNabb's . . . big fellow with curly hair?'

Mary Keziah had turned in wonder, her tear-swollen eyes wide.

'That's him! That's my William!'

The colonel had frowned, nodded her back to the town.

The poor girl had been alarmed by his suddenly abrupt manner. 'What's the matter with him?' she had screeched.

'Nothing's the matter with him. At least . . . He was taken prisoner.'

Prisoner. To poor families struggling in small villages the term generally meant their man would be as good as dead. Now, on the death-loud hill, it was like a blessing from Heaven, a generous gift from the gods.

'My William's a prisoner!' she had cried. 'Where is he, can I see him?'

'That might prove a little difficult,' the dark-haired fiend had admitted.

Mary Keziah lifted her skirts and stepped down into the dimly lit scullery, regarded her mistress sourly. Bella smiled, equally awkward with her pale servant.

'Are you all right? Where have you been?'

Mary Keziah compressed her lips.

'How's William?' Bella asked cautiously.

'He's been taken prisoner, miss. On Roundway. Him and most probably me brothers too.'

Bella's face dropped, but not very far. Mary Keziah bristled, remembered her mistress's former dalliances with the generously built printer's apprentice. She had thought little enough of him then, and had been content to let him pant along behind her like a distressed sheepdog. Imagined you were too good for him, but he was too good for you, my lady, she thought with a scowl.

'Jamie was taken as well! We're off now to see if we can't get them released!' Bella declared, as animated as ever. 'We can get William out as well as Jamie, I shouldn't wonder!' Bella cried excitedly.

Mary Keziah shook her dark head. 'Too late, miss. They've taken all the prisoners away. Nobody seems to know where. Oxford they said, but some of them left by the Warminster road according to the folk in Devizes.'

Bella understood little of this. 'Well, no matter. I am sure somebody knows where he's gone. You didn't see Jamie on your travels?'

'No, miss. I didn't realize he'd been taken.'

Bella slipped her arm beneath her maid's and guided her toward the door.

'It's partly about him I came to see you. Father has found a lord, a real-life lord, to do business with. He says he'll take me up to Oxford but Father won't let me go without a suitable chaperone, you know what he's like.'

Mary Keziah glanced at her mother, still busy with the laundry.

'And you want my Mary to go with you, Miss Bella?' Mrs Pitt asked carefully.

Bella opened her mouth, paused, then smiled.

'Well . . . if she would like to come, of course. I'm sure we'll be able to look for Eli and Zachary as well as Jamie.' Bella squeezed her maid's arm, rather disconcerted by her vacant state.

'You take her on, miss, get her out of 'erself. She's no good around 'ere frettin' and pukin' all morning. And if you see those idiot boys o' mine, remind 'em they've a mother left 'ere slavin' to keep a roof above their 'eads! I ain't 'ad as much as a brass farthin' from any of the buggers.' Mrs Pitt manhandled the starched sheets and folded them under her brawny arms. Mary Keziah stiffened as Bella continued to stare at her.

'Aren't you well?'

'I'm all right,' her maid scowled. 'I'll fetch my things, if I'm not wanted here.'

*

The happy travellers said their goodbyes and climbed aboard the coach. There was plenty of room now Captain Nybb had been ordered off on a new assignment. He was to ride on down to the coast to complete some pressing business for Lord Clavincale.

'Right klecked am I, mineer, miss'noot on the way a homer mitt der gleschlechter fraulein!' Nybb had informed Sir Gilbert with a broad wink.

The perplexed merchant had rubbed his chin, nodded enthusiastically.

'Ah, agriculture's a closed book to me, my friend,' he had replied. 'All I know is good farmers don't grow from seed.'

Nybb had given him a puzzled look and taken up his reins. Clavincale had nodded to his bodyguard, and turned his attention to the ladies. He had practically nailed Bella into the coach, hardly believing the merchant would allow him to wheel his principal asset out of his sight. He pondered the crafty trader's motives. Did he mean to set the girl up to tease and tempt him? By God, she'd succeeded in doing that already. He had pulled her arms and thrust himself at the girl the previous evening, hurried her back to his room where he had allowed himself to be tempted a little more.

He pictured the girl lying on the ruckled bed, her tired blue dress collecting further sets of jagged creases, her massed underclothing pulled about like the filmy skirts of a jellyfish. Transparent but deadly to the indiscreet swimmer. She had slapped his wrists soundly, scissored her long stockinged legs out of his numbed reach.

What did he think he was doing? What did it look like, he had hissed.

She couldn't. Not now. Not now? The wrong time of the month, my lord. My lord!

He had barely restrained himself from throwing her down anyway and satisfying his rampaging lust as if the long-legged spitfire was another simple maid in waiting.

'Don't treat me like one of your sluts!' she had threatened, her hazel eyes popping with annoyance. She had hauled herself up on the bedclothes, tearing the hangings while she was at it. They had stared at the significantly torn curtain, calmed themselves for a moment. Angry and indignant, she had looked all the more fetching to the hopelessly bewildered Clavincale, who found himself clenching and unclenching his fists as if he was at a particularly exclusive dogfight. The girl had been put on the earth for one reason – to pleasure men – and here she was playing the coquette. Bella could behave like a Parisian strumpet one moment, and be as virtuous as a nun the next. It drove the leering Lord to distraction, and whetted his already considerable appetite for the girl's charms. Oh, yes, she knew what she was doing all right, and so did her old man. Was the cunning lout expecting him to marry the girl? It would be a sight easier to force his hand if he had already disgraced himself. Think of the gossip, think of the scandal! She wouldn't be the first blushing virgin married off to her seducer. He would be playing into Morrison's hand, trying his hand with his minx of a daughter. Then again, a chap could do worse for himself. She would be a lady now, after all. Lady Clavincale! And in a year or two, if everything went according to plan, he could expect a sizeable dowry too!

Clavincale stepped back as Bella hauled herself into the coach. He watched his precocious paramour make herself comfortable alongside Mary, who gazed miserably out of the window. He was tempted to ask the sorry-looking wench to change places, but thought better of it.

'Cheer up, girl, we'll find these silly menfolk of yours,' Clavincale had encouraged, hauling himself up into his seat with difficulty. His breeches appeared to have entangled certain portions of his anatomy, and he fluttered his handkerchief in distraction as he attempted to make himself comfortable. Why on earth had he ordered them so tight?

'Keep an eye on her now, Clavincale,' Sir Gilbert called familiarly, stepping up to the window and standing on tiptoes to peer inside.

'I shall take great care of her, Sir Gilbert,' Clavincale replied, bending forward to lean out of the window conspiratorially. 'Or should I say Baron Marleward? Ha ha! I doubt we'll see any trouble, now the King's arms have cleared the roads!'

Sir Gilbert had wondered about sending Findlay with them in place of his lordship's burly German bodyguard, but decided he couldn't spare his surly sergeant major from his duties with the new troops. Well, it could only be a matter of time before the hall was over-run with eager recruits. He stood back as the driver whipped up the team and pulled the heavy coach around on the crackling gravel. Lady Ramsay and Anneliese stood quietly on the steps, and watched the coach trundle off toward the gate. The merchant folded his hands behind his back and gave them a broad grin.

'Ah, there they go! Not long now and we'll have our Jamie back with us, eh, Annie?'

Anneliese blinked at the rosy-cheeked merchant as he capered around the foot of the steps. He was in tremendously good form, what with Bella and her new gentleman friend getting along famously and his own commercial future signed, sealed and delivered. A trade agreement his merchant cronies would have sold their own mothers for! Another few months and Morrison's would be the principal trading house in the west, its ambitious and go-getting chief one of the most powerful and influential men in Somerset. He would invite all his business friends and rivals to the wedding, of course. He would parade his new-found allies for those grubby Bristol grocers. Another month and they would have cause to regret writing Gilbert Morrison off as a bad loss. He had suffered some cash-flow problems, it was true, and had been forced to reassess his allegiance. Sir Gilbert had been away from the hustle of the coffee houses and the bustle of the wharves for months.

But he was safe outside Bristol's walls now, quids in with some powerful men at court and about to be connected by marriage to the principal Royalist family in the Mendips. His knavish, quarrelling, fair-weather friends were still shut up in the city, praying those same walls would hold against the dread prince himself. He pictured the merchants at their counting tables, trying to decide how much of their preciously hoarded cash to spare for the woefully under-manned garrison. Too much and they would be ruined by the expenditure, too little and they would be sharing what was left with a greedy King! It wouldn't be Sir Gilbert's goods the Cavaliers burnt when Prince Rupert's men arrived to punish the sinful city! It wouldn't be his kinfolk put to the sword by the wild Cornishmen! He would be surprised if they stayed put, risked everything behind the dreary grey walls and hastily dug ditches. With a bit of patience and a little luck, he would clean up those that were left, perhaps use his privileged position to buy up their rotten stocks. He rubbed his hands with glee, and glanced up at the women scowling on the step. Not even these two stuffed codfish could put him off his stride tonight.

'I wager you'll be counting the days, eh?' His jolly smile slipped a notch as he regarded them, silently reminded the women of their penniless plight. 'A few short weeks and everything will be sorted, that I promise you,' Sir Gilbert said flatly. He bowed shortly and clattered up the steps past the unblinking, black-robed statues. Lady Ramsay and her daughter stood for a while, watching the tangled woodlands on the horizon smother the sun.

'She was always saying she would get away from here, that she'd travel the world until she'd met her man,' Anneliese said woodenly. 'We used to plan our journeys on Father's globe, pick all the places we would like to go.'

Lady Ramsay shuddered as dusk advanced out of the woods and ate up the deserted grounds.

'There are better ways to see the world than on your back,' she snapped.

Anneliese chuckled mirthlessly.

'We'd best go on in,' Lady Ramsay sighed, and escorted the sobbing girl back into the house. She couldn't decide whether she felt like a prisoner or a jailer.

BY
PENMETHOCK HARBOUR,
WESTERN DORSET, 19 JULY 1643

William Sparrow harboured no such doubts about his current status. He was a prisoner; worse than that, he was to be put to work like some slave from the Indies. Hacking mineral ore from some Cornish pit, they said, caged and prodded as if he was more beast than man. A suitable punishment for a vile rebel, for a common traitor.

He had overheard half a dozen campfire debates, heated arguments in which a firebrand like Gillingfeather rounded on all those who doubted their duty, or questioned the crusade Parliament had been forced to undertake to free the King from his evil counsellors.

'Let he who goes about the Lord's work with doubting heart fall out! Away with ye, the false hearted! I'd rather serve with ten true men who know the cause and love what they know than a hundred lily-livered poltroons!'

William shook his head. Serving with a hundred lily-livered poltroons? It just about summed up his military career. He hobbled on, blanking his mind against the ferocious bursts of pain from his legs – numb no longer. His toes were on fire now, burning, shooting cramps as if he was trying to trample on a wasp's nest. He ignored his agonized muscles, and concentrated instead on recalling the faces of his friends. He conjured their fiery features, pictured them as they sat smiling over their suppers, sucking their pipes as they listened quietly to the head-strong debates. Lily-livered? Perhaps. Poltroons? Maybe. But he would rather have them around him now, with their doubts and fears and faint hearts, than these silent shufflers lost in their own private agonies. It was all too easy to sit around a good fire, a hundred miles from the nearest Cavalier, and swear you would rather die with sword in hand than duck beneath the King's hated yoke. It was all too easy shouting Death before Slavery when the only ones in earshot were frightened women or shrieking children. William wondered whether it would have been better to have held together on Roundway, to have stood like rocks while the Royalists pounded them to mush with their own artillery. Better for whom, some news-sheet scribbler secluded in London? Some careless colonel safe behind the battle lines? Sparrow gritted his teeth, and let his hate feed on his pain. He had plenty of it to spare.

Sir Gilbert now. All those months preparing for war, collecting his regiment and stealing their pay. The first whiff of powder and he had scampered away up to Kilmersden Hall, claiming to have been a Royalist spy in a hostile village. His daughter, the bewitching and beautiful Bella. Another weathercock creaking and swinging in the slightest breeze, but her cause was men. Advancement. A way out from under her father's feet. Any man who could take her away from her hated home, from her pampered prison, would do for her.

Men like that house dove, that gander-necked Cavalier coxcomb, the Royal Wool-Gatherer himself. What was his name? Hugo Telling. A thin, sneering youth with a mousey moustache. He'd got the better of him on two occasions already. He wondered where his despised rival was at that minute. Did Parliament put its prisoners to work in the mines? He doubted it. Sparrow looked up from the cobbled road, scowled at the dragoon captain riding a little to the left of the shuffling column. Not much older than himself, a newcomer to the wars. What made him a party to such barbarities? The promise of a promotion or a few extra shillings? One of the other prisoners had claimed the entire troop had changed sides earlier in the year, and here they were preparing to sell their own former comrades into virtual slavery!

'They watch 'em close, see, make sure they ain't got no obligations to any of their old mates,' Long Col had murmured. 'Turncoats are the worst, always got something to prove to their new masters, mark my words.'

Sparrow realized the young captain was staring down at him, studying the filthy cavalryman with distaste.

'What are you staring at?' the captain rasped, raising his chin a notch.

'You, you damned Judas. Selling us out for a handful of silver!' Sparrow growled with more determination than he had meant. 'I hope you rest easy tonight, mate!'

The captain swivelled in his saddle to stare at the surly trooper.

'Don't come the holier than thou with me, Roundhead. I didn't ask for this assignment, I was given it. Unlike you fuckers, I obey me orders!'

Sergeant Lawton, Sparrow's particular enemy, had trotted up behind the muttering prisoners, unobserved.

'Mr Mouth again, is it? Sort the shit-stirrers out of this lot and the rest'd come meek as lambs,' the unshaven wretch leered. 'Want me to make an example of the bastard?'

'You've got my boots, you short-arsed cunt, why don't you try growing into 'em?'

Lawton's rheumy red eyes twinkled merrily as he raised his pistol. Sparrow shuffled on, one eye fixed on the furious rider. Breech turned his horse into the crowd, whacked the truculent cornet with his hat whilst he was looking the other way. Sparrow jumped in surprise and grabbed his red cheek.

'Now shut your mouth and get a move on! We're going to catch the tide if I have to flog you the last mile myself!' The captain turned his horse in tight circles, forcing the tattered prisoners to make way for its clattering hoofs.

'Get along, the lot of you, like the captain says!' Lawton seconded, cheated of his fun.

Muffet, trudging along the overgrown verge, eyed the dusty dragoon sourly. 'We'll see you again, mate,' he vowed quietly.

'What's that? See me again, will you? You'll need good eyes or a perspective glass, my friend, where you're going!'

'Sergeant Lawton, keep them moving!'

The tired prisoners had barely time to ponder the sergeant's meaning before they rounded a bend in the narrow, hedge-lined lane and emerged on a windy plateau. The cliffs reared on either side, gloomy white in the gathering dusk. They could taste the sea and smell salt fish. The road narrowed once more, descending the steep cliffs in a series of treacherous terraces. The prisoners could see lights twinkling down in the village, and a clutter of black masts in the busy little harbour. Looking up, they could see a rippled black sheet fleeced and flecked by quietly lapping waves. They had reached the sea.

The wild-eyed folk of Penmethock had stayed up late especially for their woebegone visitors. Fishermen with hands like crabs' backs and their gap-toothed wives had crowded the steep main street, jostled themselves a shoulder space on the steps of their narrow cottages as the prisoners filed in. They bawled and whistled, hooted and laughed as the Roundhead sheep were shooed down the hill and penned between the busy inn and the quay. They weren't worth looting, they had little left to take, but the villagers had sour bilges full of scorn to heap and splatter over their miserable guests. Children screeched and flapped around the fringes of the terrified mob, shouted obscenities in their own dialects. Black-bonneted grandmothers shook their fists at the rebels as if they had personally been responsible for slaughtering their children. As if the sorry company had been rounded up after burning down their homes. Yellow-haired Viking raiders, blue-painted Picts would have found no worse a welcome.

The dragoon guards took up the watch around the silent mob as the villagers crowded in to spit at and heckle the infidels.

'Ah, plot against yer King, would you?'

'Pym's brave boys, not so saucy now though!'

'Who's sorry now, Roundhead? That'll teach you London bastards to rise against your rightful masters!'

' "No bishops", is it? No mercy, I say! Throw the scum in the sea!'

'Yes! Throw 'em all in the oggin!'

Captain Breech left Lawton to prevent a general massacre while he strode up to the brightly lit inn to keep his rendezvous with the master of the *Messalina's Purse.* He had noted the sleek cutter tied up in the busy harbour, surrounded by bobbing gigs and more heavily laden yawls. The crew were busy hauling barrels and boxes over the low gunwale by the light of a dozen lanterns. Heavier merchandise was being manhandled into position, strung up beneath the creaking yards. Deckboys scampered in the rigging while the boatswain bellowed his instructions at the shore party. One of the youngsters – clumsier than the others – had tangled his foot in the coarse rope nets strewn over the deck and stumbled against the worn planking, cracking the barrel he had been hauling.

'Get a move on, you biscuit-nibbling monkeys! Caleb, damn you, not that way! Get it under your arm, you snivelling idiot! We're not paying by the hour!'

Breech paused on the short flight of steps leading up to the noisy tavern, his buttocks aching from the long ride south. Half a dozen doxies shoved and squalled past, eager to heap their threepennyworth of scorn on the unfortunate prisoners. Their excited exit released a flood of yellow light and a draft of obnoxious smoke over the worn steps. Breech pushed the heavy door open and peered through the fug.

Captain Valentine Cruickshank raised an eyebrow, studied the coughing newcomer for a moment. He was playing picquet with the Spanish agents, and losing a pretty penny too. He pushed back his chair and threw in his hand, and welcomed the astonished dragoon officer with open arms.

'Captain Belcher, is it? We'd damn near given you up as lost!' the captain called, shaking the newcomer's hand and dragging him into a vacant chair. Cruickshank was a tall, spare Londoner, a privateer with long years of experience. He had raided and robbed from Dunkirk to the Hebrides, from the Orkneys to Ireland, but had recently remembered his affection for Charles Stewart and taken up service, not so much for the King as against the Parliament. Because Parliament had richer ships. Cruickshank tore off his battered black hat to reveal a completely bald skull blistered and blackened by fierce tropical suns. He had a smudgy anchor tattooed on one side of his neck and a swallow on the other, although the poor bird's wings had been cruelly pinched by the vivid scar which looped around his throat.

'Where's old Nybb, then? Taken a touch too much grog, has he?'

'I understood he'd be here,' Breech said, looking about the devilish den with some alarm.

Cruickshank muttered something to his equally formidable mate, and nodded at the waspish clerks opposite. The senior of the two had kept his cards close to his chest although the captain had no intention of resuming play. The gentlemen seemed too well dressed for their present company, their striped scarlet and gold coats standing out alarmingly in the filthy bar. Their black hair had been neatly combed, and oiled to the brilliant consistency of their slick moustaches.

'This shark's belly-slapper is Rodriguez, his mate's Orlando, Count de Meola, don't you know?' Cruickshank waved his tankard at the tight-lipped agents.

'Was that *Count*, you said, Crooksie?' the half-drunk mate enquired, slurring his words horribly.

'Aye, count's near enough, eh, boys? Don't see the likes of them round 'ere too reg'lar these days. Got a pretty packet for 'em, have you?'

'My Lord Clavincale left precise instructions,' Breech began.

Cruickshank belched and nodded enthusiastically.

'We are well acquainted with Lord Clavincale,' the leaner Spaniard interjected, his English marvellously clear after the captain's barely understandable chatter.

'Are we to understand you have delivered the merchandise in question?'

Breech frowned, nodded slowly. 'One hundred and six men, just like his lordship said. For service in Flanders, sir.'

The Spaniards exchanged a quick look. 'Their service, sir, is our business. Yours was merely to deliver the men to us,' Count de Meola snapped.

Breech bristled. 'And collect the money, sir.'

'The down payment, perhaps. Señor Rodriguez will settle the details. The full price will as usual be made up in arms and ammunition on our return.' The Spaniard studied the young dragoon as if he expected him to argue, and nodded impatiently. 'Don't worry, Captain, your master will be well rewarded, as usual. Shall we examine them?'

The Spaniards got to their feet and picked their way out of the crowded tavern. Breech followed while the seamen linked arms and staggered behind singing a filthy song about a milkmaid and a pig. The crowd fell back respectfully as the Spanish agents clicked along the slippery quay in their expensive buckled shoes. They were a familiar enough sight around the harbour, but folk had long memories, and half expected the dark-complexioned strangers to seize their suddenly silent children for some devilish ceremony up on the clifftops. Sergeant Lawton gave an exaggerated bow, and stood aside to allow the agents to examine the wretched gang. Count de Meola took one look at their bloody foot rags and shook his narrow head in disgust.

'How far have you marched them? From Diffices, yes?'

'Diffices? Oh, De-vi-zes,' Lawton agreed. 'Diffices, that's right. Fresh from the battle at Roundway Down. Pity your lot don't wage war so quick, eh? All your troubles would be over by now!'

The Spanish count shrugged past the grinning dragoon and began a rapid inspection of the weary, red-eyed prisoners. Cruickshank stood by, casting his own eye on the sorry bunch.

'There's not a man with another march in him,' de Meola remarked. 'I've never seen such a flea-bitten crew.' Breech realized the complaints were the agent's standard means of address. The price for these men – however high or low it had been set – had already been agreed.

'We could have wrapped them all in swaddling and given them a piggyback but you're not interested in their health,' he replied frostily. He disliked the assignment more each second, the angry prisoners glaring at him like some vicious Roman centurion condemning his captives to living death in the galleys. The Spanish didn't have galleys any more. They had galleons.

The agents completed their inspection and took a quick head count. 'One hundred and six,' de Meola reckoned, scribbling some figures in the small ledger Clavincale had given Breech to take with him on his field trip. The count's surly deputy seconded his signature and passed the note over to Cruickshank. The sea captain took a cursory glance at the accounts and passed the ledger back to Breech. The bleary-eyed mate blew a raspberry to herald the successful completion of the transaction. A party of sailors armed with cutlasses and clubs appeared as if on cue, and proceeded to push their way into the silent mob, replacing the tired dragoons who opened their ranks accordingly. The bald-headed captain thumped the nearest man on the back, sending him sprawling over the cobbles.

'Whoops-a-daisy! Careful on the gangplank, you crippled stiltskin! Come along, form a line. Congratulations, Captain Breech, another company of cannon fodder for the Low Countries!' Cruickshank bellowed maliciously as Breech made his way through the muttering mass of men. He caught Muffet's flashing eye for a moment, but shoved his way on past to rejoin his men outside the inn.

'Time for a drink, eh, Captain? The boys were asking, like?' Lawton asked hopefully.

'A barrel on me, Sergeant,' Breech agreed, accepting a stone jar of rum from one of the grinning, gap-toothed whores who had appeared to serve the dusty riders. Breech thumbed the stopper out and took a long pull at the fiery liquor. He'd need it, this night.

Messalina's Purse was full to bursting, her hold emptied of every barrel and box which could be spared to make room for the human cargo. The prisoners had been packed in so hard they could barely breathe. They crouched in misery, pressed against one another with their arms folded wearily over their knees. Long Col had kept his friends away from the dark corners of the stinking hold, and had them sit beneath the heavy iron grilles.

'At least we'll get some light and air,' he said quietly, although most of the men appeared too stunned by the horrible turn of events to notice – or care about – their new surroundings. They had been herded on board like cattle, as docile as calves to the slaughter. Cruickshank's crew had struck out at every raised eyebrow, punished every scowl as the prisoners filed on board.

'That's it, my boys, down ye go!' the captain had yelled, his breath reeking of strong spirits and cheap tobacco. He stood beside the quay with his foot resting on a crate, nodding the exhausted captives up the juddering gang-plank.

'One hundred and six, Cap'n Cruickshank!' Callow reported. 'Though how many'll be standing when we get back is another matter,' he added in an undertone.

'What was that now?'

'Beggin' pardon, sir, but they'll be fair jammed down there. She weren't built for slavin'.'

'Slaving? We're trading, Ned, and mind ye don't forget it!'

The mate appeared unconvinced, shaking his rum-addled head. 'I swear this old tub'll run aground on the first spit!'

'I'll flog the helmsman if he dares miss his markers,' the captain replied.

The Spanish agents paused on the wharf, frowningly watched their servants hurry aboard with the ambassador's bulky portmanteau. They were clearly unsettled by the oafish bragging of the English pirates. Count de Meola grimaced to himself, disguising his revulsion behind his expertly embroidered handkerchief. Strictly speaking, these scoundrels were not pirates at all. They bore letters of marque signed by the Lord High Admiral, authorizing them to prey on any vessel deemed an enemy of His Majesty, and were therefore Royalist privateers. Ah, it was no matter to de Meola what they called themselves – they had until very recently been the sworn enemies of Spain, heretical English seadogs captained by a mad sow of a captain.

'We could leave a score of them here until the next time, if the crossing is as dangerous as thees,' Rodriguez offered in his accented English.

Count de Meola snorted and waved his cane.

'They can't weigh any more than the barrels we brought over with us, they are nothing but skin and bone! Captain

Cruickshank is trying to alarm you.' He added something inaudible in Spanish. The captain grinned and closed one eye to peer up at the sky. A bank of bruised clouds had scudded in off the channel, and seemed to be impaling themselves on the oak masts.

'It's freshening up, Ned,' he remarked.

'Aye. We're in for a blow.' The mate peered over the side of the creaking ship, took a professional look at the scummy seawater lapping at the harbour walls. Loaded to the gunwales the cutter would be about as manoeuvrable as a hod of house bricks.

'Half hour to high water, sir!'

'Right you are, Ned. All aboard? Let's deliver these Roundheads to their new masters!'

'Deliver them to their makers, for all we care!' a wag on the wall called, waving his arms as the *Messalina's Purse* nosed away from land, carried by the swift, swirling current.

BY
KEYNSHAM BRIDGE,

19 JULY 1643

The bony bay had belonged to a French cadet serving in Sir Arthur Aston's regiment of horse – the same man injured beside the ferry when Major Fulke's cursed command had escaped across the river. Telling had clawed his way up the crumbling bank, gasping and wretching mouthfuls of dirty water, only to spend the next hour convincing his doubting rescuers of his identity. They had frowned disbelievingly as he had spluttered out his story, turning up their noses at his ragged appearance and remarking on his hollow cheeks and unshaven chin.

'I've been kept in a cell for a week, what do you expect?' the young captain had insisted, trying to keep his hysterical outbursts under control. 'Didn't you see them shooting at me?'

'We thought they were shooting at us,' the troop commander, Major Marrow, had sniffed disdainfully. His unit belonged to the Oxford army which Prince Rupert had led west to reinforce the Western army's resoundingly successful summer campaign. The troop had been sent out ahead of the main body to scour the water meadows around Bath for any Roundhead fugitives. They were also to make contact with General Hopton's army which was known to be manoeuvring westwards along the banks of the Avon.

Major Marrow had pushed his men hard, leading them across the river to scout the wooded slopes of the Avon valley. His advanced guard had come within an ace of running down Fulke's company beside the ferry. If only they had been a few seconds earlier the Roundhead stragglers would have been hacked to pieces for sure. As it was the impetuous cavalry had ridden into a squall of well-directed musketry and the young French volunteer had been hit in the shoulder. The unlucky trooper had died before they could fetch the surgeon, and Marrow had grudgingly allowed Telling to take the dead man's horse on the proviso that the fugitive accompany the troop back to their headquarters.

'Then we can make sure you're who you claim to be, if that's all right with you.'

Telling, cold and miserable, hadn't had the energy to argue.

'Captain Telling, Maurice's horse.' He had muttered the mantra behind his chattering teeth, but they still watched him as if he had leapt out of a witches' cauldron.

The young captain had been near purple with cold, his bony frame racked with shivers before the short-tempered major had been satisfied the river line was clear and had turned his tired troop back to Bath for the night. The next morning Telling had been gripped by a chill, riding along in shivering misery as the troop rejoined the advancing Oxford army. He had been forced to wait another hour outside a staff tent while a distracted clerk noted his credentials and eventually agreed to supply him with a pass. The trembling captain had taken the chit with a gruff nod and a sorry sneeze, and spent the rest of the night nursing his streaming cold. By the time he had felt well enough to ride, Prince Rupert's army had been on the move again. A large contingent of experienced infantry regiments backed up with a smaller but powerful force of cavalry and an effective siege train which included two of the biggest artillery pieces Telling had ever seen. Great lumbering demi-cannon which required a team of more than a dozen equally lumbering horses to drag them over the dusty roads. The animals, hitched in tandem, had to be whipped and tugged and cajoled by a whole platoon of exhausted drovers wearing the ubiquitous country smocks. The idle buggers looked a damn sight tidier than he did though, shivering in his steaming coat and soggy breeches like a half-drowned scarecrow.

Armed with his precious pass, Telling had finally parted company with the Prince's Oxford army and headed south. He had picked up the trail of the Western army as it toiled up steep sheep tracks over the hills and trampled broad slopes of standing corn. If he had cared to stop and search the ditches he would have found half a dozen new outfits, although the quality of the discarded garments was hardly any better than the sodden rags he stood up in. As well as ripped breeches and torn shirts he spied heavy Dutch coats – fine for the winter but far too cumbersome for a long march in hot weather. Helmets, broken pikes and musket rests had been cast down by the advancing Cornish, only to be picked over and ignored by the camp followers hurrying along in their manured footsteps. Telling had eventually caught up with his comrades as they closed in on Keynsham, a small village nestling on a bluff overlooking a broad bend of the Avon. He had located the quarter-master's cart amongst a logjam of assorted supply wagons at the bottom of a steep, wooded slope. He had waved his pass for all he was worth but hadn't persuaded the wretch to part with anything but a selection of old junk he could have picked from the roadside.

The grumbling quartermaster had eventually agreed to replace the pale youth's sodden breeches, and had found him a spare pair of boots from the battered chest in the back of his wagon. He had sorted him out with a sword of sorts, a shapeless felt hat and a threadbare coat, and yet he still insisted on pacing to and fro, snorting and cursing in agitation. He'd have the blade back and run the bugger through with it, if he had much more of his sauce, the red-faced officer thought vindictively. He had dealt with half a hundred arrogant young pups during his six months with the colours, but this one was certainly several sizes too big for his borrowed boots.

'P'raps you'd be likin' the shirt off me back an' all?' the burly commisariat officer enquired with a sarcastic sneer. He pretended to fumble with his grubby buttons while the strutting coxcomb climbed in and out of his skin with frustration.

'Keep your shirt!' Hugo Telling snapped, stamping the worn boots against the dusty road. As he expected the sole had peeled from the square-toed leather upper, and flapped like a fish's mouth. Telling stared down at the shabby footwear and positively smouldered with anger. 'Are you trying to tell me His Majesty's Western army hasn't one pair of new boots to its name?'

The overworked quartermaster wiped his hands on a horse cloth, nodded grimly.

'That's exactly it, sir, in a nutshell. Now if you want to go barefoot you hand those back and I'll give them to some other bugger.'

Telling straightened, hands on his narrow hips. He was a

regular gamecock, this one, the quartermaster decided. A gang of Cornish infantry making their way up the hill had paused beside the stalled provisions wagon to watch the fun, enjoying the young Cavalier's obvious discomfiture.

'That's a nice coat, Jethro,' one of the pikemen commented to his enormous shaggy-haired neighbour.

The red-suited musketeer closed one eye and tilted his head. 'Clashes a bit with his white shanks, though,' Jethro Polruan declared. 'I've seen more meat on a ramrod!'

Telling sucked in his cheeks as the mob chuckled past.

'I'd put them breeches on, boy, you'll catch your death!'

'Looks like he already has!'

The quartermaster ran his dirty sleeve over his face to disguise his grin. 'Hang 'em over your saddle, sir, they'll be dry soon enough, in this weather,' he advised considerately.

'I'll hang you over my saddle if you don't find me a decent pair of breeches! I'm a captain of Prince Maurice's horse not a damned bucket boy!' Telling screeched, ducking and diving around the bulky quartermaster to see what the rogue had hidden in the back of the wagon. The quartermaster held out his brawny arms and shooed the furious youth back.

'I told you, sir. You want a set of fancy velvet you'd best find yourself a tailor!'

'Those men who passed just now, they're all wearing new boots and breeches!' the red-faced officer observed belligerently.

The quartermaster nodded. 'That's 'cus they was at Roundway. They had their pick up there, see?'

'The pick of the dead, I suppose?'

'And the prisoners. Missed it, did we, sir? The battle I mean.'

Telling rolled his livid brown eyes dangerously.

'Yes, I did as a matter of fact. I was surrounded and captured on Lansdown and held prisoner in Bath for a week. I got my clothes wet escaping from the enemy, and so now I need some more!'

'And so you might, sir, so you might. But what you see is what you get. All I've got left is what the Cornish boys didn't want. You take it or leave it.'

Telling tapped his flapping boot in anger. 'Right, then. I'll take it,' he fumed.

The quartermaster beamed, handed over the armful of assorted rags and tatters he had been carrying.

Telling pulled on his breeches and tugged at the enormously generous waistband. 'Haven't you a belt, at least?' Telling asked in a rather more piteous tone.

The bigger man shrugged, leaned over the wagon's running board to tug out a length of string. He handed it over, suppressing a giggle. Telling took the string and knotted it around his middle so tightly it was a wonder to the curious Cornishmen he didn't cut off his circulation. Telling rammed the mossy coloured hat over his greasy hair and yanked the reins of his new horse. He hauled himself up into the borrowed saddle and gave the grinning quartermaster a withering stare.

'Mind how you go now, sir,' the oaf called merrily, stepping out of the rider's way as he kicked the unfamiliar beast through the crowd of carts and barrows. The captain turned his borrowed horse into a bean field running parallel to the blocked road, and overtook the main body of the army as it made camp out on the broad summit. It took the exhausted officer another hour to locate Prince Maurice's reduced regiment, bivouacked on the edge of a beech wood which seemed to be groaning and sighing to itself, stirred by the stiffening breeze edging over the plateau. The mournful wail seemed to sap the last of his willpower, and he began to sway in the saddle like a drunken miller on his way home from market. The regiment's rather emaciated horses had been picketed in a long line just before the latrine pits, and grooms were busy carrying armfuls of hay for their evening feed. Telling's horse followed its nose along the rope as its new master sneezed uncontrollably, frightening the animals as they munched their supper. Telling woke with a start, sneezed, and wiped his mouth on his sleeve.

'Did you hear trumpets, Jack, or has one of them knackered nosebags got the colic?'

Telling squinted down at a pair of bandy-legged bandits who had been busy repairing their greasy tack beside the horselines.

'Ah, it's cruel to keep 'em in such a state. You'd not keep a dog like it,' his grinning colleague replied, pretending not to have noticed the bedraggled captain.

Telling nodded his head in annoyance. 'Cady and Jacobs,' he chuckled, recognizing a couple of his long-lost troopers. 'I wouldn't have guessed I would ever be glad to see your ugly mugs.' He slumped over his saddle bow and grinned weakly at the dirty corporals.

Cady tugged at his bony chin, nudged his mate. 'Christ on earth, your highness, but it must have been grim wherever you've been, if you're pleased to see a couple o' sorry buggers like us!'

The faithful troopers wrapped their captain in a horse blanket and set him by the fire, stoked his rumbling belly with a platter of good thick mutton stew and a hunk of double-baked bread which damn near cracked his teeth.

'Soak it in your gravy, sir, it softens it up a little,' Cady advised with a grin, crossing his legs by the fire and fishing for his pipe.

Telling felt himself thawing slowly, and relished the well-spiced stew. He couldn't remember a meal ever tasting so good. Jacobs handed him a stone jar of cider and he took a long draught, wiped his mouth and belched like a culverin. The two troopers made themselves comfortable around the blazing bonfire, and filled the officer in on the army's fluctuating fortunes since they had parted company at the foot of Lansdown's bloody escarpment.

'Well, it was all right for you, sir, wasn't it, galloping up that hill. What bollock-brained old duffer thought that one up, eh? You were a hundred yards off at least when the buggers caught us from the flank. We tried to get to you, but we had enough to do holding those Roundheads off, am I right, Ned?' Cady nudged his colleague's boot.

'We would have 'ad to cut through half of Waller's horse to get you, sir.'

Telling blinked like an owl, mesmerized by the flickering flames and the soothing drone of a dozen campfire conversations.

'Course we paid 'em back on Roundway, sir.'

'We did that!' Jacobs grinned, exhibiting what few teeth he had left.

'Rode all the way to Oxford in a night, turned round and came straight back again,' Corporal Cady went on. 'Fought a battle in the afternoon and looted their camp by moonlight, if you'd credit it!'

Telling nodded drowsily.

'You should have seen 'em, the pious bastards. Singing psalms one minute and trying to fly like angels the next.'

'Straight over the biggest cliff you ever saw,' Jacobs added.

'We barely drew rein before Chippenham,' Cady elaborated. 'I must have cut down half a dozen of 'em myself.'

'At least that, Jack, at least that.'

'Well then, Captain, what about you? Where did you hide yourself this last fortnight?'

They peered across the fire at the swaddled officer, sleeping like a baby in the gathering gloom.

PART THREE

HERE BE DRAGONS

BY SEAL SHOALS,

OFF THE DORSET COAST, 20 JULY 1643

There were old deckhands down in the hold who reckoned they could tell which direction the ship was heading by the feel of the water, and predict their heading by the shape and strength of the swell.

'Sou' westerly, or I'm a Dutchman.'

'You're not wrong, mate. We're just pickin' up the rip offshore. It's a wicked current, mind, Lyme Bay. Turn you all about as soon as piss on yer.'

The only swell William Sparrow recognized was the sour churn in his belly. He listened to the idiotic debate being held over by the latrine bucket and rolled his eyes toward the rusty grille over their heads. The sullen sky was packed with hurrying clouds which reminded him of the grey bags beneath his late master's mournful eyes. He couldn't have said which way they were blowing or how long they had been at sea, and the only motion he could detect with any certainty was the nauseating rise and fall of the hated bows, swallowing the waves like a great brown whale. The heavily laden vessel wallowed suddenly like a drowning stag in a bog, tipping the prisoners into their cursing neighbours.

'They're tacking now, man,' a Welsh voice piped up from the gloomy corner. 'Tryin' to bring her round against the wind, see?'

'Tacking'll bring her round through the wind,' another

prisoner corrected from the reeking press behind them.

William sighed and clenched his teeth. Clairvoyant Merlins who could sense the waves' intentions beneath three foot of planking were just what he needed right then. 'Give me strength,' he muttered.

Gillingfeather nodded soberly.

'Amen. We will need the strength of Samson to endure the barbarous pits of the Philistines, the vile caress of the harlots of Babylon.'

Muffet nudged Sparrow in the small of his back, raised his eyebrows in warning. It was too late. Gillingfeather shoved himself to his feet, steadied himself against Will's broad shoulder and wagged his hairy finger at the lost souls crowded into the malodorous hold. Not even the freshening wind could clear the ripe stink of the slop buckets from their creaking prison.

'Aye, they'll tempt you with sweetmeats and sweeter lips, ply you with reason-stealing liquors,' the wiry little Londoner went on, his gleaming eyes boring into their grey faces. 'They will bring you to your knees, saturate your minds with their sly innuendoes. And they will wait and watch, they will be ready when you wander. They will stuff your nose with incense and blind you with their orbs and sceptres. And when you reach your gnarled fists for mercy and salvation, when you reach out for clean water to slake your bitter thirst, they will clap you in the irons of Rome! Wind you round and round with the chains and shackles of their thrice-damned creed, the clinging weeds of Popery!' The stinking hold was silent, the captive congregation nodding in dumb resignation. Even the devil-may-cares who would generally have yawned and scratched through his fiery sermons seemed bewildered enough to believe.

'No matter what they do, no matter what they offer you,

how they threaten you, hold on to your souls. They can peel your skin and break up your bones, tear out your organs and feed them to their dogs, but they cannot steal your spirits. Woe betide him who abandons his brothers and his cause for earthly advancement.'

William swallowed and stared at his grubby hands. Earthly advancement? Mouthing a few phrases in order to avoid being boiled in lead seemed eminently sensible to this humble printer's apprentice. He thought sermons were supposed to fill you up, not hollow you out like a gutted cod. Gillingfeather's uplifting and impassioned encouragement had only succeeded in deepening his misery. He had never taken exception to another man's religious beliefs, so long as those views weren't imposed on him. It was up to every man to decide for himself how he should address his God, the right of every man to decide for himself how he would meet his maker. The ship groaned, its timbers racked by the inquisiting troughs and peaks of the choppy Channel.

The wind blew up stronger, and even William could feel its undiminished power surge through the hull, thrumming through the beams and waxy planking as if the mighty ribbing was nothing but an old drum, bobbing for ever on the wild ocean. The crabby old sailors in the corner tilted their heads to study the sky, and cautiously revised their headings as if they had a set of charts spread out over their bare-knuckled knees. Gillingfeather staggered as the vessel began to roll through the rising swell. He held on to William's shoulder, and continued to berate the quaking fugitives crammed into the chilly hold.

'Yea, if we be rocked by tempests and swallowed up by whales, if we be . . .' His high-pitched caterwauling was drowned out by the sudden dry crack of the sails as the squall switched direction once more, tossing the sleek cutter over the boundless waves. They could hear the frantic shouts of the boatswain, the strangulated curses of the mate as he strode by the hatch. William rested his tired head on the crook of his arm, and prayed to his maker for the first time since he had been a child, frightened and alone in the hinge-creaking darkness of his room.

Captain Cruickshank did not waste his breath drawing attention to the gathering storm. The officers of the watch knew as well as he did they were being blown off course, tacking hopelessly in the teeth of the sprightly gale. They had sailed seven miles and were no nearer Portland Bill than they had been the previous evening.

It was every sailor's nightmare, becoming embayed. Caught like a leaf in the treacherous Lyme Bay, they risked being blown against the leeward shore, dashed on the littered rocks and reefs by the tremendously powerful currents.

Cruickshank drummed his scarred fingers on the cross-staff, and turned to the pale Spaniard sheltering by the mast beside him. He took one look at the gentleman's white-knuckled hands clutching the rail, and winked broadly.

'I'd heard you Spaniards reckoned yourselves the best seamen in the world,' he crowed over the vicious crack and wallop of the close-reefed sails. 'Or maybe I'm mixing you up with them Portugee fellers?'

The count compressed his lips into a feeble smile, nodded his head carefully as if he was afraid it might fall off and roll about the foam-splattered deck. 'We Spaniards tend to let others do the sailing for us,' he commented. 'As for the Portuguese—'

He licked his lips and spat over the rail. The splittle was caught up by the gale and carried off into the canvas. Cruickshank gazed up at the masts, the rigging stretched like violin strings, singing siren songs in the blow.

'We do not seem to be making a great deal of progress,' the count called. The mate chuckled grimly, nodded over the grey horizon.

'The bay's a tricksy miss, Señor,' he shouted back. 'Get a contrary wind and you can get carried round by the current until it leaves off. It's like stirring paper boats round a puddle, if you take my meaning.'

The count didn't. 'And when can we expect it to "leave off"?' the Spaniard asked patiently, hanging on to his flamboyant wide-brimmed hat.

The mate shrugged.

'I don't like the look of her. It's a ripper, blowing up quick like, and they're always the worst,' Callow mouthed.

'Perhaps it will blow itself out,' de Meola wondered.

'Perhaps it'll blow us to the Americas?' Cruickshank replied, deflecting the Spaniard's inquisitive stare.

'We could run for a port, Crooksie. Torbay, mebbe. Let it blow out and follow the drift on out again.' The mate described a lazy circle with his bitten finger. Cruickshank tore off his hat and ran his hand over his pitted scalp. The skin looked like mottled cuttlefish, scathing sandpaper which had worn away its flimsy flock of hair. The mate held his tongue, waited for the moody captain to make up his mind. His master stared off over the bucketing waves, squinting against the storm.

'SAIL FOUR POINTS OFF THE STARBOARD BOW!!!!!!'

*

The desultory conversations which had eventually broken out following Gillingfeather's mind-numbing sermon died at once. One hundred and six pairs of eyes were fixed on the rusty grille, the barred window throwing chequerboard shadows into the anxious hold. They could hear the crew's bare feet slapping on the wet deck as they dashed to and fro and hurled themselves at the rigging. A sail? So what? William peered up as the shadowy sailors pushed and jostled around the hold, the officers screeching orders to the bewildered crew. A sail? By God, they were out in the Channel, what had they been expecting to see, wheels?

Cruickshank braced himself on the heaving deck, holding his perspective glass as rigid as a statue.

'It's either the *James* or the *Rainbow* . . . one of the second-rates,' he cursed, fixing his gaze on the insignificant shadow just visible against the vivid backdrop of the clouds.

The mate snatched out his own glass and quickly located the tiny ivory flag on the horizon. He stood back from the rail and glanced up at the foretop, the D-shaped structure which held the lookouts, and in battle, the ship's sharp-shooters. Seventy feet above the deck, a wind-blown platform where sails were stacked, but otherwise open to the elements. By God, they should have seen it! A bloody sail as plain as a man's thumb. Stuck out on the horizon like a pall of smoke over a snowy hillside. He peered up at the rigging, a crazy web of ropes and blocks, narrow walkways no bigger than a gentleman's cane. A man could freeze to death away up there, taking his watch so far removed from the comforting mother's belly of his ship. The gnawing, perishing wind would flake the thickest clothes and flay the toughest skin.

It was no place for a youngster, no place for a pale boy like Caleb. Cruickshank had lowered his glass a fraction of an inch, just enough to notice the mate's furtive glance.

'Who's up there? Well?'

Edward Callow knew enough not to try and influence his captain with anything so womanly as a smile. He ground his jaw and jabbed the glass to his grey eyes. Cruickshank stood as still as the mast, feet planted apart against the *Messalina*'s steadily more alarming pitch.

'Mr Callow,' Cruickshank said crisply, a razor breath on a roaring wind. 'Who's aloft?'

The mate's momentary hesitation told the master all he needed to know. Count de Meola peered inquisitively at the glowering captain.

'Your lookout missed the sail? One could hardly blame the man, a wind such as this,' he said simply.

Callow closed his eyes in silent dread. The Spaniard held on to his hat, and peered up at the exposed platform high over the deck. Every so often the sail would billow up and hide the offending platform from view.

'Yes, there you are, Captain! He is but a boy! You send a child to do a man's work!'

The mate raised his eyebrows warningly at the chuckling Spaniard. The fool seemed oblivious to their sudden peril. The officers returned their attention to the ship, cutting its way toward them. Callow could make out the foam breaking on the black bow as the great man-of-war plunged through the waves. A fearsome juggernaut bristling with cannon, and crewed by hated enemies who despised and denied the very right of existence to crews of privateers like the *Messalina*. Even as he watched, Callow saw the monstrous ship loom out of the squall, and began to make out the detail of her bustling decks. White ants scuttled around the tiny guns like insects clinging to a rolling stone.

'They've every scrap o' sail on, Christ Jesus I'd wager they've tied their drawers along the mizzen!' the mate growled, desperately attempting to divert the captain from his devilish line of questioning. The Spanish agent squinted over the vast green ocean, shaking his head disdainfully.

'I can't even see this sail of yours. Surely he cannot delay our mission any more than this foul weather?'

'Ah, he's seen us, Count de Meola, and yes, he can delay us,' Cruickshank said formally. 'You can rely on that.'

The mate cringed at his master's unusually subdued manner. Polite and formal meant a homicidal tantrum might be just around the corner.

'They've the wind and the currents in their favour,' Callow explained to the apparently ignorant Spaniard.

'As well as the benefit of surprise,' Cruickshank growled.

Callow winced.

'But we can leave him standing if we go south with the wind, see, cut across his bows and escape the bay,' the mate encouraged, demonstrating his fanciful navigation with his great hairy paws, right hand tucked in just behind his left.

'Aye, but we'll be sailing right past her, right past his bloody broadside if our luck runs out,' Cruickshank reminded him with a lazy roll of his icicle-grey eye.

The Spaniard frowned. 'A man-of-war you say? Surely we'll outrun a lumbering beast like this, eh? Why not turn back into the bay where we have come?'

'I'll not be embayed with a Roundhead potwalloper on my heels!' Cruickshank vowed.

'Might he not hold his present course across the bay, and get blown on past us?' the persistent Spaniard theorized, peering out over the leaden swell at the unwelcome intruder.

Cruickshank bared his teeth. 'Ah, he's crept up on us fair and square, and if he's any kind of a fighter he'll sail into the bay after us.'

'And risk smashing himself on the coast?' de Meola wondered.

'I would,' the Captain replied stonily.

'He's coming around after us!' Callow called, eye fixed to his glass. 'He's a fighter all right!'

Cruickshank seemed almost relieved the Roundhead had decided to risk his ship in the vast green mouth of the bay. 'There now,' he asked. 'Does that answer your question, sir?' He had more pressing matters to attend to than explain the complexities of navigation to some landlubber of a foreigner. The Spaniard lapsed into silence as Cruickshank stared at the enemy second-rate, tacking into the bay on an obvious interception course. He didn't move a muscle for a good minute and a half.

'You haven't answered my question, Ned. Who was in the top? Who missed this dog's pizzle of a Roundhead?'

Callow winced. 'Cruel hard, sir, the wind. Fair cuts my eyes to slits, sir, let alone the boy's . . .'

'Answer the question, God damn you! Was it him, my Caleb?'

'Aye, sir. He took the watch for droppin' that brandy barrel over the side, sir, just as you ordered, sir.'

'Ah,' the captain murmured stonily.

The fifteen-year-old in question was Cruickshank's eldest son. A thickset, slightly backward boy who had followed his formidable father to sea almost before he could walk. Young Caleb loved the adventure, worshipped the braggart sailors who made it their business to rove the world's oceans. But the youth was clumsy and slow on the deck and aloft, and had all the balance and coordination of a blind bear.

Captain Cruickshank – determined he would never show any sympathy or favour to his own flesh and blood – was twice as hard on the lad as on the rest of the boys, and never failed to assign his son the most oppressive duties. He was handy enough given a steady deck and some clear directions, but leave the boy to his own clouded devices and he would fall into a sort of sea-wonder, stare at the waves as if he could hear the fish singing lullabies in the deep. He was clumsy and forgetful, slipshod and accident-prone. He was the bane of his horrified father's life, but Cruickshank hadn't dared admit defeat by putting the useless boy ashore. The captain's son a good-for-nothing tavern-sweeper, a sausage-fingered pot-boy? He'd vowed to make a man of him. Aye, or die in the effort.

Cruickshank lowered the glass and studied the Spaniard, who by his nervous glances around the deck was beginning to register their desperate peril. Cruickshank held his glass out, pointed out their barely visible pursuit.

'It's the *Conqueror*. One of the Parliament's best ships,' he rasped. 'She carries forty-three guns and twice as much sail as us again. Her captain spied us before we spied him, and he's taken the best line across the bay, d'you follow me, sir, you're following me, aren't you?' he asked dangerously.

The Spaniard nodded. 'So what do we do, my captain?' he asked, swallowing drily.

'We cut and run, sir, as Mr Callow says. South, as quick as we can. If we can get in front of him on an open sea he'll never catch us.'

'A damned traitor of a psalm-squealing sailor? Catch the *Messalina*? He can sift our shite if he likes,' Callow bragged feebly.

The Spaniard grimaced. 'South? Is that what are you

proposing, Captain? A dash up the Irish Sea and around the Orkneys? The prisoners will never—'

Cruickshank coughed and spat over the side.

'We run south, never mind your destination, sir!' he barked. 'With luck he won't be able to bring his guns to bear as we pass him.'

'And if he does?'

'If he does, Señor Count Orlando de Meola, we'll be as dead as our lookout.'

Callow took a moment to register the mad captain's meaning.

'Crooksie, Cap'n Cruickshank—' he called as the furious skipper shoved him aside and strode toward the mast. 'Don't be hasty, sir, you know how you feel when you've beaten the poor scrap!'

'Mr Craig, ahoy there!' Cruickshank bellowed at a sailor poised halfway up the shrouds – the rigging stretched between the mast and the cutter's side – shielding his eyes to watch the horizon. 'Mr Craig, bring the boy down to the deck if you please! Aye, sir, now, sir! RIGHT NOW!'

Callow closed his eyes and muttered a brief prayer. By God, the captain's temper was a foul thing for a man to behold.

BY

THE ANGEL'S FINGERS,

OFF DORSET, 20 JULY 1643

The scurvy crewmen were as sick as dogs, clinging on to rails and rigging as Parliament's ship *Conqueror* plunged into the waves. The spray lashed over the deck, worn as smooth as glass by years of frenzied feet and long hours of merciless scrubbing. A spindly-legged youngster was caught by a stray gust and toppled against the gunwale. He scrambled for a hold as the man-of-war raised her beaked prow from the foaming sea, sending a great sheet of water sliding down the deck to take the legs from beneath half a dozen gun crews. Lieutenant Richard Pine hauled himself to his feet, his canvas trousers soaked through and sticking to his skin. The young officer cursed under his breath as the frightened crewmen cowered down behind the enormous gun carriages – roped up like iron oxen behind the closed ports – holding on for dear life as the great ship pitched through the sea. Pine braced himself against the straining man-ropes for a moment, and hauled himself along the deck, hand over hand. The half-drowned boy had wrapped his arms around a rail post and was clinging to the frail timber as if his life depended on it. His life did depend on it, with the captain refusing to slacken their speed for a moment. They should have stayed out to sea and reefed the sails, tried to sit the worst of the gale out. The towering sea and whirling undercurrents had carried them along the Channel like a leaf blown by the wind. But instead of slackening sail and battening the hatches Gallen Fey had ordered every sail hoisted, and every man to his station on the alarmingly unsteady deck. Pine could sense the timbers and spars, the stretched and crimped woodwork tearing and flexing under the perilous strain. The bloody captain would tear the ship in two, holding this course hard, blown by the ragged outriders of such a fierce summer storm.

Lieutenant Pine reached the boy and crouched down under the gunwale beside him. He patted the boy's soaking shirt, nodded encouragingly.

'Hold on, Pip. You could have been a goner just then!'

The miserable boy stared back at him, the bluish skin stretched tight over his chattering jaw. They froze behind the feeble barricade as the *Conqueror* hurtled head first into the next trough. The bow wave broke over their heads, turning their world white. Freezing-cold water tumbled over them, tearing at their brittle fingerholds. Pine tugged at the terrified youngster's arm.

'Come away from the bows, get below,' he urged. He slapped and pinched the boy's hands clear and shoved him, blinking and trembling, back down the wet deck. The gun crews eyed him for a moment, and then glared feverishly back out to sea. Lyme Bay, an awesome green mouth on the south coast, gaping wide for the rushing sea and the splintered ships which pirouetted out of control on its hurtling breakers. Steadying himself for a moment, Pine could make out the sabre-edged sweep of the Chesil Beach, a pale grey spit beneath the murkier slopes and tree-crowned hills. The bay swept west as far as he could see, the tranquil green horizons studded with wrinkled inlets, tiny ports. Lyme, folded in the middle of its vast belly, and then sweeping around to the western side of the bay Sidmouth, Exmouth and a dozen more tiny and anonymous harbours. And somewhere, vivid white against the rich green horizon, a tiny white sail.

'Evergreen' Slater, their most experienced sailor, hawk eyed despite his long years of service all over the world, had bawled his warning over the mournful wail of the wind, alerted his captain to the strange vessel's presence. Nobody in their right mind would have dared put to sea in weather like this. Only Captain Fey's orders and the desperate need of the garrison in Bristol had prevented them from taking shelter themselves. Pine peered up at the crosstrees, wrenched and racked by the gale-force winds. He could just make out Slater in his soaked coat, clinging to his frail nest as the storm laughed around him. Nobody else could have been trusted aloft, with the wind tearing through the sails and the masts shrieking like sweating mothers in childbirth. Slater had defied the wind and spied the sail, tacking forlornly into the same wind that had driven them so hard. Lieutenant Pine packed the frightened boy below decks, and struggled up the ladder to the somewhat crowded quarter-deck. Captain Fey, at pride of place on the rail, was a lightly built man with a shock of sandy-coloured hair, plastered darkly beneath his leather hat. His cloak had been drenched black by the rushing water, but he seemed oblivious to the weather which was all but carrying off his wretched crew. The captain stood with his legs braced, his flayed skin stretched taut as he kept an eye on their interception course. Despite howling winds and regular drenchings the sweat stood out on his features, his white teeth clenched against the back-breaking strain.

The range closed with every cable, and fuelled the argument raging as to the identity of the strange ship.

Gallen Fey had let his officers bicker. He had fixed his perspective glass on the sleek cutter, stared at the tiny stick mast until he could just make out her storm-racked colours.

'A King's privateer, out of some Cornish lobster pot,' he declared, settling the debate in a second. The younger officers, crowding beside him like wet lambs, squinted and peered toward the shore, waiting in vain for the captain to offer up his glass. All they could see was an infinitesimal speck against the murky grey-green land.

Pine straightened himself up as best he could behind Rhodes. The first lieutenant was hanging on for grim death, silently cursing their course and the fanatical captain to the pits of Hell. Fey took his eye from the horizon for a moment, and noted the return of his bedraggled second lieutenant.

'Ah, there you are, sir. Are the guns bowsed?'

'Roped and secured, aye, sir.' The cannon had been lashed into cat's cradles of rope to prevent them from rolling about on the viciously pitching decks.

'Very good, Mr Pine,' Fey allowed.

Pine glanced at Rhodes, by now green to the gills and showing every sign of immediate collapse. He winked encouragingly, eyes bright with salt and excitement.

Did the old man mean to fight, despite the weather?

God alone knew how they would keep their match alight with so much water flying about.

'As I thought. She's coming round into the wind. They're trying to cut and run!'

The junior officers swallowed, concentrated on standing straight. No one bar the captain had been in action before.

The *Conqueror* belonged to the Summer Guard, squadrons of warships and armed merchantmen which patrolled the coasts from May to October. Most of the fleet had declared for Parliament at the beginning of the war, although there had been several defections since. The King had begged or borrowed other vessels, and had fleets of Irish and Continental pirates to assist his cause. Captain Fey's assignment had been to scour the Thames estuary and patrol the Wash for smaller, faster Royalist vessels running guns and powder to beleaguered garrisons. The desperate news from the West, however, had forced Parliament to recall his ship to transport urgently needed supplies to Bristol, which they had correctly deduced must come under attack from the victorious King's men any day now. Fey had jumped at the chance of such a vital rescue mission, and hadn't allowed his tired and generally inexperienced crew a moment's rest. They would deliver the supplies to Bristol, aye, and a company of volunteers for the walls! The wretched sailors had imagined the ferocious storm would force the captain to slacken their speed, but he had praised the Lord and piled on sail until the massive ship fairly flew across the tossing waves. Now, it seemed as if he would offer battle to an enemy vessel without drawing breath.

Pine shielded his eyes against the blinding spray, and picked out the tiny enemy vessel. It had turned into the prevailing wind, but the manoeuvre had cost precious minutes. Pine could clearly see the vessel's sleek hull, painted bright red and gold. He clung on to Rhodes as the *Conqueror* belly-flopped into another trough, and came up spouting white water. They had seen sails on the horizon before of course, but had never caught up with the crafty enemy blockade runners.

'They'll try and run to the south. If he can get his nose in front he thinks he'll out-run us. Will he out-run us, Mr Rhodes?' Fey called hoarsely.

'No, sir!'

'What will we do when we catch up with him, Mr Rhodes?'

The first lieutenant, a rather pudgy merchant's son from Essex, grinned feebly. 'We'll sink the bastard, sir!'

Fey shouted with laughter, making the nervous crews crouching at the guns jump.

'Good man! Mr Pine!'

'Yes, sir?'

'We'll close up quick now.' Fey seemed to glow with delight, relishing the chance to come to grips with the will-o'-the-wisp privateer. 'Pass the order, beat to quarters! We'll close to fifty yards and put a warning shot across her bows. If she doesn't lie to, we'll yaw to larboard and try and get broadside to her!'

Fey's pale eyes danced with delight as he capered around the deck, ignoring another alarming roll into the crested sea. Pine waited for the ship to right itself and then scrambled down the ladder to the main deck.

'Beat to quarters!' he roared over the crash of the waves. A nervous youngster relayed the order with a rapid flourish on his drum, the energized crew leaping to the straining cradles which enmeshed the mighty iron culverins.

Pine struggled along the heaving planking past groups of spewing sailors, busy rearranging the complex web of ropes to allow for the loading, aiming and recoil of their devastating arsenal. He eventually arrived at the storm-lashed bows. A thoroughly soaked sailor with an immense tawny beard watched the officer secure himself on the gunwale and examine a handily mounted swivel gun. The light cannon could be swung about on its iron pivot, and was used to fire at the busy decks of enemy vessels.

'Tryin' a potshot, are we?' seaman Swale asked,

dragging his wet hands across his sea-sparkled beard.

Pine nodded. 'Get a lantern stowed there, we'll need it in case we lose the match.'

Swale frowned. 'Already have, sir.'

He held up the length of tarred match he had concealed under his oilskin cloak, the tip was glowing impatiently.

Pine nodded and swung the gun experimentally. The *Conqueror* crashed through another trough, the rigging strained to breaking point by the massive collision of man-machine and nature. He knelt down and brought his eye to the sight.

Swale watched him with barely concealed amusement. 'I think the cap'n's askin' a bit, sir, we couldn't hit a tent from the inside in this swell.'

'We'll see,' Pine muttered. 'We'll see.'

A mile ahead of the sea-sodden man-of-war, the sleeker cutter rocked and rolled as the driven waves crashed against the creaking hull. Cruickshank calculated the wind and current, tried to sense the shifting sea. Once he had altered course to the south he would cram on all sail and make a run for the Lizard, put in at one of the friendly ports dotted along the Cornish coast. He stared at the colossal warship bearing down on them. Close enough to see the whites of the captain's eyes now. He was a hard man all right, keeping the big ungainly ship under full sail in this gale. His damned crew must be puking like rats by now. One gust could carry away his masts and all, leave him dead in the water if it didn't spin him under for his impudence. A brave man. A man prepared to take risks. Parliament had few enough of those, thank God, or captains like him would never risk putting to sea. He tried to concentrate, to think his way out of their dire peril. Turning round and fighting forty guns with his ten would send them to the bottom inside an hour. He must stay out of range, and prevent the enemy ship from getting broadside to him. A lousy prospect now the enemy ship had sneaked such an advantage. Damn that boy, daring to sleep on his watch. Cruickshank turned to his quaking mate and thrust his chin out.

'I gave you an order, Mr Callow. I want the boy down here and the first twenty of those scumbellies,' he pointed at the secured hold, 'on deck, right now.'

The mate swallowed.

'On deck, sir? They might try jumping us, sir.'

'Oh, they'll try jumping all right. You said yourself, Ned, we've taken too many of the buggers aboard for our own good. They'll never make Antwerp packed in like that, spewing their guts up within sight of land!'

'They're not packed *that* bad, Captain!'

'I gave you an order, damn your eyes! Now get 'em up here now!'

Ten minutes which seemed like hours, and the *Conqueror* had closed on the gaily painted cutter like a mastiff on a baby rabbit. Pine had the hull in his sights, then the billowing sails, then the piled grey heavens. The ship seemed ready to leap from the churning water, poised at the apex of its sickening swing. The *Conqueror* fell back into the spray, and Pine stood back in helpless frustration.

'We'll never get a shot in like this!' he moaned.

Swale nodded. 'I tole you so, didn't I?'

Pine peered over the gunwale, saw jagged black rocks

reaching for the hurtling ship. The forlorn summit of a sunken reef, smeared in weeds and clogged with barnacles. The black mass reminded the young officer of a charred and twisted witch, burnt at some righteous stake. Swale grinned.

'Good job we've got most of the day ahead of us. Getting past the Angel's Fingers at night in this sea? Pah!' He spat over the side. Mostly over the side anyway. Pine looked back down the length of the foam-splattered deck. Pip Rowe, the boy who had almost been swept overboard an hour earlier, was staggering down toward them, hand over hand along the straining man-ropes.

'I thought I said go below?'

Pip gasped; his frail body convulsed in shivers. 'Captain's orders, sir. All hands on deck for boarding.'

'Boarding?' Swale exclaimed. 'In this chop?'

'Captain Fey requests you open fire, sir.'

Swale rolled his eyes. 'Might as well piss on 'em, all the good we'll do!'

Swale was typical of the bad-tempered and argumentative sailors who had swelled the ranks of the demonstrations in London in the previous years. Idle hands, jobless dockers and a swarm of nagging fishwives had converged on the capital to cry No Bishops at the fine palaces, to stone the constables and jeer the soldiers who had remained loyal to the King. Having chased his sovereign from his home, Swale was now back at sea, chasing his servants from the seas. Pine sighed, bent down over the gun. For one brief moment, the ships were level and he could see the crowds of sailors on the enemy deck. Swale cupped the match over the touch-hole.

'Wait!' Pine shoved the sailor's hand away from the tiny hole on top of the ornate breech.

'What is it now?'

The lieutenant nodded at the cutter, practically motionless as it came broadside on to the driving wind. A few precious moments more and the enemy vessel would slip gratefully into the wind.

'Fire!' Swale barked.

Pine shoved him back against the gunwale. 'There are men on deck!'

'What did you expect, monkeys?' Swale screeched.

'They're all roped together! They've brought their prisoners up on deck!'

The bawling mate had thrown back the grille and climbed down into the stinking pit with half a dozen of his hardest men at his back. They kicked and clubbed the terrified prisoners back against the dripping walls, making a small space for themselves.

'Right, I want the first dozen of you pimple-arsed bastards on deck, right now.'

His brawny fighters kicked and shoved their way into the compressed pack of men, kicking and punching the selected men into the bright light streaming down from the opened hold. Butcher, Muffet and the older pikeman first. Sparrow staggered forward as the *Messalina* rocked again, and a shaven-headed sailor clubbed him viciously about the arms and shoulders. Sparrow threw his hands over his head and fell to his knees. The sailor kneed him aside while two of his mates hauled the shouting youth out of the crowd. The mate grabbed hold of William's filthy hair and yanked his head up.

'On your feet and on deck, you Roundhead prickster!'

William clenched his teeth as the mate propelled him

into the mossy steps. A jab in the kidneys from a handspike and William was clambering up the filthy ladder like a monkey. He emerged into the fresh air, blinking against the fierce daylight. Two more ruffians clamped his arms and tied his wrists, and slipped a dirty hemp noose around his neck. William was pushed through the guards and swayed over to his friends, roped together like cattle on deck. A tall, thin youth William hadn't noticed before was crying like a child, sobbing into his sleeves and imploring the sailors to let him go.

'Where's Father, where's me father now?' he pleaded.

William was shoved in the back as more prisoners were hustled out of the hold, roped and lashed. Long Col looked grey and old, his thin face set. Butcher was blubbering. William peered out to sea, wondering if they were to be transferred to the galleon which was sailing up behind them. In this weather? Gillingfeather was dragged protesting out of the hold and forced into a dirty rope collar. He was shouting and bawling at his captors, but William could hardly make out what he was saying. The vessel lurched once more, tipping alarmingly toward the right. The mast dipped and the billowing sails seemed to brush the hungry waves. The *Messalina* had been nailed by the storm, pinned by the gale-force winds that rushed down the Channel. The crew quailed as the steersman wrestled to keep the distressed cutter on its escape course. The mate clambered out of the hold and hauled the grille back over the shouting captives.

'Line 'em up, Mr Callow, where they can see the bastards!' Cruickshank bellowed from his station on deck. 'They'll not fire on their own men!'

William cursed, stared over the choppy waters as the big warship careered toward them. The cunning captain had paraded his prisoners in order to persuade the pursuers against opening fire. A living umbrella of flesh and bone. The mate hauled on the rope, tugging the leashed prisoners along like a string of mackerel he had hauled from the deep.

'Shout, shout, you bastards!' Cruickshank bellowed, leaning over the rail to aim his pistol at the hostages. Billy Butcher needed no further encouragement.

'DON'T SHOOT! WE'RE ON YOUR SIDE!' he roared, his face contorted like a gargoyle.

The mate jabbed his elbow into William's back. 'Shout, God-damn you! You look as if you've a big enough gob!'

'I'd rather be shot down by them than be traded by you,' William snarled, practically blinded by fury. 'Shout yourself, you mangy old cunt!'

The mate looked as if he would argue the point, but shoved on through the mob to find easier targets. Long Col kicked out at him, bringing his tattered shoe down on the mate's knee. Callow collapsed as the sailors crowded in, raining blows down on the helpless hostages. The furious mate hauled himself to his feet and ran into the cursing press. He brought the hilt of his cutlass down square on Muffet's jaw, shattering teeth and splitting the skin. The old veteran collapsed to his knees. Sparrow wrenched the rope taut and yanked it to his left. The rope caught the mate's head and propelled him over the grille. A forest of hands emerged from the darkness, scrambled over the bars to pull and grasp at the helpless mate. Sailors jumped in to rescue their chief, stamping on the grasping fingers. The hold was in an uproar as the captain's intentions became crystal clear to all but the dimmest wretch.

'He's goin' to throw 'em overboard!' a frantic prisoner

screeched, his hands clawing the air. The sailors recovered their mate and helped him to his feet. Cruickshank hadn't taken his eye from his perspective glass for a moment. He could make out the pale faces of the enemy crew, less than two cables off and apparently on a collision course. He felt the hull rock under his feet, knew the *Messalina* had won the race and come about in time. Three hundred yards though, it was too close for comfort.

'Mr Callow!'

'Sir.'

'This'll give them something to think about!'

'Aye, sir.'

'Unleash those men, sir, and over the side with them.'

'I beg pardon, sir?'

'You heard me, Mr Callow. I want those men in the water, where that bastard can see them.'

Callow swallowed, weighing the notched and bloody club in his meaty paw. The prisoners pulled and kicked, shouted oaths as the sailors manhandled them to the gunwale one by one.

'You wouldn't dare! We can't swim!' Colston Muffet screamed, wrenching at the greasy hemp ropes shackling his thin arms. The burly sailors clamped him between them, cut his bonds and lifted him on to the gunwale, his bare feet kicking frantically. William watched in helpless horror, dumbstruck by the crew's utter lack of compassion. Their damned captain might just as well be ordering sacks of wool thrown over the side.

'You'll burn in Hell for all eternity for this,' Gillingfeather mouthed, the drool running down his straggling beard, his thin chest rising and falling with fury. The sailors lifted the first man to the gunwale and shoved him overboard. The old pikeman screamed as he hit the sea, and came up coughing water. Cruickshank raised his glass and focused on the enemy quarterdeck. He could see their white faces, sense their horrified outrage.

'And the next, Mr Callow! And the next!'

BY

SEAL SHOALS,

OFF DORSET, 20 JULY 1643

Lieutenant Pine let go of the gun as if it was red hot, and ran off down the rearing deck as if the sea had opened up before them, a mighty whirlpool gulping down God's creatures, sucking them down to hell. He ignored the violent pitching, slipping and skidding as he sprinted past the cowering gun crews to return to the poop deck. Another enormous convulsion sent him flying the last ten feet, and he landed with a splintering crash against the ladder. Pine ignored the blinding pain, and groped his way up the narrow steps. Rhodes leaned over and hauled him up, his brown eyes wide.

'They're throwing them overboard!' the second lieutenant gasped, jaw trembling with shock. Pine wiped his bloody nose on his sleeve, looked up at Fey standing alone on the rail.

'He's daring us to open fire. One stray shot and we'll kill and maim the lot of them,' he said quietly.

Pine strode over to him and pointed into the water. 'They're throwing their prisoners overboard, sir,' he croaked, on the verge of tears.

'I have eyes, Mr Pine,' Fey snapped. 'He wants us to give up the chase, lie to and pick them up,' he added in a hushed undertone. 'A desperado, sir, if ever I saw one.'

Pine swallowed, clenched the rail so hard he thought he might tear it in splinters.

'We've got to stop.'

'I beg your pardon, sir?'

'We've got to stop, we've got to help them,' Pine repeated, watching in horror as the first man slipped silently beneath the greedy green sea. A second and third man were hurled over the side of the speeding cutter. A flick of the wheel and the *Conqueror* would come broadside on to the helpless vessel, blast her and her unfortunate human cargo to smithereens. The cumbersome warship bore down on the smaller vessel, every man crammed along the rails to watch the vicious tragedy played out on the lee rail. Thanking their God they weren't among the helpless victims strung along the enemy deck like so much human poultry.

'By the time we've come about those men will be dead,' Fey grated, glaring madly at the callous slaughter of the unknown hostages.

'We can drop a boat, sir, save whom we can!'

'We'll lose hours, sir. Our mission must come first.'

Pine looked to Rhodes for support, but the pudgy first lieutenant seemed too stunned by the shocking course of events to even speak. Stopping to lower the boat would be extremely hazardous – perhaps fatal – but they owed it to those poor wretches to try something. God's wounds, it was no worse than the course of action Fey was proposing, yawing and firing a broadside in this swell. The *Conqueror* might be broached to, thrown on her beam ends by the greedy winds!

'An hour, sir, one hour to rescue those wretches. Think of our crew, sir, think of our men in that position! They wouldn't give a fig for the mission, if they were going down for the third time!' Pine screeched, pulling at the captain's soaked cloak.

Fey wrenched his arm away.

'I don't like it any more than you do, sir! Now return to the deck and prepare to open fire!'

'In the name of God, we can't leave them to drown! The crew won't like it, sir, they'll—'

'I don't give a God-damn for the crew, Mr Pine! You have your orders, sir!'

William Sparrow kicked his blistered feet and wrenched the flint-faced sailors this way and that, but their arms seemed to have been cut from the same timbers as the ship and he stood no chance against three of them. He pushed himself away from the gunwale with his bare feet, but was dragged back by their sheer strength. A rusty dagger bit through the umbilical rope which had connected him to the herd, severing the furious youth from his friends. He redoubled his efforts, kicking and wrenching his pinioned body against the pitiless rogues closing in on him. One of the sailors looped his arms around his left leg and lifted him from the deck.

'You bastards! You cowardly whoreson bastards!'

William screamed helpless obscenities at the shaven-headed louts, but they seemed to have blanked their minds against the outrage. Another blink of an eye and Sparrow felt himself tumbling through the spray. He hit the water with a breathtaking crash which jarred his entire body for a moment. Then he was up and kicking, shocked into action by the freezing power of the surging water. He whirled around, watched the red hull of the *Messalina* slide by. He kicked his legs hard as the swell pummelled his body, tried to suck him under the ship's white wake. Another man landed on top of him, and William thrashed underwater before coming up for a lungful of air. He kicked himself free from the other man, who was whirled away and tugged under the waves, his white hands reaching for the unblinking heavens. William broke through the surging foam and swam away from the plunging hull, kicking his cramped legs for all he was worth. He could see other heads bobbing in the waves, hands and arms held out of the water. The *Messalina* rammed through another trough, and another brace of men were thrown into the greedy sea. Long Col was thrashing wildly, screaming through a mouthful of brine. His hands clawed at the whirling waters as the sea sidled around him. Sparrow swam up to him, and held his contorted head out of the waves.

'Keep still, kick your legs!' William bellowed, collecting a mouthful of water for his trouble. Muffet thrashed wildly, a leopard in a drowning cage. Both men were sucked under by another fierce trough, and emerged spluttering and coughing. Gillingfeather was in the water now, calmly treading water and watching the *Messalina* cruise off as if he could sink the despised ship by power of prayer alone. William got a grip on Long Col's leaden coat, and kicked his legs desperately to keep them both up. Muffet had gone limp, his eyes rolling horribly in his skeletal face. Sparrow shook him hard, and the Londoner thrashed awake once again. The water swirled the survivors around, bobbing and waving as they tried to stretch their lost lives by precious seconds. The warship reared through the sea a hundred yards away, they could see the crew peering at them in helpless and horrified sympathy. William waved his right arm, and held on to Long Col's coat with the left.

'Help! Help! For God's sake!' William bellowed, swallowing another mouthful of water.

An enormous wave broke over them, scattering the survivors once more. The Welshman yodelled horribly as he was dragged under the foam. The older pikeman floated away, face down as if he was staring at the broken bottom.

Fey closed his eyes for a moment, nodded once. A dozen black heads bobbed in the waves. Ten. Eight. Another moment and they would all be dead.

'Mr Pine. Throw out all the barrels and bales we have. Mr Rhodes, prepare to come about. Lower the longboat.'

Pine had leapt to the steps before the captain had finished speaking. The horrified crew, galvanized into action, hurled anything which might float overboard. Baskets, empty barrels and old buckets. Anything which a man might cling to for another precious minute or two. Pine watched the survivors swim and thrash toward the bobbing bales, clinging to the flotsam and jetsam as best they could. A dozen men wrestled the longboat from the waist, hauling it over the gunwale using heavy tackles rigged from the yardarm. The back-breaking work took precious moments, moments the survivors did not have.

The crewmen manhandled the boat over the side, defying the heavy sea as they lowered the madly swinging craft into the churning waters. Others scrambled up the rigging to reef sails and slow the plunging man-of-war's crucifying progress. Pine leapt into the boat, cracked his shins against the thwarts and held on grimly as the longboat swirled alongside the mother ship. Swale leapt down beside him, snatched up an oar and pushed off as two men clambered down beside them.

'Secure a line there, we'll never get back otherwise!' Swale roared at the wide-eyed newcomers. Pine held on in the prow as the longboat was sucked away from the massive warship. He jumped out of his freezing skin as a white hand groped over the bow, clawed a hold in the splintered decking. The young lieutenant grabbed the hand and hauled its owner up with all his might. The spluttering stranger pulled himself over the gunwale and flopped down exhausted, half in and half out of the water. Pine got a hold on his soaking coat and hauled him into the boat, which rocked alarmingly, almost pitching Swale into the water. Pine could see white faces and waving hands all around the rescue boat, and hardly knew where to help first. One survivor was desperately holding on to his mate, holding his head out of the water while he screamed and thrashed. Swale leaned over and grabbed the man's jacket, tugging him out of the water as if he was a bag of feathers. His saviour slipped back, his arms spread out over the water, clearly exhausted by his efforts. Pine reached out for him as his white face slipped under.

'God damn you, come back!' he roared. He stretched his fingers, closed them in the man's thick dark hair. He pulled with all his might, bringing the drowning man up once more. Startled by his unexpected rescue, the swimmer seemed to make one final, Herculean effort. He flapped his arms and kicked his legs, and threw himself at the boat. Pine clawed at the man's shoulders and dragged him over the gunwale, resting the deadweight on the rail while he caught his breath. Swale leaned over and helped haul the half-drowned man into the boat. Pine looked out over the crashing waves, spotted another survivor bobbing in the foam. The man was treading water apparently unconcerned, watching the *Messalina* slip further and further away.

'Swim! Swim, you fool!' Pine yelled.

The hostage looked up as if startled, and swam unhurriedly toward the boat. He grabbed the sides and hauled himself up and into the boat, nodded at his astonished rescuers.

'You should have fired. Why in the name of God didn't you sink the Antichrist?'

Hereward Gillingfeather was alive and well.

The longboat's saturated crew snatched seven men from the jaws of the storm. Seven of the two dozen or so the inhuman fiend on the privateer had hurled overboard. The stop-at-nothing enemy captain had paraded the rest of his prisoners on the deck, daring Fey to open fire on the sad wretches. Slowly, painfully slowly, the *Messalina* had accelerated away from the heavier warship, the captain's despicable *ruse de guerre* having worked well enough.

It took the *Conqueror*'s crew another two hours to complete the rescue operation by dragging the sodden longboat alongside, by which time Pine and his men were in no better state than their speechless survivors. More men had to be sent down to help both rescuers and rescued up the heaving hull and on to the deck, where they were wrapped in blankets and sent below. Lieutenant Pine, his body racked by frozen convulsions, recognized Fey moving through the crowded deck, nodding his pale head in satisfaction.

'Well done, lad. You'd better get below and get outside some grog.'

Pine tried to smile, but his jaw wasn't working. He tried to speak, but his trembling lips wouldn't form the words. Fey eyed him.

'What changed my mind?' he asked with a small shrug. 'You were right. We couldn't let them die like rats. Wouldn't have been good for the crew. Wouldn't have been very good for us, living with it. Now get below before I throw you overboard, you insubordinate imp!'

He watched the courageous young spark helped below, and scampered back up the ladder to the poop. First Lieutenant Rhodes lowered the perspective glass, pointed out to sea. Away on the horizon, the *Messalina* was once more a frail white puff in the sea haze.

Fey took the glass and quickly scanned the sea for his quarry.

'He'll be long gone now,' he said to himself.

Rhodes nodded. 'What a blackguard, sir. Not even the Turks would have thrown men overboard like that.'

Fey smiled weakly at the naïve young officer.

'Aye, well. Prepare to come about.'

'Sir?'

'Prepare to come about. Back to our original course, if you please, Mr Late.'

'Aye, sir.'

'Coming about? I thought we were putting into the bay!' Rhodes exclaimed.

Fey frowned. 'In this weather the bay is as much a trap for us as it was for that hellhound,' Fey rasped. 'We've lost precious time already, sir. Pass the order, all the sail she'll bear. I want to be in Bristol by Monday at the latest.'

Bristol by Monday? All the way around the Lizard and back up the Bristol Channel? They would have to maintain full speed in this wretched storm, come back into the wind and cram on every square inch of sail they had. Rhodes nodded wretchedly.

'All the sail she'll bear, aye, sir,' he said flatly. The squall which had pursued them the past hundred miles finally caught up with them. Driving rain thrashed the sails and drummed the decks. Rhodes shivered as he clambered down the ladder to pass the order. Fey wiped the rain from his face, and raised the glass to his eye. The *Messalina* was no more than a white dot on the horizon, well out to sea now. One day, my friend, we'll meet again, he thought coldly. And when we do . . .

BY

KILMERSDEN HALL,

CHIPPING MARLEWARD, 22 JULY 1643

'Ah, there's nothing like a fine body of men drilling under the colours to stir the blood,' Sir Gilbert Morrison – resplendent in buff coat and Royal blue sash – declared enthusiastically. He had stepped out into the courtyard to watch the latest recruits to his new regiment put through their paces, marching and counter marching in front of the hall's abandoned defences. At least his new formation could boast a pair of robinets and a larger drake. All he needed now was a gunner who knew how to fire them. Findlay, fidgeting and frowning in his unfamiliar soldier's garb, nodded sourly.

'Aye, and this lot's nothing like a fine body of men!'

Sir Gilbert glanced at the newly promoted sergeant major of foot and wagged his gauntlet dismissively. 'There might not be many of 'em, I grant you that. Regiments don't grow from seed, man!'

This regiment certainly hadn't grown as quickly as the merchant would have liked.

He had imagined riding into the doomed city of Bristol at the head of a spanking new unit, sweeping into the city hall to accept the grateful thanks of Charles Stewart himself. And more profitably, the keys to the vital port. General the Lord Morrison, Governor of Bristol and President of the board of the Royal Westward Oceanic

Venturers. Good grief, if young Bella had got her claws into that transparent pup Clavincale he could be an earl by the end of the summer! He danced a little jig of delight, and slapped his gauntlet into his pudgy palm with rather more force than he had intended. His regiment shuffled by, pikes swaying this way and that. A thirty-legged porcupine which looked as if it had toppled into a cider barrel and tried to drink its way out again. Findlay closed his eyes in disgust.

'Lead off with your left, how many more times? Listen for the beat, you damned fool!'

Jeremiah Pitt had volunteered to provide the company signals, and was clearly enjoying himself clattering out ragged tattoos on the enormous drum he had slung over his shoulders. It was man's work really, but young Jeremiah could manage for now. Half a dozen of his young friends had also turned up at the hall, and were parading at the rear of the fanciful battalion. They copied their elders' haphazard drill with borrowed brooms and rakes, and more than made up for their marked lack of enthusiasm. Findlay had tried to shoo the noisy youngsters away but had been over-ruled by his clear-thinking colonel.

'Let 'em stay. They can stand at the back and nobody would be any the wiser.'

'The enemy would,' Findlay had protested. 'There's enough young fellers missing from the village without taking the few that are left.'

After being talked into accepting his commission by a tearful Lady Ramsay, Findlay had re-enlisted Ancient Bates and a couple of the gardening staff as corporals. To this non-commissioned core he had added a handful of odd-job men from the estate and an equal number of idle hands from the tenanted farms further down the hill. The gamekeeper had also called in a few old favours around about, and managed to persuade half a dozen loafers from the village to accept Sir Gilbert's shilling. Findlay had caught them or their children on Ramsay's land often enough. It was high time they gave something in return for all those rabbits and wildfowl they had poached. The few diehards who hadn't jumped at the chance had been offered a one-way trip to the local Assizes instead, and had grudgingly joined the queue to make their mark on Morrison's roster sheet.

Findlay had marched his newly formed company out to the main road through the hills, and set up a checkpoint of sorts which succeeded in detaining another dozen or so shifty-looking fellows who had clearly had enough of the war further north. The promise of a shilling up front and a few hot meals persuaded most of the stragglers to delay their homeward journey, at least for a few days.

'Scum. Ditch-running sneak-purses and cattle thieves. I'd shoot the lot of 'em,' Findlay commented drily as he watched his new command stumble past.

'Early days, Findlay, early days. As soon as the word goes out we're recruiting we'll have more mouths up here than we can feed!' Sir Gilbert had argued. 'We'll have another company ready for Jamie when he gets back from Devizes, and another for that idiot William, if my Bella can find him. Hello, who's this?'

The lean gamekeeper had narrowed his iron eyes and peered over the blustering merchant's shoulder at the sudden clatter of hoofs on the drive. He saw a small dark figure hunched over a knock-kneed nag ride under the gate and bounce along the gravel pathway in evident discomfort.

'Aye, and here come your cavalry, Sir Gilbert,' Findlay muttered ironically. The merchant shielded his eyes and watched the nervous rider flap his arms and kick his legs against the beast's prominent ribs like a demented toad. The tired horse picked its mucus-smeared muzzle from the grit for one more half-hearted trot, and came to a halt in front of the imposing hall. Morrison hurried over to greet the new arrival, grabbing the beast by the bridle although it had little enough energy or inclination to go an inch further.

'Christ's wounds, Starling, where have you been?' the merchant enquired, running an expert eye over his choice of mount. 'And where did you get this windbag? Brown's knackers?'

Algernon Starling, Morrison's trusted clerk and shipping agent, threw his thin leg out and slipped to the floor. He gave his master a sour salute as he rubbed his mean buttocks.

'The last he had. I'd bought every other animal I could to sell on to Waller.'

Morrison clapped the clerk on his slightly hunched back. 'Good man! How many?'

'Thirty at three pounds five shillings and thruppence.'

'Three pounds five shillings and thruppence? Do I look as if I run an almshouse?'

'There were none any better than this one,' Starling protested. 'Three pounds five shillings and thruppence was the most they'd part with.'

'I hope they rub their niggardly backsides raw ridin' 'em and all,' Morrison cursed.

'Sold 'em to a Scotch man, you know what they're like. Wouldn't part with the steam off his piss without a letter of credit.'

'Ah, you did well enough, I suppose,' Morrison allowed, grudgingly. 'What else have you been up to?'

'Spying, sir. Like you bid me,' Starling called for the entire regiment to hear.

Morrison waved his hands and raised his eyebrows, and shooed the crooked clerk up to the house.

'I don't want every Tom, Dick and Harry knowing my business! Come into the study.'

The exhausted clerk followed his master up the steps and nodded at the lady of the house, who had been waiting expectantly in the hall.

'Here's Master Starling with news from Bristol, ma'am,' Sir Gilbert called cheerily.

The clerk touched his white hand to his craggy forehead, unabashed by the lady's bristling stare.

'I thought for a moment you had landed yourself another recruit,' she observed waspishly. 'Obviously, I was mistaken.'

Her unwanted guest winked conspiratorially. 'Starling? Oh, he's no soldier. He's worth a hundred of those fools!'

Starling accepted this tribute without changing his habitual scowling expression. Lady Ramsay raised her eyebrows. 'Of great worth indeed, then.'

'Was there anything else I could do for you, ma'am?' Sir Gilbert enquired gallantly. Let the old bitch whine and gripe. He had her and her damned stiff-lipped family precisely where he wanted them. In his pocket with the rest of his creatures.

The widow shook her head. 'I was just going along to see Anneliese. I wasn't aware I had to account for my movements just yet.'

The merchant's winning smile slipped a notch. 'Still feverish? Off her food? Time of the month no doubt. Still, when her and my Jamie are joined in holy matrimony, she won't have to worry about the curse much longer, will she?'

Lady Ramsay closed her eyes against this witticism. She stalked off down the corridor like a storm cloud. Sir Gilbert chuckled.

'Remarkable woman. Full of spirit. Spirit doesn't grow from seed, you know, although I suppose in a way it does,' he went on, warming to his theme.

Starling sucked his off-colour teeth.

'Come on into the study. I was expecting you two days since.'

The clerk stared at his master's broad back.

'They're getting touchy up there, hardly letting anyone in or out. Apart from your merchant friends, that is.'

Sir Gilbert closed the study door behind his assistant, nodded him to go on.

'They're wetting their breeches, all of them.'

Sir Gilbert rubbed his fat hands enthusiastically. 'Just as I said they would! Should have jumped when I did, not now they've half the King's army on the doorstep!'

'They've had all their worldly goods put aboard their vessels. They're shipping out, lock stock and barrel!' the clerk declared.

'And run for London, eh? They won't get much of a welcome there!'

Starling shook his misshapen head. 'They're sitting in the King Road, loaded to the gunwales.'

Sir Gilbert marvelled at his former colleagues' fearful audacity. They were worried enough to order their assets stored aboard their boats, but had drawn the line at a total evacuation. It was not an ideal time to relocate one's business empire in London, not whilst the merchants in the capital were under such intense commercial pressure.

Pirates on the high seas preyed on their shipping, Royalist armies blocked their routes to market and raw materials and to cap it all the Parliament they had supported so vociferously demanded more and more in taxes and contributions to keep the tottering cause on its feet. The London trading houses were at each other's throats as it was, without fugitives from the provinces trying to muscle in.

'They can't make up their minds whether to throw in their lot with Fiennes and his Roundheads or sell the city out from under his boots,' Starling commented acidly. 'The smaller ones are the problem. They think they've nothing to lose. If they're forced out of Bristol they haven't the influence to start up in London.'

'Told you so, didn't I tell you so?' Morrison queried.

The clerk lowered his voice to a venomous rasp. 'They've fallen out over it. I heard a couple of their hands talking it over in the Cat and Compasses.'

Sir Gilbert grimaced. 'Talking in the Cat and Compasses? They're always plotting something or other in that rat's den.' He leaned forward conspiratorially, his narrow eyes shining with anticipation.

'Talking about what?'

'Betrayal. Squealing to the King's men.'

The merchant slapped the table. 'I knew it! The backsliding bastards!'

Starling thought this a prime example of the pot calling the kettle black, but held his tongue.

'Who's talking, Keeler? Rennie?'

'Fitzherbert. And the trained bandsman, Bevan.'

Sir Gilbert growled in disgust. 'Fitzherbert, eh? Selling out his friends.'

'So they said. And if they bring it off and Rupert batters his way in, they'll both be sitting pretty in Bristol.'

Sir Gilbert bit his fat lip as he pondered this distressing development. William Fitzherbert was already amongst the most pre-eminent men in the city. A coup like this could put him in an unassailable position to dominate trade throughout the west. Sir Gilbert had already been promised such a position by Clavincale, he wasn't about to see it usurped by that greasy buffoon!

Starling waited patiently for his master to release his lips from his clenched teeth.

'Right, then. You'll have to get a message to Fiennes.' It wouldn't be the first time Sir Gilbert had passed useful information to the Parliament. He was for the King now, but business was business. 'Warn the bugger what's afoot, let that Fiennes fellow nip it in the bud like he did last time. What's the feeling in the city?'

'Non-existent. Plots and counter-plots everywhere. There's a couple of hardliners from Somerset in, and a whole passel of noisy women,' the misogynistic clerk spat hatefully, 'but the rest of the townsfolk don't give a tinker's cuss.'

'Women? What women are you talking about?'

'A set of harridans who hang around the gates and bridges encouraging the soldiers and shouting advice to Fiennes. I'd have 'em bagged up and thrown in the Frome, I would.'

'What women?'

'War widows, mostly. Fishwives, you know.'

Sir Gilbert had plenty of experience dealing with them. 'Never mind the women. Prince Rupert isn't going to be dissuaded by some old trout with a big mouth.'

'Ah, they're more than that. They say it was women as foiled the plot last December, when those buggers got themselves hung up for all to see.'

'What about the garrison? Waller's off to Evesham with our horses!'

'He'll be lucky to get there, then,' Starling commented drily. 'He's taken the best of the men with him and all. I wouldn't credit Fiennes with more than a thousand soldiers, a few hundred more city militia and a couple of troops of horse.'

Sir Gilbert shook his head. 'To hold what, five miles of walls and a dozen forts? What about guns?'

'Oh, he's got guns, all right, and plenty of 'em. Trouble is, he's got more guns than gunners. They won't be doing much damage to Rupert's rogues, mark my words.'

For once in his life, Starling's predictions were about to come completely unstuck. Rupert's rogues were going to suffer torments beneath Bristol's walls the like of which Englishmen had never seen. Not on their own doorsteps, at any rate.

BY

DEVIZES CASTLE,

22 JULY 1643

'What do you mean, they let him go?' Bella Morrison snapped, increasingly irritated at the time they had wasted on this wild-goose chase around Devizes. She hadn't minded postponing her trip to Oxford for a little while, and had barely protested when Lord Clavincale had suggested stopping overnight in the rather shabby market town. It was after all her duty as a good Christian to go to her poor brother's aid. But she hadn't imagined for one moment the search for Jamie would use up all that evening and half the following day. Where had the silly boy got to now?

Lord Clavincale looked peeved at the girl's selfish outburst, and only managed to hold his tongue with the greatest of difficulty. His many mistresses had included a red-headed Parisian duchess and a fiery Spanish marquise, but they had been blushing novices in comparison with this precocious puff-adder. He clasped his hands behind his back and paced across the dingy room to the window. The street outside the inn was crowded with labourers and masons in dust-smothered smocks, and their constant chip-chip-chipping at the town's damaged stonework seemed set to continue for a few hours yet. The infernal racket had shredded his nerves almost as quickly as Bella's single-minded outbursts.

'It's really quite simple, my dear. Your brother was released from the castle a week ago. We probably passed them on the road.'

Bella bristled, staring at her reflection in the pitted glass which passed as a mirror in this hideous shambles. The grinning landlord had been so proud of his rambling ruin, leading her up the fragrant oak-panelled stairway and showing the remarkable beauty to her suite as if it was the finest set of rooms this side of Constantinople.

'Will you be stayin' long, miss?' he had asked hopefully.

'Not if I can help it,' she had snorted derisively.

Another dozen labourers shouted and bawled as they tried to straighten a chimney stack on the house next door. The roof had taken a glancing blow from a spent shot during the short-lived siege the week before, and the stack had been wobbling uncertainly ever since. Bella ground her teeth at the constant tap-tap-tapping and cracked her brush down on the table.

'Why on earth would they keep all the rest but let him go? Are you sure it was him?' she asked, watching his reflection in the glass.

Clavincale's back seemed to shudder as if he had caught a chill.

'I have just spent the last two hours with the commandant of the castle. Your brother was not amongst the prisoners dispatched to Oxford or . . . or to Sherborne.' In other words, Jamie Morrison's name had not been on the ragged list the staff officer had managed to unearth from beneath a pile of credit notes, letters of complaint and other miscellaneous paperwork. 'He seems to remember one young man being allowed home,' Clavincale growled at the fastened window.

'One young man? Jamie?'

'Possibly. I am making further enquiries.'

Bella frowned. 'It looks like it.'

The red-faced lord wheeled round and glowered at her. 'Pardon me, Miss Morrison, but there is a war on. As far as anybody can make out we took almost a thousand prisoners. I wouldn't like to say what became of every single man Jack of them.'

He could say with some certainty what had become of a hundred and six of them – they would be aboard the *Messalina's Purse* and halfway to Antwerp by now – but the fate of the other nine hundred was anybody's guess. Bella bit her lip and smiled sweetly.

'I'm sorry, I didn't mean to nag at you.' She patted her skirts invitingly, and worked her smooth shoulders in the clinging bodice as if she had developed a severe backache from the long ride in the cramped coach. Clavincale hurried up behind her, placed his pudgy hands on her cool shoulderblades and began a soothing massage. Bella purred with approval.

'How much longer will we have to stay in this horrible town? You would have thought they would have left off all that knocking by now,' she said distractedly.

The young nobleman ran his forefinger along her smooth neck, twirled her curls absentmindedly.

'You can blame Waller's artillery for the damage. I'm told it runs into thousands of pounds. No wonder the locals were so keen on buying up the goods the soldiers had looted from his camp.'

'Just like my father. Making a penny from somebody else's misfortune,' she observed quietly.

Clavincale renewed his gentle ministrations, pursing his rather too generous lips.

'He's a realist, my dear. Your father is one of the few

men other than myself who really understand what this war is all about. Money. Who has it and who hasn't. Those who want it, and those who object to them having it.'

Bella snorted. 'He wants it right enough,' she said with feeling. 'He'd do anything to get his way.'

Clavincale imagined he had felt the room tip slightly, as if the worn boards under his boots had warped suddenly. He disliked being reminded the girl's wretched father had more than one iron in the fire, more than one scheme in mind for the most profitable settlement of his daughter's future. He was just one more eligible male as far as Sir Gilbert was concerned. He would be ready enough with her hand, so long as Clavincale kept his part of the bargain, and came up with a stream of new titles and appointments for the greedy merchant. Governor of Bristol, indeed!

The girl was every bit as cunning as her father. She had played with him all the way from Chipping Marleward. Played with him, aye, as if he was a trout, not one of the richest and most resourceful men at the King's court. She would lead him on and hold him back, much to the apparent disgust of the girl's dark-haired maid. He'd had his eye on her and all, but the one time he had experimentally fondled her bottom she had given him a look which would have turned milk sour. Her mistress had been rather more subtle, ensuring the surly maid was beside her at all times, and claiming to be suffering from an ever-growing list of ailments if she wasn't. Ah, he'd have her sooner or later, or he'd die in the attempt!

'Well, we can't very well wait here until he turns up,' Bella observed in a slightly more agreeable tone. 'And I don't intend going back to Father just yet.' She sighed heavily, her bosom practically heaving its way out of her dress. 'I do so want to see Oxford,' she added longingly.

Clavincale swallowed hard, and gave her shoulders a reassuring squeeze. He nodded smugly. 'Don't you worry, my dear. You'll see Oxford.'

She'd see it, all right. She'd see every ceiling in the whole town. In the meantime, he had better find this wretched brother of hers, or he would never hear the end of it.

Lord Clavincale's enquiries into Jamie Morrison's whereabouts took him out of the inn and back along the bustling High Street to the castle. The old grey pile had made a good target for Waller's guns, and a whole battalion of eager volunteers had been put to work repairing the worst of the damage. Clavincale stepped between muttering labourers, skirted baskets bulging with dusty rubble, and worked his way into the crowded courtyard. Files of men and women sweated and strained as they manoeuvred barrow loads of pulverized stone away from the badly battered towers. A surly oaf in a dirty smock pointed him in the direction of a certain Colonel Sparkes, who had apparently been left in charge of the working party. Clavincale introduced himself and briefly outlined his mission. The distracted colonel seemed to be in the grip of some fearsome skin disease, and kept picking at his peeling face while the nobleman chattered on.

'I understand some of your men may have known the fellow, he'd apparently been a captain in the militia. I was told he had been released, although I wasn't able to establish why.'

'Whose militia?'

'Morrison's regiment. From Chipping Marleward?'

'Never heard of it,' Sparkes snapped. The scaly colonel

had more pressing things to worry about than missing Roundheads. He had a town to fortify and a newly raised regiment to knock into shape. Most of the men had only been recruited the previous week; turncoats and deserters from Sir William Waller's thrashed army. He and his officers needed eyes in the back of their heads to make sure the reluctant Royalists didn't take it into their straw heads to make a run for it. The army command had decreed that as soon as the regiment was operational it would be sent to another part of the stricken country, a quiet backwater where the officers could assure themselves of their new troops' loyalty before they trusted them in battle.

'What's he done, anyway?' the colonel enquired as he turned aside to sign a requisition form for a burly elder sergeant. The gummy old bugger tipped his hat and stalked off folding his precious order under his coat.

Clavincale waited patiently for him to finish his administrative duties, and leaned forward confidentially. 'To tell you the truth, he's the brother of my fiancée.' Well, it wasn't far from the truth.

The colonel rubbed a patch of flaking skin over his right eye, and smiled wanly. 'Been fighting on the wrong side, eh?'

'He's easily led.'

'Aren't they all? Well, I don't know. You're welcome to ask about, if you like. Most of them were fighting with Waller this time last week, they'll know your man, likely enough.'

Elder Sergeant Cully Oates waited at the castle gate while his new charges caught up with him. The hulking great farm boys were dragging a small cart which had been loaded down with every barrel and bottle he had been able to lay his hands on. He chuckled to himself, and patted the note tucked firmly inside his coat. As usual Sparkes hadn't bothered to read the requisition order. If he had the colonel would probably have had him flogged at the tumbler for his insolence. Cully was quartermaster to Captain Allington, and as such was responsible for provisioning the hundred or so newly enlisted men in his company.

But good old Colonel Sparkes had just signed a chit authorizing him to collect beer for the *entire* regiment. By God, they'd enjoy it while they could!

'Come on, you lumpy buggers,' Cully called, watching the new recruits drag the cart over the uneven road. 'We haven't got all day!'

The two soldiers sweated and cursed as they hauled the clattering cart over the cobbles after the jolly quartermaster. His great sagging belly preceded him by a good six inches as he waddled down the busy High Street, tipping his hat at the ladies of the town as if he was some dandy from the cavalry down from Oxford. The goodwives and townswomen of Devizes didn't mind his good-humoured if rather coarse tongue. He could sort them out with everything from a barrel of best French brandy to a suit of armour, so he was a man worth cultivating. Cully escorted the cart down the alley toward the Black Swan, mischievously wondering what the poor landlord would make of the order he carried. Beer and brandy for a regiment, if you please! The unlucky recipient could in theory redeem the value of the requisitioned goods by presenting the chit to His Majesty's Exchequer. In practice, very few were foolish enough wasting any more of their time (or money) on such a thankless errand. In the King's army, free quarter meant just that. He paused and looked over his shoulder, wondering where the newly recruited rogues had got to with the cart. There they were back at the top of the lane, wetting their breeches over some serving girl!

'Oy! You're not here to pick up the polecats, get that fucking cart down here now!' The sergeant's bawled instruction brought pale faces to the leaded windows up and down the narrow alley. The two recruits glanced around at him, waved like the sheep-shagging idiots they were. Their companion glowered, her pretty cheeks burning with embarrassment.

'Who are you calling a polecat?' Mary Keziah snorted, furious at the interruption. The soldiers were none other than her brothers, Zach and Eli. Gone to the wars two months since. Miss Bella's search for her missing brother was over.

Almost over.

Lord Clavincale listened to the maid's breathless report with considerable relief. So they had found the missing youth at last. Now perhaps they might get back to Oxford and allow him to resume his rather more pressing assignments on behalf of King Charles. He had sauntered back from Devizes Castle pausing only to purchase a light snack of bacon and eggs washed down with a flagon of good ale, and had arrived back at the inn expecting to see the unfortunate fugitive's charming sister hanging out of the window in eager anticipation of his heroic return.

Instead, he had found the girl closeted with a pair of smelly soldiers and the excitable Mary Keziah. Bella had leapt to her feet and clapped her hands together, but not in pleasure at seeing him.

'Mary's brothers have seen him, Jamie, I mean. He's gone to Bristol with General Hopton!'

Clavincale had smiled warmly. 'Come to his senses and changed sides, has he?' he enquired, running his wet eye over the awkward soldiers.

'Well, yes, sir, that is, not quite, sir,' Zach mumbled, rather overawed by the quality of the nobleman's expensive blue suit.

Clavincale sighed. More cannon fodder with barely enough sense to fall over.

'These are Mary's brothers, Zach and Eli. They were captured with Jamie on Roundway Down,' Bella said excitedly. 'They saw him leave with Mr Ambrosio, the Italian surgeon.'

'Well, that is good news now, isn't it, Miss Morrison?' Clavincale enquired. He hadn't minded undertaking the search for Bella's imbecile brother but hadn't anticipated spending quite so much time in the thankless pursuit. Then again, the only reason he had agreed to look for him in the first place had been to further ingratiate himself with the senseless beauty. Another half a day wasted and no good come of it.

'I'd looked high and low for him myself,' he offered rather belatedly. 'The colonel had heard some story about a prisoner and this doctor,' he lied.

'He's not gone as prisoner,' Zachary corrected him carefully, 'but as a patient, begging your pardon, sir, like.'

'He's hurt his head and the doctor is treating him,' Bella informed him.

Zachary winced. 'Well, he's done a mite more than 'urt his head, miss, I mean, he wasn't . . .'

'A well man,' Eli piped up.

Bella's features clouded momentarily. 'You said he

wasn't badly injured,' she said, her voice brittle with uncertainty.

Zachary nodded cautiously. 'He wasn't hurt as such . . .'

Clavincale turned on his expensive heels with a snort of derision. 'Oh, come now, if you saw him as you claim you must have noticed whether he was injured or not,' he snapped, losing his temper a little. 'Are you sure these rogues aren't feeding you some kind of a story in the hope of reward?'

'They're not the ones after a reward,' Mary Keziah said sharply. Clavincale glared at her.

'Mary! You hold your tongue,' Bella ordered, equally sharp.

Clavincale paced the room in agitation. Smelly soldiers and saucy servants? Why couldn't they just pack the bags and get on the coach? Standing here gossiping with a couple of cabbage-headed idiots and their surly sister wasn't getting any of them anywhere. And it certainly wasn't getting Bella into his bed, which had been the prime object of the entire exercise.

'You said he'd hurt his head,' Bella accused, looking between the brothers and their sister as if she too suspected some horrible conspiracy.

'That he has, miss, that he has . . .' Zachary was lost for words.

Eli tapped his own head in a farmyard diagnosis of the absent youth's ailments.

'Hurt inside, like, miss.'

'If he's taken a knock he's taken a knock,' Clavincale said dismissively. 'The question is, how badly was he hurt? Could he walk? Could he talk?'

'After a fashion, sir,' Zachary replied.

The young aristocrat clapped his hands ironically.

'There we are, then. He can walk and he can talk. A dry blow to the head, I'm told it's not uncommon in battle.'

Mary Keziah glanced nervously at her helplessly agitated brothers, reached out to touch Bella's arm.

'What they're trying to say is he's not well in his mind, miss. He has a numskull, miss.'

Numskull? The dratted youth was a numskull all right. Clavincale clicked his pudgy fingers in irritation.

'The fact is, Bella,' he said crossly, 'we have missed him. The commandant at the castle said he'd been released, your friends here suggest he might still be seeing stars. If he's lucky enough to be getting treatment from this Ambrosio fellow all well and good. As long as he's safe I don't see there is much more we can do.'

Bella favoured him with his first glance of the afternoon, smiled weakly. 'I suppose you're right.'

Clavincale nodded briskly. 'Now I don't wish to hurry you along, my dear Miss Morrison, but I've urgent reports to make to His Majesty. I would like to be on the road inside an hour.'

Bella bit her lip and turned to her maid.

Good God, was she obliged to ask her own servant's permission to do anything? What kind of a household did this Morrison fellow run?

'He will be safe now, won't he, Mary?'

Clavincale gave the curly-haired brunette a barbed look. She turned away, shrugging her shoulder insolently.

'Who's to say, miss?'

'Well, then, here's what we'll do,' Clavincale interrupted, deciding to get a grip on the situation before they called the stable boy up to give his opinion on their troubles. 'You and I will continue with our journey to Oxford. With a bit of luck we should be there by midday tomorrow. In the meantime I will write a letter to this doctor fellow, instructing him to have young Jamie returned to Kilmersden Hall and your father's tender care.' Bella's proud colours returned to her cheeks as she nodded her approval. 'Your maid will carry it with her when she returns to Bath by coach,' he added. 'She will find the good doctor, present the letter to him, and then accompany Master Morrison back to his beloved home.'

Mary's scowl contrasted strikingly with Bella's misty grin. Clavincale stalked between the girl and her servant, and snatched up Bella's cold hands.

'Isn't that a fine idea, my dear? Young Mary here seems eminently sensible to me, I'm sure she can be trusted to get him home and tuck the poor boy up in bed for a couple of days. By the time you get back from your holiday at the Court, he'll be as right as rain!'

Bella could barely resist standing on tiptoe and kissing him. Her hazel eyes shone with happiness, and he felt a stab of guilt slide under his ribs to see her complete trust in him. No matter. Let her trust, let her love, let her worship. He pulled his eyes away from hers for a moment, smiled icily at Mary Keziah, standing uncertainly beside her hulking brothers.

'I will see you in one hour to finalize the arrangements for your trip,' he said rigidly. 'You may go.'

Mary Keziah held his stare for a moment, but she knew she dare not gainsay the gentleman. She nodded briefly, and hurried her brothers out of the door. Clavincale ran his hands up Bella's arms, felt cool satin then warm skin. He bent over her face and planted a chaste kiss on her dewy eyelid while he slid a heavy straight-backed chair across the door with his boot. Bella returned his kiss, running her lips lightly over his puffy red neck. Clavincale reached down blindly, and turned the key in the lock, his eyes opening in delighted surprise as he felt her tongue cut a moist trail along his lower jaw, and then slip between his lips like a seasnake. Clavincale's hands flew back to her shoulders in a fit of jealous possession as she leaned away from him, smiling sweetly.

'You're so . . . commanding sometimes,' she purred as he lunged forward, his dry mouth pursuing the tiny heartbeat in her slim neck, cornering her breath inside her mouth. She was thrilled to her core, every inch of her body shrieking for the release of his touch. Swooning like a schoolgirl when she had imagined she would be as cool and collected as a courtesan. Aching with need like some dairy maid when she should be as assured as a countess. Clavincale was beyond any such ideas. He had buried his face in her fragrant cleavage, slavering like a hog at a trough. This time, this time, there would be no bashful excuses, no panicked interruptions. He strode forward, carrying her with him, spreadeagled around his chubby right thigh. She locked her slippers behind him, allowed herself to be lowered to the great piled cake of the bed.

BY

BRANDON HILL,

BRISTOL, SUNDAY 23 JULY 1643

Bristol basked under the unblinking stare of the high summer sun, the fierce heat shimmering off the many church spires towering above the mean, packed streets. The marvellous monuments looked crooked, magnified and distorted by the heat haze.

The townsfolk would normally have been making the most of the weather, strolling beside the broad green sweep of the Avon as they made their way home from church. The breezy slopes of Brandon Hill were a favourite haunt of courting couples, affording a panoramic view of the city. Families would bring baskets of bread and fruit up there for impromptu picnics on the grassy sward, take their ease as they watched the bustle down in the harbour.

The poor dock-hands and sailors enjoyed no such Sabbath holiday. The whole port was gripped in a frenzy of activity as last minute military supplies were unloaded. As fast as the holds were emptied they were refilled with plate, furniture and effects belonging to the principal merchants. Most of them had already loaded their best stock, and ordered their biggest and most cumbersome vessels out to the comparatively safe anchorage of the King Road, seven miles downriver at the mouth of the Avon. With their goods safely stowed, the self-righteous citizens had time to think about their families, crowded into the oak pews of St Mary Redcliffe and half a dozen other city centre churches. With the morning worship complete, many of the well-to-do burghers made their way straight to the quays, and boarded the remaining ships ready for an eleventh-hour evacuation.

Foremen and agents strode about the packed crates and anonymous tarpaulin tents while the crews toiled over the hot decks and greasy rigging of the ships out in the green bowl formed by the confluence of the Avon and the smaller, swifter Frome. Busy quays and stuffy warehouses had grown up around either side of the inner harbour, which had more than enough room for a dozen and more merchant ships to unload their goods.

Looking down on the waterfront from the commanding heights, the tall masts looked as knotted and kinked as the silver and bronze spires of the surrounding churches. Immense fingers stretching up out of the city stews, rather like the bright points of a mighty crown.

Major Tobias Fulke frowned at the uncomfortable image which had sprung into his mind's eye. Bristol, a mighty crown waiting patiently for its sovereign to return. Untarnished by the grubby hands which had passed it around like a market bauble.

He had paused to catch his breath on the steep slope, the commanding point on his sector of the city walls. His gravely reduced company – barely seventy strong now – had been assigned to the north-western corner of the five-mile defence line. It didn't take a military genius to recognize that his men had been spread perilously thinly behind the broad turf bank. He had walked the length of his sector with his sweating sergeant major, past redoubts and embrasures and great basketwork emplacements, and had spotted half a dozen places where an experienced enemy captain might put a company over the walls. The Royalists weren't fools. They would be watching for weak spots just as he had. And woe betide the Parliamentary garrison if the enemy found one.

Fulke took off his neckerchief and wiped his red face. The steep climb had taken it out of him, he thought with a silent curse. If he'd been twenty years younger he would have run the five-mile perimeter without raising a sweat. Now it was as much as he could do to get his breastplate on without getting himself into another lather. He had caught Matilda looking at him, pitying his fumbling efforts. She would smile and coo over him as usual, of course, but she couldn't hide the lies in her eyes. She was a whore, a whore with a heart, and her heart was set on that prickly Cavalier, that was for sure. Ever since their encounter beside the ferry, Matilda had redoubled her attentions to him, trying to convince him she only had time for her dear old major. He had coin for her, that was how he bought her time.

Fulke had taken lodgings not far from the walls, on a steep stair behind Park Row called Christmas Steps. The alley climbed in a series of switchbacked terraces between bustling shops and fat-bellied town houses, open to the elements (as well as the contents of any number of bedpans and chamber pots). The well-worn steps were used as a short-cut between the lousy sidestreets about the harbour and the grander apartments clustered on the higher ground just to the north of the city centre. A popular thoroughfare for hurrying servants and their red-faced masters – for employer and employee alike, Fulke thought vindictively.

Ah, it was no use fretting over his relationship with the bold-eyed Tilly, worrying what the girl really thought of him. She would be safe enough there for a while, aye, dreaming of her young captain. Fulke could close his eyes and picture the insolent pup who had injured his leg in the bad-tempered duel beside the river. Remember with an inward wince how the young rascal had cut him down as if he was a carpenter taking the legs off a warped old table. Those manic eyes and bristling moustaches reminded him horribly of his own youth, and of his long service with the Swedes in Germany. Battling the forces of Tilly and Wallenstein halfway across Europe. At least today's youngsters didn't have to sail hundreds of miles to find suitable sport. The wars were being fought in their own back yards now, not in Bohemia or Pomerania or Saxony or Westphalia. They were fighting in front of their family and friends, and so, maybe, they wouldn't last so long. Ah well.

He braced himself on the firestep, the walkway cut into the parapet of the broad turf barricade, and peered over the top.

Bristol's extensive defences began alongside the River Avon at Hotwells, away to his left as he gazed out from his breezy eyrie on Brandon Hill. The wall ran north to the Water Fort, the first of the many works which studded the line. The fort's guns overlooked the river, and could be brought to bear on any ships coming up the Avon. From there the wall rode up to his position on Brandon Hill and linked with a second, more formidable bastion. It then turned slightly to the east, and ran across a shallow dip to a large, squat stone barn which had been cleverly incorporated into the defences. The wall then turned sharply east and followed the ridge of Windmill Hill, arriving at the most northerly point on the line at Prior's Hill Fort. From there the walls swung south-east, encompassing the eastern suburbs before reaching the banks of the Frome. The defences on the southern side of the city weren't visible from Fulke's lofty eminence, but he knew the broad wall ran from the Frome to the Avon beside Tower Harratz, and then swung round Bristol's vulnerable underbelly, reaching the river not far from the awkwardly truncated spire of St Mary Redcliffe. He could see the massive structure throbbing in the bright sunshine, and remembered with a twist of concern the city governor had installed cannon under the soaring arches, turning the church into a formidable bastion just outside the city wall. The townsfolk who had packed into their pews that day had shared the aisles and knaves with gunners and musketeers, engineers and captains.

Any assault from the south would have to bypass the obstacle, or be subject to enfilading fire from the grandiose structure. And even if an invader forced his way in there, he would immediately come up against the heart of the city's defences, the great squat pile of the castle, Nathaniel Fiennes' strongpoint headquarters.

The walls were impressive enough on paper, and quite formidable to the untrained eyes of the pious citizens. The more vulnerable sections had been beefed up with star forts and gun emplacements, and surrounded by deep ditches which the labouring townsfolk had filled with sharpened stakes and assorted household refuse. More than one hundred pieces of artillery had been sited around the perimeter, cunningly dug into the basketwork emplacements. With ten thousand men and a few score gunners who knew their business, Bristol would have been virtually impregnable.

But with around a thousand half-hearted soldiers and a few hundred surly townsfolk, she was as easily defended as a maid's honour on a ship full of Turkish pirates.

The old veteran shook his white head as he wandered

along the almost deserted wall. A couple of stragglers from the militia lounged beside an antique gun, peering out of the tumbledown hovels crouching around the marshy slopes at the foot of the hill. A third man was striding carelessly along the parapet, balancing himself with his pike held out like some Oriental acrobat. His two companions had been laughing and jeering at him, but subsided into respectful silence when they heard Fulke's spurs jingle on the walkway. They touched their hats as Fulke strode up, peering at the idiot on the wall.

'God's wounds, man, this is a citadel not a circus!' Fulke snapped, red faced. The youngster stared straight ahead, maintaining his balance on the turf wall. Fulke noticed he had removed his boots, and that his feet were particularly filthy.

''Nother 'undered yards, sir, and I'll be there,' he declared in a strong local accent.

Fulke waved him down. 'Get down, sir. I'll not have clowns playing tricks on my walls!' He reached up and grabbed the wavering pike butt, and tipped the youth off balance. The youngster staggered and jumped down to the firestep, his pike clattering over the wall. The major looked over his shoulder for his absent sergeant major.

'No harm, sir, I used to rope walk a while, back at home, sir!' the simpleton said with a grin. Fulke shook his head.

'There's a time and place for everything, but not in the middle of a blasted siege.'

'I hadn't seen no one, sir, d'you want me to get up and 'ave another gander for you, sir?'

Fulke waved his neckerchief dismissively. 'In my lot, are you?' he growled, not recognizing any of the players from his old company. Farmhands by the look of them, about as much use with a musket as a one-eyed baboon.

'Whose lot would yours be, sir?'

'Fulke's. Attached to Colonel Fiennes' regiment now.'

The acrobat's companion pushed his felt hat back and scratched his head. 'Ah, that's the feller. We've 'ad so many colonels it's a job to tell who's who,' the taller of the two observed, climbing to his feet with difficulty.

'I'm Pitt, sir, that's Mordecai, in case you're wondering. This 'ere's Michael Bart who don't talk much on account he's dumb, and this,' he pointed to the vacantly staring youngster, 'is Sidney Virtue of Shrivington, sir. D'you know Shrivington at all, sir?'

Fulke didn't. He watched the talkative soldier as he fussed and slapped at his heavily bound leg, wincing as he flexed the stiff muscles. One monkey, one mute and one cripple, Fulke fumed.

'Took a pike point on Lansdown, sir, can't do a thing with it since,' Pitt said matter-of-factly.

'On Lansdown, were you? My lot were in Malmesbury, missed it altogether. We took a batch of prisoners back to Bath and missed Roundway and all,' the veteran went on, revising his hasty opinion somewhat. He waved the men back to the crates they had set up beside the lonely gun to watch their comrade's performance. The young soldier with the wounded leg frowned unhappily.

'Ah, sir. Me brothers were there, sir, and I haven't seen either since.'

Fulke sighed. 'I hear they took more than they killed. They'll be safe enough, God willing.'

'Aye, sir. God willing,' the youngster repeated.

Fulke slapped the breech of the ancient drake, bent down to squint along the barrel.

'You've a good spot here, lads, keep your eyes skinned if they come this way.' Fulke pointed to the gate below the hill to their right. The road ran out into a broad hollow studded with furze bushes and large loose stones.

'I don't like the lay of the line just yonder,' Fulke mused. 'See the way it dips between the forts? They'll not be able to bring a gun to bear.'

The two soldiers looked sheepish. 'We ain't gunners, sir, plain pikemen, us.' The old veteran frowned, drummed his fingers on the equally ancient gun. He had walked the walls with the hope of finding a suitable spot to station himself. The obvious command post was in Brandon Hill Fort itself, directing operations from the well-defended strongpoint. But if the enemy made a surge toward the gate, under the lee of the guns further up the line, there would be nobody to stop them besides these few bewildered sheep herds.

This was where he was needed. On the curtain wall between the forts, just above the hollow gate. All he required was a good supply of powder and ball. He turned and peered back down the way he had come. As usual the younger if somewhat stouter Sergeant Grantly had run out of puff a good fifty yards back down the line. He whistled him over, and pointed out the dead ground to the panting baker.

'I want musketeers in the barn there, and a gunner for this drake,' he instructed.

Grantly snorted. 'A gunner? There ain't a gunner on the whole bloody line worth the name,' he growled, spitting over the turf wall.

Fulke frowned. 'Well, get me a barrel of powder, a dozen two-pound balls and a couple more volunteers. A blind man with a dog could force the line here, look at it, man.'

Grantly looked, and nodded glumly. 'Tain't any worse

here as anywheres else,' he muttered crossly. The baker had it about right, and all.

By three in the afternoon the sun had driven most of the remaining townsfolk into whatever shade they could find. The courting couples had rolled themselves deeper into the hedges and bushes, the picnicking families had drained the last of their beer and packed their baskets. The compacted streets of tottering, bulbous-eyed houses seemed almost deserted under the braying heat.

Up on the walls Fulke's visit had sparked a brief flurry of activity as musketeers were moved from one strongpoint to another, and a supply of powder and ball secured for the ancient, half-forgotten gun. Mordecai Pitt had pulled off his breeches to let the sun warm his stiff thigh bones, while Michael Bart took a nap on the firestep. Sidney Virtue was up on the walls again, shielding his eyes to peer over the suburbs and broad downs beyond. Unusually, he had been silent for some time, pondering the hazy treeline, a shimmering snake on the horizon.

'There's a deal of folk come out of that church yonder,' Sidney reported at last.

'Some minister kept 'em back for an extra long sermon,' Mordecai thought.

'Brightest set of Puritans I ever did see,' Virtue commented.

'They're not that strong for religious ways up here,' Mordecai argued, wiping the sweat from his forehead. To his simple Chipping Marleward geography Bristol, London, York and the north were all simply 'up'.

'Looks more like a set of Flanders tarts, riding about in their finery.'

Mordecai Pitt narrowed his eyes, sat up on the firestep and followed the youngster's inquisitive gaze. A mile to the west, the shallow valley beneath the walls was overlooked by the majestic sweep of Clifton Downs. The open grassland changed colour, flushing with life as a broad band of sunlight swept over the plateau. The grass was studded with trees and bushes, and the grey spire of Clifton church rose like a swan's neck from a girdle of poplars and tall elms. Mordecai's gaze came to rest on the shimmering collage of colours beneath the sober grey walls of the church. Bright red banners, blue coats, white plumes and yellow sashes. A congregation of Kingfishers enjoying the bright afternoon sun, parading in their brilliant plumage. Mordecai swallowed hard.

He'd seen the same plumage at the foot of Lansdown. A hundred and more Cavaliers, trotting slowly around the church, changing direction to follow the line of the city walls.

And then, out of nowhere, an enormous, ear-splitting crash.

Mordecai jumped out of his loose shirt, stumbled on his bad leg. He looked left to see a plume of white smoke rise from the fort a hundred yards along the hill. Five hundred sets of eyes watched the graceful trajectory of the ball as it boomed over the valley and collided with the green down a good half-mile away from the Royalist scouting party.

'Hah! Will you look at that?' Sidney Virtue yelled. 'That's told 'em good and proper!'

'That told 'em good and proper we're trigger-happy buggers who can't judge range,' Fulke growled, hobbling along from his afternoon rest. He had gone to take a cat nap in the fort, and had hurried back at the first whispered word of the enemy movement. He stood in his shirt sleeves, cracked a perspective glass to his eye.

'Ah, it's no good,' he complained, thrusting the glass up at the youth capering on the wall. 'Your eyes are better than mine. What do you see, boy?'

Sidney Virtue steadied the glass, then held it away to squint at it as if it was a magic totem spewed out of the belly of some African witch doctor.

'Hold it to your eye, man, what do you see?'

Virtue followed his instructions cautiously, swinging the glass to and fro.

'A whole passel of 'em. All colours. A big feller on a black horse out in front. Is that him then, King Charles?'

'No, it's not King Charles. I wish it were,' Fulke muttered under his breath. 'Take a good look, lad. That's Prince Rupert, Count Palatinate of the Rhine, His Majesty's trusted nephew.'

Sidney Virtue stared through the glass at the legendary commander, half expecting him to sprout wings and fly around the walls like the demon he surely was.

'God save us,' Mordecai said quietly.

'Amen. Pray to God you don't see him any closer. And if you do, boy, you turn this gun on him, d'you understand?'

Fulke grabbed at the boy's leg, tugged him hard. The youth nodded dumbly.

'I will, sir. Straight at 'un.'

The sun had long since sunk behind the trees, silhouetting them sharply for the first time that blistering day. Fulke had struggled back into his armour and had his whole company mustered along the wall. Sergeant Grantly counted fifty-six. Fifty-six? They had mustered seventy the previous day.

'They'll be back, sir, in the taverns, likely as not.'

Fulke ground his teeth in frustration. 'Take a dozen men and round them up. I'll shoot any bugger deserting my colours,' he snarled. Sergeant Grantly hurried off on his assignment while Fulke completed his inspection. He arrived at his new lookout post on the curtain wall and nodded to pikeman Pitt, leaning on his weapon as he watched a party of horse tightening girths in the crowded road beneath the wall.

'Are they off then, sir?' Pitt asked glumly.

'Not off, no. Raiding their battery up on the downs.' The garrison had watched in fascinated horror as the Royalist intruders dug a gun emplacement in the lee of a couple of old houses near the church. Another few hours and those guns would be lobbing rounds at the works.

'I wish I were with them,' Fulke breathed. 'Can you ride, Pitt?'

'After a fashion.'

Like most countrymen, he knew how to stay on at canter. Just about the only requirement for a cavalry trooper, these days, Fulke thought with a sigh.

They watched the small troop check their weapons and soothe their stamping horses. The men looked like evil steel crabs in their rusty back and breast armour, their dull coats shining greasily in the torchlight. Evidently satisfied his men were ready, the lieutenant in command ordered the gate opened. Pitt and Fulke crossed to the parapet to follow their progress down the hill and into the darkness.

'Twenty of 'em ain't goin' to do much good,' Mordecai said.

The men on the walls watched and waited. Shadowy figures could be seen moving about in the shabby suburbs, but most of the townsfolk had locked themselves away in their homes at the first report of the enemy invasion. Dogs barked and cats prowled. Sidney Virtue watched a bat flitter about the eaves of a house near the wall. No doubt some dark familiar of Prince Rupert's, come to have a closer look at the defences, he thought superstitiously.

A sudden flurry of shots and the men along the wall stared up at the darkened down. Bright orange flashes erupted around what they guessed was the enemy battery. They spied darting orange flames and a moment later, heard the dull report of a musket. The skirmish was over as quickly as it had begun, and the garrison fell silent once more.

The raiders galloped up the hill a sight faster than they had gone down, clattering beneath the hastily opened gate. Fulke watched them trot down the dimly lit street, twisting in their saddles to look out for any pursuit. The gate was closed and the men along the wall relaxed, leaning against the parapet once more. Fulke had just turned to make his way back toward the fort when the horizon erupted with sickly orange light. In the sudden glare he could see half a dozen and more palls of white smoke. He was still focusing on the gaudy fireworks when the first balls whistled in from the batteries on the downs. He threw himself flat, winded, and covered his head as the explosions tore up a great heap of stones and turf and hurled it over the wall. A shower of gravel clattered over his black armour as he lay prostrate.

'Get down! Everybody down!' he yelled. The astonished troops dropped behind the parapet as the first rounds bracketed the ditch, tore huge holes in the green slope where the townsfolk had enjoyed their Sunday afternoon picnics. The smoke drifted raggedly over the walls and the major pushed himself to his feet to peer out over the black valley. There was a second eruption away over the downs as the Royalist gunners corrected their range. Fulke clapped his hands over his ears as the guns in Brandon Hill Fort blazed back. He doubted whether any of the gunners had marked their targets during the last light of the afternoon. They were firing at the night, the empty night which seemed to have swallowed the city whole.

The duel went on until dawn. Hundreds of rounds tore into the dark slopes or sailed overhead to smash the tiles from the nearby houses. A couple hit the turf walls and sent up great gouts of scorched sod. The garrison had taken cover from the wild fire, some men had slipped away into the anonymous safety of the streets. Fulke patrolled the line incessantly, reassuring the men the enemy fire was as ill aimed as their own.

By dawn he was short of breath, stumbling about the wall like a blind man. The acrid smoke had snatched the spit from his mouth, dried him like an old prune. The fifty-odd men who had endured the deafening barrage peeped over heaps of sullenly fuming rubble, and stared nervously at the eighteen-foot walls of Brandon Hill Fort, which had taken several direct hits. Sergeant Grantly arrived with a stone jar of cider, just in time to take the men's minds from the frantic bombardment. Fulke accepted a mouthful and passed the jar back. Grantly was staring over his shoulder, his fingers groping vainly for the handle.

'Here you are, man . . . What's the matter now?' Grantly nodded his chin slowly, working his mouth without making a comprehensible sound. Fulke twisted around and shielded his eyes to follow the sergeant's awestruck gaze.

Away across the smoky hollow, up on the broad grey downs, Prince Rupert had paraded his entire army for all Bristol to see.

A dozen regiments of foot with colours flying in the

early morning haze, countless troops of horse, trotting by cocksure of their own dreaded reputation. Drummers and fifers could be heard over the hoarse shouts of the sergeants and the catcalling officers. The mighty host had been drawn up in a line two and a half miles long. Fulke knew the enemy commander had spread his men thinly, but he could not deny the awesome spectacle's effect. His troops gaped and pointed, struck dumb by the display of might. Even the seagulls wheeling about the docks seemed silenced by the impressive parade of firepower.

It was perhaps lucky for Fulke his reeling troopers could not see the southern approaches of the city from their lofty works on Brandon Hill. Prince Rupert's brother Maurice and his respected colleague Sir Ralph Hopton had drawn up their Cornish army in exactly the same fashion. Four thousand foot and a thousand and more horse. Every man jack a veteran of the long summer campaign. They had also worked through the night to dig batteries for their formidable artillery train. The emplacements overlooked the river, the bastion of St Mary Redcliffe and the quiet walls beyond.

Bristol woke up slowly, and found itself completely surrounded.

Matilda Dawkins had been sitting at the narrow leaded window of her narrow and rather sparsely furnished room, idly watching the few townsfolk who had ventured out puff and pant up the steep stair below. She had an excellent view of the busy alley, and could make out their assorted red faces as they paused on the broad landings, the tall houses rearing up above them like three-tiered cakes baked by some backward child. It was as if each successive floor, each timbered layer, had been taken out of the oven too soon and squashed down flat onto the floor below, squeezing out the mortar filling so that each storey bulged like a fat man's belly. There were plenty of fat men running about on last-minute business, haranguing their poor clerks and carriers as they hurried down to the city with handcarts loaded with their personal goods. She had heard the rumours about the wealthy merchants making a run for it, trusting their goods and families to their miserable fleets out in the King Road.

These were lesser men: grocers and soap makers, shop keepers and other petty tradesmen. They weren't rich enough to be able to stow their stuff on board ship, so they were hurrying it down to the castle, and storing what they could in the great medieval cloisters behind ten feet of good stone wall. Trusting to God their precious hoards would be safe there from the horrors of the storm. Matilda shook her head, running her long fingers through the thick auburn mane. It needed a wash, but there wasn't much chance of adding to her own precious hoard today. Old Toby was obviously concerned for her, and kept hurrying back down from his position on the walls to make sure she was all right. And to make sure she hadn't pulled in some greasy butcher for a quick one, no doubt. Poor old Toby, he'd not quite forgiven her since she had tipped his arm at the river, spoilt his aim as he tried to shoot down poor Hugo. She hoped the boy was all right. That water had been devilishly cold, he might have caught a chill or something. Better a chill than a ball in the back of the head though, which is what he would have got if she hadn't been there to save him. She grinned. He could pay her when they met again.

She looked down the press of narrow hovels, each floor bulging with windows like cod's eyes on a fishmonger's slab. The woman opposite was hurrying about her room, alternately moving her heavy furniture and peering out over the busy stair. The Christmas Steps was a popular shortcut from the heart of the city beside the river to the suburbs built in great terraces into the surrounding slopes. Errand boys would race each other up and down, their baskets flapping against their bare legs. There were inns and hot-pie shops on the ground floors of the towering tenements which did a brisk trade with porters and passersby. The delightful aroma sidled along the oak and mortar canyon, reaching Matilda's pretty nostrils as she sat at the open window, her skirt drawn up to air her long brown legs. She wiggled her bare toes, and noticed the old bag across the way scowling in at her.

'What are you looking at?' she snorted, catching the woman's stern glance.

The bonneted matron shook her pale head. 'There's men out there fighting for their lives, and here's you sitting up for customers,' the woman snarled back, leaning out of her own window to make herself heard. 'Out, you strumpet, you carrion! Feeder on men!'

Matilda jumped up and stuck her wild red mane out of the window. 'I'd feed on yours if you had one, you miserable old trout!' she shouted back.

'Witch!'

'Hag!'

'Whore!'

'Who are you calling a whore? You've got a face like a pig's arse! Get on and bar your door, you good for nothing old nosebag. Not that there's a man within the walls or without who'd come knocking for you!'

The beetroot-featured matron gave a snort of anger and clapped her window to. Matilda stuck her red tongue out and sat back down at the window. Cheeky mare, calling her names in front of everybody. If she had been back at camp she would have gone over and boxed the old bag's ears, she would true! She tapped her foot and watched the stairs, the smell of cooking making her belly rumble. She'd only had a bit of stale loaf that morning and she was damned hungry. Perhaps old Toby would be hungry too, up on the walls on his own. She clicked her fingers. A good mutton pie and a jug of ale! If you couldn't fuck your way to a man's heart, you could always feed the bugger!

Matilda had clambered up the ladder, the heavy basket swinging against her gently rounded hips. Every man on the wall turned to watch her as she straightened her skirts and flounced down toward the fort. Toby said he was in the tower on the left of the wall. It couldn't be far.

'Goar, Dinny, would oi or what?' a white-haired musketeer asked his grinning mate.

Matilda was used to their ribald comments. She could always tell the time wasters and window shoppers from the boys with a spare copper or two.

'Flop it out and let's have a look at it, you old turkey,' she called back. The old musketeer's jaw dropped in surprise, revealing a set of spitty pink gums. Matilda made a face and strode by, much to the delight of the man's companion.

'She had you there, mate! Go on, flop it out if you can find it!'

The raucous chorus built up as she strode along the wall, dragging their attention from the worrying preparations over the valley. Wagons were lumbering up with all sorts of supplies, great bundles of brushwood they would throw into the ditches, and long scaling ladders to get over the walls. More batteries had been dug, and great guns rolled into position to batter at the long turf wall. Some of the guns had been moved, to test alternate sections of the defences. The fearful defenders forgot the awesome spectacle for a moment, whistling and cheering as Matilda took the wall by storm.

'Flop it out for her, lads!'

The call was passed along the sparsely manned embankment as far as Mordecai Pitt, who tipped his hat back to admire the captivating redhead.

'Michael, Sidney, for the love of Christ! Come and have a look at this little beauty,' he called over his shoulder.

Sidney Virtue snatched off his cap and peered down at the smiling whore, swinging along the wall as if she was out for a Sunday stroll. He leapt up on to the battlement and danced a little jig, stopping the girl in her tracks.

'You daft bugger,' she called up at the energetic youngster. 'What's he doing up there?'

Mordecai blushed to the roots of his hair. Even his hat went red. 'Well . . . oi . . . that is . . .'

'Where's Toby . . . Major Fulke? I've brought him his lunch, look,' Matilda said, holding up the basket.

Mordecai's red nose twitched at the succulent aroma. 'Wouldn't be mutton would it, miss? Mutton's my favourite,' he said.

'I bet it is,' she sniffed, and looked up again at the fool on the wall. He had tiptoed toward the fort, holding his arms out for balance, yelling and hallooing to wake the dead.

'Come down, you silly sod. If Toby sees you up there he'll throw a—'

Her good-natured advice was drowned out by a whistling scream. Mordecai ducked down like a startled hen, making a grab for the dumbstruck girl at the same moment. Matilda was staring straight at the capering youngster when the cannonball tore through his billowing white shirt. The ragged cotton turned crimson, and then exploded in a slithering rainbow of blood and bowels. Sidney Virtue was torn away by the screaming ball, thrown off the wall like a slaughtered duck. He seemed to fly for a moment, his bloody arms beating the air as his kicking legs were snatched out from under him, scattering droplets of blood and handfuls of anonymous flesh over the horrified defenders. The ball carried his body a few more feet, and then deposited it like a bag of bones over the sagging roof of the nearest hovel. The splattered tiles buckled but held, spreadeagling Sidney's lifeless body like a surgeon's plaything. Matilda held her white hand to her face, and hardly dared look at the fragment of warm flesh which had stuck to her cheek. The men on the wall fell silent. Even the gunners on the downs opposite stood back from their belching culverin, as if they couldn't quite believe what they had seen. A daft fellow capering in his shirt, blown away like a scrap of paper in a tempest.

The great killing of Bristol had begun.

BY

THE MARSH,

BRISTOL, MONDAY 24 JULY 1643

Prince Maurice's cavalry regiment had been assigned to billets in the villages crowded like stepping-stones along the southern banks of the Avon. The widely scattered horsemen were to cover the south-western approaches to Bristol, resting and refitting while their brothers in the infantry bore the brunt of the storm. The horse had covered two hundred miles in a fortnight, had fought and won a pitched battle against overwhelming Parliamentary forces and reckoned they deserved some respite from the rigours of war. Tired quartermasters had ridden down the dingy main streets inspecting the mean hovels, eager to pick the best billets for their units. The careless troopers had left their hungry horses cropping the verges while they scrambled over tumbledown fencing to pick peas and beans from the neglected garden plots stretching down the slopes toward the muddy river bank.

Their noisy arrival had not endeared them to the citizens, who as usual greeted their requests for free board and lodging with a terrifying arsenal of reasons why the soldiers should seek shelter elsewhere.

'Ah, sirs, the plague's been bad 'ere, cruel bad, my eldest Alan as was taken just this morning.'

'They say the back room's haunted. You wouldn't get

me sleepin' in there if 'twas last place in all Bristle.'

'You're welcome to stay, my boys, but the house carries a curse, sure enough,' one woman warned, peering through the crack of the door at the cavalry troopers who had arrived on her step.

'Oh yes. What sort of curse?'

'Ah, a terrible curse, sir, put on the house by a notorious witch hereabouts!'

Jack Cady stifled a guffaw as he stood waiting, his saddle slung over his shoulder. 'What's the curse?' he repeated.

'Tis a dretful curse for men to hear, sir, proper dretful.'

'Go on,' Cady invited.

'Well, sir, tis said any man sleepin' in the back will wake with hairy palms and never another pulse in his pizzle, if you'll forgive an old woman's rough words!'

Cady burst out laughing while his mate kicked the door back in on the muttering crone.

'If there's any witches round here it's you, dear. Now stand aside for the King's cavalry!' Ned Jacobs shouted, shouldering his way past what he fully expected to be a cursing hag.

In fact the cursing hag turned out to be a handsome woman of thirty-five, her wild auburn hair clamped and pinned beneath a rather grubby bonnet. Ned and Jack dumped their belongings by the fire and squabbled over the bed.

'What, you're not going to turn me out of me bed and all?' the woman demanded, looking from one to the other. The villagers had been expecting Cavaliers, not grinning apes in dirty boots. Cady eyed the woman as she wiped her hands on her apron, shook his head craftily.

'Well, I'm willin' to share if you are, me beaut,' he replied winningly. 'Yer man around, is he?'

'Away with the fleet,' she said gruffly.

There was a loud sneeze at the door, and the goodwife looked up to see a thin youth with pale features stumble over the threshold.

'Three? Three in two tiny rooms not big enough to swing a cat?' she wailed, bunching her hands in her apron in simulated distress. Hugo Telling peered blearily at her, his eyes bloodshot balls of weeping mucus. He swayed from side to side as he ran his sleeve across his running nose.

'I than't take up mudge room,' he said thickly.

'Got a bit of a cold, ain't we, sir?' Cady asked kindly, stepping to one side to allow his captain to stagger into the hovel. Telling nodded, depositing the few items of clothing he hadn't wrestled over his shivering body on the cluttered table.

'A cold? He looks as if he's been dead a week! You'll put us all in our graves bringing your bastard agues here!' the housewife cried miserably.

Cady took off his greasy felt hat and ran his fingers through his flaxen mop. 'Cut the cackle and get the soup on, darlin',' he called. 'Can't you see he's over the worst?'

Telling stepped uncertainly over the well-swept flags and sat down beside the remains of the fire with a heartfelt sigh. The woman's expression softened instantly, and she held a blotched red hand to his cheek.

'Ah, he's burnin' up, the poor lamb! What's he doing out with you scoundrels?'

'He's cap— colonel to the prince,' Jacobs invented, making himself comfortable beside the table and helping himself to a hunk of fresh bread.

'Prince? What, Rupert? The Devil incarnate himself?'

'His brother. Maurice,' Cady replied. 'But he's devilish important, all the same. As God's my witness, I wouldn't want to be in this village if his right-hand man takes a chill and dies. What's the place called again, Ned? Bugminster? Bellminster?'

'Bedminster,' the woman snarled, wiping Telling's sweating brow with her apron. 'What do you mean, "if he takes a chill"? He's got river fever or I'm the Queen Mother. Fetch us that blanket and set some more sticks on that fire. We'll have to sweat it out of him,' she ordered. Lisbeth Swale hadn't had many visitors lately.

The argumentative cartel of senior officers assigned to run the King's Western army had been in broad agreement for once, allowing the cavalry to stand down and disperse about the hill villages. Although the Royalist commanders had not anticipated the enemy would attempt to relieve the besieged city by land, they had not ruled out the possibility of a seaborne rescue mission. The broad and boggy-banked Avon was tidal as far as Black Horse Ferry and beyond, the muddy waters rising ten feet and more in Bristol's busy harbour.

In order to prevent any attempted relief from the sea the Royalist commanders had ordered gun emplacements dug to overlook the basin and command the western approaches. Anyone fool enough to risk the passage in or out of the city docks would now have to run the gauntlet of a dozen cannon of all calibres. The toiling gunners and engineers had worked through the night by the light of a dozen fiercely bright torches, the glowing beacons an insolent challenge to the invisible garrison over the water. They had completed their emplacements that dawn, fortifying the gun pits with heaps of spoil and bulging gabions. The great baskets of earth and stones would protect the crews from any counter-fire from the forts beginning to take shape in the early morning haze across the river. Carts rumbled over the muddy works bringing barrels of powder and a supply of cannon balls, which were feverishly unloaded and set out beside the newly completed batteries.

If the Royalists had completed the works a few days earlier they would have trapped a dozen and more merchant ships riding at anchor out in the basin. But the canny merchants had evacuated their prize fleet to the King Road, and all the gunners could see when the mist began to clear were a few old coasters and barges, and a handful of decaying sloops whose disaffected captains were more interested in playing cards than putting to sea. They remained at anchor in the broad basin, so many sitting ducks for the King's greedy guns.

Algernon Starling paced to and fro along the cold chamber, his muddy shoes stamping a confused trail on the stone flags of Bristol keep. The castle seemed remarkably quiet for a military headquarters, even at that early hour of the morning. The few clerks at work in their narrow cells adjoining the landing seemed completely indifferent to the urgency of his business.

Sir Gilbert had ordered his dogsbody back to Bristol as fast as his knackered horse would carry him, with instructions to ensure word of the imminent mutiny of his brother merchants was brought to the Governor as soon as possible. Starling had slipped through the Cornish lines, hunched over his coughing nag like a diminutive Grim Reaper. The ruffians were too busy preparing for the storm to worry too much about the sorry-looking old fellow, and had let him pass without any serious attempt to question him.

'Gah, boys, look at that sour-faced old coot. Where d'you think you're off to, matey, lending a hand with the garrison, are you?'

'Let the bugger go, Simon, he'd curdle their milk from twenty paces!'

'What if he's a play-acting spy?' a giant one-eared musketeer had challenged suspiciously. 'He bleedin' well looks like one!'

'Get on, Jethro, you daft bugger, spies don't *look* like spies, do they?'

'Well, what about that feller on Lansdown? He didn't look much like a spy either,' the giant musketeer challenged gruffly.

'What's that, Jethro, before or after you shot 'un? Ged on, boy, if he's a spy my prick fires roundshot. On you go, Father, but you'd best keep your 'ead down when we gets in with yer Roundhead mates!'

Starling had slipped through the gradually tightening cordon around the southern approaches and entered the city through the Wells Gate. He had then used his not inconsiderable knowledge of the labyrinthine backstreets of Bristol to get into the inner citadel, and had searched out the busy alehouses where city gossips generally outnumbered the bona fide customers by several dozen to one. That night, though, the smoky inns seemed full of reluctant warriors rather than tale tellers. The weary soldiers didn't have time to listen to his venomous warnings, and moved deeper into the gloomy corners away from him. He tried to strike up insinuating conversations with several likely looking big mouths, only for the suddenly suspicious drinkers to finish their beer and stalk out. You couldn't trust anyone these days. There was nothing else for it, he would have to go to the Governor's headquarters and see Fiennes himself. A tricky task given his master's late adjustment in allegiance, but still, desertion was desertion. Fiennes could hardly stand by and let the merchants sell the city out from under his boots.

Starling looked up sharply as a crowd of red-eyed officers clattered up the broad stairs, arguing and gesticulating amongst themselves. The bold clerk recognized Nathaniel Fiennes, a rather pudgy, red-faced man strapped tight into a worn breastplate. His tawny sash had been tied around his middle, the gigantic knot sagging like some unsavoury growth on the back of his buff coat. Starling took off his tall black hat and bowed as steeply as his crooked back would allow him. Fiennes paused on the ill-lit landing and wearily massaged the bridge of his nose. Starling pounced.

'Algernon Starling, my lord, merchant's clerk of Temple Street.'

The Governor glanced at the pale shade, the stranger's enormous beaked nose twitching like some carrion bird's bill. Fiennes had been up all night touring the defences, staring morosely at the gun flashes from the surrounding hills and trying to estimate how many pieces Rupert had brought up. At least a dozen, and well placed too. The enemy batteries had been carefully sited to threaten the weakest portions of his line, clearly the work of some damned professional in the Prince's service. Rupert's dawn parade, the massive display of might on Clifton Down, had reduced his officers to stunned silence, God only knew what it had done to the men. There was barely a company left on the walls which could boast more than half its official strength. The men seemed to be melting away with the early morning mist. He glared balefully at the crow-faced clerk, nodded him to continue while his staff officers shuffled on into his headquarters in the rocky heart of Bristol keep. Starling leaned forward conspiratorially, and whispered under his rank breath.

'Sir, it grieves me sore to bring you ill news at a time like this, but it has come to my notice that certain disaffected individuals are planning to desert your cause.'

Fiennes stifled a yawn, holding his gauntlet to his slack mouth. 'More plots? I thought Whitehall was bad enough, but you Bristolians would make the blasted Venetians look honest.'

Starling ignored the Governor's despondent jest, pursing his thin grey lips.

'The merchants, sir, plot your undoing even as we speak.'

Fiennes raised his rich ginger eyebrows in exasperation. 'If I had a man on the walls for every plot I'd heard about this last week, they'd be standing on each other's heads for want of room,' he snapped. 'I can't sort out the wretched merchants as well as the defences!'

The vile, money-grabbing traders had done their best to line their pockets, supplying the humble garrison with everything they might need, so long as they had good coin to pay for it. The city elders had at the same time cawed and quailed at the prospect of paying their own militia, with the result that Bristol's trained bands had become perilously weak, with only the most notorious ne'er-do-wells remaining with the colours. Nathaniel Fiennes was heartily sick of Bristol, its mean merchants, its surly soldiery and its wailing womenfolk. The wretched harridans would accost him in the street as he went about his business, ordering him to have a care for this stretch of wall or that blasted gate. Offering up their services as if they were some fantastical breed of West Country Amazons. If he never saw Bristol ever again, it would be too soon.

'I have heard rumours, sir,' Starling persisted as Fiennes strode past him toward the great oaken door to his private chambers. 'The talk in the quayside inns is all of mutiny and desertion, sir. They mean to sell their fleet to the enemy!'

Fiennes paused on the threshold, looked glumly at the excitable clerk. 'I hear they're waiting in the King Road. An understandable precaution, I would have thought.'

'The merchants are plotting to go over to Rupert,' Starling insisted.

'They're out of my jurisdiction,' Fiennes growled, as if he were back at the bar arguing some obscure point of ownership before a gin-blossomed judge. 'I can't spare men to go gallivanting along the coast after a few grocers, can I?' He clicked his chubby fingers in the clerk's mean face. 'Now, sir, I have an appointment with my officers. If you'll forgive me?' Before Starling could hiss any further objections, Fiennes had closed the heavy, worm-holed door firmly on his thin face.

The flock of peacock officers poised above the guns ran their perspective glasses to and fro over the ship which lay at their mercy a few cables out in the quiet basin. The sloop had originally been tied up across the broad bay, but its master had apparently decided to make a late dash for the sea, and had slipped his moorings on the rapidly ebbing tide. Its somewhat erratic progress downstream had come to a grinding halt two hundred yards upstream, the overladen hull having stuck fast on a sandbank. The deck was swarming with sailors and dock-hands, hurrying about knots of gesticulating gentlemen and their bawling children. The captain was shouting to make himself heard above the din, stamping about in circles like the queen bee in a smouldering hive.

'What in the name of hell is going on now?' the senior gunnery officer muttered to his lumpen assistant, crouching beside him on the pit's rubble-strewn parapet.

The heavily built German master gunner tilted his tousled head, but clearly hadn't heard the question. He was reputed to be one of the finest gunners in the world, lured at great cost from his last assignment with the Swedes to take a part in England's ever more vicious struggles. He had served the Parliament for six months, only to be among the crowd of prisoners taken on Roundway. The Royalist high command had quickly realized the German's professional potential, and had promptly recruited him into the Cornish army. The King's forces needed all the experts they could get. The only trouble was that Jacob Kreutzfeld's long and distinguished military service had left him as deaf as a post.

Colonel Augustus Potts, in charge of the Cornish batteries nearest the river, turned in despair to the young lad who acted as the master gunner's ears.

'They must think they're safe lying beneath the castle walls.'

The sooty-faced powder monkey smiled politely. 'Or they've run out of water, sir.'

'What?'

'Run aground, sir.'

Potts bristled, and followed the youngster's gaze while the alleged master gunner hummed a drinking song at least an octave out of tune, apparently immune to the nerve-racking battle of wits being played out along the river.

'Ah, the canny buggers. Look, sir, they're chuckin' stuff overboard to float 'er off!'

The colonel snatched up his perspective glass and studied the furious activity out in the bay. The boy was right. The crew had leapt about as if they had accidentally dropped a grenade into a hold full of gunpowder. They scrambled up the rigging like ragged brown rats while their fellows turned crates and barrels of God knew what over the side. The abandoned ballast bobbed away on the tide, tantalizingly close to their position.

Potts watched in growing frustration as a gaggle of officers and black-jacketed gentlemen clambered down the oaken gunwale and into the sloop's longboat. The over-loaded craft was carried away from the stuck sloop, revolving gently in the swirling currents.

'They're trying to get out on the flood tide, the rogues! Leaving it to the last minute to throw us off,' Potts cried. 'Damn it all, I've had enough shilly-shallying. Put a round across the bow.' The colonel pointed out the isolated merchantman with his calipers, simple compasses he used to size the roughly cast balls. Deaf Jacob tilted his head like a great flaxen-headed parrot, looked quizzically at the distracted colonel. The young interpreter jabbed his dirty finger at the renegade vessel, and mimed its imminent destruction. The German scrambled down the parapet on his backside, waving his weary assistants to their feet. The distracted gunners breathed a sigh of relief. They had worked like demons to dig their pits and dearly wanted to see a fat Puritan merchantman blasted to Kingdom Come.

'Mr Kreutzfeld,' Potts bellowed. 'One round across the bows, if you please!'

The jolly youngster relayed the order to his master and the crew manhandled the cumbersome culverin around a few degrees. Kreutzfeld bent down to take one last look down the barrel, and held up his fat thumb at the lieutenant with the linstock.

'Ready!'

They were just about to open fire when a frantic staff officer galloped up on a lathered horse, and practically threw himself in front of the loaded cannons.

'For God's sake,' he gasped, waving his gauntlets at the astonished crews. 'Don't fire on the ships, don't fire on the ships!'

Potts stormed up to the breathless messenger and jabbed him in the shoulder. 'What do you mean, don't fire on the ships? Can't you see they're making a run for it?'

'Didn't you get the message? The masters have handed every ship in the King Road over to Rupert! That's our fleet you're looking at!'

The perilously poised plot to betray the vessels to the King had come to fruition at last.

BY

PILL FERRY,

NEAR BRISTOL, 24 JULY 1643

Another hour was all they had needed. Sixty minutes more and the *Conqueror* would have caught the tremendously powerful tide, and ridden the scum-crested waves into Bristol docks exactly on schedule. Captain Fey had barely left his post these last few days, staring out at the sullen brown breakers which dappled the murky surface of the Severn estuary as if sheer willpower could succeed where the winds had failed. The weather which had blown them around the coast had given out at the last minute, leaving the weary ship cruelly close to the mouth of the Avon, the last lifeline of the Bristol garrison. Fey had glared down at the dirty water lapping around the bow, and felt the contrary current sliding away beneath the hull – dragging them remorselessly back the way they had come. He had immediately dropped anchor between the seal-stacked sandbars of the Bristol Channel, cursing the lost time. Now they would have to wait six hours and more for the tide to turn, and complete their epic voyage to the beleaguered city towed behind the ship's longboats.

Fey slapped his calloused palm on the worn rail and turned to his tired officers, gathered dutifully behind him.

'Well, gentlemen, we've missed the tide, and I don't need to tell you what that means. The garrison must hold out another day without our help.' The hollow-eyed junior officers looked suitably gloomy at the wretched news. All those sickening hours plunging along the south coast on the outriders of a mighty gale, and they still hadn't reached the city on time. Captain Fey had pushed both his men and his ship to breaking point, insisting on full sail throughout their voyage, but even their Herculean efforts hadn't been enough. Miraculously, the storm which had speeded their progress the length of the south coast had given out as they negotiated the Lizard. If it had continued to rage, it would no doubt have blown them halfway to the Americas. Instead, they had languished on a mirror-smooth sea for a few hours, tacking hopelessly toward the north many miles short of their destination. The exhausted crew had slumped where they could, barely able to tie the simplest knot. The foul weather had pummelled them remorselessly for twelve hours and more, and the unfamiliarly stilled sea robbed them of what was left of their sense of balance. In the silent lull following the squalling storm the wretched crew suffered new torments, staggering to the rails to empty their heaving stomachs.

Gulls wheeled and dived over the sour mess, gleefully mobile in contrast to the stranded man-of-war. The sails hung miserably on the creaking masts, the tortured timber groaning after the ordeal on the storm. That evening a light westerly wind had sprung up, and carried them gently along the rugged coast of north Devon. The mild breeze had continued into the following day, propelling them at last into the critical switchback of shoals and currents in the Severn estuary. The muddy mouth of the river opened wide as if the smudged brown coastline was laughing at their pathetic efforts.

The King Road was unusually crowded, with eight big merchantmen anchored offshore surrounded by a busy fleet of attendant sloops and brigs. The *Conqueror* anchored up a mile or so away, a timber wolf bedding down in a sheepfold. First Lieutenant Rhodes ran his glass over the crowded anchorage, marvelling at the furious activity their arrival seemed to have occasioned. Bewildering sets of colours were run up and down the packed masts, as if the contents of half a dozen laundries had been hung up to dry.

'That's the *Cormorant*, look, and behind her the *Pious Reformation*,' Rhodes commentated as Fey stood by rubbing his red-rimmed eyes. 'By God, sir, it looks as if they've got women on board!'

Fey reclaimed his glass and studied the huddled fleet. He could see crowds of people lining the rails, waving enthusiastically. Many of them were indeed women and children, cloaked and bonneted against the offshore blow. The families of the Bristol merchants, no doubt, out of harm's way aboard their masters' ships.

Rhodes frowned. 'What are they waiting here for? They might just as well go on back to London.'

Fey lowered the glass and eyed his second in command. 'It's bad enough they've run this far,' he snapped, his usual good temper hardly restored after their late arrival at the King Road. 'Sailing on to London is hardly likely to inspire the garrison to greater efforts, is it?'

Rhodes shook his head glumly. 'Sorry, sir.'

Fey turned to accept a mug of rum from Pip Rowe, the undernourished galley hand. The youth was making his first wary appearance on the deck since he had damn near been washed overboard during the storm. The frightened boy looked about the unfamiliar coastline as if they had sailed to the moon.

'A fine sight, lad. D'see those merchantmen yonder? They're the backbone of the cause.'

Fey ruffled his hair encouragingly and climbed down from the poop deck, leading the exhausted officers into his barely furnished and infrequently used cabin.

He took off his hat and collapsed onto a narrow bench, waving his junior officers to their places around the crowded map table. Rhodes shuffled the charts, and pointed out the *Conqueror's* position. His dirty fingernail was barely an inch from the green coastline, teasingly close to the narrow mouth of the Avon. Fey leaned over the map, following the meandering blue path of the river between the clustered villages to the west of Bristol. Pill, Portishead, and nearer the city walls, Sea Mills on the northern bank and Bedminster on the southern. If the city had been closely invested the villages must have fallen to the enemy, and if the banks were held in force, their passage would be a one-way ticket to hell itself. A gauntlet of guns not even the Avon's notorious tides could carry them through in safety.

He sat back with a sigh, loosening the collar of his damp shirt.

'Judging from the presence of the merchantmen, gentlemen, I would hazard our journey has not been in vain.' Richard Pine said nothing. He stared morosely at the map, tried to superimpose complex siege lines, valiant forts and formidably fortified batteries of guns onto the greasy chart. He gave up his thankless imagining and glanced at the captain. If they had left the wretched prisoners to their fate, sailed on by while the sorry fugitives screamed and drowned, they would undoubtedly have reached the Avon in time to catch the all-important tide. The currents round about were more powerful than any other in the world. Sailing against them would be like trying to swim up a waterfall.

Fey caught his eye and grinned feebly. 'Don't look so miserable, Dick. I'm not sure I could have let them die like dogs,' he said, reading the young lieutenant's thoughts.

Pine nodded gratefully.

The few sea-shocked survivors they had whisked from the waves had looked like dead men when they had finally lifted them back on board the madly heaving deck. They had been taken below and plied with hot rum, their shivering blue bodies shrouded and packed with blankets and spare clothing.

'And they'll be worth a hundred men apiece, when we put them ashore,' Fey had encouraged.

Pine brightened at the prospect. 'Permission to command the landing party, sir?' he piped up on a sudden burst of enthusiasm for their desperate mission.

'By all means, Mr Pine. By all means.'

Five and a half hours later, and the bright summer day was waning as fast as the hopes of the trapped garrison of Bristol. The *Conqueror*'s longboat had been lowered into the dirty, frothing water, and the men who had volunteered to man her scrambled down the netting and took their places on the thwarts. They cast off quickly, slipping away from the vast bulk of the man-of-war shortly before the turn of the tide.

Captain Fey had decided to scout the winding Avon as far as he could before trusting his ship – and her valuable military cargo – to the narrowing gorge which carried the broad river into the busy port. If the city had fallen the ship would be at the mercy of every gun on the wall, and their desperate mission would become a grim battle for simple survival.

Lieutenant Pine went in command, with Swale and Slater as senior hands. Pip Rowe had also volunteered for the shore party, glad of the respite from the hateful sea. The rest of the party consisted of the survivors from the *Messalina's Purse*, Captain Cruickshank's unwanted passengers, expendable ballast.

The former prisoners had hardly noticed the last furious lashings of the storm which had so nearly swallowed them all up. They had shivered and coughed in their borrowed blankets, thawed themselves with hot liquor. Three days of warmth, rations and rum had restored their bodies if not their minds. None of them had managed to sleep a full night without waking up in sweat-drenched terror, lashing and kicking in their hammocks like the lost souls of Bedlam as they relived those vile moments on the deck of the pirate cutter.

Now they sat grim faced and red eyed, paired on the worn thwarts of the longboat and wrestling with the unfamiliar oars. Pip Rowe turned to his neighbour, a silent, heavy-boned boy about his own age. The boy rowed like a man possessed, his stepping-stone spine stretched beneath his sweaty shirt. William crouched on the thwart behind, struggling to keep pace with the furious youth. He dipped the heavy and awkward oar into the turbulent water in an ill-balanced bid to match the youth's colossal strokes. Swale, perched at the tiller, had to hold on to the gunwale to steady himself as the boat pitched in the slow swell. Pine peered down the rocking boat at the grey-faced crew.

'Caleb,' he called. 'Caleb!' The startled boy looked up sharply at the sound of his name. He wasn't used to hearing it without it being accompanied by a selection of colourful expletives.

'You're rowing too fast. Mark time with the man in

front.' The slow youngster frowned, and pulled the oar back in an exaggerated parody of Gillingfeather's determined but rather haphazard oarsmanship. Pine glanced at Swale, who raised his bushy black eyebrows in unspoken agreement. He was an odd one, Caleb, this daft pirate boy they had adopted. It was hardly surprising though, Pine mused as he made himself comfortable on the prow. He wondered how he would have turned out if his father had treated him like a runty pup all his life. This madman Cruickshank obviously hadn't spared the rod but he'd certainly spoilt the child. Taken aboard the *Messalina's Purse* when he was little more than a toddler, he had been at the mercy of his drunken father's despotic rages. Hounded and heckled through his denied childhood, he had seen sights which would have cracked the most tranquil and sensible of minds. Beaten and abused, the clumsy boy had been unable to complete the simplest task to his father's satisfaction.

Caleb had found himself huddled below decks with the rest of the survivors, barely comprehending the tragedy he had by some freak chance endured, sharing the rum ration with the men his own father had hurled overboard.

William had been the first to recover his voice, glaring at the shivering stranger in their midst.

'I didn't s . . . s . . . see you below,' Sparrow had stuttered, teeth chattering, his bones pulsing with brittle ice. 'Were you with us on the walk south?'

Caleb had stared dumbly at his fellow survivor, his lips forming words which wouldn't quite come. Muffet shook his gaunt head, his lank grey hair plastered around his white face like seaweed on a washed-up corpse.

'He's not one of o . . . ours,' he muttered. 'It's the ship boy.'

'Ship boy?'

'I heard the bastard captain call him d . . . d . . . down from the top. He m . . . m . . . he missed the sail, seemingly.'

Caleb nodded at the familiar terms. Terms which had been battered into him with a thousand idle cuffs and kicks.

'Made Father angry. Always mekin' 'im angry,' the boy said flatly. 'Missed the sail, see. Missed the sail, Caleb.'

The boy's blank distress silenced his fellow survivors. Pine, overseeing the distribution of the rum, had shaken his head in disbelief. The lad had missed the sail so his own flesh and blood had thrown him overboard with no more thought than he would have emptied a bucket of slops. None of his half-drowned companions could trust their tongues, staring at their tin mugs in abject misery. United by their horrific ordeal, they thawed in silence, stoked by the fires of their hate for the inhuman wretch who could have ordered such a thing. Not even the nauseating passage of the *Conqueror* could jolt them from their traumatic contemplations, their imagined revenge.

'We thought you were goners, thrown over like that. I've never seen such a thing,' Pine said as he waved Pip Rowe onto the cramped quarterdeck. All eyes were fixed on the galley boy as he braced his legs, balancing a steaming tureen of broth. The young lieutenant distributed rough wooden bowls to their frigid blue fingers, but hesitated before offering one to Caleb. Muffet reached over and took the bowl, handed it to the dumb boy without a word. There had been nothing more to say.

*

Early evening, and the murky waters of the Severn had given way to the brown rush of the Avon. The horizon behind them had merged with the sullen cloudline, dim glints of yellow light showing along the coastline where the merchantmen rode at anchor. Every ship was leaking light, each porthole and hatch flung open wide. The gloomy banks closed in slowly as they rowed along the quiet river, making good progress on the slowly rising tide. Pine crouched in the bow with a pair of loaded pistols in his lap. He nodded to Swale as they negotiated the swirling waters at the mouth of the Avon, and struck out hard for the Somerset bank. Swale peered over the dim fields and murky woods, trying to get his bearings. He knew the country of old, but had been away a good while now. It was three years since he had shared a bed with Lisbeth, his handsome wife. With luck, he'd snatch a moment or two with her now.

'Another mile or so and we'll round the bend, coming up to the gorge,' he told the young officer fidgeting beside him. 'There's a ferryman of my acquaintance, he'll know the score.'

They rounded another broad loop and saw a cluster of lights and some low-slung cottages on the Somerset bank.

'Pill Ferry,' Swale said, turning the tiller to bring the long boat nearer the shadowy destination. 'This is where we'd pick up the pilots, in peacetime that is. Ship oars, boys, and quietly does it,' he called. The boat grounded softly on the glutinous bank, and Swale slipped over the side, up to his knees in the sucking mud. He waded off as quietly as he could, clambering up the bank toward the dim lights. The crew crouched quietly on the benches, gradually becoming aware of the dull thumps and rumbles on the horizon. Swale was back in a moment to tell them what they had already guessed: Bristol was closely besieged, but had not yet fallen. The ageing ferryman had followed the sailor down the bank, hardly bothered by the thick mud which closed about his bare shanks. He held a lantern aloft to illuminate the silent crew of the longboat, and clicked his tongue in annoyance.

'Gwoar, Davey Swale, 'alf a dozen ain't goin' to turn the odds,' he sneered indignantly.

Swale ignored the old man's remark and nodded upriver. 'The Cornish have closed in on the south, Rupert 'isself's on Clifton Down. Peter 'ere,' he nodded to the cantankerous ferryman, 'reckons they called on 'em to surrender this morning, but Fiennes sent 'em off with a flea in their ear.'

'Good for him,' Pine called enthusiastically. 'We're in time, then.'

The ferryman frowned miserably, and pointed a crooked finger to the east.

'Three mile or so further on they've dug in their damn guns. Half the bliddy merchants have turned their coats, sold their ships out to the blasted prince.'

Pine looked up sharply. 'Sold out? When?'

The ferryman spat into the slowly oozing mud around their feet. 'Eight of 'em slipped anchor, got out of the harbour with a bare hour to spare. Your gunners must have been dippin' their bliddy wicks 'cus they just let the buggers go merry as you like!'

The lieutenant cursed under his breath. The *Conqueror* had unknowingly anchored alongside the rebel fleet for six hours! One shot across their blasted bows and the lousy cowards would have struck their colours all over again. He ground his teeth, thinking quickly. Maybe they would catch the turncoats on the way back – if God granted them a way out of this damned gorge.

Pine peered upriver, the surly Avon writhing black along its muddy channel. Desertions and mutinies. What could all their bravery achieve if the merchants who bankrolled the war behaved like rats leaving a sinking ship? Damn their faint hearts.

'The last of 'em tried pulling out first thing this morning. Cap'n Stanton of the *Mercy*, d'you know the man? Got in close as he could to the Zum'zet bank and took shelter under the King's guns. Sittin' pretty they are, waitin' for the town to fall. And fall it will if those bliddy gunners are all as is 'oldin' the walls!'

The lieutenant pondered this unwelcome intelligence.

'We've a second-rate waiting for the tide. Is she going to get in or not?' he asked the surly old crank.

The ferryman spat again and rearranged his genitals in his worn breeches.

'Gwoar, I dunno, do I? The *Mercy*'s not carryin' much more than a few peashooters, and they've anchored up in front the battery maskin' their fire somewhat. If you catch the tide and put out all yer lights, you can try your luck, but I wouldn't fancy it meself.'

Swale clapped the old man on the back. 'We're not asking you, Pete.'

Pine took a moment to make up his mind, and then clambered out of the gently rocking boat. He got his balance in the clinging mud and turned to the mate resting over his oar.

'Slater, you get back to the ship and bid Captain Fey come on. We'll go ahead and scout this battery.' Evergreen Slater nodded. Pine turned to the ferryman, and glared at him with all the authority he could muster. Eighteen years versus eighty.

'If it's as dangerous as you say, we'll get back here and

hang two lanterns from the ferry post. If it's safe, we'll hang one. Is that clear?' Slater nodded again. Pine turned to the experienced Swale for confirmation of the old ferryman's trustworthiness. Swale slapped the old crock on the back and winked broadly at the officer.

'Oh, aye, sir, Pete's as hot for the cause as any round here,' he declared.

'That's not saying much,' the ferryman grunted. 'But I'll 'ang yer lanterns for 'ee.'

'Right, then, it's settled. Out of the boat, you lot, and steady as you go.'

Slater stuck his oar into the mud, and held the boat steady as the rescued prisoners clambered over the gunwale and balanced themselves in the filth.

'Off you go then, Slater, and don't forget the lights.'

'I won't, sir. Two is stop, one is come on. I have it, sir,' the old sailor nodded and pushed the long boat away from the muddy bank. The shore party followed the ferryman as he clambered up the steep bank, and paused in the yard to straighten their gear.

William brought up the rear, the cold mud sucking at his new shoes. His feet were hurting already, the blisters he had collected on the long march from Devizes still weeping adulterated blood. The ship's doctor had slapped poultices on his sores, and given him an evil-smelling concoction to rub on his toes, but a nice long rest with his feet up was what was really needed. He paused at the summit of the mud cliff, and peered toward the dull glow on the eastern horizon. Bristol was burning. His home city. All that he had known – up until that summer – bombarded with shot and shell. If they destroyed the city, they would by definition be destroying him, all his old self anyway. This was all he would have, the borrowed clothes he stood up in and the leaden cutlass he had taken from the ship's well-stocked armoury.

It seemed to William as if the war had stolen his past, made him an outcast in his own backyard. He could only hope to live, or get a living, from the war which had orphaned him in the first place. The brooding soldier stood away from the others, talking in undertones as they made ready to set off. It was the first moment he had had to himself since he had been captured on Roundway, good God, was it just a few days before? It felt like an age, as if his brutalizing adventures and terrifying ordeal had been inflicted on somebody else. The old William. He was racked with conflicting emotions: fear and rage, hope and despair. Much more of this and despair would get the upper hand for good, drive his quaking spirit out of his body and fling the useless shell back into the turbulent waters. The bewildering twists and turns which had carried him to this spot, a few short miles from his home town, were little more than a barely remembered blur. Fragmented images of night fires and sudden alarms, of hedges of pikes and great pulsating caracoles of brilliant cavalry. Galloping flat out on a wild-eyed horse for the edge of a precipice. He thought of the drunken pirate crew, wrestling with their poor prisoners on the heaving deck, laughing like madmen as they heaved their charges overboard.

By the blood of Christ Jesus, somebody was going to pay for that.

'You all right, mate?' Long Col had noticed William's silent preoccupation, and stepped on over to him.

Sparrow blinked rapidly, for one terrible moment imagining he was going to burst into tears and run off into the darkness. He was aware of Long Col's fatherly hand resting on his shoulder, calming his restless spirit as if he was a nervous horse ready for a steeplechase. Muffet shouldered the musket he had taken from the *Conqueror*'s lavishly stocked hold, and nodded encouragingly.

'I know how you feel,' he said quietly.

William swallowed hard, located his voice in the jumble of butterflies which had been rammed like black powder into his throat.

'If it wasn't for this fucking mud I'd get on my knees and kiss the ground,' he said hoarsely.

Muffet chuckled.

Rounded up and penned like cattle in Devizes, driven like sheep to the coast and loaded on to the filthy privateer like so many slaves, and then dumped overboard for good measure.

'Don't hold back, lad.'

'I won't,' William growled.

Muffet pulled at his long nose absentmindedly.

'I hadn't, you know, had a chance to thank you, for back there,' he said stiffly, as if the thought of their ordeal by sea was too powerful to be contemplated too closely.

Sparrow nodded blankly, and lifted the heavy cutlass in his right hand. The razor blade weighed a good six pounds, far heavier than the useless tuck he had carried on Roundway and had snatched away by a belligerent Cornish musketeer. He swung it experimentally, enjoying its whistle as the blade flayed the night air.

'We won't get taken like that again, Colston,' he said menacingly. 'They might beat us a thousand times, but I'm not going aboard any more slave ships.'

Muffet's considered reply was interrupted by the arrival of Ferryman Pete with a string of rough-coated ponies. It would take half the night to walk to Bristol, this way they could with luck be there and back inside two hours. The newest marines in Parliament's fleet mounted the shaggy beasts and tugged their borrowed clothing straight. Calico trousers with thin red stripes, seamen's jackets and borrowed buff coats which hadn't been cured properly and so smelt worse than the mud-caked ponies. Pine waved, and urged his mount on down the lane with a series of bow-legged kicks to its hairy belly. Ferryman Pete stood in his yard and watched them trot off down the lane. Bliddy madmen, the lot of 'em.

BY

THE KING ROAD,

BRISTOL, 25 JULY 1643

If it hadn't been for Swale, Pine's patrol would have gotten itself hopelessly lost in the tangled allotments and gardens fringeing the village. The veteran sailor might have been out of place riding the shaggy pony, but he knew the quickest ways over the dark dewy fields and through the dripping woods, and led the intruders to within earshot of the enemy positions without mishap. They had steered away from the filthy road, expecting it at least would be well guarded. By the look of the sleepy village, though, Swale's cautious approach had been unnecessary. They could have marched along the deserted main street with a twenty-piece band at their head for all the notice the Royalist troopers seemed to be taking in their backwater billet. It was only the fragrant presence of a score of cavalry horses hitched along a trampled fence that convinced the shore party the enemy were present at all.

They retraced their steps to the bottom of the row of allotments, and dismounted in silence. Pip Rowe held on to the greasy lengths of rope which had been pressed into service as bridles. Swale shook his head in bewilderment.

'Well, they're here, but God knows where,' he whispered. 'The battery'll be further along toward the river, but you'd have thought they'd have had an eye on the place.'

Pine hunkered down beside his nervous patrol, glanced at their barely recognizable features.

'That's their lookout,' he said quietly. 'I counted twenty-two horses, so they're hiding up somewhere. We'd better not leave them in our rear, if we've got to go on down the road.'

Swale nodded in agreement.

'Drive the buggers off,' Billy Butcher piped up from the shadows.

'Drive those bloody ponies off, we'll keep the horses,' William modified.

Pine waved them silent. 'He's right. Pip, you stay here with Robin and Andy.' He nodded at two of the younger men, Wiltshire farmboys who had thrown in their lot with Waller and been thrown overboard with the other prisoners for their trouble. 'Get their horses out of that garden and hitch them nearer the wood.'

Swale pointed out the cluttered lane which would lead them back the way they had come.

'We'll go on, and leave two more men at the other end of the village. If there's trouble, you'll hear it. Get back to the ferry and warn the ship. Two lanterns, remember?'

Pip Rowe nodded, his eyes glistening with nervous anticipation. The three youngsters watched the rest of the patrol double back towards the sleeping village, Swale leading the way like a great bearded gun dog, a pistol in one fist and a cutlass swinging in the other. Muffet and Butcher marched with muskets ready, followed by Lieutenant Pine and William Sparrow with drawn swords. Caleb had a stout club – all that Pine had decided the boy could be safely trusted with – and Gillingfeather ranged along in the rear, ducking and diving behind hedges and bins as if every shadowed cottage concealed a hundred and more mad Cavaliers.

'Where are we going now? The water's that way!' Muffet hissed, as Swale diverted them from the weedy path which ran parallel to the main street and led the way down a narrow alley. He paused beneath the peeling shutters of a particularly unkempt hovel.

'This is my house,' Swale hissed angrily, his bushy beard framing his small red mouth. 'If you'll wait a moment I'll ask my Lisbeth how the land lies.'

Billy Butcher blew on his smouldering match, eyed him suspiciously.

'We wait 'ere while 'e pops in and slips 'is missus one, is that it?'

Swale bristled up in front of the saucy Londoner, but Pine patted his shoulder reassuringly. 'A minute here might save us ten later, but be quick and quiet, Davey, for the love of God!'

Swale nodded, stepping quietly along the alley and slipping around the side of the careworn cottage. Muffet followed, taking up a position at the corner. Butcher slipped across the dirty street, and crouched in a lopsided doorway.

William was about to ask Pine how long they were planning on staying in the middle of the enemy-held village when the peace was shattered by a loud thump and a crash. The cottage wall bulged and the hiding men were covered in flaking plaster.

'JEZEBEL!' Swale roared from the interior of the quaking hovel. The astonished patrol heard a scuffle, and a pistol shot cracked the night. Pine cursed under his breath and doubled down the alley. He emerged into the street just as the door behind Butcher was dragged open with a loud creak of rusty hinges. Butcher ducked to his knees, musket ready, as Pine raised his pistol and fired. An enemy trooper in a flapping shirt clutched at his chest and fell back inside his gloomy billet. Butcher swung his musket down the street as shutters and doors were flung open and the alerted Cavaliers bawled the alarm. Muffet fired, and ducked back into the alley, waving Gillingfeather and Caleb along with him.

'We'll go round the back or the buggers'll cut us off,' he hissed, leading the way back down the alley. Sparrow was about to follow when he heard a muffled crash of crockery from within the cottage. Swale! He wrenched the shutters from their lousy hinges and peered inside the gloomy cave. A shadowed figure ran from right to left, closely pursued by another.

'You fornicating bitch!'

Swale, all right. William doubled along the wall and around the corner, and was knocked down by the wild-haired madwoman in the gaping shift who rocketed out of the open door and sprinted off down the street. Bullets whistled over her screaming head and thudded into the dirty road at her bare feet, bringing her to a shuddering halt in the middle of the desultory firefight. Swale bounded out of the cottage like a rabid bear, and bore down on the senseless woman in righteous wrath.

'Billeting them is one thing, Lisbeth, lyin' backwards for the bastards is another!' he roared.

William paused in the doorway, watched the burly sailor gallop down the road after his handsome wife. She gripped her shift around her thighs and sprinted off down another alley, closely followed by the irate seaman, bawling obscenities. There was a groan from within the hovel, and a patter of hands on the cold flagged floor. William raised the cutlass and peered into the room. He saw a thin man in a baggy shirt crawling from the overturned bench near the dying fire, patting the dusty corners as if he was searching for something. Another man lay huddled on the hearth, either dazed or dead. William strode across the room toward the groaning fugitive, tripped on an overturned stool and measured his length over the floor. The stranger scrambled into the corner, hiccuping and spluttering in his terror. William jumped to his feet, kicked the stool across the room in fury. He stepped over the cowering cavalryman, who caught his breath and sneezed violently. In the gloomy half light, William could make out shiny snail trails of snot over the man's downy moustache. The enemy trooper wiped his nose in his sleeve, and looked up miserably at his conqueror. His red-rimmed eyes widened in recognition.

'You! The bastard with the piebald!'

William squinted, and recognized the pinched features of Bella's old beau, the Royal Wool Gatherer himself.

'Telling. That's three times I've floored you, you prickless wonder!'

Undaunted by his half naked and unarmed state, Telling roused his strength and tried to push himself up from the floor. William kicked him back against the wall and lowered the wicked point of the curved cutlass to his rival's running nose. Telling sneezed and cursed pitifully. Sparrow chuckled, felt the anger ebb from him like a slow tide. The Cavalier captain glanced up at the suddenly thoughtful Roundhead, and kicked out as hard as he could. His bare foot caught Sparrow on the side of his knee, and tumbled him over the corpse sprawled over the hearth. Telling prised himself to his feet and leapt through the bare doorway into the adjoining room. Sparrow got to his feet with a curse, and strode after the unarmed fugitive. He saw Telling bend over a heap of bedclothes, trying to wrench a sword from the dead fingers of the slaughtered cavalryman whom Swale had caught abed with his wife.

Sparrow had met Ned Jacobs very briefly earlier that summer, when Telling's patrol had ambushed Sir Gilbert's wool wagon on the high road over the Mendips. Jacobs had been among the unlucky ambush party, a bandy-legged little braggart with bad teeth. Sparrow wouldn't have recognized him now though. Swale's cutlass blow had cut the impish face from its white skull, the remains of his features hanging like a bloody pancake from the side of his head. His lifeless body was hanging half in and half out of the rumpled bed, his dead arms reaching for the sword he had leaned beside the bulky dresser. The sheets were splattered with bucketfuls of his blood. A great crescent of gore over the badly plastered wall a red question mark behind his shattered head.

Telling whirled around, the blade free in his right hand. Sparrow brought the cutlass down with shattering force as the Cavalier raised the borrowed sword to parry the killing stroke. He diverted the heavier cutlass but staggered back with a grunt, exhausted by the effort. His bare feet tangled in the sheets and he fell against the bloody wall, cracking his head. The young captain slid down the wall and came to rest on the floor, smeared by his corporal's sticky blood.

'Christ Jesus, what's happened?' Pine called, running through the devastated room and coming to an astonished halt in the doorway. Sparrow backed out of the room, the gorge rising in his throat.

'Swale caught him in bed with his wife,' William croaked. 'He must have brained the other and killed this one.'

Pine tugged him out by the sleeve of his borrowed coat.

'Come on, then. The rest of them seem to have run

for it. They must have thought there were hundreds of us.'

The pale lieutenant dragged the hulking soldier out of the cottage, and waited in the front doorway as the rest of the patrol trotted back. Muffet, Gillingfeather and Butcher were already reloading their muskets with quick precision, their eyes running up and down the deserted street for signs of the fleeing enemy. They had caught three men staggering out of the back doors of the dreary hovels, and a fourth squeezing his way out of a back window. The fleeing Cavaliers hadn't made it to their tethered horses.

'Where's that idiot Swale? He could have got us all killed,' Pine cursed fluently.

Muffet snapped his musket to his shoulder and aimed down the alley. A youngster hurried along into his sights, looked up with a small shriek of fright at the jumpy patrol.

'Pip! I told you to stay with the horses!' Pine called hoarsely, recognizing the young galley hand. The boy looked as if he would fall in a faint at any moment.

'We heard the shots! We moved the horses further over to the wood,' he explained shakily.

Pine clapped him on the shoulder, and looked up to see Swale trotting back down the street with the boy Caleb at his heels like a two-legged hound. The sailor looked sheepish as he stood averting his eyes from his comrades' furious glances.

'They're off down the main road,' he muttered apologetically. 'And my missus with 'em.'

'Back to the ship, Lieutenant?' Muffet suggested. 'It won't be long before they realize they've been duped.'

Pine glared balefully at the hitherto trusted Swale, shook his head grimly.

'You've got us into this mess, Davey,' he said threateningly. 'You get us out. I want a quick way to this battery, right now.'

Swale, wise enough to recognize a lifeline when it was being offered, nodded eagerly.

'Right. Down the hill awhile. Pip, you take those horses along that wood till you join the road. We'll come back along the bank and meet you there.'

Pip nodded and raced back up the alley. Lights were appearing in the slovenly hovels as the fearful residents peeked out to see the damage. Their unwanted house guests had run for their lives, but they'd be back all right. They could already hear trumpets in the distance, dull clangs around the sleeping camps. Pine ground his teeth in agitation, nodded Swale to lead the way. On through the growing tumult to the battery by the river.

Jacob Kreutzfeld hadn't heard the alarm, but he had certainly felt the kick. He sat up with a start, his blanket unpeeling from his bulky body, and squinted at young Walter, the powder monkey. The boy signed the alert, and stepped back as the big German gunner threw off his blanket and crawled out of his narrow leather tent. He had brought it with him from Germany, a handy little bivouac which could be stowed into a small pack and carried with ease. So much more civilized than sleeping under the hedges, which was where most of his gun crew had been forced to find shelter. He peered over the black water toward the brightly burning horizon. Red-hot shot had ignited houses in the mean streets beneath the battered walls, illuminating the forts and redoubts for all to see. Plumes of white smoke showed over the gunports as the garrison kept up a determined – if rather ill-aimed –

bombardment. Jacob frowned. A waste of powder, firing blind in the middle of the night. Not one ball had landed within half a mile of their newly completed battery, and he had retired for the night ready to rise early to give them a taste of their own medicine. Soldiers were hurrying around with spluttering torches, apparently unaware they had stored ten barrels of powder in the adjoining pit. The bunker's rubble walls had been reinforced with soaking wet sandbags and a thick leather tarpaulin had been stretched over the roof, but the sparks were still too close for comfort. He grabbed one of the frightened troopers, snatched the torch from his trembling fingers and hurled it away into the gently lapping Avon, where it sizzled out in a tiny plume of vapour.

'Have a care for the powder!' Walter screamed, catching on at once. 'There's powder here, you fucking idiots!' the youngster screeched on behalf of the lumbering gunner. The alarmed troops stopped in their tracks, and disappeared on a dozen errands into the surrounding night. The alarm had brought Colonel Potts from his billet in a netsman's cottage a way along the bank. The sleepy officer was strapping on his sword over his bare shirt as he marched up to see what the commotion was about.

Half a dozen half-naked cavalry had sprinted into their laager as if all the fiends of Hell were after them, pointing back the way they had run and screaming that the Roundheads were upon them. Potts strode into the agitated mob, cuffing the most distracted troopers into shaky silence.

'Roundheads? They've made a sortie across the water?' Potts cursed under his breath. Those double-dealing merchants were behind this, he thought furiously. All that fuss about changing sides had been a complex cover for a night attack! He could have told them this would happen, allowing those scoundrel turncoats to come and go as they pleased, changing their minds like the weathercocks they were!

It had been a bitterly frustrating day for the hard-working gunners, obliged to stand idly by while the complex negotiations continued under their noses. They had watched in agitated frustration as the lone merchantman had weighed anchor that morning, and flounced out of range of Bristol's guns. The fugitive vessel had promptly run aground along the Somerset bank, cravenly taking refuge beneath the newly dug Royalist batteries. The gunners had shaken their heads in resentment as gaggles of officers and civilians had gone to and fro throughout the day, boatloads of local gentry hurrying between ship and shore to complete the sordid negotiations. The stranded vessel, the aptly named *Mercy*, had been no more than a clumsily handled intermediary – the real prize lay seven miles downstream in the King Road.

Potts had heard the merchant fleet had been loaded down with plate, money and commodities of all sorts, as well as the families of many of the leading merchants. What a set of rascals, fair-weather rebels who hadn't even had the courage of their convictions. They had run out on the garrison, but the poor fools seemed determined to stick to their walls despite the defection of their betters. Potts had shaken his head in disgust, and been tempted to turn his guns on the lousy sloop anyway.

Later that same eventful morning, Prince Rupert had sent a trumpeter in to Fiennes to demand his immediate surrender. At least the Governor was made of sterner stuff than the merchants. He had politely declined to give up the treacherous, ungrateful city, until 'brought to more extremity'. Good for him, for making a fight of it despite the cowardice of the grasping tradesmen.

Now, though, it seemed to him as if Fiennes might have put one over on the besieging forces. Those blasted merchantmen could have been loaded with his best troops – delivered to the enemy-held bank in perfect safety, they had clearly doubled back through the screen of cavalry for a night attack!

'With me! With me! Fetch your arms!' he shrieked, desperately excited and determined to nip the unworthy attack in the bud. 'Mr Kreutzfeld, to your guns, please,' he called to the dozing German, blinking like an owl in his nightcap. Walter translated, and Jacob grunted a question in his strangely distorted and heavily accented English.

'He wants to know what the target is, sir,' Walter said.

Potts pointed a trembling finger at the *Mercy* lying along the bank, the masts starkly silhouetted by the fires burning bright over the water.

'The sloop, of course! They've landed a party from the boats and they've worked their way around behind us!' Potts declared. He drew his sword and shouldered his way through the mob of confused and befuddled troops, leading the way down the bank toward the river. At least two dozen armed men pressed in behind him while the gunners set to work preparing their pieces. Messengers galloped off into the night as the alarm sounded from one billet to another, all along the bristling siege lines to the south of the city.

The sleepy defenders on the walls around the Water Fort stood to for the umpteenth time that long night, wondering if this noisy preparation was the long anticipated attack. They watched the signal fires glimmer from one horizon to another, and waited impatiently for the howling assault.

'Where are they going now?' Pine whispered. The depleted patrol had taken refuge in a stand of timber a hundred yards from the battery. They could see a big culverin and a couple of smaller sakers dug into a half-moon work, surrounded by wagons and baskets of stores. They had been on the verge of giving up their mission, seeing at least fifty Royalist troopers standing to their arms beside the formidable work. There was no way they could take on such a force, three muskets wouldn't stand much chance against thirty and more. Just then, however, a rather stout officer had appeared on the scene, shouted for order and led the company off to their left.

'They're off to guard that ship, look, gone aground on the flats,' Swale said.

The lieutenant stared in disbelief as their objective was evacuated. The battery was wide open to a sudden attack from the rear! 'They must have a powder store somewhere! We could blow the whole thing off the face of the earth!' he exclaimed.

Swale nodded eagerly.

'I'm yer man, sir. I could have got us all done in back there!'

Pine scowled at him for a moment, and then nodded. 'We'll all go in. We need to spike those guns somehow.' He cursed his own stupidity for neglecting to bring along a hammer and nails to ram into the touch-holes, effectively preventing the guns from being fired. They would have to blow them up or burn them instead.

'You and Caleb will come with me, Mr Sparrow and his

men will cover us,' Pine decided. The nervous shore patrol followed him through the bushes and brambles down the slight slope towards the riverside track where the Royalists had set up their guns. The gunners looked busy enough around their weapons, hurrying to and fro with rammers and buckets. The intruders took cover behind an unlimbered wagon and waited for a moment while a youth in his shirtsleeves hurried by tugging a pair of handsome cart horses on a rope rein. Muffet squinted over at their unsuspecting target.

'By God, Gilly, do you recognize the feller in the hat? It's that scoundrel from Roundway!' he whispered.

Gillingfeather nodded grimly.

'The deaf and dumb bastard. Taken sides with the Cornish, has he?'

'Doncher worry about 'im,' Billy Butcher promised.

Swale spied the well-fortified powder store, pointed it out to the excited officer. Pine smiled, opened his snapsack and drew out the grenades he had taken from the ship's store, plain clay flasks filled with an unreliable mixture of well-pounded powder, Greek pitch, sulphur and salt. The tops had been carefully sealed with coarse linen, and a fuse inserted through the waxy seal. Well lit and smouldering, the grenade could be lethal to everyone within a twenty-yard radius – including the bomber. They waited another moment, peering out from behind and beneath the huge spoked wheels of the stalled wagon. Swale held the grenade in his palm, and Pine borrowed Butcher's smoking match to light the short fuse.

But before the errant seaman could move Caleb had snatched the sizzling bomb and darted out under the running-board. Swale shouted a warning, inadvertently alerting the busy crew in the gun pit. Pine cursed and hurled himself forward, praying to God the others would follow.

He saw Caleb run to the leather-covered dugout to the left, duck down and lob the grenade into the narrow hatch. Swale had set off after him, while the others doubled forward with muskets ready. Pine held his pistols out as a gunner brandishing a long-handled rammer rose out of the ground like a ghoul, shouting a warning to his mates. Pine shot the man in the face and he writhed back against the rubble wall clutching his ruined mouth. The officer turned his other pistol on an open-mouthed gunner, back bent as he cradled a heavy ball. Pine fired, hitting the man at point-blank range in the chest. He shrieked, dropped the heavy round on his bare feet and collapsed in agony over the culverin's heavy limber. The three musketeers raised their guns and fired a quick volley at the rest of the gunners as they scrambled up the loose rubble parapet and tried to escape over the gabions. The turncoat German clutched his thigh, slipping and sliding back down the wall in a small avalanche of stones. Two more slumped over the basketwork emplacement.

Pine turned as more shadowy figures rose from the next gunpit along. One fired a carbine, the shot going wild. William rose from the back of the wagon, and seconded their attack. He screamed his own terror in their equally terrified faces, covering the short distance to the gunpit in seconds. He landed on two of the half-dressed gunners, knocking them over the heavy limbers. The man with the carbine swung it at his head. William parried with the cutlass and kicked the man between his bare legs. The gunner contorted in agony, flopping down clutching his crushed genitals. Another grabbed at William's leg and toppled him into the wall. Butcher leapt down into the struggle, upending his musket and laying about the survivors with the bloody butt.

Pine looked up from the captured gunpit just as Caleb's grenade went off. It was the last thing he ever did in his short, blameless life.

The sandbagged bunker with its treasure house of powder exploded with a cataclysmic roar which shook the river bank to its foundations, brought the gunpit walls toppling down in a flurry of stones and dust. The blast blew what was left of the young lieutenant clear across the devastated pit and hurled his shattered body over the cold barrel of the culverin. Muffet and Gillingfeather were sprayed with fragments of sacking and splinters of wood, blasted with ash as they crouched behind the feeble cover of the wall. Butcher was knocked senseless by a twisted piece of hooping from one of the barrels. William was hurled into the saker, badly winded, his limbs twitching in uncontrollable spasms.

Swale had caught up with Caleb as he stood like an idiot before the bunker, and dived full length to send the boy rolling down the bank seconds before the fatal blast. They scrambled back in a storm of dust and grit, and watched the surviving musketeers haul themselves from the demolished pits. Lieutenant Pine had taken the full force of the blast. His face and chest had been scorched black to the bone, his boyish features barely recognizable in the charred mask. The dazed intruders stared at his grisly remains for a moment until Muffet cuffed them to their senses. He pushed Gillingfeather past the smashed corpse, which slipped over the barrel and came to rest face down in the rubble. Muffet looked down at the bulging snap-sack the lieutenant had carried, and realized with horror the canvas bag was smouldering maliciously.

'Out! Get out!' he roared, scrambling out of the hellish hole. Gillingfeather lent William a hand to drag Billy Butcher away, Swale and Caleb taking to their heels toward the sheltering trees. There was a flurry of shots and shouts behind them, as the Royalist commander hurried back with his troops.

Back in the hastily evacuated gunpit Jacob Kreutzfeld clamped a hand over his spurting thigh, gritted his teeth and propelled himself toward the smouldering snap-sack. He balanced himself on the barrel of his beloved gun and bent to lift the bag from the Roundhead officer's rag-doll body. He heaved, lifting the charred corpse with it. He cursed in German, tugged the bag open and thrust his hand in to retrieve the glittering bombs and throw them into the river. One of the grenades went off with a frightful crash deaf Jacob heard all too clearly. The explosion tore off his arms and hurled what was left of him over the smoking pit. The blast ignited three more bombs, rocketing the ragged gunner and the charred body of the lieutenant around like bloody puppets. The culverin sank on its smashed wheels, fragments of spoke and lumps of smouldering rubble landing all around the ill-fated gun platform and splashing into the water twenty yards away.

William got a grip on Butcher's torn collar, and dragged the coughing youth into the trees. Gillingfeather slipped the sniper's loose arm over his shoulder and boosted him along. Muffet doubled along behind as Swale and Caleb clawed their way up the bank behind them. The returning Royalists, astonished at the hellish din, saw them running for the sheltering bushes and gave them a ragged volley. Caleb ducked down into the brambles and scuttled away on all fours while Swale took great cumbersome leaps, staggered, and fell to his knees. Muffet whacked his men with the butt of his musket.

'Run! Run, you bastards!' he screamed.

Colonel Augustus Potts stared at the devastated gun position, mouth agape. He hadn't been away more than a moment, and it had been reduced to heaps of blazing rubble! His men shouted and bawled as they dashed off into the woods after the wicked Roundhead firebombers, but he stood rooted to the spot, barely able to register the devastation they had wrought. The ship must have been another clever ruse, a trick to get him to lead his men away from the vulnerable guns. He had reached the riverbank to see the merchantman lit up like a floating ballroom, the decks crowded with half-dressed and inquisitive spectators, men, women, children and all. There was no sign of any landing party, or the boats they must have come in. He had cursed in bewildered fury, stamping along the muddy bank looking for clues that weren't there.

Then they had heard the shots behind them, and the sudden explosion which had seemed to lift the whole hill and throw it back down again in disgust. He had hurried back to his precious guns to find them wrecked, the barrels half buried in smashed gabions, leaning drunkenly on their smashed carriages. The gunners had been slaughtered or left for dead in the smouldering graves, the German master gunner chopped to pieces and hung out to dry by the exploding grenades. His fearful soldiers were hurrying this way and that, shouting and calling to each other as they closed in on a wounded survivor. The musketeers hauled Swale to his feet despite his smashed shoulder, prodded their muskets into his belly. Potts hurried after them, knocked the soldiers away from the grimacing seaman. His striped coat and calico breeches were scorched and smeared, splattered with blood. The blood of his own gunners! The colonel glared at the defiant rogue, hardly able to speak in his impotent fury.

'Where are the rest of them? He didn't do this on his own!' he snarled at last.

'Off into the woods, sir.'

'God's wounds, get after them, you miserable shits!' Potts bellowed.

A troop of cavalry cantered along the blazing path, and reined in beside the devastated gun position. Potts looked up to see Prince Maurice, his buff coat flung on over his bare chest, reviewing the situation with a Germanic sneer. He waved his troopers on down the path, and regarded the colonel with evident contempt.

'Vere did zese fiends come from?' he asked in his heavily accented English. 'Had you set no guard?'

Potts swallowed with difficulty, the sooty air catching in his throat. 'We had guards, sire,' he said hoarsely.

Maurice regarded the wrecked gunpit, his lip quivering in anger.

'We thought you were guarding the rear, sire,' Potts added cautiously. The burly Prince frowned darkly. He had thought so too.

'Vere is Capitan Tellink's troop?' he barked to a quaking staff officer.

'Further along the road, sire. In the village.'

'We've caught one of them, sire,' Potts offered, pointing out the prisoner slumped between two none too gentle musketeers. Maurice gave Swale the briefest of glances, thrust his chin out belligerently.

'A pity your men did not match his efficiency,' he said shortly.

'We'll hang the bastard as an example, sir!' Potts suggested.

The Prince wheeled his prancing horse about and pointed his drawn sword at the sooty officer.

'You have done enough for one night, sir. You'll not rob me of my honour as vell as my reputation,' he snarled. 'I shall expect to see this man with the rest of the prisoners in the morning. Now get him to the surgeon before I lose my temper!' The furious Prince jammed his spurs into the black horse and galloped off to find the errant captain who had supposedly been holding the village. And woe betide him when he caught up with the lazy scoundrel!

The depleted patrol kept to the woods, ducking behind trunks and bramble outcrops as the enemy cavalry pelted to and fro along the tracks. The feeble pursuit had been called off in the trees, the enemy musketeers apparently reluctant to get to grips with their demonic quarry. Muffet led the way through the quiet plantation, taking the long way around the wide-awake village. They could see clusters of cavalrymen trotting to and fro, the villagers peering out of their doors in fascinated horror as the bodies of the Royalist sentinels were dragged out of the streets and laid out in an alley under the disbelieving gaze of their officer. A thin youth in a torn and bloody shirt, sneezing and coughing as if he had the vapours.

Muffet and his men worked their way around the back of the village, and reached the trampled fence where the unwary Cavaliers had left their horses. The beasts had gone, all right.

'We'll have to leg it back to the ferry,' Muffet told them. They hurried behind as he led the way down the trampled path toward the dark mass of the woods, listening with alarm to the gathering tumult in the village. A clatter of hoofs as another party of horse arrived to take up their trail. Long Col followed the overgrown path further into the woods, stepping over a heap of steaming horse droppings. Good God, the boy had left a trail a blind man could read! They hurried on, and caught up with Pip Rowe a mile or so further into the wood. His nervous companions had slipped away into the night. They had done enough for one war and had sloped off at the first chance, leaving Pip struggling to hold the nervy horses. The galley hand looked sheepish as the sooty strangers strode out of the trees, nodded to the ten horses they had tethered to the branches.

'The rest of 'em took a panic and ran off when we heard that bang,' he said apologetically, looking over their shoulders for the missing lieutenant and Swale.

Muffet clapped him on the shoulders and strode to the nearest horse.

'Good lad. Good lad,' he said shakily.

Pip Rowe looked around questioningly. 'Where's Mr Pine?' he asked.

Muffet swung himself up on the bare back of the chestnut he had chosen, and bent over to retrieve the rope reins.

'Mr Pine'll be staying, lad,' he said flatly.

The boy thought for a moment, lost and alone in the middle of the clearing, and then burst into tears.

BY

THE MARSH,

BRISTOL, 25 JULY 1643

The swollen tide had crept up the broad mud banks, extinguishing the shore party's trampled tracks and carrying away the splintered wreckage they had left behind. The same surging current had lifted the *Conqueror* as if she was a biscuit barrel, and helped shoulder the man-of-war into the city docks. Crewmen who could be spared from the busy hold had manned the longboats, and had helped tow the great ship upriver.

By God, they had broken half a dozen of the port's complex regulations already, Captain Gallen Fey thought with a wry smile. Had he been negotiating the seven mile stretch of the Avon in peacetime, he would have waited for the tide at the mouth of the Avon, secured to one of the enormous stone bollards built along the bank. He would have been obliged to hire teams of hobblers – professional gangers from the villages nearby – to handle the heavy hawsers, as well as sparing a few shillings for the rough and ready boatmen who would have piloted the vessel into the city harbour. It was demanding but very lucrative work, and the only way to join their jealously guarded guild was by stepping into a dead man's shoes.

Dead men's shoes. Fey frowned at the all too apt expression, wondering how many volunteers he would be needing if and when he took the *Conqueror* home. No time to think about that now. He had to press on regardless, and to hell with the formalities of marine etiquette. Fey had been ordered to get the cargo to the beleaguered city, and that was what he meant – if it lay in his power – to do. His men might be expendable but his ship was certainly not. Fey had been instructed to save the *Conqueror* for another day rather than sink her in some bloody bid for glory under Bristol's walls. They had ventured into the river, but he was not to sacrifice his ship for a lost cause.

Fey paced the rail, calculating the risks as the crew toiled and sweated the early hours away. He had been on the poop deck for three hours now, scanning the dark banks for the glow-worm match which would reveal the remaining Royalist positions. Listening to that Sparrow character, he could have been forgiven for thinking the entire King's army had melted away in blind panic, every gun they possessed having been destroyed by the firestorm the intruders had unleashed along the Somerset bank. The scowling soldier they had pulled from the teeth of the storm claimed to be a cavalry cornet. He seemed to have inherited the command of Pine's depleted shore party efficiently enough, but could he really trust his startling report?

An entire battery wiped out, its crews killed or run off, and a troop of enemy horse scattered to the four winds? Another few boatloads like these dour dogs and the war would be won in a month! Fey gripped the rail and stared at the alleged officer as he shambled along the crowded deck. Too big for his borrowed coat, his face was as black as an African with soot and smoke. But somebody would have to see the supplies ashore, and he couldn't spare any more officers from the ship no matter how keen they were to take the fight to the enemy – on sea or on land.

They had retrieved the burly cornet's grievously reduced shore party from their lonely lookout beside the ferry. Evergreen Slater had rowed them back to the warship as she continued her majestic progress down the river, every light and lamp extinguished from the prying eyes of the alerted Royalists. Fey had known there were men missing long before the survivors had hauled themselves up the netting and slumped exhaustedly on the crates stacked under the gunwale. He had hurried down the ladder to meet them, realizing from their subdued stares their mission had not been without incident. Sparrow, their argumentative spokesman, had mumbled a brief and bloody report about their crucial scouting mission, numbed by the furious firefight they had witnessed. He had wiped his mouth and stared at his palm, repeated and then corrected himself, backtracked and sidestepped in his dry mouthed confusion. Fey gathered the vital battery had been silenced but that Pine and Swale were dead. Two more of their number had simply melted away into the woods.

'He didn't know much about it, the lieutenant I mean.'

'The lad did well,' Muffet added soberly.

'Never flinched from his duty nor his maker,' Gillingfeather said, his iron features clamped as if he didn't quite believe the good Lord could ever have wished such a wasteful rendezvous.

'And those merchant ships we saw back at the King Road?' Sparrow had added with a disbelieving shake of his head. 'Deserted to the Prince this morning, lock, stock and barrel.'

Fey had listened to their plainly phrased and poignant tributes as he stared out over the swift black waters, but wheeled back round on the dull-eyed shore party at the mention of the defected fleet. He glared at the bone-weary cornet, his white fists clenched in fury. God's wounds, they must have laughed themselves silly watching him steer the *Conqueror* past their treacherous anchorage! Danced little jigs of relief as the loyal man-of-war cruised into the river they had just fled from with such shameful haste. The sea must have turned black beneath their craven hulls! He strode around the deck, his vile temper threatening to ignite the stack of powder barrels the crew were busy hauling up from the hold.

The loss of two of his crew members had been cheapened by the hateful defection of this turncoat fleet. What was the point in such sacrifice if the gentry who had countenanced and then financed the rebellion in the first place had so little stomach for the fight? Fey felt particularly stung by the fact they had sailed right past the deserting merchantmen on their way into the channel. They had assumed the ships had evacuated women and children from the city, instead they had sold themselves like the cheapest whores to their gloating enemy. Six hours anchored alongside as if they had been bashful lovers sharing a picnic! By God, he'd finish their game on the way home. Malignants and traitors laughing and drinking while his own brave men died for the cause, he'd not stand for it.

'Well, if you're right and the battery is out of action, he will not have died in vain,' Fey said woodenly. 'Thank you, gentlemen, you have helped me make up my mind. We go on,' he said heavily.

Gillingfeather nodded as if the decision could never have been in any doubt.

' "Why are ye fearful, O ye of little faith?" ' he quoted. ' "Then He arose and rebuked the winds and the sea, and there was a great calm." ' Matthew, verse eight line twenty-six.' Fey caught the agitator's glinting eye for a moment, smiled coldly.

'I have faith, Mr Gillingfeather, but I also have a punishing responsibility to the Parliament we all serve. I cannot lose the *Conqueror*, no matter what the need of the garrison.' He paused, nodded at the crew busy unloading the well-provisioned hold. 'You men will be joining the second party, to escort the cargo into the city,' he said briskly. 'I suggest you rest up while you can, we'll be another hour yet, at least.' He touched his hand to his leather hat, and strode back towards his lonely lookout post on the poop deck. Sparrow nodded wearily, and followed his colleagues as they threaded their way through the gangs of deck hands to the relatively deserted bows. Billy Butcher set up his musket and made himself comfortable beside an old hand taking depth soundings with a lead plummet. Caleb crouched a little way off, as if a distance had opened between the pirate's boy and his fellow orphans now they were back aboard. Sparrow glanced at the boy's face, but his glistening eyes were fixed on the far bank, lost in his own private contemplations.

William's muscles were stiff and sore from the long ride. He felt drained now the savage excitement of the night's furious fighting had worn off, leaving his mind's eye free to gloat and roam at will. He couldn't help piecing together scenes he had thankfully forgotten in the heat of the battle and the fearful chase through the woods.

The Cavalier trooper slaughtered in Swale's bed, his face hanging off like a discarded mask. Pine, blown across the gunpit like a bloody rag. Swale himself, shot down and staggering, his heavy legs tangling beneath his holed body as he fell further and further behind the rest of them. They hadn't dared stop for him. One day it would be him lying in that bed, him blown across the gunpit, him falling behind his fleeing friends. He closed his eyes and tried to halt the cascade of fearful images but he could not.

He might never swill his mouth free of the war's vile afterburn, the sour and increasingly familiar flavour of battle.

William opened his eyes a few moments later and stared at the shadowed bank. He must have been asleep longer than he had imagined, because now he could see bright gouts of light on all sides, burning outbuildings and wrecked wagons. Pillars of slow smoke obscuring the stars. He looked back down the deck, and watched the crew hauling crates of muskets, cases of pistols and swords up from the jammed hold. They stacked them beside the gunwale ready for unloading. Evergreen Slater had wandered down to join them, taking a deserved break from the boat he had rowed all night. He fished for his pipe but thought better of it as he watched ten barrels of powder being hauled on deck and covered in waterlogged tarpaulins. According to Slater the crew would have less than an hour to complete the disembarkation of the precious cargo. One hour to put her volunteers and their arms ashore before riding the ebbing tide back down the gauntlet gorge.

'If we're still here break of day we'll be a sittin' target. They'll be fishing us off those flats yonder,' he predicted gloomily.

William nodded his head although he had barely heard the old sailor's summary. Muffet and Gillingfeather seemed to have fallen fast asleep, while Butcher, their irrepressible sniper, optimistically scanned the banks for a target.

'We tole you, din't we? The fire's still burning, look!' The young musketeer pointed towards the Somerset bank, the demolished gunpits hellishly illuminated by sullen flames as outbuildings, wagons and supplies continued to burn into the night. Bright beacons which lit the whole bank and the furious Royalists as they scurried to and fro.

'Looks like they're still searchin' for us!' he called.

'And they'll bleedin' well find you if you don't stow that bawlin',' Slater hissed angrily.

He followed the boy's excited gaze, chewing the stem of his pipe in agitation as he studied the battered battery. Well sited to command the harbour basin, the guns would have blasted them out of the water before they had gone another cable.

'Mebbe you boys did all right after all,' he allowed grudgingly.

Captain Fey raised his glass and studied the isolated merchantman stuck fast on the starboard bank, gangplanks laid to connect it to the land as if it was to take part in some Royal review. Maybe it would at that, maybe King Charles himself would ride down the bank waving to the turncoat merchants, throwing handfuls of coins to the mutinous crews. He scowled at the heavily laden merchantman, the slim black superstructure starkly revealed by the flames crowding behind. Only a fool would have taken a well-loaded vessel so close to the mud. In their haste to get out of range of the castle's guns, they had risked running aground on the notorious spits and banks which laddered the tricky channel. Now they had thrown open every hatch and porthole, crammed the sloop with lights and lanterns like some witch ship, luring the unwary into its oaken embrace. He glanced aside, noting with satisfaction his first officer was ready and waiting at his elbow. A good man, Rhodes, even if he hadn't shown Pine's restless spirit. Fey would miss the lad, they all would. Pine had been a shipping clerk in the bustling East End of London, before he had joined the mad flock to Parliament's colours. He would have to get word to the boy's poor mother. She had cried and wailed as he had trotted up the gangplank back at Chatham. She'd have something to wail about now, all right. Fey frowned, and quickly shut the thought away.

'Mr Rhodes, roll out your guns on the quarter-deck, forecastle and poop, but quiet as you do it, sir!' he whispered. There would be little room for powder, match and shot while they were trying to unload their cargo, and the gun-crews from the main and lower gundecks would be needed elsewhere.

'Longboats to boat oars, we'll tow them the last mile.' He held his finger to his pale lips. 'And pass the word to the men. No firing until I say so. We'll slip in as far as we can and hit the treacherous buggers on the way back. Is that clear, sir?'

Rhodes saluted, and slipped down the ladder to the busy hold.

'Mr Late, bring her into the port bank if you please, steady as she goes.'

The silent mate turned the whipstaff to his left, easing the prow away from the unwary merchantman across the river.

Another hundred yards of steep dark bank slipped by, Mr Late adjusting their silent passage with an occasional clench of his fists. They followed the broad bank as it curved around to the north, and suddenly the whole of the city opened up before them, rearing above the broad river like the gateway to hell itself. A horrific panorama of fire and flames, searing smoke and shrieking shot.

The broad walls were girdled and illuminated by dozens of isolated blazes, as if some demon had strode along the perimeter flicking a fiery whip and setting fire to his ragged footprints. The turf bank had been holed and patched, scorched and shaken, but as far as the speechless crew could see it had not yet been breached. The long wall ran up and down the surrounding hills, the summits crowned with defiant redoubts which kept up a one-sided battle with the Royalist batteries on the escarpments opposite.

The *Conqueror* glided into the inner harbour, the black waters splashed and smeared with blooming explosions, the silent reflections of the firework displays which cartwheeled across the night sky. Fey felt the subtle change in the current as they passed the mouth of the swift River Frome, emptying into the broad bay from the north. He looked up and saw the slim spires of half a dozen churches, the grim tower of Bristol Cathedral encircled by flaming buildings around College Green. The hellish din had grown in intensity. Whistles and shrieks, the sudden staccato crash of falling walls and toppled chimneys. They gazed forward into the heart of an inferno of shot and shell, shattered masonry and grubby smoke. Directly before them the rivers divided about a broad tongue of low-lying land called simply the Marsh. Scattered hovels crouched beneath bleak warehouses, bounded by cobbled quays and crisscrossed with lousy lanes and rubble-strewn alleys. Outcrops of stunted lilac and bramble dissected by the three roads built to carry the merchants' wares across the wasteland and up to the bustling heart of the city. A skirting wall had been built across the neck of the Marsh to divide it from the built-up commercial centre beyond. It was through this smoke-clogged maze of alleys and gutted halls that the *Conqueror's* shore party would have to haul the vital cargo. Powder, ball, muskets and match and all.

The shore party had been divided into two groups. The first was made up of roughneck deck hands who would bowse the supplies ashore. This would require the rigging of a light cable from the yard-arm to the quay, from which they could sling the cargo using a block and tackle – letting gravity do the work of tired muscles. The first party would port the goods as far as the gated wall and then hurry back to the ship. The second, smaller group was made up of well-armed volunteers who would escort the goods into the city, and stay behind to assist the hard-pressed garrison. Sparrow had prised himself to his feet and was taking a quick head count. Some of the original volunteers had taken one look at the burning city and swapped their muskets and cutlasses for a barrel or a case. In and out was one thing, staying behind in this devil's kitchen was quite another. Sparrow's depleted section shook themselves out and checked over their weapons.

'No rest for the wicked, eh?' Muffet asked drily.

'You'd have thought we'd done enough for one night,' William agreed.

Gillingfeather bit the top from one of the wooden powder bottles dangling from his bandolier, and tipped the charge into the sooty eye of his musket.

'The wicked deserve no rest. Let them roast in Hell with the malignants yonder,' he snapped, jerking the weapon to his shoulder to take imaginary aim at the stuck sloop full of Anti-christs.

Sparrow eyed the fanatic warily. A man couldn't be expected to fight for ever, after all. They would all have to rest a while, sooner or later. The wiry little agitator glared back with his usual unblinking intensity.

'If you're tired of the service, you could always stay aboard,' he suggested.

Sparrow thrust his bearded chin out defiantly.

'I've had enough life on the ocean wave, thanks very much,' he growled. 'You can stick it, if you want to know.'

'Service afloat or on land, it makes no difference to me,' Gillingfeather replied.

The boarding party lapsed into silence as Pip Rowe trotted along with a jug of rum, a tumbler for every man going ashore. Gillingfeather waved the liquor away without a word, but William slurped his ration and the agitator's for good measure. He felt the fiery, sickly sweet liquid scour his throat and warm his bowels. Muffet drank his and smacked his lips, Butcher burst into a fit of dry coughing.

'Gor blimey, this'll rot yer guts quicker than a red-hot roundshot,' he complained when he had finally controlled the fit. The prospect of further combat didn't seem to bother the game apprentice. Muffet and Gillingfeather also seemed to take fighting and killing in their stride, a punishing but predictable routine of loading and firing, loading and firing. Sparrow glanced at Caleb, idly carving patterns in his belaying pin. God only knew what he was thinking, after the business at the bunker. There was no question of the boy's courage, but he certainly hadn't demonstrated much in the way of brains, dashing off like that with Pine's spluttering grenade. Swale had been operating to a plan, a carefully judged balance of risk and probability. The pirate's boy hadn't seemed to have cared whether he was blown up or not. A definite liability, Sparrow decided.

They had held their breath as they passed by the grounded merchantman, and were nearly halfway across the open bay when the dreaded alert was bellowed from the shadowed bank to their right. A swivel gun mounted on the sloop was dragged about and fired, the wild shot bouncing over the open water. The warning was seconded by a squall of ill-aimed musketry, as the Royalist guards picked out the stark superstructure of the intruder as she was silhouetted against the burning city.

'Mr Rhodes, beat to quarters!' Fey roared from the poop deck, breaking the tense silence on the ship. The drummed signal galvanized the guncrews, who sprang to their posts relieved the frightful waiting was over. Ten thirty-two-pounder demi-cannons along the upper gun-deck roared at once, the great ship reeling away from the tremendous recoil. The shells crashed into the busy bank, sending up great fountains of slimy mud and gouts of earth. The besieging Royalists ducked down behind what cover they could find, the officers shouting and bawling to their troops in demented fury. The swift tide and change of course had carried the *Conqueror* out of range of their small arms, and her momentum lifted the lumbering warship closer to the critical quays along the Marsh.

The shore party clambered down into the longboats which had been towed into position along the broad hull. The sure-footed sailors scampered up ladders and hurried to secure the ship to the shore, slipping the heavy hawsers over the bollards and standing back as the slow progress of the ship took up the slack. Fey watched from the poop deck as the shore party quickly rigged their cable and began hauling and heaving the barrels and cases over the gunwale and down to the quay. William stared at the burning skyline, recognizing individual buildings holed and gutted by the flames. Old haunts reduced to skulls of sooty bricks. Muffet jabbed him in the back, breaking his dry-mouthed reverie. He clambered down the netting and stepped warily over the bobbing boats. The old stone steps up to the quay had been hollowed out by centuries of use and were slimed with green weed. Sparrow slipped, clutching a handhold in the treacherous algae. He cursed, scrambling up the ladder like a monkey. He drew the cutlass and led his grim-faced squad toward a burning warehouse, the tiny reptilian windows billowing with smoke as its forgotten contents went up in flames, ignited by the red-hot cannonballs the Royalist gunners had let fly from the opposite bank. William coughed on the filthy air, tiny glowing smuts bobbing and dancing in the hot smoke. He saw a bulky figure stagger out of the ruins, waving the shore party down a narrow lane beneath the blazing mausoleum. The officer was wearing one of the older issue black jackets beneath a badly scorched buff coat. He had dipped his felt hat in a bucket of water as a feeble protection against flames and sparks, but the steam was already rising from the sooty crown. He grinned broadly, his teeth showing up remarkably white in comparison to his blackened features.

'I'm Birch. Who in Hell are you?'

'Sparrow, McNabb's horse,' William bawled over the furious crackle of the flames. 'From the *Conqueror*.'

He gestured back over the broad quay at the warship, the patient vessel dwarfed in turn by the glistening basin and the black hills beyond. Birch shook his head in amazement, releasing more tendrils of steam from his hat. His soaking wet hair leaked thin rivulets of grimy water through his sooty mask.

'We'd given you up as lost! A story to encourage the boys,' Birch replied, leading the way into the relative calm of a warehouse courtyard. Bales and boxes had been stacked high on all sides, and half a dozen broken-down wagons had been abandoned beside the warm walls. Birch coughed and spat onto the glimmering cobbles.

'We've brought powder and ball, muskets and all sorts,' Sparrow reported as the first of the rather reluctant porters hobbled into the yard and deposited their precious loads between their bare feet. Birch watched them work, a living umbilicus coiling over the quay toward the proud ship.

'You'd best keep to the road, look, they'll let you in through the Marsh Gate.'

Sparrow nodded. The gate and the taverns nearby were one of the favourite haunts of the city prostitutes. The wall protected the girls from the busybody Puritan gentlewomen on the other side and was a handy spot to intercept sailors on their way into town. William doubted any of the girls would be plying their trade that night though.

'I know it,' Sparrow said, wiping a glowing smut from his lip.

'I've had to move my lot back, got a little hot for the musketeers!' Birch went on. 'I'm going to check on that battery and I'll follow you in,' he said, giving Sparrow a resounding slap on the back. He loped off across the burning yard toward a small gun emplacement which had been built to cover the quays. The guns had kept up a steady fire against the massed batteries opposite, but the crews were tired and the small minions and rabinets were too light to counter Prince Maurice's culverins. Even as Sparrow watched the one-sided duel, the Royalist guns opened up once more, aiming for the insolent bulk of the *Conqueror*. A stray roundshot hit the cobbled quay and ricocheted into the emplacement, splintering a gun limber and pinning two men under the red-hot barrel. Sparrow watched Birch leap into the pit to help drag the shrieking wounded out.

'Pick up those boxes, we've not got far to go!' William bawled for the benefit of the latecomers. He pulled up his collar and doubled off up the deserted lane, the shore party struggling along behind him, one eye on the ship they had left behind.

The toiling, sweating and cursing crew came to a sudden halt at the foot of a set of broad, well-worn steps. The hovels seemed to have closed up around them, shoulder to shoulder as the flames cracked and ate the roof tiles and then gobbled up the dry beams beneath. The fish market was belching flames and stinking smoke into the steep steps, effectively barring their progress to the Marsh Gate. The coughing sailors set their loads down once more, looking up at William as if they expected him to take the stairs three at a time, pissing the flames down as he went.

'We'll have to go round,' he called. 'Follow the wall to the right and seek out the smaller gate nearer Bristol Bridge.' The fearful sailors took one look down the narrow street and shook their heads. Several roofs had already caught fire as the flames danced from one hovel to the next. Another hour and the whole lot would be burning behind them, preventing their return to the ship.

'You can't just dump it,' William roared, striding down the stalled column staring at their anonymous faces. 'All this way for you lot to chuck it on the fire!'

'Traitors,' Gillingfeather muttered for all to hear.

'We're no traitors, you pigeon-toed landlubber!' a brawny deck-hand shouted back. 'This is black powder, not salt fish. One spark and we'll all be goners!'

'You want the stuff, you fucking carry it,' another snarled, dropping his end of a crate of muskets onto the cobbles. Half the surly sailors followed suit, barging their way back along the street and setting off the way they had come.

'Typical bloody Jack Sprats,' Butcher called after them.

'Is that right? If it wasn't for us you lot would be feeding the gulls on Chesil Beach b' now,' one of the remaining seafarers declared. He dropped his barrel and stalked off after his mates.

Sparrow stared in dismay at the logjam of boxes, and peered back down the street after the fearful crew. The flames had already taken hold on the last hovel in the row, bursting its grimy windows in its haste to devour the wretched contents. They couldn't manage this lot through the storm of sparks and smuts blowing hungrily down the dockside alleys.

'We'll go back and get one of those wagons,' William decided.

Muffet leaned on his musket and shook his head despondently. 'And where are we going to find the horses?'

Sparrow showed his teeth. 'We're the bleeding horses,' he said flatly.

They left half a dozen of the more determined sailors to begin moving the abandoned cargo further along the street, and doubled back toward the burning warehouses along the quay. Several buildings had collapsed, the fierce heat having sucked the strength from their damp foundations. Burning rubble had gobbled up the larger wagons in the adjoining courtyard, but Sparrow picked out one flatbed trolley used to carry goods about the busy port, and bent down to lift the empty shafts. Muffet and Gillingfeather lent a hand while Butcher and Caleb pushed the unlikely contraption from the back. There was a mad screech of bursting bricks as the nearest warehouse erupted, spewing flaming debris over the entire quay. The shore party ducked their heads, sucking themselves into their coats as they redoubled their efforts with the wagon. They arrived back at the blocked stair to find the last of their colleagues about to make a run for it. Sparrow glared at them, his black-rimmed eyes reflecting the fires all around.

'What are you waiting for? Get the bastard loaded!' he roared, breaking the momentary spell. The leaping flames speeded their labour, and soon the precariously balanced cart was creaking along the street, each towering hovel blowing smoke from its windows, each chimney snorting showers of sparks. Muffet took off his hat and wafted the worst from the wobbling barrels, every eye fixed on the murderous cargo.

They dragged the trolley past the worst of the fires and met up with Captain Birch at the relatively unscathed Water Gate. He had called his gunners back from their demolished emplacement, and ordered them up to the medieval wall which divided the marsh from the built-up heart of Bristol. Birch watched them push the overloaded cart safely under the gate, and grinned at the exhausted cornet as he leaned against the cool stonework.

'Well done, lads. That little lot'll keep us going for a couple of days.' He slapped Sparrow on the back and followed the tottering officer into the city. Soldiers and civilians were running to and fro with leather buckets, extinguishing fires and soaking vulnerable roofs. Carts were being trundled down the steep streets as townsfolk moved their belongings to safer quarters and made their way down to the castle to store their valuables. The gunfire and flames had turned night into day, and most of the city seemed to be up and about. Sparrow stared at the frantic activity, bewildered by the smoke and noise and spluttering torches. Birch called a halt outside the Beaver, a busy inn on Corn Street which seemed to be doing a roaring trade despite the imminent storm.

'I reckon you lot deserve a drink,' he called cheerily. 'What'll you have?'

Sparrow couldn't think. It seemed an age, an eternity ago, that he had last drunk at the notorious den. Squandering some of the small coin his master allowed him each week on a flagon of ale and a meat pie. He stamped up the crowded steps and followed Birch into a riotous miasma of stale beer and tobacco, every bit as thick as the choking smokes they had just left. William recognized several of the belligerent drinkers present, although none of them held his stare long enough to pick him out of the sooty and bewildered mob.

'What'll it be, boys? Beers all round?'

William Sparrow gulped the frothy brew, closed his eyes in delight as the beer cleansed his parched throat. I'm home, he thought simply. Although home didn't seem an adequate word for the burning city he'd found round the bend of the river.

PART FOUR

THE CHRISTMAS STEPS

BY

THE MARSH,

BRISTOL, 25 JULY 1643

A damp and dreary dawn did little to lift Hugo Telling's sagging spirit. He was dimly aware of the dappled grey light filtering through the dripping trees, flickering across his consciousness. He didn't know whether it was a particularly misty morning or merely that his vision had been dimmed by his hateful cold. The shaggy pony's bow-legged gait hadn't helped, catapulting the snivelling youth up and down on its broad bare back. He clung on grimly to the rope reins, his spine jarred by the beast's hideously unpredictable rhythm. What was left of his pitiful troop shambled along as best they could or doubled up on the ragged ponies they had caught in the woods that dawn. Others limped along lending a hand with the more seriously wounded. At that precise and most miserable hour of his war, Telling's troop wouldn't have passed muster charging a party of saucy schoolgirls, let alone a sober block of God-fearing Roundheads. Hugo felt like death. If he had been able to concentrate for more than a moment, he would indeed have wished for its divine release from this latest cruel torment. He hadn't been the first captain to suffer his quarters being beaten up by the enemy, and he certainly wouldn't be the last, but the complete eclipse of his unit as a fighting formation would take considerable explaining. It wasn't as if he could argue his men had been severely outnumbered. There could only have been about twenty of the bastards after all. Twenty-one if you counted that hulking great oaf Sparrow. He had barely recognized the gaunt warrior, his red eyes glittering madly behind that enormous curved blade. Had he been away serving with the Turk, to arm himself in such a fashion? A typical lout's weapon, heavy, cumbersome and completely devoid of any style. He had been lucky to deflect that savage blow though. His arm still ached from the brute, almost elemental force the fellow had unleashed. And yet Sparrow had paused, held the wicked blade glinting in front of his nose when it could have been juddering through his throat. Telling realized with a start the bloody oaf had spared him. He had had the captain at his impudent mercy, and walked away and left him lying there in his feeble-minded misery. Hugo shivered at the truly appalling prospect.

The goodwife's river fever had wasted the little flesh he carried, sucked his bones and spat out his watery blood. He hadn't the strength left to grip his worthless pony, let alone stand upright unaided. His clothes were damp, blotched and spotted with blood from the hated hovel where he had set down to rest his aching body. Telling had left Cady and two other badly injured men back at the village, promising to send the surgeon as soon as they had relocated the regimental headquarters.

The pony picked its way down a crumbling earth bank which had been raked and sieved by creepers and weeds, and trotted out over the rough stones which littered the riverside track. Prince Maurice had ordered gunpits dug along the road to face the enemy defences across the water, and Telling knew the dour German wouldn't have strayed too far from their demonic bellowings. He blinked miserably at the frantic activity along the shore, and eased the ragged beast aside as a loaded wagon rumbled down to feed the hungry iron mouths of the cannon. For all their desperate efforts all he could hear was a low-pitched hum and the occasional shrill whistle. He cupped a hand over his ear and tried to clear the blockage, swallowing repeatedly as his eardrums popped and pinged. His dismal troopers sauntered to a halt and threw themselves down onto the soaking wet verges. The early morning dew had settled over the smouldering ruins on the other side of the river, quenching the dying flames but releasing a huge pall of sullen grey smoke in their place. The manmade cloud twined and writhed with the thin mist rising from the water to draw a sullen shroud over the battered warehouses and wrecked quays. The red-eyed observers on the Somerset bank could pick out the defiant forts which crowned the high ground, and the occasional slim finger of a church spire, but the low-lying wharfs around the harbour and the deep green bowl of water were invisible behind a sluggish grey curtain.

Somewhere in the tattered shroud was an enemy ship. A big black battleship which had slipped into the harbour in the dead hours of night, and blazed away at the furious Royalist gunners with every gun it carried. The King's culverins had roared in response, and the deadly fusillades had filled the sky with smoke and ash. Every officer and man along the misty river had watched in fury as their quarry was slowly eaten up – not by fire and flame but by a greedy cloud of fog. The harder they had tried to sink the intruder, the more they had stoked the smokes which had saved it from certain destruction. They had stared at the swollen shroud, willing it to lift from their insolent enemy so that they might send her steaming to the muddy bottom.

Prince Maurice hadn't slept at all. The weary crews would

have wagered he hadn't even blinked, bending down to direct the guns with his usual grim determination, as if the very presence of the enemy vessel was a direct challenge to his personal honour. He had ordered up braziers to heat the cannonballs, and sent red-hot roundshot ploughing into the billowing mists after the ghostly warship. The incendiary shells had torn through warehouses and ploughed whole ranks of hovels into smouldering heaps of rubble, but the enemy vessel seemed to have a charmed life. Their final few shots had plummeted into the water or whistled through the rigging, and before they could reload the ship's masts had been swallowed by the constricting fogs.

Prince Maurice clenched his fists, pulled at his black moustache in frustration. A sooty powder boy gave him a nervous smile, but the stony-faced German looked straight through him, his dark eyes fixed on the torn curtain, glowing with wildly blowing smuts.

'Gone, sir. Would you believe the bugger's luck?' Colonel Augustus Potts enquired, offering the prince a goblet of wine to refresh himself.

Maurice regarded him coldly.

'The tide moves at walking speed, yes? He will be in the gorge in less than fifteen minutes.'

Potts raised his partially singed eyebrows at the prince's calculations.

'And away out to sea in an hour or two, cah, what luck!'

'That sloop, the ship that was stuck on the mudflat. She has guns,' Maurice breathed, hauling himself out of the gunpit, further smearing his already filthy blue suit.

Potts sucked his teeth miserably.

'The *Mercy*. I am afraid the captain managed to refloat her at dawn, sire. He put the women and children ashore, you see . . . '

Potts looked up nervously as the stocky commander stamped his mud-caked boots in fury.

'Sir! There she is!' the powder monkey called, pointing out into the foggy basin.

Maurice took a flying leap into the pit, and gripped the rubble-strewn parapet of the gunpit in excitement as the enemy warship nosed its way into the middle of the river. The fog seemed to tear about the great black masts, picking up long streamers of sooty smoke. The captain had manned his longboats, and the desperate fugitives were rowing like demons to tow the heavy man-of-war into midstream, where the ebbing tide was swiftest. Maurice cuffed the bleary-eyed crew aside and jumped behind the red-hot saker. He ordered the hot barrel spiked and scoured to remove any debris from the previous shots. The youth with the ladle then inserted the powder into the hungry barrel, and rammed the charge home.

'And another,' Maurice snarled. Potts blanched. Double loading a cannon could in theory increase the range and velocity of the ball. It could also split the barrel and mince the unfortunate crew. The youth added the second charge and stood back apprehensively while another gunner fitted the heavy ball into the barrel and rammed it down with a dull thunk. The Prince snatched a smouldering linstock and took one last look down the barrel. The warship had detached itself from its tattered blankets and was slowly picking up speed in the middle of the river. He could hear the frenzied shouts of the mates as they dipped their oars into the smooth green water. Now.

He dipped the glowing match to the small heap of powder on the touch-hole and the heavy saker roared into life, leaping back on its creaking wheels and driving the heavy limber into the loosely piled bank of the gunpit. The gun position was wreathed in acrid white smoke, which Maurice waved away with his hat. The black balls rocketed over the smooth water and bounced between the bow of the ship and her many-oared daughters, clipping the timbered stern of the right-hand longboat. A seaman on the stern thwart slumped over his oar, his jacket and back torn open by a razor-sharp stave. Another toppled overboard into the path of the mother ship. The rest of the crew jumped to their feet as the river rushed in over the shattered stern, lifting the longboat's bows out of the water. Their brothers in the second boat stuck to their task grimly, backs bent as they took the strain. The survivors swam for the side netting their shipmates had hung over the heaving hull as their massive thirty-two-pounders roared in response. Another shattering broadside straddled the Royalist gunpits, sending up great gouts of hot mud and flying chips. A team of gunners hurrying up with a fresh supply of cannonballs were caught in the open and cut to pieces, shrieking wretchedly as they writhed in stony puddles of their own blood. The prince was drenched by a waterspout as a thirty-two-pound ball gouged into the muddy bank not ten yards away from his post beside the grumbling saker. Before they could bring the heavy gun around, the jealous wind blew up once more, lifting the escaping ship into the strong current and quickly stitching the great torn sheets of fog back about the black masts. The boiling shroud swallowed the ship once more, as if the elements had allowed the prince one shot and one alone, and then whisked the offending vessel from under the apoplectic prince's nose.

'Oh, bad luck, sir. What a shot,' the grovelling colonel offered.

Maurice was about to reply when he heard Telling's ragged pony clatter along the bank, its scarecrow rider swaying from side to side in imminent danger of being flung off. Maurice peered at the newcomer, and then scrambled out of the hole sobbing with fury, soaked to the skin and drooling for blood. He straightened up, arms akimbo, as the young captain brought the shaggy pony to a halt a yard in front of him.

'Capitan Tellink,' Maurice breathed dangerously.

Hugo lifted his trembling leg and slipped gratefully to the ground. He steadied himself against the gently steaming beast as Maurice shoved his face to within an inch of Telling's dripping red nose.

'Vot's vong vid you?' he screeched, his accent becoming more pronounced as he lost control of his notorious temper.

Telling limped from one foot to the other, trying to focus on the prince's unblinking black eyes.

'Are you drunk, sir?'

Telling frowned, tilted his head slowly. 'I beg your pardon, sire?'

'I said, are you drunk, sir?'

Telling shook his head dumbly, wishing for the hundredth time he had Cady and Jacobs with him. They always knew what to say, whether they were sweet-talking Roundhead goodwives or sucking up to some cutpurse of a quartermaster.

'River fever, sir,' he said, running a finger under his nose.

'River fever? River fever slaughtered your men and drove off your horses?' Maurice snarled.

Telling's skull shone through his translucent skin as he mumbled apologies.

'Six dead, sir. Three wounded. The enemy patrol drove off our horses.'

'And where were your guards?'

'Run off, sire,' Telling croaked, ordering up a full battalion of lies in a desperate rearguard action against the pop-eyed prince. 'They fell on us at midnight,' he offered feebly.

'Fell on you? They fell over you, you mean!' Maurice snorted, white with rage. 'You were drunk, sir, sleeping off your debaucheries with some village woman! There is no need to deny it, sir, I had it from her own lips!'

Telling swayed against the snorting pony, his mind awash with horrifying possibilities. The wretched woman had bleated her story to the prince! God damn Jacobs for talking her into bed! It had been the death of him.

'You set no guard on your camp, sir! Caesar would have fed you to his dogs!'

Caesar might have sent his poor centurion to the sickbay, Telling thought crossly.

'I was sick, sir. I had left orders that guards were to be set. River fever . . . '

Maurice clicked his dirty fingers for all he thought of river fever, and shoved the tottering officer to one side to stare at his bemused troopers.

'You have ruined my troop, sir. A whole troop! What am I supposed to do with these scoundrels?' Maurice snarled, his waxy figure fixed on the bewildered captain.

'There was no warning,' Telling mumbled. 'I tried to get them out . . . ' His sore throat rubbed like sandpaper, his hands vibrating at his sides as if he was a saucy boy caught in an apple orchard.

Prince Maurice, a few short months older than his wretched victim, had no time for excuses, no time for trifling inconveniences like river fever.

'You're out!' he hissed. 'Out out out, do you hear me, Tellink? Major Atkyns will take over your troop.'

He strode past the fearful captain and snatched the reins of his horse back from a nervous groom, and spurred off down the dismal track. Telling blinked dumbly, not quite sure whether the boorish prince had been addressing him or some horrible doppelganger that had risen out of the mud like a ghoulish shade. He turned in confusion to his men, chattering like magpies amongst themselves now the demon prince had cantered off down the track.

'Atkyns? That candle waster?'

'They say he's a right tyrant!'

Telling's cloudy vision darkened by the second, the perimeter of his vision narrowing as if he was peering out of a musket barrel. His ears whistled and his teeth ached, his heart pounding like an overstretched drum inside his wheezing chest. Out? What did he mean, out?

Prince Maurice was still fuming over his shattered troop when he arrived at the handsome town house on Pine Hill which had been selected as the Western Army's head-quarters. He left his horse in the bustling garden and took the steps three at a time, noting with annoyance his brother Rupert had not yet arrived, and with even greater annoyance that the doddering Marquis of Hertford – his theoretical superior – was not even up yet. He snatched up a pile of ink-smeared dispatches from the scrofulous clerk in the hall, and digested their news as he strode down the hall towards the dining room. He found the comfortable chamber wreathed in tobacco smoke horribly reminiscent of the fog which had stolen his prize away not an hour before. Buck, Slanning, Porthcurn and Basset were already present, other senior officers had been sent for. Maurice glared at them, lounging about swishing the dregs of the previous night's excesses around in fluted goblets. One grenade in that reeking room and the Western Army would have collapsed like a decapitated pullet. They were veterans all, equally at home in the splendour of a requisitioned Roundhead mansion or lying under a hedge with their men. Every bit as tough as the Cornish troops they commanded, and with good reason. The Cornish were the most mutinous crew in the entire army. His infantry commanders lapsed into giggling silence as Maurice strode about clicking his heels and drumming his fingers on the mantelpiece.

The door opened at last, releasing a stream of smoke into the corridor. A fearful maid carrying a tray of empty tankards down the hall gave a tiny cry and dropped the pewter mugs to the floor with a nerve-racking clatter. She swooned against the wall as Rupert strode into the room with his usual manic scowl. The Cornish officers clambered respectfully to their feet, but the six-foot general of horse ignored them, making straight for his brother. He tore off his gauntlet and held out his hand, which Maurice clenched with dogged devotion. He muttered something in German, and Maurice nodded sheepishly, reduced once more to mere mortality by the drop-jawed arrival of his elder brother. Rupert lowered his forehead and gave his sibling a gentle nod, an oddly touching greeting for the reputed Prince of Robbers.

'Where's Hertford?' Rupert snapped, breaking their reverie in an instant.

Maurice raised his eyebrows toward the stuccoed ceiling.

Rupert frowned, and tossed his hat onto the cluttered map table.

'Well, we've got them penned up like drunken hogs,' he

said quickly, running his index finger around the black-inked siege lines on the spreadeagled chart. 'All we need to decide is whether we're going to sit it out or get in after them.'

It didn't take the council of war too long to decide on the latter course of action. Scipio Porthcurn had risked their everlasting scorn by pointing out the ground on the southern side of the city would be ideal for a more cautious approach, mining and trenches and so forth.

'The soil's soft as butter, and the walls are higher on our side,' he had argued, looking from one unblinking prince to the other.

'Well, they're a damn sight lower on our side, and the ground's like rock,' Rupert countered. They looked up as the door creaked open and the elderly Marquis of Hertford limped into the room, supported by half a dozen simpering servants and cawing surgeons. The white-haired old buzzard nodded gruffly.

'You've started, then,' he muttered. 'Sorry I'm late, touch of the gout you know.'

Rupert and Maurice eyed each other significantly. Porthcurn marvelled at their shared perceptions, it was as if they could communicate by thought alone, warlocks in arms just as the scurrilous Roundhead pamphlets maintained.

Gallen Fey had lost count of the guns which had been wheeled out against him, the laughing crews working like furies to reload their wretched pieces as his battered ship ploughed on through the slowly shredding mist. His own crew matched them ball for ball, scouring the fuming barrels of their thirty-two-pounders and ramming home new charges before the previous shot had hit its target. Not that any of his bleary-eyed officers could tell whether their broadsides were impacting anywhere near the invisible enemy positions. The frantic gunnery kept them busy though, and took their minds from the hellish passage downriver. God knew they needed some distraction from the nerve-racking escape, or they would have been leaping overboard like rats, and swimming to the miserable fog-cloaked shore.

'Captain Fey, sir!' Rhodes yelled from the smoky pit of the gundeck. He was waving his hat furiously to attract the scowling master's attention. Fey leaned over the rail as his first officer pointed furiously towards the mast.

'The cliffs, sir, we're in the gorge!' Rhodes bellowed as the enormous cannons rolled over the bloody decking. Fey looked up sharply, and made out the merry chain of lights which stretched along the dark cliff, illuminating the enemy artillery positions. The ship was a hundred and fifty yards below the commanding heights, tucked in beneath the grim cliffs. The furious gunners couldn't lower the elevations of their guns to register such an awkwardly positioned target. Little by little, the enemy bombardment died away astern, the last wild shots sending up angry spouts of brown water.

'Very good, Mr Rhodes!' Fey yelled. 'Recall the boat crew, if you please!' They had already recovered the survivors of the first crew, who had been thrown into the water by the chance shot from the Somerset bank. The terrified oarsmen had scrambled up the netting and shivered in the smoke-racked lungs of the mother ship while their colleagues in the second boat toiled like slaves to tow the *Conqueror* into the main channel.

Fey watched from the pock-marked poop deck as the

second crew boated oars and slumped at their benches, the longboat slipping alongside the battered warship like a young whale nuzzling its mother. The exhausted oarsmen had barely enough strength to haul themselves back on board, but a flurry of ill-aimed musketry from the northern bank soon persuaded them to one final effort.

'Cease fire, Mr Rhodes!'

'Aye, sir.'

'Mr Slater, I want a complete damage report and a list of casualties. Mr Late, you'll steer us for the King Road if you please. I believe we have some unfinished business with those whoreson merchants!'

BY

CHRIST CHURCH,

OXFORD, 25 JULY 1643

With those handsome braggarts Rupert and Maurice up to their stiff German necks in the trenches outside Bristol, lesser mortals like Anthony St John Dyle had flocked to the King's high-spirited court to revel in His Majesty's undivided attention. Well, perhaps not quite undivided attention. There were after all whole battalions of velvet-smothered courtiers and entire troops of buff-coated buffoons waiting in the wings for an opportunity to earn the King's fickle favour. The miserable princes usually stuck beside their uncle like wasps round a jam pot, offering their interpretation of any information laid before their sovereign, and substituting their own opinion where they could. They were untouchable, unassailable. Every victory they earned helped swell their already enviable reputations and cement their unquestioned status as His Majesty's right and left hands, his most trusted and reliable servants.

Clavincale would generally have needed steel-reinforced elbows to barge his way to the King's closely guarded side, but tonight he had deployed a secret weapon. A totem so powerful there were few men (real men at any rate) who could have withstood such a diversion. An irresistible force which would have brought even the mighty Rupert to his knees.

Bella Marguerite Morrison.

He silently formed her name, rolling the smooth syllables around his mouth with his moist tongue. A deceptively demure name for such a fiery, passionate creature. Clavincale prized a maidenhead above all things, never mind the lass to whom it belonged. Thin or fat, tall or short, lady or maid. He had had his choice, the pick of the bunch from Oxford to Antwerp. Some cried with cramps, some howled like cats, but he would thrust away like a battering ram, and frequently black out with the intensity of his climax, collapsing in a dead faint over their assorted breastworks.

Bella, though, she had been different. At first he had been disappointed, was she going to give up her virginity with the same lumpen astonishment as some parlour girl? Lie there staring over his heaving shoulder as if she was spying out the cobwebs?

No she wasn't. She had endured his initial rasping attacks as if she had been taking the measure of his abilities, coldly calculating his performance as if she was minded to award him marks out of ten. Then she had come alive, thrust him back on the bed as if he had activated some infernal appliance, a shamelessly fascinating Venetian apparatus he had heard his cronies boast about.

'Not so fast,' she had breathed huskily, further inflaming his already ardent affections. She had turned him over and sat astride him as if she'd been trained in the arts of love by a bow-legged Parisian courtesan, and flogged him past the winning post like some jaded jockey. He had been catching up with his disturbed sleep on the coach back to Oxford when he had become aware of her fumbling in his breeches, and opened an eye to find the girl bunching her skirts about her bare midriff, her underwear discarded under the seat! A living breathing masterpiece leaping from its wooden frame to twine itself about his astonished face.

He felt himself blushing again, and ran a pudgy finger around his constricting collar as he watched the throng of hangers-on manoeuvring in the narrow cloister which ran around the busy quadrangle. The eager flock had been gathered from all over the overcrowded town, packing into the gradually narrowing arteries and capillaries of old stone which radiated in all directions from the vaulted heart of the venerable college. The main hall, the heart of Christ Church, which had become the King's official throne room.

Clavincale tugged at the girl's limp hand, leading her through blustering packs of wolfish noblemen, belligerent bishops and second-rate soldiers – quick enough to strap on a sword now the Princes weren't about to call their bluff and put their military prowess to the test. Bella tugged her hand back, insisting on making a dignified and serene entrance to the packed court.

'There's no time for that now, my dear, just stick close to me and kick anybody who puts so much as a toe in front of yours,' he advised over his shoulder.

'I can't see a thing from back here,' Bella complained, standing on tiptoes to peer over the flamboyant crowd of gaily turned out toadies. Clavincale glanced at her once again, and almost swooned. She was hot and excited, her perfect complexion enticingly flushed without resort to the cosmetics favoured by many of her jealously staring rivals. They had rouged their nipples, altered the necklines of their dresses to reveal a tiny strawberry suggestion. Bella had scorned the Oxford fashion, and tucked her unquestionably superior breasts away as if they were too good for such vulgar exhibition. Her gown had cost him twenty guineas, the jade ear-rings and heavy choker a further ten, but the expenditure had been well worth it. She looked stunning. The jewels set off her hazel eyes, and the finely fingerable bones of her chest and shoulders. The choker accentuated the slim and graceful lines of her neck. Tendrils of hair which had escaped from her imperfect coiffure coiled about her pretty pink ears. It was all he could do to stop himself leaning over and taking a bite out of her there and then! Her skin was outstanding, several shades darker than that favoured by the Oxford matrons, who preferred frosted limbs and translucent shoulders. She turned every head in the hall, from the bored serving boys in their crested tabards to the most fabulously appointed commanders in their lawn and lace. From powdered whores who had been pressed into service on some drunk's arm for the night to the glittering damsels who fluttered about the royal couple like superb birds of paradise, fantastic butterflies from some unspoilt rain forest.

'We won't see them from here,' she whined, frantic she would miss her chance at court after waiting so patiently all these months.

'The trick is to let them see you,' Clavincale explained, nudging some joker in a hunting outfit. The raven-haired rogue in the outlandish garb glared over his padded shoulder at the intrusion, his thin mouth creased in irritation.

'My Lord Clavincale, reduced to scrimmaging with the likes of us now?' the man snorted in a strong but melodious Scots accent.

Clavincale nodded a greeting as Bella huffed and puffed herself a narrow chasm alongside her lover. The Scots laird's china-blue eyes flickered from Clavincale to Bella, and remained fixed on the girl as his narrow mouth widened into a broad and winning grin.

'Tell me it's your sister, Clavincale, and I'll give you the keys to my hold at Strathcraigie, aye, and the salmon stream and all!' the dark hunter offered.

The portly nobleman was becoming rather tired with the attention his companion was attracting. Making an impression was one thing, courting half the blades in the kingdom was quite another.

'And what brings you here?' he asked waspishly, deciding against introducing the beauty to a notorious roué like Ross Dunblane, Laird of Tullymallock.

The Scots laird tapped his cruelly hooked nose, refusing to take his bright eyes from the girl.

'The usual. Feuds and factions, factions and feuds. Will you not—'

'Sorry, Ross. Pressing appointment and all that.'

'Where are you staying? I'm at the March Hare, what a sty, but it was all I could get!'

'We're at the Rainbow,' Clavincale replied, shouldering a passage through the bad-tempered stampede toward the royal couple.

'The Red Hart, not the Rainbow,' Bella corrected, giving the handsome Scot a discreet smile.

Dunblane raised his bristling black brows, stretching the unusual white scar beneath his eye. The young Scotsman fingered the puckered skin.

'Lochaber axe, the dog caught me with the hook, but wished he hadn't a moment later! Where did ye say ye were staying, miss?' the laird asked, touching her arm for a moment as Clavincale hurried her away, deeper into the rock pool of precious people.

'Morrison. Bella Morrison. We're at the Red Hart. It's not too far . . . '

'Will you be back . . . '

The Scotsman's call was lost in the growing tumult as Clavincale propelled his prize through the jealous throng, nodding to his many acquaintances bent on the same mission. He sidestepped and shoved his way to the front of the queue, a rank of smugly smiling old fogies whose white hair and crooked backs hadn't prevented them from picking the best spot to intercept the royal couple as they made their way to their table.

The King and Queen of England, acknowledging their loyal servants with gracious waves and smiles as they negotiated a gauntlet of adulation, meandering along toward their waiting supper.

Bella stood on tiptoe, and peered over Clavincale's stooped shoulder. She saw a slightly built unprepossessing Scotsman with thin legs and a forked beard. He took small, precise steps as if he was afraid he might slip, his small white hands patting his wife's slightly darker fingers. The Queen was even shorter than her husband, but she seemed more solid somehow, made of sterner stuff than the melancholic monarch.

So this was who all the fuss was about, Bella thought. They radiated calm, every moment measured and dressed with plain, unaffected dignity. She couldn't call anybody to mind who had ever exhibited such single-minded serenity. Her father would gush and pant and bluster over the slightest trouble, a broken barrel, a spoilt sheepskin. Here was a king who had almost lost his kingdom, who had been chased out of his own capital by his impudent subjects, and yet he seemed indifferent to everything but radiating glacial calm as his fawning courtiers clustered about him.

Clavincale held on to Bella's arm, feeling her smooth flesh flushed with expectation. He leaned over her bared shoulder, and renewed his acquaintanceship with her delightfully provocative fragrance.

'Don't go to them, let them come to you,' he hissed. The perfumed dandy had been a familiar player at the excitable court long enough to know when to speak, when to strike and when to cut some imposter dead with a superior sneer. Bella, anxious she had come so far and would get no further, looked imploringly at him.

'Watch the Queen's fingers carefully. See how she leads him along? A quick pinch and on again?' Clavincale whispered against her delicate rose-hued ear.

Bella watched closely as Henrietta Maria, the Catholic Spitfire herself, steered the King from a slack-mouthed marquess and on down the hall. The diminutive couple stepped closer, great ladies with ridiculously elaborate hairpieces struggling to keep their backs straight as they curtsied, their husbands or lovers bowing low and causing a panic in the pressing rear ranks as the swords they had worn for the evening skewered unsuspecting crotches. The Queen's eyes flashed along the waiting ranks, choosing her husband's course like a ship's captain over rocky ground. Bella caught her eye for a moment – surely she hadn't seen her in the crowd – and the Queen looked away, tugging her husband over to the eager courtiers ranged to their right. She squeezed Clavincale's pudgy hand, then glared at him as he tugged her behind a marble pillar, hiding her from view as if she was a gap-toothed old crone. The slightly built Scots laird slipped into his place gratefully.

'Let go of me, what do you think you're doing?' Bella hissed at her patron's maddening manoeuvres.

'She's seen you, don't worry, my sweet,' Clavincale

replied with a wink. The royal couple seemed to spend an age with the choleric earl opposite, receiving his petition with rapt disinterest. Henrietta Maria gave her husband a gentle tug, and escorted him toward the gracefully fluted pillar. The Queen looked at the crowding faces, expecting to find the beauty who had caught her eye. Instead she found Ross Dunblane, Laird of Tullymallock, grinning like an undernourished pirate. He bowed deeply, and straightened up to find the Queen peering over his shoulder. Clavincale eased his companion forward, and bowed as low as he was able. The Queen recognized the nobleman, one of her allies in the increasingly acrimonious campaign between her faction and Prince Rupert's for the ear of the King. While the princes were away fighting, she generally held sway. When they returned her rapacious advice was often ignored.

'My Lord Clavincale.' She showed her small white teeth, but there wasn't even the slightest flicker of warmth in the smile.

'Your Majesty, I am honoured you remember your humble servant so. May I present Miss Morrison, eldest daughter of Sir Gilbert, the wool factor?'

Henrietta Maria turned her bitter-almond eyes on the blushing girl, who curtsied clumsily. She noted her unfashionably tanned skin and cheap paste choker around her taut throat, but knew true beauty when she saw it. Beauty a man would fall over his boots to win. Beauty a man would sell his soul to possess. A useful ally, then. A handy tool in her never-ending war of whispers with the kaleidoscopic cabals which ran the court. The Queen gave the girl a scorching smile, and tugged her husband alongside to meet the beaming couple.

'Clavincale! We've certainly m–m– we've missed you

these last fe–fe–few weeks,' King Charles stammered quietly, smoothing his forked beard with his free right hand as if he would massage the words from his troubled throat. 'How was your t–t–t–trip?'

The portly lord bowed, straightened up with a smile. 'Very well, sire. The West Country merchants, of which Miss Morrison's father is a crucial co-ordinator, have jumped at your proposals. If you could spare me a few moments of your time I would be delighted to bring you up to date with developments.'

Charles nodded. His queen hadn't taken her eyes from the succulent creature he had brought with him. Man bait, Henrietta Maria thought shrewdly. As tasty a morsel as ever graced a hook. She was as rough and ready as a milkmaid, a diamond dug deep from the earth set off in her vulgar gown and cheap jewels. But talent like hers could be honed and trained, aimed like a pistol ball for the heart of a man. Earl, marquess, lord or prince.

'I'm not familiar with your family, my dear,' the Queen observed kindly.

'From Chipping Marleward, ma'am, my mission to the West Country included a particularly pleasant diversion with Miss Morrison's father,' Clavincale interrupted.

The Queen glanced at him, as if reluctant to take her eyes from the silent girl. A pretty face was always an asset when one was obliged to cut cards with devilish men.

'Sir Gilbert is busy raising new regiments to serve your majesties,' Clavincale went on. 'He regrets he could not tear himself away from his personal engagements to pay his respects, but affairs in the west are so delicately poised, the matters we discussed at a crucial juncture.' The King glanced at his wife, who was already tugging him along to the next toady. 'Jolly go–go–good, Clavincale. You must come to s–s–supper. Be so g–good as to have a word with Sir Edward to f–fi–finalize the time.'

The portly young lord bowed deeply.

Henrietta Maria paused, and leaned forward to whisper to the speechless girl. 'And you come along and see me in my chambers, my dear,' she said. 'It gets so tiresome listening to the men chatter on!'

The royal party swept on down the crowded hall, surrounded by blushing acolytes.

'He didna see me!' Ross Dunblane complained, turning on his heel to frown at the delighted girl and her smug companion. 'Three hundred miles and I'm sent to see secretaries.'

'Bad luck,' Clavincale crowed. 'But you've just had your first lesson at court. Don't try and catch Their Majesties' eyes, let them catch yours!'

Dunblane scowled.

'Away, man! I'm a soldier, not a speaker! Mebbe His Majesty will have more need o' me some day,' he muttered darkly.

Bella had pressed in against her beaming lover, looking up at him as if he had laid the world at her feet.

'An audience with the Queen,' she breathed disbelievingly.

Clavincale wondered what the fickle Henrietta Maria could want with the girl, but smiled benevolently.

'What did I tell you? Her Majesty doesn't grant such favours to every girl on her first visit to court.' Not unless she had something in mind for them, he thought.

Bella blinked, overawed by the heaving crowd and the dizzy excitement of it all. Why hadn't she spoken? Why had she stood there like a dumb serving girl while Clavincale blustered for both of them?

'She asked me about my family,' she said slowly, turning her embarrassment onto her more worldly companion.

'And I stepped in before you gave the game away, my dear.' He reached down to pat her bottom familiarly. 'The King is well aware of your father's previous, er, dispositions. Your brother caught on Roundway in arms against him, it's hardly likely to endear him to you, is it?' he snapped. The girl was here to hang on his arm and make him look good, to smile and curtsey when she was told, not question his mastery of court etiquette.

The surly Scotsman hadn't paid any attention to their whispered debate, lost in his own gloomy assessments. He perked up again when Bella brushed past him. 'Ah, Miss Morrison, are you off for your supper now?'

'Mind your own business, you lecherous heathen,' Clavincale advised, rather hotly.

'Heathen, is it? Heathen's all very well until you need saving from this Parliament of yours,' Dunblane answered. 'Another year or so and I and others like me'll be esteemed Highland gentlemen, aye!'

Clavincale tucked the girl behind him as if she was at risk from the laird's flashing good looks.

'We'll take care of our own Parliament. Haven't you heard the news? Waller smashed, Essex immobilized by typhus, Bristol about to fall like a ripe plum? By God, man, the war's as good as over!'

The Scotsman's lip hovered under his hooked nose. 'Ye reckon so? I've two thousand swordsmen in my glens, waiting on my word. They don't seem to think it's finished, not by a long chalk!' The rangy laird in his curious highland plaids and leathers manoeuvred himself into Bella's sight, walking in circles to keep up with her.

'I'll mention your name to His Majesty for you, put in a good word,' Clavincale offered, wishing the wild-eyed barbarian would make himself scarce. He guarded his prize jealously, achingly aware he would be the talk of the town tonight. The envy of all these sad-eyed pot-wallopers and second-rate soldiers. They were a formidable team, Bella with her looks and him with the brains. Captivating the Queen as well as her gullible guests.

He had been chewing over his next move since they had got back, pondering his future as he watched the girl climb into her new dress. Her eyes had shone with gratitude, she hadn't realized the favour she was doing him, how his stock would rise on the back of the rumour and gossip of the jealous court. But she was no fool. One day she would realize she could go it alone, swim these dangerous currents by herself and leave him high and dry. There was no shortage of young blades ready to whip her away from him. For the first time in his young life, Anthony St John Dyle needed something more than it needed him.

Clavincale coughed, coming to a decision at last. He inserted his bulky body between Bella and the lecherous laird, leaned over to whisper in her bewitching ear. 'Bella, my dear. Would you marry me?'

BY

PINE HILL,

NEAR BRISTOL, 25 JULY 1643

The soldiers had used the bramble-choked ditch as a latrine, cutting gaps in the needle-sharp coils with their blunted swords. Mary Keziah, imagining they had evacuated the neat dugout behind the hedge as some sort of defensive work, straightened up at once with her hands clamped to her mouth. Why hadn't she smelt it before she had clambered down the crumbling bank? The stench was strong enough to floor a horse, and her unwary tread had disturbed a cloud of bluebottles which circled her in annoyance, rattling her senses with their incessant buzzing.

She turned away toward the towering hedge and retched over a squad of drooping dockleaves, thin strings of yellow spittle hanging from her slack mouth. She had felt giddy on the road, but not as bad as this. Perhaps it had been the strain of the walk, a good six miles from the inn near Keynsham where she had spent the night – and the last of the money Lord Clavincale had packed her off with. Well, there goes my breakfast, she thought, straightening up slowly and blinking rapidly to clear her thick head. The weary maid hoisted her skirts and pulled herself back up to the rough track, rubbing her hands vigorously on her mud-splattered cloak. She reached inside her dirty woollen tunic and felt the reassuring crackle of Clavincale's letter safe beneath her fingers. She had already produced it half a dozen times at various checkpoints and military headquarters along the road, although none of the King's officers seemed to have heard of her elusive quarry. Surely they would have remembered a five-foot Italian surgeon and his numskull patient? The soldiers seemed more interested in her than in her mission, and she had been forced to rap a number of them on the knuckles for their insolent suggestions. All the lecherous rogues could say with any certainty was that the Western Army had crossed the river and was approaching Bristol via the southern suburbs. There had been some desultory fighting at the bridge and the wounded had been sent on to the army headquarters in commandeered wagons.

'You want to find the surgeon, that's where he'll be,' a grubby trooper in a tight green coat had told her. 'No place for a girlie, though, you stay back here with us,' the drunken dragoon had suggested with a wink and a gap-toothed leer.

Mary Keziah had hurried on down the road, lost among the flotsam and jetsam of the advancing army. Wives and children, carters and hawkers, pedlars and whores. A noisy, argumentative rearguard in looted coats, their bare legs black to the knee with caked mud and clay.

She had felt the first waves of nausea a few miles back, a sour ache in her belly which had given way to a series of ever more painful cramps. Another mile further on and she had made a dash for the ditch, emptying her stomach into the soldiers' improvised sewer. She thought she must be sickening for something. Perhaps the eggs she had eaten for breakfast had been off. Mary Keziah wiped her mouth and trudged on up the hill. She was halfway to the top when she made out the faint rumble and thump of the guns. Not far now, she told herself.

The Cornish soldiers sat around the surgeon's unlimbered wagon, bleeding quietly into their filthy dressings as they waited their turn under the knife. A burly pikeman with a ball lodged in his ribs bit a length of old leather rein as the surgeon eased his scalpel beneath the mauled lead bullet, and gouged it out with a loud plop. Ambrosio di Meola St Corelli bent over and retrieved the ball from the trampled grass as the pikeman spat the wad out with a curse.

'A spent ball. Your buff-acoat took the worst of it,' the surgeon said in his heavily accented English, examining the bloody ounce in his palm. The pikeman picked the misshapen round up and nodded grimly.

'It still 'urt like buggery,' he growled.

'You'll live.' The surgeon strode over to the wagon, and selected a large stoppered jar from the rack of pots and potions he carried with him. He tipped some of the evil-smelling concoction onto a rag and held it to the oozing wound. The pikeman winced as the mixture got to work.

'By God, that's worse than bein' shot in the first bliddy off,' he hissed. Ambrosio stoppered the bottle and tucked it under his arm as he made a brief tour of the bloody crowd. Most of the injuries seemed to have been caused by shell splinters or spent balls, missiles fired from the lively garrison over the river. The bullets hadn't caused many serious wounds, indeed, the Cornish soldiers could consider themselves unlucky to have been hit at all at such extreme range. He looked up as a pale girl in a flapping cloak made her way down the line of groaning and muttering men, stepping carefully between their outstretched legs.

'Mr Ambrosio, is it?' the girl asked him.

The Italian nodded. Some goodwife come to reclaim her injured husband, no doubt. She produced a crumpled letter from her gown and passed it over with a small curtsey.

'Lord Clavincale's compliments, sir,' she added, as the surgeon held the brief note in his bloody fingers, and digested the spidery message.

'James Morrison. Si, si, Master Jamie,' he said quickly, gesturing toward the wagon. 'He is much better today,' he said, taking the girl by the arm and guiding her through the bloody waiting area to his bulky mobile surgery. A shaven-headed assistant sharpening knives on the running-board looked up with a grin.

'I know you, don't I? Kilmersden Hall, am I right? You remember, sir, couple o' weeks ago now, after the fight at Chewton?'

Ambrosio glanced at the tall but rather wan girl, and shook his head.

'You know, sir, the girl in the blue dress. The one with the . . . '

'Ah, si si, I remember her now,' Ambrosio said, clicking his bloody fingers.

'I'm her maid,' Mary Keziah said flatly. 'I'm looking for Mr Jamie, her brother.'

'Brother?' the surgeon exclaimed, taking another look at the crumpled note.

'Jamie Morrison, Miss Bella's brother. We was led to understand he was with you,' she said nervously. Had something happened to him?

The assistant dropped the knives into a dirty leather bucket and nodded around the back of the wagon.

'Ain't exactly got his sister's way with words, has he?' he

asked, scratching his black stubble. Mary Keziah gathered up her skirts and followed him behind the wagon.

Jamie Morrison was squatting on a shaft, rocking back and forward like a child on a swing. His hair had grown, a mass of matted brown tangles stuck with bits of straw and feathers. His chin was covered in gingery down, a growth he would have been proud of, showing off back at home. They had taken his clothes away and left him in a dirty shift, thrown a thin blanket around his twitching shoulders. He had been tied to the wagon with a loose hemp rope, like some mangy cur fond of running amok about the camp. Mary Keziah had to bend down to examine him, to satisfy herself they had the right man. They had the right man all right. Jamie stared at the worn boards as if he was reading closely printed script. His red-rimmed eyes flicking from one bent nail to another.

'What's wrong with him?' she asked over her shoulder.

The assistant sighed. 'Don't ask me, lovely. He's the expert.'

Ambrosio strode along the wagon rubbing his hands on a towel.

'Say good morning, Jamie.'

'Good morning Jamie, baa!' Jamie recited without taking his eyes from the intriguing panelling.

'James, it's Mary. You know me, don't you?' Mary touched his shoulder, horrified by his wild and unkempt appearance. James had always been so fastidious about his clothes, he had refused to join their rough games in the woods for fear of ripping his breeches or dirtying his stockings. Here he was now, a drooling maniac in a borrowed smock.

'Where's his clothes?' she snorted.

The assistant rubbed his stub nose thoughtfully.

'Made a bit of a mess of 'em. Besides, that was a damn good buff he had on.'

'What about his shirt? His breeches?' Mary cried.

'Shat 'em. He can't help it.'

'His mind is locked up like an orange in a box,' Ambrosio told her, clenching his fist in front of his thin face. 'He has no sense of anything. He cannot feel pain, cold, heat . . . '

'Well, how long'll he be like it?' Mary Keziah demanded, staring at the pitiful creature.

'Well, that is the question. Sometimes, a blow on the head, in some precise spot, will break the lock and set him free. Sometimes, the mechanism will seal over altogether, lock his mind away for good.'

Mary closed her eyes, wondered what horrifying amusements they had practised on the poor wretch to come to such a conclusion.

'The colonel at Devizes was going to march him off with the prisoners, I persuaded him to see reason,' Ambrosio said smugly.

Reason. Reason?

'You've read the note, he comes with me,' Mary growled, straightening up in front of the bemused surgeon. He frowned, his black eyes searching her pale face. The girl did not look at all well.

'You know of some other doctor, some surgeon who will trepan him?'

'Trepan him?'

'Open his skull to release the fluids. His mind is swollen with evil humours. They must either be sweated out with a steaming bowl or a hot, what is your word, "pol-u-tice", or cut open and drained away like a saucepan of your lovely turnips.'

Mary Keziah clamped her lips together and tugged the note out of the surgeon's hand. 'He's coming back to his family. We'll look after him.'

'Yer bloody welcome to him, miss,' the assistant said cheerily.

Ambrosio shrugged. He had enough to do with the other wounded to spare any more time on the foolish youth. He had hoped he would be able to unravel some of his drooling mysteries, but he had neither the time nor facilities to undertake such a study.

'Take him. We've done all we could,' he said casually, adding something under his breath in Italian.

'I'll take him, you bloody butcher. T'weren't a mark on 'im till you got your hands on him,' she snapped, dragging the floppy youth to his bare feet. She tugged at the coarse rope, picked at the knot in agitation. The crop-haired assistant looked from the flustered girl to the weary surgeon, but his master appeared to be in one of his more indulgent moods.

'There are marks on him you will not see,' Ambrosio said resignedly. 'He is past your help, my dear.'

'We'll see,' Mary growled, easing her arms round the bony youth's shoulder.

'Baa! Baa!' Jamie called, the muttering Cornish squatting around the wagon silenced by his pitiful distress. Screaming and groaning they could live with. Losing a limb, an eye or an ear was a hazard they had all learned to accept. But losing your mind, reduced to being spoon-fed and arse-wiped by some maid, scared them stupid. They looked away as the determined girl carried the daft boy back toward the busy road.

*

Jamie seemed full of life, springing along beside her or bounding up the verges to peer at the fields beyond. The farmers thereabouts had either sold their livestock off to the armies or hidden their cows and sheep away, and so the green slopes seemed peculiarly lifeless after the frantic activity in the camp. Mary wasn't alone on the road, however. Bands of ragged soldiers seemed to be wandering at will, while furtive individuals could be spotted hurrying along the hedgerows, hungry for their homes. She paused to get her breath, looking back over the vast bowl formed by the rearing green hills. A dirty pall of grey smoke hung about the city, highlighted here and there by a sudden puff of white as the besieged forts sullenly bombarded the advancing Royalist lines. The slim spires of half a dozen churches speared through the drifting curtains, as if they were oblivious to the shots and shells. Perhaps God had crossed his invisible fingers in front of the vulnerable towers, to protect them from the raging, man-wrought tempests. He would surely punish those who turned guns on his own houses, she thought. She stared at the distant, dull green walls as they trembled under another shattering broadside, and wondered where William could have got to. Taken prisoner on Roundway and marched off with the rest. The rest? Half of them seemed to have changed sides, her own brothers amongst them. Why hadn't the stubborn bugger seen sense like they had, and made his peace with the King's men before it was too late? The rich counties of Somerset and Wiltshire had been all for the Parliament this time last year. Now it seemed King Charles and his terrible cousins had scoured the rebels out, chased them and penned them up in Bristol like so many sheep.

William was no rebel. Not one of those troublemaking bishop-bothering loudmouths like the ranters she had seen in Parliament's forgotten army. She could barely credit it. A few short weeks ago she had been marching with them, strolling through the psalm-singing encampments and marvelling at the number of finely equipped soldiers General Waller had led. He'd led them up that bloody hill all right, and left them there for dead. She shuddered at the memory, those broken men and dead horses heaped at the bottom of the cliff.

'Baa!'

Jamie's croaking call caught her wandering attention. She glanced round at the youth as he trotted out in front of a creaking cart, his arms swinging by his sides in the shit-smeared shift. The driver pulled up sharply, cursing the idiot dancer as he jigged about frightening the horses. Mary strode out after him, grabbed the shift and tugged him back.

'Bliddy fool there, jumpin' out on folk like a March hare!' The cantankerous driver shook his fist at the girl.

Mary frogmarched the daft youth to the side of the road and looked up sourly. 'Hold your water, you old pot-walloper. Can't you see he's hurt?'

She glared up at the drowsy occupants who had peered over the side of the wagon to see what the fuss was about. Mary Keziah was about to offer them some spicy advice when she realized with a start she recognized them. At least, she thought she recognized them. Miss Bella's blushing captain, wasn't it? Looking as miserable as sin in a dirty old coat and a greasy felt hat. What had he done with his fine coat? Kingfisher-blue velvet with a startling red sash, according to Miss Bella. He'd fair made her mistress's eyes water in all his rainbow finery. He looked as if he had lost a few stone since the last time she had seen him, and all. Pale as a roach's belly, his slit eyes rimmed red as if they'd just been cut in his cheesy skin. His batman wasn't any better either. He was lolling uncertainly on the bench beside his master, an enormous bandage tied about his head. The maid scowled at the silent pair.

'It's Captain Telling, isn't it?'

'Not any more,' the youth said miserably, wiping his nose on his dirty sleeve.

Mary Keziah decided against any further enquiries. She smiled shortly, peered down the rough track which dropped away between the hedges and followed the Wells road over the hill opposite. By God, she had a fair way to go.

'You wouldn't be heading my way would you? Back to Kilmersden?' she asked wearily.

Telling shrugged. 'We might as well. It's all the same to me,' he moaned.

Mary helped Jamie clamber up beside the surly driver, who eyed the mad youth warily.

'He's all right, is he? He ain't going to throw a fit on me or nuthin'?'

Mary Keziah hauled herself up into the wagon, the sad-sacks in the back making room for her.

'He'll be all right. Had a bit of a bang on the head like your man here,' she reassured him.

The driver nodded, and clicked the reins. Telling and Cady lolled alongside each other, pointedly avoiding eye contact with the girl as she made herself comfortable.

'Well, we're a fine crew ain't we?' she asked. 'Sick as dogs or mad as hatters, I shouldn't wonder.'

Telling glanced at her for a moment, and then hung his pale head over his hollow chest. Mary clicked her tongue and nudged the driver.

'Do you know Kilmersden Hall at all?'

'Oh, I know it a'right,' the driver replied. 'I used to drive for Morrison, had a place down them parts. Wouldn't pay yer the steam off his piss, that bugger.'

Mary nodded.

'He'll pay you for this journey, mark me,' she said smartly. 'That's his son sitting alongside of you. Back from the wars with his head all wrong.'

Telling looked up sharply, and watched the mad boy jabbering to his feverishly flexing fingers, as if he was clutching a handful of butterflies.

Telling stared at the hedgerows for mile after mile, lost in gloomy imaginings. He looked up every now and again to steal a look at the wild-haired lunatic bleating beside the driver. Morrison's boy home from the wars. He tried to picture his own mother and father, waiting anxiously at the gate as they brought him home to them. Brought him home like that. He had imagined losing his troop and being relieved of his command had been the worst thing which could ever have happened to him. He had conjured his own death, run away like a beaten cur rather than endure the shame and humiliation of the contemptuous camp.

Now, looking at the wretched creature on the running-board, he felt a thousand times worse, hideously ashamed of his own insignificant troubles. Pride and position, it didn't count for piss.

He didn't dare look at Mary, fidgeting and muttering on the creaking bench in front of him. He didn't want the girl seeing him cry, and crying was just about all he had left.

The fog which had helped deliver the *Conqueror* from the fearsome gauntlet of the Avon gorge swirled thicker and thicker around the creaking warship until Fey could barely hear the hoarse shouts of the boy lying along the bows, casting and retrieving his greasy lead line.

Three fathoms. Two fathoms. Three. The shoals and sandbanks crowded around the mouth of the Avon like sharks around a blood bucket, their grating teeth ready to snap up the barnacled timbers of the ship. Rhodes sweated over the charts, tracing a dirty fingernail along what he thought and prayed was their current course. Fey couldn't blame the first officer for his befuddled reckonings, he could barely keep his eyes open himself. They had all been drained by the nerve-racking night, and were ready to drop at their posts. A moment's relaxation however, one second's inattention to the precarious passage, and the *Conqueror* could be lost. Washed up along the rocky coast or stuck fast in some gluepot sandbank, at the mercy of the enemy's guns.

Fey pinched the top of his nose, and wiped some of the soot from his black eyes.

Two fathoms. One.

'We're going to run aground, sir,' he said curtly. Mr Rhodes swallowed, his compass poised in his trembling fingers.

'I . . . that is . . . I'm not sure, sir, where we are, sir.' The first officer bit his lip as he caught the captain's beady eye. 'I've lost my bearings,' he said stiffly.

'Then, sir, we had better trust our ship and ourselves to God.'

Pip Rowe cast his leaden plummet again, the line going slack almost as soon as the weight had hit the water.

'Less than a fathom!' he shrieked.

BY

ST MARY REDCLIFFE CHURCH,

26 JULY 1643

The Royalist assault on Bristol had been carefully planned to follow as precise a timetable as the troops could manage. At break of day Lord Grandison was to fire his two enormous demi-cannon from his reinforced battery overlooking Prior's Hill Fort on the northern wall to signal the attack. To ensure there were no mistakes in identification the Royalist troops were to wear a sprig of leaves in their hats or a length of green ribbon about their arms, and nobody was to wear a neckerchief. The password was to be 'Oxford'. Both the Western Army and their colleagues along the northern defences were to advance in three or more columns, dividing and confusing the shell-shocked and completely bewildered garrison.

They would be over the walls before the dozy Roundheads realized they were under attack.

Scipio Porthcurn and his brother officers had spent a good hour explaining all this to their eager captains and lieutenants, who in turn had informed the elder sergeants of the gist of the plan. Reveille would be at 3 a.m. The carts, ladders and faggots they would use to negotiate the ditch and walls would be in place by 4 a.m, and the general assault would begin promptly at 5 a.m, when they heard the double blast of the signal guns.

Porthcurn had satisfied himself his men were ready, and had spent another hour or two creeping about the open ground beneath the quiet walls, trying to identify a weak spot in the broad turf banks. He had positioned his men behind Redcliffe Hill, in a barren wasteland between rows of abandoned hovels, half a mile from the oddly truncated tower of St Mary Redcliffe. The storming party which would spearhead the attack was concealed from the small enemy garrison in the church by an abrupt fold in the ground. The rocky gully offered some protection, but emerged at the bottom of the bluff within musket shot of the fortified Redcliffe Gate. They would have to break cover and turn right, hurrying into the dead ground beneath the walls before the surprised defenders could bring any concentrated fire to bear.

Porthcurn wandered back to his breezy bivouac in the pestilential shanty town behind the hill, and settled down to while away the night, fortifying himself with an occasional swig from a stone jar of cider. The fiery apple juice slowed his agitated ponderings, dismissed all his imagined manoeuvrings. Trust yourself to God, and don't worry about a thing, he told himself for the hundredth time. The enemy would break before his Cornish would.

The wild men from the moors of Bodmin and the salt-crusted Cornish coasts couldn't be doing with signals and suchlike. God knew they had waited long enough to get into this well-spread whore of a city – a Roundhead honeycomb oozing with loot.

Never the most patient troops in the world, the fighters had shot the gun, rushed the defences as if their miserable lives depended on an immediate victory. As if Bristol's dumbfounding defiance had raised dreadful questions about their own martial prowess.

The moment the slow summer night loosed its feeble hold on the sky hundred upon hundred of them had leapt out from their gullies and holes and sprinted for the sleeping walls, howling like demons and screaming oaths in their own incomprehensible dialects. There was no ordered advance, no straight line nor careful coordination of effort. The carefully synchronized plan of attack blew up at once, the sudden conflagration hurling soldiers against the damp turf barricades like razorbacked chaff flying on a fiery tempest, splinters and smuts tumbling from a raging brush-fire.

The Cornish berserkers tore over the broken ground yelling and shrieking, their vaporous breath belching from gaping mouths. Their weapons glinted in the eerie glimmer from the fiery pits which opened up before them. The mobs of men pulsed and contracted about the hidden obstacles, ran over the deserted wastelands like the wildest spring tide.

Porthcurn leapt to his feet with a curse as he realized what they were about, clenching his fists as his insomniac soldiers dashed down the narrow neck of land between the shadowed church and the abandoned suburbs. One hundred and fifty of his bastard brawlers had unleashed themselves upon their section of the walls, joined the frantic steeplechase across no-man's-land.

He snatched up his pistol and jammed his burgonet helmet over his slick black hair, peering around the empty laager. There was no sign of his ensign with the battered black colour. Sergeant Major Rice and the rest of his idiotically eager junior officers must have been overwhelmed by the surge or more likely decided to join it, shouldering their way to the front like demented boys let out of school for the holidays. Damn them all to the blackest pits of Hell!

Porthcurn doubled over the broken ground after the shadowy host, hesitating to call the buggers back now. They wouldn't listen anyway, and their premature descent might, might, take the enemy by surprise. He ran on, and immediately tripped over an outstretched wagon shaft. He measured his length on the stony ground, levered himself up with a curse. The wagon had been left behind the rickety wall of a demolished cottage. The men had spent most of the previous day loading it with bundles of lashed twigs and sticks, the faggots they would throw into the yawning ditch in front of them. They had laid their eight-foot siege ladders over the top of the bundles in a bid to flatten them down. Porthcurn cried out loud. The stupid bastards had left the lot behind in their haste to get to grips!

The apoplectic colonel hurled his pistol into the deserted wilderness, popping the rivets from his breast-plate in a teeth-grinding rage. They were gone now, it was too late to bring them back. He strode back the way he had come, cursing and spitting like a demon. The supporting party wandered up out of the dreary mist, and were about to shoot their livid commander down in hot blood before they recognized his hatchet-faced scowl.

'They've not waited for the signal,' he growled. 'And they've left the faggots behind. You'll have to pull the wagon down yourselves.'

He strode through the mob of musketeers, who turned their heads from his pop-eyed stare. Most of the pikemen had set aside their clumsy weapons, preferring drawn swords, gleaming daggers or crudely fashioned clubs. They took one look at the heavily laden wagon and tried to push on past the irate colonel. He grabbed the nearest offenders by their coats, and dragged them back with a hoarse curse.

'I said, you'll have to drag the wagon with you, unless you want to join the other buggers getting slaughtered in the ditch!' The officer's dire threats and the growing tumult from the walls stopped the Cornish in their tracks. Fifty of them crowded about the nuisance wagon, while another twenty grabbed the shafts and tugged it out from its cover. Porthcurn strode to the front of the muttering mob, and led the way down the crooked gully. He could hear the great wagon creak and grind over the stony ground, the enormous wheels thudding over any obstacles as the heavily laden wain picked up speed.

Porthcurn ran on, the crackle and snap of gunfire growing louder every step. He stepped aside as the wagon trundled by, and hauled himself over the running-board ready to oversee the distribution of the crucial ladders. From his vantage point on top of the hellish engine he could see the dark mass of the walls opening wide for them like a giant whale. Suddenly, the tower was lit up in the ghoulish flash of a hundred muskets. Now he could see the shadowy storming party milling beneath the broad turf bank, running one way and then the other as they tried to negotiate the steep ditch. To their left, the black mass of the Redcliffe Gate, the battlemented tower glowing orange and blood red as the defenders crowded behind the stonework to pour a steady fire into the stalled attackers. To their right, the turf bank stretched away to the squat pile of Temple Gate. In between, six hundred yards of well-defended walls, the ditch beneath six foot wide and eight feet deep, occasional heaps of rubbish and refuse and studded with cunningly fixed tree trunks, the branches pruned back to form a bitter barrier of sharpened stakes. The Cornish had scrambled down into the ditch or knelt down to fire back at the shadowy figures behind the defences. They couldn't get anywhere without the carefully prepared faggots and ladders they had left back at the top of the hill, but they weren't about to give up the accursed ground without a fight. Men screamed and fell on all sides, toppling into the damned ditch. Another half an hour and they could have bridged the moat with their own bodies.

Jethro Polruan reloaded his musket, cursing steadily as he tipped another charge down the hot barrel. He threw the gun to his shoulder and squinted through the belching smoke to find a target. All he could see was a black bank and shadow defenders, running this way and that with their matches glowing like will-o'-the-wisps at midnight. The musketeer to his left took a ball in the jaw, and fell to his knees gurgling on his own blood. Another ball clipped his musket barrel and slashed into the next man's arm. He dropped his musket and grabbed the spurting wound, howling in agony. Polruan felt the mob behind him break up. He thought for a moment the dogs had run, but they had merely hurried out of the way of the wagon being rolled down toward the ditch.

Ah, the wagon.

He knew they'd forgotten something! The colonel didn't look too happy either. The black-headed devil had clambered up on the speeding wain to direct operations, his panting soldiers hurrying up behind.

Porthcurn had bent down to get his bearings in the dirty drifting murk, and realized with horror their impetus had carried them too close to the wall, the deadly ditch opening up beneath them like the mouth of a conger eel.

'WHOA!' His scream of warning came a moment too

late. The laden wagon careered over the crumbling edge, the flailing shafts lancing into the bodies heaped at the foot of the ditch. The dumbstruck wounded screeched in agony as the shafts snapped like matchwood and the enormous oak wagon nosedived into the ditch on top of them. Porthcurn was catapulted from the running-board, and landed with a stomach-churning thud, spreadeagled against the turf wall. He toppled back into the ditch, hitting his head on the wain's oak rim, and came to rest on top of a pile of bloody bodies.

The reinforced storming party ignored their losses and surged forward over the debris, clambering over the obstruction lifting the ladders from the wreckage as they went. The ringleaders balanced the hastily strapped ladders against the wall, and held them steady as their comrades scrambled over to get to grips with their invisible enemy.

William kept thinking it must be a trick. Surely they wouldn't simply have run at the walls, and hopped around like startled rabbits? His improvised squad had been assigned to a length of wall adjoining Redcliffe Gate, just over the water from the burnt-out wasteland of the Marsh where they had come ashore. He knew the cramped network of streets as well as his own face, and he had spent the best part of the day wandering about his old stamping grounds, looking up his friends and acquaintances.

He hadn't been able to get into his lodgings. His master had locked and bolted the tiny squalid print shop, and all he could see through the grimy windows were loose trays of lead type, scattered about the dusty benches. The leaning shelves he would have expected to see jammed and piled with smudged pamphlets and grubby news-sheets had been cleared. Percy Greesham had always been a canny master. He had obviously disposed of the incriminating documents, the evidence his shop had been a close ally of the Parliament. William himself had helped write and produce the slanderous pamphlets, and had been a familiar figure on Bristol's streets, hawking copies at a penny or two each.

William stood back from the window and shook his head as if he had been mesmerized by phantoms, a shimmering vision of his old self. A curly-headed youth with a loud mouth and a quick pen, casting secretive scowls at his crooked-backed master. The arguments they had had in this tiny shuttered shop seemed foolishly unimportant now. The disputes over what they dared print and what they didn't, as if it mattered a damn either way. William had grown up here and had begun to assert his own opinion more and more forcefully, until the inevitable break.

He had snatched off his inky apron and joined the army. Well, Morrison's sorry militia, at any rate. He would have liked to have thought he had done it out of a strong sense of duty, that he had embarked on a sacred mission like Gillingfeather, or because he genuinely believed the running of the country ought to be a matter for more than one man. Colston Muffet said he was for a republic, that he would have no king at all. Gillingfeather said no king but Jesus, and Billy Butcher hated bishops, so he said, anyway. William had joined up in a feeble effort to impress Bella. The clearest route to the colonel's daughter was to become his right-hand man, after all. Two weeks after he had been rather fancifully commissioned as a captain of militia, Morrison had changed sides, leaving him high and dry.

Now he found himself back on his own doorstep. He seemed to have assumed command of his small squad, but nobody called him William, much less Captain Sparrow or sir. He was plain old Will, one of the lads. In it with them come good or bad, in it for ever.

He hadn't known whether to feel angry or elated, whether to tremble with terror or puff himself out with pride as he showed off his old haunts to his new friends. Swaggering down the narrow streets, the three-tiered hovels bulging like great brick toads over their heads, he had pointed out people and places he remembered.

The smoky inns seemed to be doing a roaring trade, full of shouting soldiers, temporarily idle dock hands and surly sailors. If the energetic Captain Birch could have emptied the taverns the men wouldn't have had room on the walls. The trouble was, the fickle garrison seemed to drift off and wander back at their own accord. William didn't recognize any of the townsfolk who had volunteered to defend their homes either. A slant-eyed and shiftless crowd, as far as he could make out. They had taken down their working coats as if they were terrified of getting their best suits dirty. Jammed worn-out old hats down on their heads and wandered along to their assembly areas, grumbling to anybody who would listen. The only people with any stomach for the imminent fight seemed to be the women. A formidable battalion of stern-faced Puritan matrons who toured the streets and emptied the inns, haranguing the idlers back to their posts. William had recognized old Mrs Hazzard – a notorious local busybody – and a squad of her lieutenants in blinding white aprons and bonnets, marching down the street towards some rabble-rousing rendezvous.

'It's a pity they don't arm them,' Billy Butcher had

quipped, as William steered them into an alley while the scowling amazons hurried past.

'With their tongues, they don't need muskets,' William said with feeling. The little squad had continued to the Dog and Drake, where they had used up the last of the few pence William had managed to borrow from Captain Birch. As well as a small sum to tide them over for food and drink, Birch had issued them with boots, stockings and new shirts, all that he had left in store.

'You might as well, no use letting the bastards have it new,' he had commented gloomily. The well-equipped and tipsy troopers had wandered back to the wall at midnight, and settled down to rest, huddled in their salt-stiff sea-jackets.

Billy Butcher had refused to sleep, peering over the wall at fleeting shadows.

'There's some bugger pissin' about down there,' he had reported to his dozy colleagues.

'Gah, it's a bat or an owl or summat,' Muffet said from under his hat. 'You'll know soon enough when they're havin' a go.'

They were having a go now all right, thousands of them, all along the line.

Storming parties had erupted out of the jagged trenches along the opposite slopes, a seething mass of men clawing and barging their way through cluttered ruins and ransacked gardens. An immense, shrieking horde vomiting down the broken hillsides turning the fitful dawn into a screaming nightmare of fright and chaos. Turning suburban Bristol into ancient Rome, quaking under the rushing boots of countless bloodthirsty barbarians.

The entire Western Army – veteran Cornish brawlers all –

seemed to have dug themselves out of the spewed earth with hateful urgency, undermining their frail perch on the south wall. The heathens had hurried down the bluffs, coagulated out of the shot-battered suburbs and rushed at the turf wall like an army of beetles. The defenders had leapt to their posts, feverishly blowing on their match or laying their pikes on the parapet to deter attackers. William had his cutlass ready, and had tucked a nailed club into his broad leather belt and a knife into his stiff new boot. He had peered out fearfully, watching the screaming monsters sprint toward the ditch as if they would leap like Greek athletes, jump right over the yawning chasm. But they hadn't leapt or jumped anywhere. They had come to a sudden, staring halt, shaking their fists and firing their muskets at the walls while the defenders calmly aimed and fired, reloaded, aimed and fired again.

William glanced around his section of wall, watched Gillingfeather, Muffet and Butcher pour shot after shot at the milling Cornish while Caleb and a couple of trembling townsmen reloaded their pieces, spilling powder and dropping bullets, their chins smeared and sooty, their red-rimmed eyes bulging in alarm. William couldn't imagine what the bawling attackers were hoping to achieve. They were woefully short of the wall, and for every wild shot they let fly at the bobbing hats along the parapet the defenders could return a dozen aimed shots at their furious faces. William realized with a surge of excitement they were winning. They were holding the wall! He bent down to the basket of rocks the womenfolk had thoughtfully provided along the firestep, and chose a particularly jagged flint. He threw it with all his might into the mass of stampeding Cornish.

'That's for the *Messalina's Purse*!' he shouted, demented, drunk with savagery. The others took up his hooligan chorus, loading and firing with enraged delight.

'That's for throwin' us overboard!' Butcher bellowed.

'That's for loading us in the first place,' Muffet laughed.

The others seemed caught up by the infectious killing spree. Caleb dropped the musket he was reloading and snatched up a handful of rocks. He leapt up on the firestep and hurled the missiles at the quaking crowd below, his face lit up like a fiend as he laughed and whooped with the rest.

The despairing enemy rolled a wagon down the slope at them, filled with faggots and stacked with ladders. A mad officer with streaming black hair bawled obscenities at his maddened troops. They watched the rumbling wain hurtle into the ditch, the unfortunate officer turning cartwheels into the wall. His men scrambled over the obstruction, dragging out the ladders as they came.

Hand over hand, the desperate assault parties clawed their way over the reeking ditch. Friends and foes toppled screaming into the thorny debris below. Their sheer impetus and weight of numbers carried the leaders through the obstacles, over the wagon and on to the wall itself. An ensign waved a torn flag from the bloody summit, bawling his fellows to follow. They caught their breath and surged on, determined to tip the balance, force the ill-timed assault through the tottering defences.

Gillingfeather was first on the wall to meet them. He swung his musket like a scythe, tumbling the first two wild-eyed attackers into the bloody ditch. Muffet shot down a third, who fell back into his companions crowded into the faggot-filled wagon. William clambered up on the step beside Caleb, hurling stone after stone at the frenzied logjam of bodies. A musket shot thudded into the turf in front of him. Another whistled over Caleb's head. Muffet and Butcher leapt up onto the parapet and kicked the flailing ladders away. Gillingfeather praised the Lord and jumped into the overturned cart, knocking the dazed Cornish aside. Without thinking what he was doing, William leapt after him, landing awkwardly on a half-crushed Cornishman. He pulled and tugged at his jammed cutlass, and realized the hungry blade had pierced the dazed Royalist trooper, skewering him to the splintered running-board before he had drawn breath. The wounded man had been lying haphazardly on the tightly lashed bundles of sticks, and William had jumped right on top of him. Sparrow tore the blade back with a sickening hiss and scrambled away as an arc of warm blood splashed his face. William balanced himself on the precariously poised platform as the rest of the squad leapt over the turf wall to join the slaughter. Captain Birch had seconded the attack, leading his own picked force down into the ditch and attacking the bewildered Cornish from the flank. With one last yell of frustrated fury, the Cornish turned and ran.

The bloody defenders swayed drunkenly among the dead and wounded, and watched the enemy storming parties hurry back over the hill, dragging their wounded with them. A dazed Royalist officer sat with his head on his knees, surrounded by half a dozen of his slaughtered soldiers. Others crawled away clutching their bellies, or hobbled off on crutches improvised from abandoned muskets. Billy Butcher knelt on the demolished wagon, and peered out through strands of bitter smoke. He raised his musket and picked his target. A red-faced officer in a bright coat and matching sash, loudly haranguing his bareheaded junior.

Butcher didn't know what he was saying, but he guessed

the gist from the officer's twitching moustaches. Butcher squinted along the dull barrel, and gently squeezed the trigger. The heavy ball tore through the smoke and hit the furious colonel in the face. Butcher yelped with excitement as his victim sat down with a thud, clutching his dented helmet. The wretched captain wheeled around clutching his arm, the deflected bullet having smashed into his already dislocated shoulder.

'By God, Billy, it bounced off the bastard's helmet!' Muffet called admiringly.

The cockney dyer's apprentice in his calico coat and coarse breeches shook his fist at the cursing colonel away over the bloody wasteland.

'Piss off out of it, you Cornish cunt!' he screamed at the top of his voice. The wretched survivors of the abortive assault took his foul-mouthed advice.

'We've won! They've given up!' Muffet shouted along the walls, the defenders waving their hats and cheering at the tops of their hoarse voices.

They looked down as a bewildered officer climbed out of the smoking pit beneath their feet, swaying from side to side as he peered up at the delighted defenders. Muffet nudged Billy Butcher's arm.

'Oy! It's the bastard from Devizes, look! The one they put in charge of us!' he declared.

Their sharpshooter rattled another charge of powder into his musket as the enemy colonel stumbled away over the broken ground, his booted feet tangling beneath him.

'He's taken a knock, the bugger,' William leered.

'He's handed enough out,' Gillingfeather ruled. 'Shoot him down, Billy. For the *Messalina*.'

Butcher dropped a ball into the barrel and feverishly rammed it home.

'Go on, lad, he's goin' to be off if you don't look lively!'

Their quarry was weaving between heaps of dead men and smoking shell holes, the blood running from his bruised forehead and into his crossed eyes.

'Have a care, lad!' Muffet called.

Butcher threw the musket to his shoulder and closed his eye. The enemy officer staggered into his sight and he squeezed the trigger.

He rarely missed, and he wouldn't have done then if Scipio Porthcurn hadn't tripped, measuring his length over a heap of splintered pikes. The ball whistled over his head and thumped into a fuming corpse, lifting the waxy body over the bloody stones.

'Shite. Missed the sod.' Butcher straightened up shaking his head, his pale lashes blinking rapidly over his colourless eyes.

'They've had enough anyway,' William reassured him, 'one more ain't going to make a difference.'

'Depends which one it is,' Gillingfeather said grimly. 'Shoot down that Antichrist prince, and they'd crumble, aye, soon enough.'

William smiled wearily, ready to indulge the gimlet-eyed fanatic. He strode about disbelievingly, tipping the leaning wagon as if it was a slowly sinking ship. He could barely comprehend it. A victory. They'd won. They had only gone and bloody well won!

BY
BRANDON HILL FORT,

26 JULY 1643

The incessant crackle of musketry and the dull thump of Roundhead cannons brought Rupert striding out of his headquarters in his shirt. He stood on the edge of the broad, dark down, and peered through his perspective glass at the fires and flares away over the southern rim of the defences. The first faint streaks of dawn had lightened the horizon to the colour of old pewter, and in the feeble glimmer the cursing prince could make out thick columns of men making their way toward the ghastly illuminations on the walls. He muttered Germanic oaths under his breath, and slammed the glass shut with such force that the flimsy lens shattered into a thousand shards.

The Western army had jumped the gun, and launched their assault hours before the appointed deadline. His staff officers rushed about pulling on their boots and strapping on swords, imagining the garrison had launched a sortie. Bernard de Gomme, one of the prince's expert retinue of warrior engineers, ran his own glass over the enemy works.

'Their ambition misleads them, they want to win the works first,' the undernourished Dutchman said drily. Rupert shook his dark head, staring at the flames and smoke. The suffering city was wreathed in foul mists and bitter fumes, its slim towers and spires reaching for the clean heavens like a drowning man's fingers. He waved a young captain over and told him to ride around the line to Lord Grandison's battery. Let him fire the signal guns immediately. Perhaps the rest of the army would obey its orders, the prince wondered, biting his lip in frustration.

Sparrow's depleted company had climbed over the defiantly held south wall to pick over the dead and wounded heaped beneath. The ditch had been bridged by tangled bodies and smashed weapons, a hateful logjam of flesh clamped in a rickety scaffold of broken pikes, splintered scaling ladders and fantastically warped musket barrels. They were fiercely excited, bawling to one another above the despairing pleas of the injured and lamed, congratulating themselves on their stunning triumph as they pulled swords and pistols, purses and lockets from the broken-backed officers, finely tooled leather boots from the feet of the well-to-do corpses packed like rotting sheep in the bloody moat.

After a while, their raucous shouts subsided and the searchers – arms bloodied to the elbows – lapsed into a sullen silence. The very scale of their victory seemed troubling, as if each man realized the slaughter would not – could not – go unpunished.

If Bristol was to fall, they would pay dearly for killing so many Cornishmen.

William tilted his head, still ringing from the deafening dawn battle, and listened to the growing tumult behind them. Instead of slackening as he had anticipated, the barrage seemed to have grown even more intense. The roaring cannon reminded him of the demented barking of distempered dogs.

They had held on to a half-mile of carefully constructed defences, perhaps the strongest sector of Bristol's walls.

But Bristol's walls were five miles long, and not every sector boasted defences as formidable as the massive Redcliffe Gate.

Sparrow's men hauled themselves back over their corpse-lined barricade and listened to the guns hammer and crack the defiant walls. They gulped water from fire buckets, munched stale bread as the Royalists redoubled their efforts on the rest of the line.

The Cornish assault might have been thrown back, but black legions of enemy troops still swarmed to the north and west of the trembling town. Whole brigades of veteran foot drawn from all over the King's divided realm waited patiently for their orders, their peacock officers waving them on down the surrounding hills toward the ghastly illuminations boiling up in the great cauldron of Bristol.

Broken ground and burning cottages, tangled vegetable plots and steaming refuse pits fragmented the swift and sure assault, breaking brigades down to regiments, companies into tumbling squads of yelling men. They swooped out of the darkness like imps of the underworld into the hateful glare of the burning city, hurrying down the uneven slopes and over the barren wastelands before the walls.

Trotting, barging, slipping, running. A steeplechase to a slaughterhouse.

Major Tobias Fulke had paced his length of wall like a caged panther, encouraging his men through the witching hours of the night, and exhorting them to remain at their posts until daybreak. If they could stand a few more hours, they would save themselves another day.

'They'll be on their way, the Earl of Essex won't forget you,' he told his disbelieving soldiers. 'He's marching here now with a relief force. He'll drive the bastards into the river!' he elaborated, desperate to lift their gloomy spirits.

It was no good. He might as well have lined so many sacks of laundry along the parapet. Another dozen men had slipped away, making themselves scarce in the quaking bowels of the expectant city. He had no more than forty men left to man his section of the wall. It was almost as if the formidable turf bank was stretching under their feet, the guardian forts at either end moving further and further away, isolating his pitiful company on a lonely breakwater. A windswept reef about to be swamped beneath the massive breakers of a rushing tide of Royalists.

The hideously lonely watch ended with a blare of trumpets and spectacular eruption of gunfire from the surrounding emplacements. The dismal soldiers as were left cowered under the parapet or peeked between their fingers as Rupert unleashed his fearsome assault forces, thousands of his screaming familiars careering out of the shadows at them.

'On your feet!' Fulke yelled, striding along the broad bank between knots of knavish washerwomen. Frightened farmboys and surly townsmen, doubtful volunteers and the rag-tag remnants of a dozen decimated regiments. He reached the ancient robinet snug in its well-fortified embrasure, and looked around for its errant crew. He spied them sheltering behind a basket of roundshot. Two terrified men to hold a hundred yards of wall!

'On your feet!' Fulke repeated, kicking the reluctant

warriors out from their hidey hole. The man with the limp was visibly trembling, his dumb partner wide-eyed with terror. The crash of the cannon from Windmill Hill Fort made both of them jump out of their coats. Fulke grabbed them by their greasy lapels and hurled them behind the gun. They staggered and stumbled, taking cover behind the awkward and angular limber.

'Where's the other idiot?' Fulke snarled.

'Dead, sir, killed on the wall on Monday, if you remember, sir,' Mordecai Pitt answered, staring over the parapet at the enemy storming parties hurrying through the furze bushes towards the wall. He watched in fascinated horror as furtive individuals led the way, gundogs drawn to the wall by the reek of blood and fear. Errant knights followed by tightly knit squads of rather more thoughtful soldiers, bristling with muskets and grappling hooks, ladders and faggots.

'The bloody fool. Showing off in front of her,' Fulke muttered, apparently untroubled by the hideous assault gathering steam beneath their horribly exposed eerie. He smoothed his goatee beard between his thumb and forefinger, frowning at the thought of his poor mistress falling prey to the heathen King's men. He had tried to spare her from these horrors, but she was a war child, as grimly suited to her occupation as he was himself. Matilda had seen it all, parading herself on the wall as Rupert had paraded his men on the down. And she had been splattered by the daft acrobat's hot blood for her trouble. He had escorted her back to their cramped lodgings as if she had been blinded by his smoking flesh, murmuring endearments as she stumbled along beside him, neither hearing nor seeing anything but the poor lad's frightful death. Fulke hadn't dared spend any more time with the bewildered girl, and had returned to the wall in a foul temper, bitterly frustrated by their hopeless plight.

All he could do was stand by grimly while the enemy probed and jabbed the over-extended defences, holding his men to their posts by the force of his will alone.

Vastly experienced, an expert in death, Fulke took one look along the frail line and knew in his bones all was lost. But he dared not communicate his fear to these lost souls penned with him. They would defend these walls, and he his honour, or die in the attempt.

As far as he could make out the only determined resistance came from the forts, strung like beads along the higher ground. They maintained a constant squall of fire against the invaders, who rapidly recoiled from the deep ditch and fiery walls. A handful of determined defenders further up the line had actually sallied out into the deep moat, and were firing at the bewildered enemy, driving them along the turf walls like a flock of sheep. The perilously thin line between the forts, though, seemed practically deserted. Whole lengths of wall vulnerable to renewed Royalist attack.

And there were always more of them. Brigade after brigade, filtering down the slopes and filling the gaps in the line, probing, harrying, rushing forward once more.

'Are you loaded?' Fulke asked the mesmerized youth beside the gun. He slapped his shoulder. 'I said, are you loaded?'

The farmboy nodded. His dumb companion held up a length of match. The fool hadn't even bothered to light it!

'Sergeant Grantly?' Fulke roared over a sudden crescendo of shots. The portly sergeant hurried along the wall, his broad head tucked deep within the collar of his coat. Fulke grabbed his glowing match and lit the dumb soldier's charred end. The panting major tipped the wide brim of his helmet away from his eyes, and squinted into the slow dawn. To his right, the vulnerable turf bank dipped away towards the Brandon Gate and then rose steeply to follow the ridge of Windmill Hill. The enemy assault seemed to have latched on to the battered fort on the summit like a multi-coloured octopus, each grasping tentacle made up of a company of musketeers and swordsmen led by a gaggle of shrieking officers.

The Royalists endured a sudden squall of musketry and then leapt down into the ditch beneath the defiant fort, working their way around the moat to the fortified gate. The officers worked feverishly as snipers picked off the struggling attackers, screaming men falling on all sides. They clambered over the mounds of dead and wounded, and managed to attach a petard to the barred gate, fixing the bomb to the barricade by means of a board called a madrier, firmly fastened to a rope and pulley they had carried up with them. The explosive device would blow the door off and kill the defenders crouched behind – according to the pristine diagrams in the drill books.

'Take cover!'

The Royalists doubled down the ditch away from the impending blast, and ducked behind whatever cover they could find.

The stunning explosion lit them up like demons, silhouetting them against the fiery skyline.

'Charge!'

The Royalists surged back up the ditch, clambering over their own dead as they hurried towards the demolished gate, clawing over the bodies of the fallen in their determination to get to grips. They scrambled up and ran pell-mell toward the flames, squinting into the billowing smoke to see what damage had been done. The blast had torn away or twisted half of the iron bars, but the rest held firm, holding the battered structure upright. The demented attackers wailed with dismay, hacked at the pitiless oak beams and tried to manhandle the twisted portcullis, but it was no use. They threw hand-grenades over the wall and fired pistols through the honeycombed gate, but for every shot they fired the defenders gave them a dozen, picking off the officers one after the other.

'Retire!'

The stalled attackers fled back down the bloody ditch, a dirty brown tide receding around the battered ruins of an old barn.

Fulke rubbed the filthy smoke from his streaming eyes, peering into the sinister wasteland where the attackers had gone to ground. He had watched the vicious fight ebb and flow along the walls, wondering when the wretched enemy would try their luck against his section. Blinded by fumes and squinting against the flying smuts, Fulke knew they hadn't gone far.

'Sergeant Grantly, I want every other man on the wall back here, with me. They'll be after us next,' he shrieked, his throat burning from the bitter fogs drifting down the line.

The sergeant noted his increasing anxiety with alarm, nodding dumbly as he gripped the peculiarly warm stone wall. It was as if the whole city had been lit from beneath, every hovel and town house a steaming pot on an open range. He swallowed, wiped his wet mouth. Good God above, if the Old Man was getting his breeches in a tangle they were all done for! He hurried off fretting towards

Brandon Hill Fort to collect the pitiful reinforcements, leaving his anxious master peering over the ancient gun towards the spluttering heart of the battle. He didn't have to look far to find trouble.

The Royalist attackers had disappeared from view into dead ground they had found – partially obscured by the squat grey mass of the stone barn. The wall had been built around the massive pile, incorporating the building into the defences. The barn had been filled with Roundhead musketeers.

Fulke, thin neck extended as he peered over the defences, ducked down as the defenders opened a furious fire. The massive structure seemed to tremble, bursting its beams as the garrison loosed a salvo at the Royalist troops hurrying away from the larger work up the hill. Their commander fell to his knees clutching his thigh and cursing. The captain hurrying to his aid was hit in the face and fell in the damned ditch. The dazed assault party, shorn of its officers, recoiled from this new terror, the milling mass breaking up into smaller and smaller groups as they ran back down the slope dragging their cursing colonel with them. Fulke closed his eyes against the sudden surge of smoke, thanking God the line had held. He straightened up and peered around the deserted wall. Where had Grantly gone? Where were his men? It was no good holding the barn if the walls around were abandoned!

'To me! To me! Have a care!' he yodelled and bawled to the empty emplacements, the abandoned stairs and draughty towers. Smuts and sparks danced in the devilish winds whisking about the tortured stonework, whistling and popping in the sinister silence.

Suddenly, there was a blare of horns followed by a thunderous roll of drums in the darkness. He had no men left but the enemy did. Fulke wheeled around and peered back out through the stinging fog, groaning with helpless dismay inside his boiling armour.

He knew the hellish symphony must herald yet another attack. The biggest and most brutal of all. Fulke groaned, fingers trembling on the hot stones which seemed to sway and quiver in sympathy with the accursed music of war.

And then, out of the boiling smoke, came a man on horseback.

A tall commander in a fiery red suit, rising up in front of his fleeing troops on a prancing stallion. Radiating imperial power and authority, arrogantly surveying the walls which had defied his legions.

Rupert!

Prince Youth, prodigal son born to war on a continent split to the brisket by his own father! A scowling Alexander, grimly determined as Caesar and as fiendishly calculating as Hannibal, bred to war and reared on blood.

Fulke prickled with anger as he surveyed the arrogant general – he'd give him blood, the coxcomb, the arrogant puppy! He'd been fighting before Rupert had been crawling, learnt his trade before the legendary prince had learnt to walk! The two men seemed aware of one another that moment, calmly weighing the other up against the pestilential backcloth of flame and blood, deafened by the crackling shot and whistling shells.

Fulke shook his fist and bent down behind the ancient robinet, grunting with the effort as he dragged the ungainly carriage about. He squinted along the thin muzzle, and watched the despised prince trot forward into the red glare of the reflected flames.

Rupert waved his arm furiously to drive the attackers back to the wall, apparently oblivious of the shot and shells which rent the air all about him. The arrogant rogue seemed convinced there wasn't a bullet in all the world which could harm him. The charmed prince rounded up the fearful stragglers and herded them back to the attack, absorbing stragglers and survivors from other units as they went. They made straight towards the dead ground they had located beyond the stinging fire from the barn.

Fulke felt as if he was holding the wall by himself, that the fate of the entire city rested on him alone. He grabbed the dumb soldier's match and dipped it on the old cannon's powder-caked touch-hole.

The explosion was out of all proportion to the modest barrel. It knocked him off his feet, his face blackened with burnt powder. Fulke prised himself up, astonished at his own survival and blinking like an owl behind his crisped black mask. The muzzle had split down the middle like a pod of peas, the scrap barrel landing with a clatter on the tiled roof of a tottering town house fifty yards from the threatened wall. He shivered inside his scorched armoured shell, stared at the trembling hands protruding from his lacquered carapace as if he could not believe they were still attached to his shocked body.

The ungainly carriage had been hurled sideways by the blast, knocking the dumb soldier over the firestep. He had fallen over the side and landed on a heap of rubble, his neck broken. Mordecai Pitt had been knocked flying, landing on his back five yards down the wall. Fulke recovered his shattered wits and crawled over, lifting the dazed youth by his lapels. Pitt stared up at the furious major, his white hair scorched to black toffee, his face a smoky mask.

'How much powder did you use? Treble charging a piece like that!' Fulke croaked furiously.

Grantly hurried up and hauled the roasted major to his feet. 'Good shot, sir! Did you see the bastard go down?' the sergeant asked, pointing his pistol over the trembling hill.

The pebble-sized roundshot had caught Rupert's horse in the face, knocking out its right eye. The horse had reared in agony, tipping the tall prince onto the broken ground. Fulke's eyes were streaming, he couldn't see the dead horse or the downed prince or much else besides. He felt only a muted throb of elation, too tired and stretched to crow over the fall of that black-hearted bastard of a sorcerer's apprentice.

'Thank God, thank God,' he said, still bewildered by the blast which had damn near killed them all.

Grantly pushed him down on an upturned barrel and held his water bottle out. The major took a swig and patted his face experimentally.

'Looks worse than it is, sir,' the sergeant said encouragingly.

Fulke nodded, slowly getting his breath back. 'Where did they go?'

'Who, sir?'

'The buggers he was bringing up. Did they run?'

Grantly peered over the littered slopes, shook his plump head. 'Can't see 'em. Must have done,' he concluded.

Fulke levered himself to his feet. 'There's dead ground the other side of the barn. If they keep going, they'll be over.'

Grantly peered through the thick smoke churning from the battered fort on the hill, trying to make out the dead ground the dazed colonel was talking about. Why didn't they just give up and have done with it, racing about like headless chickens? He glanced at the bristling commander and knew the old bird wasn't about to give up just yet. He'd get 'em all killed, sure as eggs was eggs.

Fulke drew his sword and led the way, Grantly, Mordecai Pitt, Ebenezer Bell and half a dozen others grimly following along. The turf bank seemed deserted. All that effort further along the line when the enemy could have gotten a regiment over on their section without losing a man. They hurried on down the wall toward the gate. A handful of demoralized defenders jumped in fright as the blackamoor colonel appeared out of the smoke. Fulke led his tiny force on around the back of the formidable stone barn, giving the nervous musketeers within a wide berth, and headed back for the wall fifty yards further on. A set of rough steps had been gouged into the embankment. Fulke was halfway up when the wall above his head was bracketed by explosions. A live grenade rolled and bumped down the step towards him, the fuse spitting and sparking with vicious vigour. They seemed paralysed with fear, petrified limbs frozen to the stone as the horrible pot bounced and hissed between their feet.

The enemy had found the dead ground at last.

BY

THE CHRISTMAS STEPS,

BRISTOL, 26 JULY 1643

The shattering explosions from the grenades the Royalist pioneers had flung over the wall blew Fulke's patrol over like brittle leaves in a thunderstorm, gusts of shrapnel razoring along the deserted firestep. Poleaxed by the concussions above their heads, they sprawled against the pock-marked wall and stared in horror as the last grenade rolled about the rubble at their feet. Sergeant Grantly leapt up like a scalded cat, and kicked out wildly at the hateful flask. The panting sergeant straightened himself and then looked down at his heavy boot. The shoddy grenade had been sealed with so much wax the fuse had not been able to burn through and ignite the murderous contents. The flask was splattered in molten wax which had stuck to the sergeant's worn leather boot like hoof glue. Grantly kicked out frantically, the sparks dancing around his feet like some infernal goblin trap. The survivors threw themselves down and covered their ringing ears as he stamped about, screaming like a butchered pig. The grenade went off with an ear-splitting crash, catapulting the horrified sergeant into the rickety wall of a nearby tool shed. Mordecai Pitt was kicked in the back by the sergeant's blackened leg as he ran for it, the force of the shocking blow clattering him over a heap of rubble. He scrambled away from the vile missile, his eyes bulging from his head like a choking haddock. Grantly levered himself up in a glowing lagoon of his own blood, taking the weight of his torn torso on his locked arms. His slack mouth opened and closed in dumb horror as his scorched senses registered the fatal wounds. By the time his starting eyes had focused on Fulke's pale face, the major had already lifted his pistol to the whimpering sergeant's blackened brow. Grantly nodded his pain-racked head. What was left of Fulke's company took to their heels, overwhelmed by the pitiless carnage, sick of the senseless slaughter. The shot rang out into the night, silencing for a moment the frantic activity Fulke could hear on the other side of the wall. Muffled curses and the dull thud of picks and axes as the Royalist attackers tore at the exposed turf embankment. There was nobody left to hold them now.

Colonel Washington's dragoons had left their ragged little ponies at the foot of the slope, midway between Brandon Hill and Windmill Hill forts. One man in every ten had been left to hold on to the stamping beasts as their dismounted comrades doubled forward between the furze bushes. They had been detailed to support Colonel Wentworth's attack, rushing into the breach once his men had clawed a foothold. Once over the wall they were to exploit the long-awaited breakthrough and spread panic behind the penetrated defence lines. But the breakthrough hadn't materialized, and the dragoons had found themselves thrown into the assault as emergency reinforcements for the bewildered storming parties. They had gone to ground in the dead zone between the forts, throwing every grenade they carried over the apparently deserted wall. In the sudden, eerie quiet they could hear the crackle of flames and the groans of the wounded, scattered haphazardly around the deadly ditch. They listened for the clatter of Roundhead reinforcements rushing up to the threatened sector, but the curious scouts couldn't hear any movement. One by one, inquisitive troopers rose out of the ground like moles, suspiciously sniffing for the expected ambuscade.

But there was no sudden shout and killing volley. They doubled up to the wall, spreading their palms over the pock-marked stonework as if they were crouching before some icon, bewildered at their own miraculous deliverance.

They could hardly believe their luck, daren't speak for fear of alerting the sleeping enemy within. The dragoons hoisted each other up, clawing feverish footholds in the battered wall and scrambled over the parapet like so many buff-coloured monkeys. They hurried along the deserted embankment, shooting at the shadows as they went.

This was it. They were in!

A squad of bewildered defenders hurried down from the defiant fort on Windmill Hill, but they turned and ran when their pale lieutenant was cut down. Another squad had taken cover in a narrow alley, but seemed reluctant to come to grips. A bow-legged dragoon captain lobbed a grenade onto the tiled roof above their hidden heads, and ducked down as it clattered over the drainpipe and landed in amongst the fearful fugitives. The sudden sulphurous blast seemed to knock the heart out of what was left of the defence. In a moment, it was over. Victory hadn't been snatched from the iron mouth of defeat – it had dribbled from its slack lips into their gratefully cupped hands.

The bloody remnants of a dozen regiments didn't give a tinker's cuss how the breach had been won, whether five men or five thousand had died to win it. They hurried along the wall to the hard-won breach, tearing the loose turf bank apart with their bare hands or using their musket butts and half-pikes to prise open the battered planking which had held it together. A bare-headed ensign clambered onto the crumbling parapet, throwing his tattered blue standard up into the smoke to mark the vital bridgehead.

The desperate attackers – on the verge of flying back the way they had come – were electrified by the news and converged on the God-given gap in the defences from all points of the broken-pointed compass. The murmured intelligence – scarcely credited at first – was whispered, shouted, bawled along the line. This was no trick to encourage them to one final effort, this was a breach, a breach which would drain Bristol's lifeblood as its hitherto defiant defences had drained theirs.

The ensign on the wall stood back as more men arrived to widen the gap, hurling great slabs of cracked stone down into the ditch.

A narrow causeway into the city, a lance into its Roundhead heart.

A tall cavalier spurred his snorting horse over the makeshift bridge and over the piled rubble into the city. Prince Rupert peered down the deserted wall, suspecting they were being lured into some foul trap or ambuscade. He waved his sword towards the expectant suburbs, hurrying the bloody attackers on to the next strongpoint. He knew a determined counter attack by fresh parties of defenders could seal the hard-won breach, flush his cheering men back out of the city and extinguish his slim chance of victory. There was no time to shout and cheer, to stand by and await developments. Rupert knew he must go for the jugular, pinch out the desperate resistance before his men began to wilt with the crazed effort, crack under the strength-sapping strain of the siege.

He ordered them on, grimly determined on his patient new horse, ignoring their howls of adulation. The Royalist musketeers and pikemen crowded around their idol as if he could shield them from the bullets and the shells, and marched on toward the erratically beating heart of the city.

The badly mauled Royalist armies had attacked all along the five mile line, and had only managed to claw a foothold on one isolated section. But the six-foot breach was hacked wider every moment, and was to prove Bristol's undoing, bleeding her resistance as effectively as if the entire city wall had come tumbling down like some modern-day Jericho. Prince Rupert had snatched his chance, jamming every available man through the pin-prick breach, and scouring the alleys and passages which radiated away from the wall into the inner suburbs. With so many officers already dead captains and lieutenants found themselves at the head of packs of up to two hundred anonymous stragglers, eager to sack the rich rebel city. The trickle became a flood, dividing about the isolated strongpoints and pouring down the terraced suburbs like water through a grate. One column headed straight for the city centre, taking the steep main road toward the Frome Gate. Another column turned right toward the river, and hurried down towards College Green and the city docks. The third force took the more direct route to the low-lying city centre, packing shoulder to shoulder into the steep stairs known as the Christmas Steps. If they could get to the low-lying castle before the bewildered defenders making their way back from the holed walls, the city would be as good as lost.

William Sparrow's quietly rejoicing company had been struck dumb by the hideous dispatch from the northern wall. For all their triumphant efforts around the Redcliffe Gate the enemy had penetrated the defences to the west of them and were even now rushing down the hill to cut them off from the castle! Forts had fallen, although nobody was sure which ones, and the cavalry reserve had either failed to charge or had made absolutely no impression against the Royalist tide, depending on which pale-faced rumour-monger you cared to listen to.

'What, all that for nothing?' Billy Butcher had rasped, hurling his musket against the wall in agitated disgust.

They were still chewing over the demoralizing intelligence when Colonel Birch had hurried along the wall calling for volunteers to stem the Royalist flood. But his dismal tidings had snatched what little heart they had left, and dozens of defenders had melted away into the honeycombed town, leaving their muskets and pikes stacked behind them. By the time he had arrived at the hard-held Redcliffe Gate, Birch could only offer Sparrow another dozen or so men to add to his grim-faced few.

'The rest have scuttled for the alehouses, the scrofulous dogs,' Birch growled, swinging his soot-smeared sword in impotent rage.

'You know the backways, lad. Get this lot over to College Green as quick as you can, I'll round up the reserve, wherever in the bowels of Hell they're hiding themselves. They're coming down Park Row, and you know what that means. If they get to the castle before we do, they'll have cut us all in half,' he explained, in case Sparrow lacked the imagination to work it out for himself.

William hadn't time to argue or ask for further instructions. If they weren't stopped soon, the city would fall like a crab apple in a gale. He eyed his wretched desperados, the sweet victory souring rapidly in their empty bellies. He wondered if they were thinking what he was thinking: that there was no way they would be taken again. Not aboard that bloody boat.

Sparrow's blistered feet felt like molten lead, his torn toes rubbed raw by his stiff new boots. He hadn't had a proper night's rest since God knew when, and he led the way through the bewildering backstreets like a sleepwalker. He shook his head, and blinked his stinging eyes for a familiar landmark. He was away from his old stamping grounds now, lost in a maze of pestilential streets which had never earned a name, hopefully heading toward the troubled western defences.

He must have been on the wall too long, and before that on the *Conqueror*, becoming accustomed to seeing wide open spaces and magnificent horizons. Now, in the heart of the city, the hovels and houses had ganged up on him, towering overhead cutting out the few feeble strands of dawn. Trapping him in narrow alleys where he had no idea what was around the next corner. He imagined a sniper at every dimly lit window, rubbing spyholes in the greasy leaded panes. A gaggle of screaming Cornish capering about the lofty rooftops like an army of gargoyles vomited from Hell itself. He strode on, wishing he could hide himself away in one of the crooked alleys or bury himself in some well-stocked cellar until it was all over. If they would only let him sleep a while now, he'd fight later, God's truth.

Muffet, Gillingfeather, Butcher and quiet Caleb panted along behind, imagining their captain's confusing route was some clever short cut through the inner city. William closed his eyes and whispered a grateful prayer when they finally emerged on the edge of College Green, the broad lawn in front of the squat cathedral. The green was overlooked on the remaining three sides by brooding town houses belonging to absent merchants and city financiers. A glorious amphitheatre gatecrashed by an unseen enemy, who crept and crawled along every creaking timber, flitted past the night-weary windows. They could see flames and smoke welling up behind the houses, some of which had clearly been occupied by none too choosy snipers.

'Well what are we supposed to do now?' Butcher wanted to know. 'Sit around and wait?'

Colston Muffet had tilted his greying head to listen to the sounds of battle. Loud and unmistakable on the higher ground to their right.

'Up there, top of the hill,' he told William.

Sparrow nodded glumly. They would have to cross the green and go up Park Street. Bloody tricky if they got caught halfway up the steep hill. They would have to batter their way into a cellar if the enemy had gotten into the perimeter in any strength. And then what?

'We could take a short cut up Christmas Steps, and then double back up Park Row. If they're in that far we've had it anyway,' he predicted gloomily.

'Listen to that firing. Somebody's givin' 'em what for,' Muffet argued. William bowed to his greater judgement, and led the depleted company across the churned green. They could see small groups of shouting soldiers making their way along the glass-strewn streets beneath the formidable houses. Some slipped into alleys or disappeared through darkened doors, their warlike intentions overwhelmed by their urge to plunder the grand houses. Some were wounded, hobbling away without weapons, while others were seeking some cover before the storm broke over their bare heads.

William's squad threw themselves to their knees as a squad of cavalry clattered down Park Street and accelerated off across the green towards the river. The terrified riders were being pursued by a squad of musketeers and a handful of officers wielding fire pikes – blazing spears which sparked and spat like Satan's torches, lighting up the ghastly faces of the screaming soldiers. The enemy company seemed to be charging straight for them when a roundshot whistled over the green and tore up a great heap of turf twenty yards to their right. The enemy mob veered away toward the cathedral, their bandaged officer urging them after the defiant gun crew, and left the battered lawn to William's relieved command. William was panting hard as he ran across the last hundred yards of exposed grass and ducked under a drunken doorway, the old timber beams bowed with age and busy worms. There was a quiet thump from the alley nearby. He held his breath and listened for a moment, and then peered around the corner of the empty house. The curious captain watched a couple of unarmed men heaving an enormous clock along like a battering ram. Hopelessly lost, the looters dropped their prize and ran off when William's well-armed company jumped out on them. They pursued the fugitives past looted shops and piles of discarded goods. Dresses and hats, brand-new boots, sacks of sugar. The enemy – or the enemy within – had been through the rank like a tornado, scouring the shelves for anything of worth and trampling the rest under their feet. They followed the devastated row for another hundred yards and then turned left into a black canyon of three-storey hovels, poised precariously above a broad flight of steps. The steep alley wound up the hill between the cunningly stacked houses, climbing up away from them like a dried-up cataract towards the smoky suburbs and broad plateau where the enemy had forced their way in. They could hear frantic footfalls and incoherent screeching as a dozen or so men came tumbling back down the echoing stair toward them.

'Come back and fight, you dogs, you hounds, you worthless apes!' A sprightly old gentleman in sooty armour hobbled down the steps after them, waving his fist at his spineless crew. The fugitives took no notice of the bawling major or anybody else. They pushed and prodded their way through William's scanty reinforcements, their pinched faces and shiny eyes eloquent testimony to the ferocity of the fight they had fled.

Major Fulke sat down heavily on a well-worn step, blowing hard. He could do no more. His old heart fluctuated beneath his dented breastplate, his blackened face alternately flushing and blanching as he struggled to catch his half-choked breath. William, who had served with the gallant pensioner earlier that summer, wasn't even sure he recognized the old devil under his scorched mask.

'Sparrow, sir, you remember,' William reported nervously, glancing over the old man's heaving shoulder up the alarmingly quiet stairway. 'Colonel Birch sent us over to help.'

'Don't just stand there,' Fulke gasped, pointing his notched blade at the hunched hovels. 'Get under cover. They'll be upon us in a moment. They're using the stair as a short cut to the city!' He covered his mouth, coughing on the insinuating smoke. 'Get a table out here, make a barricade, we'll have to stop 'em here or they'll be swarming over the castle! If they get there first we're done for!' he croaked.

Sparrow stared up the evil chasm formed by the closely packed houses. His depleted company crouched at the bottom of the steep passageway, the broad grey steps worn smooth by thousands of hurrying feet, winding up between the leaning buildings until they were swallowed by the sullen smokes which washed this way and that between the sooty brick walls of the man-made gorge. William had been up and down the familiar pathway a thousand times, delivering leaflets or sharing a joke with one of his long-lost cronies, dawdling before he made his way back to the molten hell of his master's print shop. Now he could hardly credit he knew the place at all. It was a mad stair from his worst nightmare, a crazily paved graveyard. He pictured the cold stone slabs tearing themselves up from their mortared beds and creaking into place above blackened pits of half-burnt bodies, attackers and defenders alike stripped and bundled into the greedy earth.

He tilted his head at the sudden flurry of footfalls, wondering if the energetic Fulke had flushed another batch of deserters from their holes further up the stair. William listened, swallowed nervously as he picked out the subtle difference in sound. This was no pell-mell evacuation, no panic-stricken stampede. The measured tramp of hundreds of boots rang down the stair, louder and louder every step. The grimly determined rhythm tightened like a cold fist of fear about his thumping heart. Drummers beat thunderous tattoos, officers yelled at the hotheads to dress their lines. Rank after rank, packed in close between the narrow walls, advanced toward their feeble barricade. Boots crashed on the stones, the quaking defenders could sense the hateful throb through the ribs of the hill.

A stairway to the heavens pressed into service as a short cut to Hell.

BY

KILMERSDEN HALL,

CHIPPING MARLEWARD, 26 JULY 1643

Findlay tugged at the broad blue sash Sir Gilbert had presented him with, wondering for the umpteenth time how the tricky tradesman had ever managed to persuade him to wear it. Or any of the other clutter, come to that. They could stuff him up with titles and flatter him with nonsensical commissions, but he was a gamekeeper all the same. If the fat owl didn't like it he knew what he could do and all.

He was a woodsman, born and bred. Left to himself he would have been prowling the leafy lanes now, gliding like a grey ghost along the deer paths which crisscrossed the deep dewy woods. All he needed was his carefully cleaned musket, a handful of bullets and a horn of fine-milled powder. A good trail and a moonlit night. He sighed deeply, a plume of vapour steaming in the dawn's chill bite. Moonlit night my arse, he thought. The sergeant major general of Sir Gilbert Morrison's regiment of foot had chosen to stand guard through the witching hours, keeping a pale eye on the road which meandered about the hill and over the downs to Wells. He couldn't trust the cross-eyed devils Morrison had pressed into service with his fanciful formation, let alone the vagabonds who were making their way west in belligerent packs. The sly buggers would help themselves to anything that took their eye along the way, just like those scum-bellied dragoons had made sport with the boy and his wayward mistress the other week. He wondered for a moment where the flighty piece had got to, perhaps as far as Oxford as her damp-eyed father maintained. Aye, and if he judged that slimy lamprey Clavincale right, they had stopped at every hayrick along the way into the bargain.

Findlay didn't need grubby news-sheets or gossipy goodwives to tell him there was trouble away over the hills. Bristol had been surrounded, two armies of reluctant warriors had finally come to grips to settle the fate of the entire West Country. It wasn't surprising the roads would be choked with cowards and cut-throats who found the work too hot for their liking. Wherever the army went it dragged a filthy tail of thieves and tinkers, troublemakers and tarts with it. None of them seemed able to stick to anything for more than a few days at a time. He had followed his father and his father before him into service at Kilmersden Hall. It would take an earthquake to lever him out of that duty. The trouble was, Lady Ramsay wasn't any more the master of the place than he was. Grossly in debt to the grovelling merchant, she had to dance his tune and endure his vile wit night after night. Stand by and watch her home being usurped, brick by brick, tile by tile, from under her very nose. No wonder the mistress preferred to keep to her room, or shut herself up with her wretched daughter. He had had high hopes for Anneliese, once. Now she was nothing more than a washed-out shadow, an ill-drawn watercolour of her old self. Maybe the match would do her good after all. Morrison's boy had been made of sounder stuff than his revolting sire, but then again, he could hardly be any worse.

He clamped his elbows around the dewy barrel of his

long-shanked fowling piece, and blew on his cold hands. Time to turn the shifty guards out, let them watch each other while he had a rest. Morrison had wondered aloud about marching on to Bristol to join the siege, but had seen reason when he had reviewed his cherished troops. A few dozen of the very basest scoundrels, the laziest, craftiest, shallowest bunch of thieving cutpurses in the entire army. They would hardly cut much of a dash paraded against the veteran Cornish or Prince Rupert's experienced infantry. Better to wait. Their day would come, God help them.

The sudden slow creak of a loaded wagon caught his wandering attention, heavy horses making heavy work of the long haul up the hill. Findlay righted his musket and doubled past the formidable gatehouse to take a closer look at the intruders. The dripping woods and dewy fields were shrouded in a light mist, the flimsy grey tendrils torn and trampled by the toiling team. Two big-boned cobs dragging an open wagon full of men. Findlay watched the huddled driver flick the reins over the tired team, and stepped out into their path with his musket levelled on the old crock's rheumy eye.

'All right, old timer. That's far enough,' he called, jarringly loud.

The frightened driver hauled on the reins while his somewhat smaller companion looked up sharply, tipping the dew-black cloak from her bedraggled curls. Findlay closed one eye, recognizing the girl's bold brown eye. Miss Bella's maid, what was her name?

'Mary! What! Where's that dratted daughter of mine got to now?' Sir Gilbert Morrison looked up from his steaming oats as the tired girl was shown into the kitchen. There was always a good fire made up in the parlour and the cook seemed to have taken a bit of a fancy to the jolly merchant. He was a cheerful sort, despite what the mistress said behind his back, and she certainly didn't mind him coming down for a warm and a few slices of toast first thing in the morning. Sir Gilbert laid his spoon on his plate, and pushed his chair back from the well-scrubbed table as the cook rushed over to help the dripping maid get out of her heavy travelling cloak.

'You've never traipsed all night, girl?' the red-faced matron scolded, pinching Mary's pale cheek. Mary held her hand up, turning the well-meaning cook away.

'Sir Gilbert.'

The merchant rose slowly from the warm chair by the fire, his twinkling grin fading rapidly as he registered Mary's miserable scowl.

'Mary. Come on in and warm yourself, girl, you look like death.'

Mary Keziah stepped gratefully into the cosy kitchen, her cheeks blushing at the welcome warmth. The merchant tugged his robe tighter, tilted his night-capped head in concern.

'Whatever is the matter, girl? Where's Bella?' he asked hurriedly, looking up as Findlay ducked under the low door, leading some dirty waif wrapped in a blanket. He looked from the gamekeeper to his charge, humming unconcernedly and staring at the floor as if the worn flags had been inscribed by some filthy-minded Roman poet. The scoundrel's hair was wild and matted, crawling with lice, he wouldn't wonder. Sir Gilbert frowned, looked quizzically at the sobbing maid.

'Mary, girl, whatever is the matter?'

Mary Keziah held her belly in anguish, the hot tears stinging her red face.

'It's Jamie, sir, it's how I found him,' she cried suddenly, the cook rushing in to comfort the distraught maid.

Sir Gilbert swallowed nervously, glanced at Findlay for an explanation. The scarecrow in the dirty blanket looked up, his merry eyes glittering with unfocused animation.

'Where is he?' Sir Gilbert asked drily. 'Is he not with you?'

Findlay growled under his breath, patted the wild highland youth into a hard-backed chair and clamped his big hands on the boy's twitching shoulders.

'Here's your boy, sir. Back from the war,' the gamekeeper answered for the numskull son. 'Didn't you say you'd never recognize him now? Didn't you say that?' Findlay barked dangerously.

Sir Gilbert ran his pudgy pink paw over his rather tangled grey curls, looked around the room nervously as if he suspected some vicious prank. Mary Keziah's obvious anguish told him all he needed to know. He took one step closer, then another, and peered down at his absent-minded son.

'Jamie?' he croaked. 'It's not you, is it?'

The household was up and about by seven. The cook had breakfasts to prepare for the staff as well as their unexpected visitors, and a poorly maid to look after and all. The girl was dog tired and hungry, and something else too, if she wasn't very much mistaken. She had stood by, holding the girl's shoulders as she retched the oats she'd just eaten into the sink.

'How long is it, girl?' she had asked Mary knowingly.

The puzzled brunette had looked over her shoulder, her brown eyes starting from her drawn features.

'How long's what?' she had asked, wiping her mouth on a flannel.

The cook had crossed the kitchen to turn the toast, pursing her generous lips. 'You know very well, you saucy piece, and you'll lose it just as quick as you got it, wandering about the country at dead of night, and all!' She may have been at home diagnosing the early stages of a pregnancy, but whatever ailed the silly girl's wretched companion was beyond the corpulent cook. Something wrong with his head all right, but his feather-brained antics were beyond her limited powers of understanding.

'Looks like the work of a clever woman to me,' she had hinted darkly, as Sir Gilbert had helped Findlay get the boy up to his room. The merchant was lost for words for once, bundling his offspring out of sight before the mistress came down to see the state of his sorry son.

'A clever woman?' Mary Keziah had asked woodenly.

The cook clicked her tongue in annoyance. 'A witch, a witch I mean. By the saints, this brain fever's not catching, is it?'

Lady Ramsay would normally have kept to her room, leaving her unwanted guest the run of her house. She despised him a little more each passing day, blaming the merchant for entrapping her husband, snarling him in this web of debt and decay his widow couldn't ever hope to untangle. The loyal gamekeeper's news brought her out of her room like a warship under full sail, her sooty widow's weeds blowing like a pirate's standard over her battlemented brow. She paced along the landing to Sir

Gilbert's quarters, rapped loudly on the door and strode straight in.

The red-faced merchant was slumped on the side of his enormous four-poster, his merry face creased in misery. He was practically unrecognizable, with his impudent eyes steamed with tears and his busy hands clamped to his thighs as if he was having trouble quelling his legs. The merchant looked up, scowling horribly but unable for once to summon up any suitable summary of his situation.

Lady Ramsay crossed the room in a trice and peered over his slumped shoulder. The thin youth had been swaddled in sheets, wrapped tight in the blankets as if his father meant to sweat any illness out of him. A cotton straitjacket which clamped his twitching arms safely away under the covers.

'I suppose Findlay told you,' Sir Gilbert accused hoarsely. 'I suppose he told you all about it.'

'He is my gamekeeper as well as your sergeant, Sir Gilbert,' Lady Ramsay intoned. 'And this,' she nodded about the choice room, 'is my house. I think I am entitled to know when you invite guests to stay, don't you?'

Sir Gilbert nodded grimly, avoiding her flashing eye. She peered down at the bewildered youth, who seemed to be trying to blow an invisible feather from the end of his nose.

'He is hurt,' she said flatly. The merchant nodded grimly. 'But he has no outward injuries,' she went on. 'So the hurt would appear to be within rather than without.'

'Apparently so, ma'am,' Sir Gilbert grated, flashing her a warning look.

The formidable widow was not going to be dissuaded that easily.

'I am sorry for your son,' she announced. 'I didn't know the boy well, you understand . . .'

'He's not dead!' Sir Gilbert exclaimed. 'Look, he's breathing! There, blowing like a whale, strong as a horse,' he babbled disjointedly. 'A little rest, madam, and he will be as right as rain,' he pronounced rather more slowly.

Lady Ramsay nodded slightly.

'We would all wish him a speedy recovery, of that there is no doubt,' she continued. 'Of course, until he recovers his wits there can be no question of any marriage with my daughter. The wedding you had set your heart on must be considered cancelled, forthwith.'

'Postponed,' Sir Gilbert answered, dragging the syllables from the sour bilge of his round belly. 'Postponed, I'll grant you.' Lady Ramsay's flashing features turned to iron. Beaten, burned and beaten again like an old horseshoe taken down from the doorway to be pressed into service once more.

'I must insist, sir, that you put any idea of a marriage out of your head. I absolutely forbid any wedding until such time as I am assured of your son's complete and unreserved return to his full capacities.'

Sir Gilbert rose to his feet from the piled bedclothes, his fleshy lip trembling as he studied the unblinking widow.

'Madam. He has been thrown into a stupor by his first experience of battle. I am told it is a not uncommon occurrence on the field. He has received treatment from the most eminent surgeon in the land, you remember Mr Ambrosio—'

'Nevertheless, sir. The wedding is cancelled until further notice,' Lady Ramsay interrupted, picking a dish of water from the bedside cabinet.

Sir Gilbert closed his chubby fist about her narrow wrist

and fixed her with such a look of unadulterated menace she thought for a moment he would strike her.

'You forget yourself, madam. Your grief misleads you. My son will make a full recovery. A good rest and some proper grub and he'll be as right as rain. And if by some evil mischance he should remain the drooling idiot you see now, then I will absolve you of our arrangement.'

Lady Ramsay scowled into his glittering brown eyes, but nodded slowly.

'If my son is not fit to wed your daughter by the end of next month as we planned, then I shall marry the girl myself or demand the immediate repayment, in full and with interest, of all monies owed by your family to me.

'Do I make myself understood, Lady Ramsay?' he added as an insolent afterthought.

The widow could not hold his piercing gaze. She twisted away and stalked out of her room, the idiot boy heralding her departure with a loud, reverberating cockadoodledoo.

Not one of the *Conqueror*'s bleary-eyed crew could bring himself to cheer as the morning tide lifted the heavy warship from the silver sandbank, and carried the battered man-of-war off like a leaf on a mill-race. Mr Rhodes, the red-faced first officer, had allowed himself a small sigh of relief at their release, but had modified his exclamation into a rasping cough when he caught Captain Fey's rigid stare.

'Prepare to make sail!'

'Aye, sir!' Rhodes yelped, making himself scarce from the poop deck where he and the surviving officers seemed to have endured an infinity of tortured soul searching. They had been stuck for the best part of twenty-four hours in the mouth of the Avon, the heavy hull grounded on one of the sandy spits which radiated out into the estuary like the vaporous blue markings along the flanks of a mackerel. They had run aground in thick fog the previous morning, running out of luck as they negotiated the narrow channels between the mudbanks.

When the wretched, spirit-sapping mist had finally rolled away, they had found themselves stuck fast in the middle of an expanse of sluggish brown pools, more sand than Severn. To add insult to injury, the mortified crew had been forced to watch the insolent manoeuvres of the merchant fleet as they took up new positions further out in the King Road, safely out of range of their wrath. The turncoat captains had steered their laden vessels between the shoals to take up a new anchorage a few miles downriver, under the guns of the newly captured fort on Portishead Point. They had crowded together like great brown water-buffalo, anchored in echelon so that each ship's guns covered the stern of her immediate neighbour.

To Captain Fey's further annoyance, the eight original defectors had been joined by another half-dozen smaller vessels, including the *Mercy*, the sleek sloop which had raised the alarm as the *Conqueror* had attempted to run the gauntlet of the river two nights before.

Fey estimated the mutinous fleet could boast at least sixty guns, with a further four heavy cannon mounted in the rocky fort at their backs. He had spent an entire day running his glass to and fro over the treacherous vessels, grinding his teeth to powder as he contemplated their serenely indifferent activities. Ah, they were busy enough now.

He had anticipated the fast-moving sloops would have taken advantage of his precarious position, and circled around his stricken ship like wolves. A well-directed and determined flotilla could have probed the grounded man-of-war for a weak spot, and pressed home its attack just as the old fellows had fought the Spanish Armada a couple of generations before. The fact they had remained idle, cowering like a flock of frightened sheep beneath the fort, had heightened Fey's frustration, rubbed salt into his wounded reputation.

The captains and crews must have been wetting their breeches at the prospect of the *Conqueror*'s return, praying to their disgusted God the Roundhead battleship would succumb to the Royalist guns further upriver. The wretched fog had saved his ship, but stolen the prize he had set his heart on, the destruction of the traitor fleet.

The heavy warship slowly picked up speed as the huge sails billowed, the surging current whisking the vessel away down the broad estuary. Fey ran his glass over the detested colours of King Charles' newly won ships, his moustache twitching as his thin lips formed silent oaths.

'Another time, gentlemen,' he breathed, as the wind tore across the battered deck and worried at his damp black coat. 'Another time.'

BY

THE CHRISTMAS STEPS,

BRISTOL, 26 JULY 1643

The sun had been up an hour or so, but hadn't penetrated the gloomy depths of the timbered canyon. What little light there was had been filtered through clouds of rancid smoke which sank slowly down the steep stair, extinguishing one cramped landing after another. Fulke's conglomerated command could hear shots and shouts from the top steps as the Royalist invaders winkled snipers out from beneath the dank eaves of the tall houses, turfing the few men who had stayed to defend the stair from behind their improvised defences. The one-sided firefight gave the small squad of sooty musketeers assembled at the foot of the steps precious moments to improve their flimsy barricade. Sparrow and Caleb had manhandled a heavy chest out of the broken-down front door of a deserted town house, and used it as the foundation of a formidable obstruction. Grim-faced soldiers had added mattresses, chairs, sacks and pillows. Legless tables and empty barrels were hauled out to stiffen the new wall.

Sparrow ducked beneath an overhanging doorway as the musketeers on the second and third floor of the ransacked houses chose their spots overlooking the narrow stair, smashing leaded windows to improve their field of fire.

He stared through the storm of shards at the mouldy wall opposite, uncomfortably aware he was being watched. Half a dozen refugees from the ferocious battle had taken refuge in the cellar of the squat, sloping house on the corner, pressing their pale faces to the rusty iron grille like so many condemned prisoners. A gap-toothed goodwife shouted at him to leave them be, take their fight elsewhere. A heavy-cheeked tradesman yelled obscenities.

'We've children in here! Women and children!'

Sparrow stared at their sorry sanctuary, and leaned forward to take a quick peek at the fog-clogged stair.

'Get out of it!' he shouted back. 'They're coming this way!'

Fulke peered round the corner, ducked his head and doubled over to Sparrow's rather vulnerable hidey-hole using the improvised barricade as cover.

'There's no time for that now. Back inside and bar the door,' Fulke gasped.

Sparrow pointed at the contorted faces behind the bars, and immediately felt the searing breath of a bullet over his wrist. He snatched his hand back as a sudden squall of shots peppered the barricade, holing an old bucket somebody had inadvertently left hooked over a chair leg. Fulke grabbed the astonished youngster by his calico coat and dragged him under the low doorway, hitting his head. Sparrow ducked down and threw himself behind the plastered wall as the game old major hurled the door closed. Muffet and Gillingfeather pushed the heavy oak table across the parlour, the ornamental legs scraping over the well-polished flagstones. Sparrow peered out of the fish-eyed windowpanes at the distorted steps, and then turned to study his unwelcoming surroundings. A plainly furnished sitting room had been stripped clean by the soldiers, who had then proceeded upstairs to take up more secure quarters.

'They're safe down there,' Fulke muttered distractedly. It was Matilda he was worried about. Shoved back into the narrow room at their lodgings at the top of the steps, barely aware of her cramped surroundings or the immediate departure of her patron and protector. He hadn't had time to take more than a cursory glance at the silent sanctuary as he had fled down the steps pursued by wildly aimed pistol shots, his few remaining troopers hurrying along beside him, pike eyed with terror. Surely the girl would have had the good sense to make herself scarce when she had heard the firing?

'You and the boy hold the door,' Fulke ordered the scowling cornet. 'We'll trap them in front of the barricade like trout in a barrel,' he predicted.

The musketeers followed Fulke up the narrow stairs, leaving Sparrow swinging his cutlass in dry-mouthed anticipation. Caleb stared vacantly about the bare walls, used to the confinement of cabin and hold. He held a nailed club, the business end already sticky with blood. Sparrow frowned, looking about the stripped room for anything else of use. A bronze coal scuttle and an ashen poker, a cracked cup on a splintered shelf. At least the Royalists wouldn't be after the loot. There wasn't any left.

Outside, the tramping boots reached a hellish crescendo – each appalling clatter of leather on stone jarring the defenders' frail nerves a little further, stretching their rapidly evaporating enthusiasm for the fight. The terrible, deliberate rhythm ate up their resolve, each measured pace promising certain death to those few who had remained to dispute their dreadful progress. The defenders clapped their hands over their ears against the din, their fear rising like bile-baked dough into their slack mouths.

Just when they felt they could take no more, the Royalist ranks broke open as the disciplined legion dissolved into a howling mob and the front rankers charged the hastily assembled defences.

The assault troops swarmed over the obstacles as if they were frolicking in front of fresh-faced maidens at a summer carnival, throwing themselves at the barred doors of the cramped inns and squashed shops which overlooked the stair. A couple of ensigns dashed ahead waving ragged banners into the drifting smoke, prodded and propelled by a gaggle of red-faced officers and seconded by a pack of screaming rank and filers eager to finish the one-sided street fight. They had cleared two landings already, breaking down the doors to throw grenades into people's parlours, poking their musket barrels through the rusty grilles to clear the infested cellars. The Roundheads who hadn't been holed up like moles had been forced back down the stairs, and had thrown up a flimsy barricade in a feeble attempt to stem the roaring flood. The attackers watched their footing as they descended the deadly stair, surging over the third landing. Another short flight and they would emerge into the packed streets of the city's commercial centre, and turn left toward the squat hulk of the castle. Cellar, attic or medieval tower, the damned rebels were trapped now, wherever they were.

And then all hell broke loose about their cheering heads.

Empty windows suddenly bristled with muskets, gaping cellars spewed volleys of shot, overlooked balconies erupted as desperate men hurled stones, slates, anything which had come to hand onto the mob below.

The furious barrage snapped about the head of the rushing column like an iron sprung trap closing about the unwary paw of some wild animal.

The stampeding invaders were stopped in their slippery tracks by the sudden salvo, muskets and pistols emptied into astonished faces by furious defenders and fanatic snipers, backs to the wall of their own homes. Shutters were thrown back, glass shattered and tiles hurled from the sagging rooftops as the desperate defenders sprang their trap. Bullets tore through the shredded colours and dropped captains and colonels in colourful heaps. The ensigns tottered back, staggering under the stinging volleys, their torn colours sliding and clattering down the blocked steps. The angry Royalists raised their muskets and fired back at the massed windows, so many black mouths in the mouldy brick and timber frames of the surrounding houses, each mouth spouting an angry red tongue as the cunning snipers moved along the fume-laden landings to find new vantage points. The reeling Royalists shoulder-charged doors or smashed ground-floor windows with their musket butts to shelter from the deadly storm.

Sparrow watched in horror as their feeble barrier sagged under the ferocious pressure, the oaken beams bulging, forcing the heavy table back with a horrifying squeak over the worn flags. The table cracked against the plastered wall, jamming the door ajar. A brown-sleeved arm groped through the gap followed instantly by a terrified face. William brought the heavy scuttle down on the youngster's head, knocking him back over his fellows. A shot thudded into the oak door, another punctured the fish-eyed panels in the parlour window scattering glittering shards over the floor. Caleb hurled his young bulk behind the table and heaved it back against the door as William fended off a thrusting half-pike with the deadly cutlass. A volley of shots from the Roundhead defenders in the house on the corner cut down three more Royalists and broke the spirit of the rest. They turned back up the stair, dragging their wounded with them.

The brief respite allowed William some time to reconnoitre their battered post. He left Caleb by the door and peered up the stairs. He could hear the musketeers calling across the pockmarked rooms to each other, apparently none the worse for the brief assault. He pushed the scullery door open and peered round the cramped kitchen. The room had been brushed and tidied by the fastidious owner, the stone flags swept clean. William found a tub of biscuits, unstoppering the handy find and helping himself as he strode across to the back door and took a quick look at the yard. Six months ago he wouldn't have dreamed of knocking on the back door for alms, let alone plundering the quiet kitchen. The army had banished any such reservations. He had to look out for himself, because himself was all he had. The ravaged house was surrounded on three sides by a six-foot brick wall overgrown with drooping lilacs. The black faces of the houses opposite leered down at the exposed back yard like immense stone ravens. It might provide a handy escape route if the Royalists got into the house from the front though. William eased the door open and crept out, hungrily munching the honeyed shortbread. He pushed over the mouldy rain barrel standing beside the door, emptying several gallons of mossy water over the neatly brushed flagstones, and rolled the empty container over to the rear wall. Set on its broad base once more, it would allow a quick evacuation if escape proved necessary. He paused for a moment, wondering how many more bolt-holes Bristol could boast. The only obstacle remaining was the Frome, and behind that the cold grey towers of the city keep. William hurried back into the house and rejoined Caleb in the front parlour. He held the biscuit jar out, and leapt back with fright as it suddenly exploded in a savage puff of clay and crumbs. Razor-sharp splinters cut into his thick coat, stinging his arms as he staggered back in shock.

The Royalists had regrouped on the next landing, and advanced down the street like timber wolves, crowding into every angled doorway, behind every creaking beam. They chose their targets carefully this time, a dozen and more musketeers picking on one exposed window. There was a loud crash from the room above, and a broken body crashed to the steps and rolled away into the barricade. The fusillade from the floor above filled the house with choking smoke. Several enemy sharpshooters slumped down wounded while the rest rushed the doors once more, shouldering the rickety barricade out of their path. The parlour door crashed open, the battered table sagging as one of the legs collapsed under the pressure. Caleb fell back against the wall as a couple of Royalists shoved their muskets through the breach and fired. The bullets sped around the plastered walls, clipping William's coat as he stood paralysed with shock. Caleb dived to the floor as the enemy soldiers forced the door wider. William stared down the sooty eye of a musket and ducked just in time. A third shot ricocheted from the plaster behind his head and buried itself in the doorframe. The broken table tipped over, trapping Caleb beneath. A Royalist in a dirty grey coat leapt into the room, swinging his musket like a club. William backed away, menacing the snarling soldier with the cutlass. The black-haired Royalist shoved the musket at his chest with a grunt of anger. William knocked it aside and dragged the heavy blade back before his opponent could react. The gleaming blade bit into the man's skull, releasing a splash of scarlet over the well-swept floor. The disabled musketeer sagged against the wall, his hands twitching violently in his sopping wet lap. Another man tried to clamber through the blocked doorway but Caleb kicked out with all his might, jamming the table up into his face with a ferocious crunch. The man fell back over the threshold as William strode forward and slashed at a third man, hanging back with a loaded musket. The reluctant warrior yelped, dropped his weapon and fled back into the street. William snatched up the discarded gun and fired from the hip as an officer rushed forward brandishing his half-pike. The shot caught him in the thigh, dropping him to the ground with a curse. William changed hands feverishly, and thrust the bloody cutlass into the wounded man's ribs. The wicked blade sank into the man's chest like a hot knife through butter before Sparrow could think. He pulled it back with a horrified oath, and stared for a moment at the officer's contorted face. His blue eyes fluttered under his girlish lashes, his thin face fluted with agony.

The barricade was swarming with Royalists now, kicking and shoving the assorted wreckage out of the way and rolling it on down the steps in a jumble of splintered woodwork. More wild-eyed invaders poured down the steps, ignoring the patchy fire from the windows. William blinked at the dead officer and darted back into the doorway as a crowd of sweating soldiers fell on pell-mell, their brass-bound musket butts dancing in front of William's terrorized face. He waved the cutlass at the screaming mob, almost losing his footing over the upturned table.

'Drop it – you rebel scum!'

'Take quarter, you bastard, or we'll run you through,' the desperate Royalists bawled.

Caleb leapt out from the other side of the doorway, catching them by surprise. He dropped one man with the nailed club but couldn't tear the horrible spikes from the man's split skull. A musketeer jammed his weapon behind the boy's ear and Caleb toppled down. A shot rang out from the stairway and the musketeer skidded to a halt, hit in the face. Gillingfeather leapt down into the room, upending his musket and beating the last man back out of the weary door.

'Get out of it quick, they're coming over the rooftops,' he panted, snatching at his bandolier to reload his hot gun. Fulke led the survivors down the stair as the house was rattled to its core by a grenade. Plaster flaked from the walls in feeble puffs of tired powder as the Royalists tore and hacked at the roof, leapt down into the empty attic.

The enemy had forced their way into one of the houses further up the deathly row and had forced a skylight. They had scuttled along the frail guttering, balancing themselves against the mossy chimney stacks. The adventurous enemy had descended the steps one house at a time, leaping over the narrow chasms between the buildings until they had worked their way down to the defiant Roundhead strong-point. A flurry of shots and a sack of grenades had cleared the upper floor, killing the distracted musketeers crouching by the window and blowing a frantic lieutenant clear through the shattered glass. They had leapt down to the cluttered floor and thrown more grenades down the stairs, forcing the defenders on the first storey down into the besieged parlour.

William wiped his face, the bloody sword hilt trembling in his fist.

'Out the back and over the wall, it's the only way,' he said shakily.

Billy Butcher strode past with musket ready, followed by Muffet and a couple of pale strangers. Fulke helped William drag Caleb from the floor, his dull head rolling this way and that on his broad shoulders. Gillingfeather had reloaded, and watched their backs as they retreated out of the smashed and bloody chamber of death, out into the fire and smoke of the stricken city. He threw the musket to his shoulder and drilled his shot into the first man over the bloody threshold. He tottered back and stumbled over the heaped corpses of a dozen and more men.

The Christmas Steps had been dearly bought.

BY

THE FROME GATE,

BRISTOL, 26 JULY 1643

The pitiful remains of Fulke's company fled the steps like soot-smeared alley cats, clambering over the back wall and hurrying through a darkened alley between a pair of broad-shouldered town houses. William turned to the right, and led the bewildered survivors through a broken-down gate into another almost identical alley. The firing died away behind them as they followed the brick tunnel past a reeking tannery. William sighed with relief. He knew where they were now, a stone's throw from the built-up bank of the River Frome, a few hundred yards from the Frome Gate. He waved the weary squad out into a broader street, partially blocked by a convoy of abandoned carts and wagons which evidently hadn't made it to the sanctuary of the gate. The stricken vehicles had spewed their contents across the street. Clothing, food, trinkets and plate had been torn from splintered boxes or rifled chests.

Thirty or more Royalist soldiers had fallen on the plunder, draping themselves in bolts of cloth and stuffing their pockets with handfuls of cheese from a broken barrel. The famished looters looked up in alarm as the blackened devils sprang out of the alley like tarred imps, their bloody features twisted into ghastly masks, a lost tribe of Puritan bandits. A grinning musketeer was guarding a trio of prisoners, slumped with hanging heads beside an overturned crate. He stopped smiling and wrenched up his musket a split second too late. Muffet's brass-bound butt caught him in the jaw, laying him out over the straw-packed coffin. Butcher fired, knocking another from the running-board of a looted wagon. The Royalist clutched his belly, dropping the ornate vase he had been admiring to the floor.

In another moment the street was packed with struggling men as the surprised enemy leapt down into the fray to protect their plunder. Fulke was knocked over by a thin officer with a mane of chestnut hair. The handsome captain stepped over his breathless victim, aiming his rapier for Fulke's scorched throat. William pushed a frightened Royalist pikeman aside, the sixteen-foot pole practically useless in the savage street fight, and lunged instead at the arrogant officer. The cutlass clipped the man's expensive slashed doublet, and he leapt around to parry Sparrow's stroke. William wrenched the blade back as the officer recovered his balance in an instant, thrusting his slim sword at Sparrow's ungainly bulk. His opponent switched his sword to his left hand, and brought it around in a vicious arc, cutting into William's calico sleeve. Sparrow yelped, felt his fingers tingle as the officer pirouetted neatly, switching his bloody blade back to his right hand. William staggered back as the tigerish Royalist lunged forward, stumbled and dropped to his knees. Fulke's pistol shot had caught him beneath the left armpit, tearing a neat hole in the man's ruined coat. William slammed the heavy hilt of the cutlass into the man's twisted features, knocking him against the tannery wall.

The unguarded prisoners, galvanized into action by the

unexpected rescue, fell on the Royalist soldiers hurrying around from the far side of the wagon. They tripped the careless musketeers into the cluttered cobbles, and battered them with stools and candlesticks, whatever they could wrest from the stuffed straw box behind them. The rest of the Royalists fell back from their prize, grimly reloading their muskets as a bare-headed ensign screamed at them to stand.

'There's no time for that,' Fulke hissed, clambering to his feet with difficulty.

William swallowed hard, the pain in his arm beginning to sound throbbing alarms in his numbed brain. Slow worms of dark blood ran over his wrist and between his icy fingers, dripping onto the glistening cobblestones. The surviving Roundheads edged away from the smashed convoy, eyeing the truculent enemy.

'Run for it!' Fulke yelled, doubling around the last wagon and leading the way down another back alley. The frightened squad galloped after him, William stumbling along in a blur of pain and agitated imaginings. He could still move his fingers. The wound couldn't be that bad, he thought furiously. A flurry of shots pittered and pattered into the stonework around their heads. One of the prisoners lurched into the wall clutching at his back.

'Leave him!' Fulke yelled, ducking into another alley.

'You all right, then, Will?'

Sparrow looked up at the sound of his name, the filthy prisoner hobbling alongside nodding his tangled head in evident recognition.

'Get on, boy, you know me, don't you?'

'Mordy? Mordecai Pitt? What the bugger are you doing here?' William gasped, his bloody arm cramped by frosty-fingered spasms. They hurried on as best they could, but they were overtaken by the rest of the survivors one by one, and quickly found themselves hurrying along at the rear of the desperate pack.

'Gah, that bloody wound on Lansdown, you remember? Here, you ain't seen me brothers, have you?' Mordecai enquired, wincing as he staggered and hobbled, red faced and slack mouthed.

William peered back down the narrow alley for signs of pursuit. They would have to hurry or they would be caught like rats in a trap.

'They're safe enough,' he growled, holding his numb arm to his bloody side.

'That bastard back there was goin' to shoot us down, afore they found those wagons,' the unarmed farmhand said disbelievingly.

The two of them had dropped further and further behind the rest, too exhausted to catch up with the fleeing fugitives.

'Come on, Mordy, another hundred yards and we'll be home and dry,' William encouraged. He forced the hilt of his sword between his bloody fingers, and eased his good hand under Mordecai's arm, boosting the bemused man onto his good leg. They hadn't gone another yard when a shot rang out behind them. The ball clipped the brickwork and ricocheted into Mordecai's left hand. He howled in agony as the Royalist musketeers doubled down the alley after them. Sparrow felt a surge of panic, knowing in his bones the damned place would be the death of them if they didn't hurry. He clamped his teeth, ignoring the angry throb in his arm, and hauled his groaning companion on, bouncing between the narrow brick walls with the shrieks of the pursuing Royalists ringing in their ears.

They emerged from the alley into a broad square,

dominated by the squat grey pile of the Frome Gate. The massive structure squatted over the swift river, linking the busy suburbs around St Michael's Hill on the northern bank with Broad Street on the southern. The square was littered with more wagons and abandoned boxes and chests. Knots of soldiers were hurrying this way and that while a troop of cavalry pranced over the cobbles as if they were trying to direct the panicked traffic. Muffet had held back to give William a hand, hurrying the wounded pair toward the shelter of the gate. Fulke stalked toward them, his eyes starting from his black powder mask.

'They've blocked the gate, we'll have to go round!' he shouted to the frantic survivors.

Royalist soldiers had already emptied into the square, firing indiscriminately at the bewildered Roundheads. The troop of horse cantered off toward a smoke-shrouded churchyard, the ragged remnants of a dozen companies hurrying after them. William peered at the formidable gatehouse, the battlements crowded with musketeers who kept up a spirited fire against the encroaching Royalists. Beneath the grim towers the heavy portcullis looked as if it had been shored up with great bulging sacks of wool. The formidable obstacle had kept the Royalists at bay, but prevented the survivors from the walls and the forts from rejoining their units in the inner city. Their only hope now would be to get within the fortress – and hope the Earl of Essex would get off his arse and venture west to their relief. But too many men had been lost in the retreat from the walls, and those that were left had had the fight knocked out of them by the relentless assaults. Outnumbered, short of ammunition and completely surrounded by a rising sea of Royalist troops, the majority of the garrison trod water while the officers pondered the inevitable surrender. Prolonging the agony would only attract sterner terms and freer plunder. Bristol would be burnt down about their Roundhead ears, if they continued the one-sided fight.

If they gave up now, they might still save some scraps of their honour, and a scratch force to shore up the next city due to face the King's men's wrath.

Sparrow's men hurried on, well aware of the precariousness of the position but unable to bring themselves to give up while there was a chance – however slim.

The steady fire from the gatehouse drove the Royalists back for a moment, and gave the fugitives time to hobble across the square and tumble over a low wall into the crowded churchyard. From there the stampeding survivors hurried along the bank and turned right into Broad Mead. William peered ahead over the bobbing hats and rusty helmets, and breathed an enormous sigh of relief as he saw the smaller Pithay Gate had been left open. The flock of beaten defenders rushed under the gloomy gatehouse and clattered across the bridge into the medieval heart of the stricken city.

The defenders dared not leave the gate ajar for long. They pulled the last few bewildered soldiers into the town and shouldered the massive door shut. Great studded planks were dropped into the iron catches, and the exhausted troops slumped down where they could, shuddering with exhaustion. Wounded slumped, bleeding slowly over the trampled flagstones. Fulke sat on a step, his scorched head in his trembling hands. Caleb lay at his feet, his dull eyes flickering under their heavy lids. Gillingfeather, Muffet and Butcher, the untouchable triumvirate, leaned their weapons against the wall and bent down to lend a hand with the wounded. Muffet eased William's calico coat from his bloody arm, and frowned at the gaping slash across the younger man's forearm. The Royalist officer's blade had bitten an inch-deep wound, parting the bloody skin and exposing the raw muscle.

'It's a good clean cut, anyway,' Muffet said, looking around for a water bottle. Mordecai Pitt lay on the flagstones at his feet like a dead man, his bloody hand folded on his chest like a badly dressed red crab. The relief of finding some shelter seemed to have drained what little strength they had left, drawn a welcome blanket of sleep over their pinched and pale faces. William blinked heavily, the streets and houses and broad wall draped in gauzy films of smoke and mist. Through the gathering twilight he thought he saw swans paddling toward him as if over a great mirrored lake. The white-bonneted womenfolk of Bristol, having built an impenetrable barrier of woolsacks across the Frome Gate, had come to the aid of their ailing menfolk.

William opened one wary eye, and focused slowly on his surroundings. He was lying against a red-brick wall, a bulky snap-sack thrust under his leaden head. He sat up with a wince, and nervously examined the heavy dressing which had been tightened around his bloody arm. Fulke was sitting alongside him, what remained of his hair standing up at odd angles from his filthy face. They were lying in a quiet courtyard, fifty of them at least. Soldiers in bloody aprons were hauling dead men out to make room for a queue of wounded waiting patiently in the adjoining alley. A red-faced woman with a bloody handprint on her broad starched collar peered over at him.

'Ease the binding off for a minute or two, and then tighten it up again,' she advised, hurrying off with an armful of torn linen. Fulke watched William pick at his tourniquet, leaned over and helped the drowsy ensign loosen the dressing.

'You've bled a lot. They thought you were a goner, but I had the surgeon take a look at you,' Fulke said gruffly.

Sparrow was too exhausted to thank him. He slumped back down and listened to the silence, and sat up again with a start.

'They've stopped. The guns have stopped!' he exclaimed.

Fulke sat back with a scowl. 'They've sent out a drummer,' he said, shaking his blackened head. 'The inner walls are intact but they've lost their nerve.'

Sparrow took a moment to digest this information.

'They're talking terms now,' Fulke said resignedly.

William closed his eyes, felt bitter tears welling from his whole body, as if his belly was awash with brine. Giving up? Surrendering? After their deadly adventures on Roundway, the horrific march to the coast and their miraculous rescue from the waves? Risking fire and brimstone to get into the damned city only to have it handed over to the enemy. It was too grim, too enormous to contemplate.

He looked over at the commotion in the corner of the yard. The waiting wounded had crowded into the narrow gate, peering out into the street with evident excitement. They could hear shouts and cat-calls, officers barking orders at unruly men. Fulke prised himself to his unsteady feet, and picked his way across the strewn courtyard. He gave up trying to force his way through the scrummage at the gate, and climbed instead onto an ornamental flowerbed bordering the neatly kept courtyard. William had stumbled after him, gingerly holding on to his throbbing arm. He joined the gallant major on his improvised grandstand, and watched the noisy procession in the street below. A troop of dismounted Roundhead horsemen was escorting a flock of officers down Wine Street toward the castle. By the splendour of their dress, William guessed several of them were Cavalier lords, come to dictate terms to the beaten garrison. They were chatting casually with the escorting officers, grim-faced colonels in greasy buff coats, their tawny sashes hanging limply around their tightly buckled waists. The crowded soldiers and townsfolk stared at the gaudy parade, lining their route as if the King himself had arrived to oversee the surrender of the city.

'Is it Rupert?' William asked.

Fulke shook his scorched head.

'One of his creatures. Rupert's a soldier, not a messenger boy,' the exhausted major growled. 'He doesn't dirty his hands doing deals with the likes of us,' he added.

Sparrow, standing shakily on the flowerbed, didn't know whether it was meant as a criticism or a tribute. It didn't seem to matter now.

They marched out just after dawn the following day. Like their ferocious Cornish conquerors, the garrison had jumped the gun and opened the gates before the appointed time. Hundreds of bloody and muddy Royalist soldiers packed the streets and houses, leaned out of the leaded windows to jeer their beaten enemy. Some belligerent characters shouldered their way into the bemused Roundhead mob, snatching bags and peering under the tarpaulins tied down over the creaking wagons.

'What have you got there, you bastards? Who said you could take yer sword with you?'

'Ah, you had sport with us when we left Reading, you dogs.'

'Where's your King Jesus, eh? Forgotten you again, boys, just like at Runaway Hill!'

'Hang the rebels!'

'Who said to let 'em go? They'll only fight again!'

William stumbled along with a regiment of weary wounded, listening to the caterwauling Cavaliers pour scorn on their hanging heads.

Their pale commanders rode in front, staring straight ahead through hails of spit and bellowed oaths. The dumbstruck Fiennes was dreading his ignominious return to London almost as much as the storm itself. Excuses and blame and explanations and accusations bubbling in his fevered brain. Oh yes, they'd blame him all right. Let Waller bleed the men from his walls, and then call him a traitor for not holding on. They had put up a good fight, damn near held the wretched prince at bay. But once the wall had been breached, the men had haemorrhaged away to bed or alehouse. The cavalry and reserves had hardly budged, their feeble counter-attacks easily fended off by determined Royalist musketeers firing from behind the hedges. Hedges? What sort of an obstacle was a hedge? Rupert had gotten his men over a ditch and wall, and yet his bloody horsemen hadn't cleared a row of damned twigs!

His scowling brother John rode beside him, with Popham, Strode, Stephens, Fulke and Birch bringing up the rear. Some of them had insisted on locking themselves in the castle, and defying Rupert to do his worst as the city burnt down about their ears. But half the garrison had already gone home and the rest had been scattered all over the turbulent city. Further resistance would only have resulted in their eventual slaughter. Look what had happened to Magdeburg in Germany, when the foolish generals had refused to surrender in time. The diehards had been voted down. The city would take terms.

The vanguard of his army of lost souls shuffled nervously under Lawford's Gate, more and more Royalists shoving their way through the crowd of dispirited shadow men, pulling and punching their dumb victims in frustrated rage. The terms of the surrender had denied them the plunder they had set their hearts on, and the men who had bade them such defiance were being allowed to march off, scot free. The furious Royalist rank and file closed in on the tattered column, gloating over their helpless enemy. The ghostly survivors might have been pulled apart like carrion if it hadn't been for the sudden pistol shot which stopped them in their bloody tracks.

William glanced over his wounded shoulder as a tall Cavalier on a black horse spurred along the shouting ranks, brandishing his smoking pistol at the enraged soldiers.

'Leave those men alone, you dogs! Get away from them or I'll flog the lot of you!' the dark stranger bellowed.

To William's lasting amazement, the would-be looters fell back like naughty schoolboys, dropped the plundered sacks and weapons to the floor with hateful scowls. Their commander turned his horse along the stalled column, and muttered an apology to the bewildered Roundhead officers. He swept off his hat and tugged the prancing horse about, trotting back down the line in his insolent splendour. William stared at the grim-faced prince, dressed for the ball but ready for battle, his lank black hair hanging over his scowling face. For one frozen moment, Rupert caught William's eye. The staring Roundhead was six inches taller than most of the shuffling mob, standing out with his matted hair and calico seaman's coat. A ragged giant with a broken pike from one of his brother's Cornish regiments had snatched William's sword, and had gone to hide the prize under his coat. Rupert's eagle glance spitted the man like a stuffed hog.

'Didn't you hear the terms, you dog? Officers to keep their swords!' Rupert barked. The surly Cornishman seemed less impressed with the terrifying German than his cowering companions. He glanced at the hulking Roundhead in the bloody coat, shook his curly head.

'If this one's off'cer I'm the bliddy Pope,' Jethro Polruan snarled back. 'And look at it, sir,' Polruan added, holding up the offending cutlass. 'What sort of a bastard carries a chopper like this?'

Rupert rolled his dark eyes menacingly, and turned to the bewildered rebel.

'Well, are you an officer or not?'

William wondered. Morrison had made him a captain, but the commission hadn't been worth the paper it was written on. McNabb had appointed him his cornet, but he had dropped the flag during their disgraceful show on the downs above Devizes. Since then he had been prisoner, hostage, fugitive and victim.

Colonel Birch had turned his horse to see what the commotion was about. He tipped his helmet and nodded at the slack-mouthed prisoner.

'Your Highness, this is Captain Sparrow, second in command to Major Fulke,' Birch said steadily.

Rupert nodded, unimpressed.

'Then he can keep his cutlass as was agreed,' he snapped.

Polruan growled under his breath, and thrust the fearsome weapon back at Sparrow's limp fist.

'Another time, Roundhead,' he hissed, his breath reeking with looted brandy.

William winced as the surly giant accidentally elbowed his wound and strutted back to his muttering companions. Rupert nodded, pulled his horse about and trotted off. The sorry column shuffled on once more.

'Few more cock-ups like this and you'll be a general by the time they 'ang us,' Billy Butcher said chirpily, falling in beside the dumbstruck officer, apparently unaware of the disaster which had befallen them.

'Watch yourselves, lads, it's *Captain* Sparrow now!'

ACKNOWLEDGEMENTS

The Christmas Steps still exist today, and the claustrophobic short cut makes a good starting point for a tour of Civil War Bristol. The steep stairway is overshadowed by timber-framed buildings (including a near-legendary fish and chip shop!) and readers can locate the plaque erected by the Sealed Knot in memory of Colonel Henry Lunsford, who fell leading his men to assault the Roundhead defenders. Turn left at the top of the steps and you will be heading toward Park Row and the top of Park Street, where the large stone barn formed a formidable bastion in the seventeenth-century defences.

The dragoon colonel Henry Washington (great-uncle of George Washington) slipped his men past the barn and made a breach near the present day Victoria Rooms. You can still make out the traces of old earthworks at Brandon Steep, and imagine the commanding view of the city and river the defenders would have enjoyed (or not!).

An excellent account of the city's experiences during the Civil War is given in the Bristol University publication *Bristol and the Civil War* by Patrick McGrath.

For the most exhaustively detailed accounts of the Civil War in the West Country I remain indebted to Stuart Peachey and Robert Morris, whose fine set of pamphlets from the Stuart Press are available at Sealed Knot musters or from the Stuart Press at 117 Farleigh Road, Backwell, Bristol BS19 3PG.

For those wanting a slightly more general view of the Civil Wars and a good idea of uniform, tactics and weapons, look out for Philip Haythornthwaite's *English Civil War* (Blandford Press).

For the military minded who want the details on the many skirmishes and battles of the three civil wars, then Brigadier Peter Young and Richard Holmes' *The English Civil War* is essential reading. I am particularly indebted to Richard Holmes and John Lee for casting authoritative eyes over my manuscript as well as providing early encouragement. Peter Young's *Civil War England* (Longman Travellers Series) provides a pungent guide to the best battlefields and castles to visit, as well as thumbnail sketches of some of the lesser known combatants.

C. V. Wedgwood's *The King's War* (Penguin) provides the full political and strategic overview of the conflict, and further details of the bloody struggles on the Continent can be found in her excellent *Thirty Years War* (University Press).

The Osprey Elite series on infantry and cavalry of the civil wars provides good background on uniforms and organization, as well as including sets of excellent illustrations by Angus McBride.

While I have endeavoured to make 'The Shadow on the Crown' series as historically accurate as possible, there are inevitably occasions when a little journalistic licence is required. Please forgive any unintentional errors as to when and precisely where certain events took place.

Nicholas Carter, pikeman and pamphleteer.

All Pan Books are available at your local bookshop or newsagent, or can be ordered direct from the publisher. Indicate the number of copies required and fill in the form below.

Send to: Macmillan General Books C.S.
Book Service By Post
PO Box 29, Douglas I-O-M
IM99 1BQ

or phone: 01624 675137, quoting title, author and credit card number.

or fax: 01624 670923, quoting title, author, and credit card number.

or Internet: http://www.bookpost.co.uk

Please enclose a remittance* to the value of the cover price plus 75 pence per book for post and packing. Overseas customers please allow £1.00 per copy for post and packing.

*Payment may be made in sterling by UK personal cheque, Eurocheque, postal order, sterling draft or international money order, made payable to Book Service By Post.

Alternatively by Access/Visa/MasterCard

Card No. ☐☐☐☐☐☐☐☐☐☐☐☐☐☐☐☐

Expiry Date ☐☐☐☐☐☐☐☐☐☐☐☐☐☐☐☐

Signature ____________________

Applicable only in the UK and BFPO addresses.

While every effort is made to keep prices low, it is sometimes necessary to increase prices at short notice. Pan Books reserve the right to show on covers and charge new retail prices which may differ from those advertised in the text or elsewhere.

NAME AND ADDRESS IN BLOCK CAPITAL LETTERS PLEASE

Name ____________________

Address ____________________

____

____

____

8/95

Please allow 28 days for delivery.
Please tick box if you do not wish to receive any additional information. ☐